## Flight to Darkness

I murdered my brother with a sculptor's mallet. But it was only a dream. It was a dream I always had. I hated my brother.

I was going home to see him now, get it out of my system, and then spend the rest of my life hunting Leda. She was my wife and she belonged to me.

All I remember of that searing journey was the sun blazing down, and there, framed in the doorway, were my brother Frank and Leda, my lovely Judas wife. So when they found my brother with his head battered in by a sculptor's mallet, they said I had murdered him. But did I?

## 77 Rue Paradis

It began here for Baron–the whole grotesque skein of terror–here in this Marseilles street of despair, the street called the Rue Paradis.

There was Gorssmann, fat and corrupt, who waited until Baron scraped bottom–and then blackmailed him into treason. And Lili, the dark, lovely gamin, who fell in love with Baron--and worked for the man determined to destroy him.

Altogether for Frank Baron it was a small hell on the street called Paradise!

# Gil Brewer Bibliography

Love Me and Die (1951; w/Day Keene, published as by Day Keene)
Satan is a Woman (1951)
So Rich, So Dead (1951)
13 French Street (1951)
Flight to Darkness (1952)
Hell's Our Destination (1953)
A Killer is Loose (1954)
Some Must Die (1954)
77 Rue Paradis (1954)
The Squeeze (1955)
The Red Scarf (1955)
–And the Girl Screamed (1956)
The Angry Dream (1957; reprinted as The Girl from Hateville, 1958)
The Brat (1957)
Little Tramp (1958)
The Bitch (1958)
Wild (1958)
The Vengeful Virgin (1958)
Sugar (1959)
Wild to Possess (1959)
Angel (1960)
Nude on Thin Ice (1960)
Backwoods Teaser (1960)
The Three-Way Split (1960)
Play it Hard (1960)
Appointment in Hell (1961)
A Taste for Sin (1961)
Memory of Passion (1962)
The Hungry One (1966)
The Tease (1967)
Sin for Me (1967)
It Takes a Thief #1: The Devil in Davos (1969)
It Takes a Thief #2: Mediterranean Caper (1969)
It Takes a Thief #3: Appointment in Cairo (1970)
A Devil for O'Shaugnessy (2008)
The Erotics (2015)
Gun the Dame Down (2015)
Angry Arnold (2015)

**As Harry Arvay**
Eleven Bullets for Mohammed (1975)
Operation Kuwait (1975)
The Moscow Intercept (1975)
The Piraeus Plot (1975)
Togo Commando (1976)

**As Mark Bailey**
Mouth Magic (1972)

**As Al Conroy**
Soldato #3: Strangle Hold! (1973)
Soldato #4: Murder Mission! (1973)

**As Hal Ellson**
Blood on the Ivy (1970)

**As Elaine Evans**
Shadowland (1970)
A Dark and Deadly Love (1972)
Black Autumn (1973)
Wintershade (1974)

**As Luke Morgann**
More Than a Handful (1972)
Ladies in Heat (1972)
Gamecock (1972)
Tongue Tricks! (1972)

**As Ellery Queen**
The Campus Murders (1969)
The Japanese Golden Dozen (1978; rewrites by Brewer)

**UNPUBLISHED NOVELS**
House of the Potato (autobiographical novel, late 1940s)
Firebase Seattle (Executioner novel, 1975)
The Paper Coffin (spy novel, 1970s)

# FLIGHT TO DARKNESS

---

# 77 RUE PARADIS

## by

## Gil Brewer

**Stark House Press • Eureka California**
www.starkhousepress.com

FLIGHT TO DARKNESS / 77 RUE PARADIS

Published by Stark House Press
1315 H Street
Eureka, CA 95501
griffinskye3@sbcglobal.net
www.starkhousepress.com

Gil Brewer in the Shadow of French Street ©2018 by David Rachels

Flight to Darkness ©1952 by Gil Brewer
First Printing, 1952 by Fawcett Publications, Gold Medal #277

77 Rue Paradis ©1955 by Gil Brewer
First Printing, 1955 by Fawcett Publications, Gold Medal #448

ISBN-13: 978-1-944520-58-8
Book design by Jeff Vorzimmer, ¡caliente!design, Austin, Texas
Cover illustration by Mel Crair, 1960

First Stark House Press Edition: April 2018
0 9 8 7 6 5 4 3 2 1

## Gil Brewer in the Shadow of French Street

In overviews of Gil Brewer's writing career, two facts often get special attention: He once wrote a million-selling novel, and he once wrote a novel in three days. As Brewer's career declined and his publications dwindled, these facts had special significance for him, too. When things got bad, he could look back at these successes to remind himself of what he could do–or, at least, of what he once could do.

Brewer began writing with aspirations to literary greatness, but first he had to make a living. To put food (and, unfortunately, alcohol) on the table, he turned to genre fiction. He found his niche as a writer of sexually-charged crime novels, and his career seemed to be going according to plan. He joined the roster of Fawcett's Gold Medal Books, which pioneered the publication of original paperback novels and paid better than the many competitors who soon crowded the field. His first contract with Gold Medal, dated March 26, 1951, was for the novel *Satan's Rib*, which the publisher re-titled *Satan Is a Woman*. By the end of the year, Brewer had already published three novels with Gold Medal. The third of these, *13 French Street*, had a first printing of 300,000, and would go on to become his million-seller.

Brewer had done it, and he had done it fast. After less than a year as a published novelist, he had achieved financial success and even a degree of financial security. No longer would he need to write and publish so quickly in order to support himself. He could slow down. He could take his time and chase his dream of literary greatness. At least that was the plan.

About the time that *13 French Street* was published, Brewer's drinking got so bad that his wife, Verlaine, put him in the hospital. While Gil was drying out, Verlaine took over Gil's correspondence with his literary agent, Joseph T. Shaw. Shaw was in New York, while the Brewers were living in St. Petersburg, Florida. Only Shaw's half of their correspondence survives. (Shaw's papers are held at UCLA. Brewer's papers are at the University of Wyoming. Brewer kept Shaw's letters. Shaw did not keep Brewer's.)

On November 19, 1951, apparently having been informed of Gil's hospitalization, Shaw wrote a note to Verlaine in which he reassured her, "Have no doubt of it. We'll pull Gil through." On the same day, Shaw wrote in a longer letter to Gil, "[T]hanks again to [Verlaine], I know what you are up against. You have my understanding and my sympathy, Gil. I wish I could give you more; the will and the strength to overcome this handicap which is so unfair to yourself, to your wonderful partner and to your proven talent." On December 3, Shaw wrote again to Verlaine, "I wish I could do something to help you, but it isn't very clear how I could."

But there was one thing that Shaw could and did do to help his client: He counseled Brewer to relax. With the success of *13 French Street*, there was no need for him to rush back to his typewriter. In Shaw's letters to the Brewers, he never mentions alcohol by name, but his hope is evident that if Gil would only slow down and stop pressuring himself, then he would no longer need the bottle. Shaw meant well, but he was, of course, naïve about the challenges of alcoholism.

By the middle of December 1951, Brewer had announced that he was sober and ready to write again. Shaw was still concerned about his client's health, but he also expressed unrealistic optimism. He responded to Brewer, "Thanks a million for your letter and the good news you give me. I didn't want to say it, Gil, but I've been told there is very great danger in reverting now. But we can put aside our worry over that for good and all."

The next novel that Brewer published was the one he wrote in three days–and it would also be the last book that Joseph T. Shaw would ever read. On August 1, 1952, Shaw finished reading the manuscript Brewer had titled *Night Follows Night*, and then he went to lunch at his favorite restaurant in Manhattan. On the way back to his office, Shaw fell over dead of a heart attack in the elevator. Malcolm Reiss, who worked for Shaw, sent Brewer a telegram that day with the sad news. Four days later, Reiss wrote a letter to Brewer to assure him that the agency would "keep things moving and carefully look after your interests."

Writing a decade later, Brewer remembered Shaw as "the very best:–a gentleman, a fine editor, an excellent agent–and a 'come hell or high water' friend. To my knowledge, he was one of the very last men of heart in the publishing [and] editorial world who understood, sympathized with, and believed in what an honest writer could do no matter how long it look–if the real talent was there." By the time Brewer wrote this tribute, his writing career had started a steep decline. Brewer's career might have been substantially different if Shaw had lived longer, but it seems safe to assume that Shaw would not have been able to keep him sober by remote control.

Four weeks after Shaw's death, Gold Medal issued a contract for Brewer's three-day novel, which they would re-title *Flight to Darkness*. The contract shows that Brewer had already signed with a new literary agency, Littauer & Wilkinson. *Flight to Darkness* was published in December 1952, roughly one year after the publication of *13 French Street*. The front cover of *13 French Street* had not mentioned any of Brewer's previous work, but the cover of *Flight to Darkness* proclaimed, "More startling than 13 FRENCH STREET / By the same author."

*13 French Street* had been a psychological sex drama whose plot revolved around a pair of World War II veterans and a femme fatale. On the opening page of *Flight to Darkness*, Brewer took pains to show readers that he would be mining the same material. The novel's initial setting is a veterans hospital, and its first named character is nurse Leda Thayer. Brewer wastes no time in identifying Leda as a dangerous woman. Just before the obligatory drooling description of her body–still on the novel's first page–he writes that "her eyes were full of hell."

Narrator Eric Garth, home from the Korean War, was wounded in battle, but his damaged leg is not the reason for his hospitalization. Rather, his problem is PTSD–"battle fatigue" in the parlance of the day. Eric's nightmares, however, are not about war but about his brother, Frank, whom he dreams of bludgeoning to death with a wooden mallet. Eric's poor mental health is reflected in his willingness to run off with Leda. He compares his nurse to "a lush, tropical flower blooming poisonously through a crack in a stretch of hot cement sidewalk." And it is not just that he can intuit her dangerousness. She freely admits that she is after his money. She says, "I love you so damned much. Because you're going to be a great sculptor and because you're just a little nutty. And, of course, you're going to be very, very rich." Leda has such control over Eric that she does not even bother lying to him.

After *Flight to Darkness*, Brewer again published three novels with Gold Medal in less than a year, all three of which billed him as the author of *13 French Street*. The first of these, *Hell's Our Destination* (1953), had essentially the same title as *Flight to Darkness*, but the next two titles were noticeably different. *A Killer Is Loose* (1954) told of a spree killer with delusions of building an eye hospital, while *Some Must Die* (1954), set in nineteenth-century Wyoming, was the only time Brewer would ever publish a novel-length western. Brewer seems to have forgotten Shaw's admonitions to slow down as well as their plan for him to leave genre fiction behind, but at least he was trying new things.

Brewer's sales, however, were flagging. While *13 French Street* had multiple printings, *Flight to Darkness*, *Hell's Our Destination*, *A Killer Is Loose*, and *Some Must Die* had just one each. With his next novel, then, Brewer unabashedly attempted to recapture his million-selling glory with the title *77 Rue Paradis*. While the title *13 French Street* had hinted at stereotypes of French debauchery (and accompanying bad luck), *77 Rue Paradis* promised the sexual paradise of France itself (but with "paradis" being used ironically). Brewer's decision to set a novel in France suggests a desperation for success, especially given that he did not like writing that required research. Remarkably, however, the cover of *77 Rue Paradis* did not bill Brewer as the author of *13 French Street*.

The first edition of *77 Rue Paradis*, with its cover painting reminiscent of *13 French Street*, proclaimed, "He met a gutter angel on the roadway to hell." This may put readers in mind of Leda in *Flight to Darkness* or Petra in *13 French Street*, but while Leda and Petra are merely promiscuous women, the opening pages of *77 Rue Paradis* suggest that "gutter angel" may be coded language for a prostitute. France really *is* different.

But once the novel has introduced its protagonist, Frank Baron, and his prostitute lover, Elene Cordon, it takes a sharp turn into a tale of espionage in the aeronautics industry. Readers in 1954 who expected another lurid love triangle would have been disappointed. Anthony Boucher, reviewing *77 Rue Paradis* in *The New York Times*, complained of Brewer's "resolute inserts of gratuitous sexuality and sadism," which is to say that the author did throw some bones to readers who wanted another *13 French Street*. However, given the disconnect between the packaging and contents of *77 Rue Paradis*, no one should have expected another million-seller.

Gil Brewer published his first eight novels with Gold Medal Books, and *77 Rue Paradis* was the last of these. His next three novels would have three different publishers: *The Squeeze* (Ace Books, 1955), *–And the Girl Screamed* (Crest Books, 1956), and *The Angry Dream* (Mystery House, 1957). After this, Brewer would return to Gold Medal, but his peaks as a professional writer–the book that sold a million copies and the book that he wrote in three days–were glories he would never recapture.

David Rachels
Newberry, South Carolina


*A Note on Sources:*

Joseph T. Shaw's letters to Gil and Verlaine Brewer are in Box 2 of Collection 8184, Gil Brewer Collection, American Heritage Center, University of Wyoming. Brewer's tribute to Shaw is in Box 9. Anthony Boucher's review of *77 Rue Paradis* appeared in "Criminals at Large" on page BR21 of *The New York Times* on January 9, 1955

# FLIGHT TO DARKNESS
# by Gil Brewer

## Chapter 1

You know how it is when you believe you should do a thing, rushing ahead toward it because it's a kind of adventure, before your realize you should have stayed in bed? Well, it dawned on me too late. That last day at the veteran's hospital in California was rugged. But I'd waited a long time. I was optimistic.

Leda Thayer stood just at the head of the stairs as I came down the corridor that morning. I wanted to stop and talk with her, maybe touch her, but I had to see Prescott. It would be the last time.

She came up to me and her eyes were full of hell.

"Eric, you sure look different."

"No bathrobe or pajamas." I grinned, took her hand and felt that way. She was wearing her white nylon nurse's uniform. It was the one that was always too tight in exactly the right way beneath her breasts and across her hips, and she was lovely. She had long shapely thighs, and her auburn hair was bright, full of light even in the somber, clinical nakedness of the hallway. There was in her face, in the damp turn of her lips, a secret lasciviousness. Deep-breasted, vigorous, Leda was like a lush, tropical flower blooming poisonously through a crack in a stretch of hot cement sidewalk. Her hand was warm.

"You going in there?" She nodded toward the chief neuropsychiatrist's office.

"Yes."

"Anyway, it's over with."

"All but the good-bys."

"Baby can't wait." Her deep blue eyes got smoky as she watched me. "I like you in a suit of clothes. My big old Viking. Wish you'd grow a beard. A big blond beard."

"So I could tickle you?"

"Much."

"I better go."

"All right." She leaned in close, kissed me, her lips soft and hot, and for that brief instant we said something against each other not alone with lips. "I'm not so patient any more."

"Good for baby." Inside I was scared but still optimistic. I watched Leda go on down the hall. She moved quickly, lithely, in her crepe-soled shoes, and I liked to hear the very soft hiss of her dress.

Dr. Prescott seemed to have changed. Only I knew he hadn't. He'd been the ogre with whom I'd spent a good share of my time during the past year.

He didn't rise from behind his desk. "How's it feel?"

"Damned fine, Doc."

I went over and sat in the good old chair beside the desk which seemed a little different now.

We looked at each other for a while. He smiled in his calm way and folded his hands on the desk blotter. The office had changed, too. There was the table up against the wall where Prescott administered the electrotherapy treatments but the table no longer held that cloudy vision of terror. At least not for me. The windows with the partially closed Venetian blinds were the same, only like everything else–different, somehow. There'd been a time when I had stared at those blinds and watched them grin at me, wink–even speak.

"You're going home. You feel O. K. about that?"

"Sure," I told him. It was a lie. I was scared, but it had to be all right because it was the only way. My stomach burned and my nerves were like banjo strings.

Prescott looked at his folded hands and pale sunlight ricocheted off the tiny bald spot on his skull. He wasn't much older than my twenty-eight, but I imagined he supposed he was old as hell. His manner had always been a trifle supercilious. He had washed-out gray eyes, straw-colored hair and he sported a mustache of perhaps nineteen hairs, which was incessantly scraggled. He always wore a blue polka-dot bow tie and, as now, a wrinkled gray gabardine suit. He didn't have too much chin, but his overlarge Adam's-apple helped compensate for the lack. His voice was rather high and, to me, irritating.

Prescott and I had been through a lot together.

"Anything happen since I've seen you?"

"Nope."

"Sleep well?"

"Fine."

"Dream?"

"Usual."

"Thought we'd get rid of that. Intervals are longer, anyway. How long is it this time?"

"Been a week and a half."

"How did you kill him?"

"Same way, Doc. With a wooden mallet."

He let that coast for a while. Then he cleared his throat. "We can't allow you to run around being haunted."

"Like I told you, Doc—it doesn't bother me any more."

"Yeah. Only you still go right ahead killing your brother every once in a while."

I shrugged. "It's a dream." Somebody strummed the banjo strings. It *had* to be a dream....

"I remember very clearly how you acted when you came in here," Prescott said. "At least we've helped you some."

"That or it's wearing itself out."

"You always doubted we could help you."

I didn't say anything.

"Eric. You're sure this dream no longer bothers you?"

He was very serious and I suddenly felt sorry for the poor devil. How could he really know? He couldn't. How could I tell him? I had to lie eight-tenths of the time now, because I was leaving the hospital today and this was I good-by. I'd been passed, I was O. K. Sure.

"It doesn't bother me. I don't get in a sweat any more. If I pound in my brother's head with a wooden mallet in a dream, it's all right. Isn't it?"

"Just dandy." He sighed, shook his head. "Only he's not even your brother, really. Adopted into the family."

"I've always known him as my brother."

"Only you knew he wasn't. Eric, we've done all we can—"

"But you don't really know a damn bit more than you did when I came in here. Right?"

It was his turn to keep quiet. We sat there for a time without speaking. Then he looked at me. "You say you hate your brother's guts. What's going to happen when you see him?"

"Nothing." God, I thought, suppose he won't let me go. "So we hate each other," I said. "We've been over all this, Doc."

He went on just the same. He always would and perhaps someday he'd write a book, as many of them did. "There was this man–" maybe it would be the last time–"this new man, who came up to the third platoon as a replacement. He looked like your brother."

I sighed. A spider was building a web under the table where they gave the electrotherapy. Maybe it was a black widow.

I knew what he was thinking. He would be going over the same old story in his mind searching for the loose ends that weren't there, and my mind raced back, too. I'd been in charge of the platoon a buck sergeant because it was down to that and Oh God all the rest of it, the platoon wiped out on a ridge all but myself and this new replacement who looked like Frank, my brother, in the bloody twilight with the guns, so the two of us tried to get back to our lines only this other man was now thinking two would draw enemy fire so he lost his head and he tried to kill me and get back alone then I knocked him on the head with a rifle butt and started shouldering him back but I remembered how I hated Frank, damn him, and this was suddenly Frank on my back hating me while they laid a barrage just for us boxed in and then the man Frank came to so I hated him all my life and I picked up the wooden mallet and smashed his head in.

–Claim you killed him only it wasn't your brother and you know that now.

–Still worse that way.

–You got hit then too machine-gunned through both legs slow *tick-tick-tick-tick-tick* not ours and shell fragments in your back but you brought Frank in carrying him on your back and he was dead.

–Yes.

–Raved around telling them what you had done.

–I killed my brother.

–Came to in a hospital.

–Yes.

–Only it wasn't your brother and you hadn't killed him; there was *no wooden mallet!*

–Yes there is!

–Where in God's name would you find a wooden mallet on the battlefield in Korea where countless men saw what happened saw this man killed by enemy machine-gun fire while he was being hauled and carried by you killed by the same gun that got you in the legs *because he melted the soap carvings....*

Prescott had said nothing.

I tried to control my heart and breathing. They were very rapid. Perspiration brightened the backs of my hands. I didn't brush it away because Prescott would notice.

His voice was quite calm. "I swear you still believe you killed him. With that damned wooden mallet. And you dream it all the time. Only now it *is* your brother."

I stared at the floor. "I don't believe it any more."

"All right." He sighed. He didn't believe me, either. "Because of hate. You hated each other all your lives. Because you want to be a sculptor; you are now. But then you had these prize-winning soap carvings on the shelf in your room. Six years old. You came home from school and Frank had melted them down in a pail. He was pouring the melted soap over the shelf. Kids. And he said–"

"Not that alone, Doc. We fought all through childhood. I still hate his guts."

"All right. The thieving, the lies. You tried to kill him time after time when you were kids. Malarky. But he didn't stop. But not to kill him, Eric. There's no reason for that. Even thinking you had–out there. Dreaming it all the time–with a wooden mallet."

"It's a wooden mallet I use when I work with stone. With a chisel. It's hanging on a rack back home right now."

"And for a time you went after people. Fought with them. You go berserk, Eric. Probably a defensive attitude of some kind stemming from the obsession." Again he sighed. "It'll be a good while before you lose that damned dream."

"It's all right."

"We wouldn't let you go if we didn't think it was all right. *It was a dream on the battlefield, Eric.* Battle fatigue–could happen to anyone. The recurrence of the dream is because you still feel yourself guilty, dream or not, and not only of the dream, either. You hate your brother. But not enough to kill him. It frightens you, back there someplace in your mind. Until that part of you is convinced it's a dream, that the man was machine-gunned by an enemy apart from you–until that time, Eric, you'll continue to dream and go through your own particular hell. Because you could never kill him."

Some fiend played havoc with the banjo strings. My jaws ached from being clamped together so tightly.

"Permit me, Eric. It could be you're the son-of-a-bitch." Prescott colored slightly. "You have all, he had nothing. Yet you slaughter him in your dreams. Guilt, Eric. Damn it, we can't do anything more. Unless you want to live here for a few years. You're oriented. The dream's wearing itself out, as you say." He paused, breathed deeply. "Just that you're a little crazier in a more positive way than I am, or anybody else." He lifted his hands, dropped them to the desk, stared at them. Then he slowly raised his eyes beneath his brows and watched me. "You sure there's nothing new?"

"Nothing." My voice was hoarse.

"You'll be seeing Frank before long."

I didn't say anything.

"You're leaving here. That means there's nobody to grab you if you go after somebody."

I'd always felt he exaggerated this. If I went after somebody–as he put it–it would be because they needed just that. Maybe I'd got out of hand in the past but that was finished.

"I've said too much and said it wrong, maybe. But you'll have to take more than this. You're intelligent enough. You'll have times of mental depression. Ups and downs–normal to everyone but you. You'll imagine they're something else. Ride it through. Battle fatigue is just a name that covers countless variations from a specific norm. It can be tough."

"O. K."

"You going ahead with the sculptoring?"

"Yeah. It's all I ever really wanted."

"You're going home to a pile of money."

"Well, there's the business, a loan business. It's worth close to a half million right now. Frank's running it for the time being. God knows how. That's supposed to be split between the two of us when mother dies." I hesitated. "Then there's more money, inheritance, that comes to me when she dies. My father's will."

"Frank's out of that?"

"Yes. But I want to get to work, Doc. I want that business so I can get straightened out. It'll give me the money and time for my sculptoring. Maybe eventually–"

"Never hear from your mother?"

I shook my head. "I told Frank in a letter I was leaving California, heading for home."

"I talked with Frank on the phone, Eric."

I went tight all over, forced myself to relax. But Prescott noticed. He noticed every damned thing.

"I haven't told him anything about what you've been through; it didn't involve him. That's for you to work out. Not the first time I've talked with him. He doesn't know what you dream, only that you do. Your mother's very ill. Sorry. It's her heart, as you know."

I was wearing a light tan suit. It was getting hot. A fly lit on my left sleeve I flicked him off, watched him buzz in an angry circle.

"You're driving home?"

I nodded. "Bought a car. Going into L. A. for it this afternoon."

The fly pulled a vertical bank and if he'd had machine guns he could have strafed Prescott's skull neatly. Prescott reached out with that irritating calmness of his and plucked the fly from mid-air. He thoughtfully squashed it inside his fist, dropped it into the waste basket.

"Leda Thayer–"

"Driving back with me, Doc. She's through nursing; her hitch is up."

"Yes. Going to marry?"

"Soon as I see–get things straightened out."

He sighed again. "She's a good nurse. Make a good wife. Knows what to expect. Fine girl." He paused, then said, "You know she planned to make Army nursing her career?"

I hadn't known. But right then all that mattered was getting out of there. I didn't want to talk with Prescott any longer, answer his questions, wonder what the hell was going on behind his eyes. I knew why he'd kept me here so long. Just to make sure old Garth was headed straight.

He rose, walked around his desk. I stood. We looked at each other. I wished to hell he hadn't killed that fly. "How do your legs feel?"

"Fine."

"You walk all right. Back bother you?"

"No–a little."

"Still a few pieces of metal in there for you to tote around."

"Well," I said. "I guess this is it."

We shook hands. "Don't have to warn you. But stay away from the bottle. No telling what alcohol might do to you. Might start knocking people around just for the noise." He was quite serious. He'd told me about that before.

I forced a grin to let him know nothing bothered me. Because he was trying to bother me–and succeeding. He always had to make sure. I wondered what he'd told Frank over the phone. And what Frank had said, damn him.

"If you feel like things are falling apart, take a walk. Especially if you feel like tearing anybody apart. Take it quick and take it far. I'll always be here." He smiled wryly. "Until I die–or until some guy like you smashes me with my desk."

I began to like him now, after it was too late. "Well, so long, Doc. And–thanks."

"Good luck, Eric."

I went on out. The tenseness that had been with me in the office became worse. I stopped there in the hall, took some deep breaths. It was as if this were some kind of trial. I tried not to think they were just giving me a chance to see what I'd do, that they'd come along after me in a minute. But I couldn't stop thinking that way. It was bad.

One of the men in the ward said there was a guy out on the sunporch who wanted to see me.

"What kind of a guy?"

"A guy! A guy. St. Peter, maybe. Just a guy!"

He was an excitable patient. I noticed Leda down at the other end of the room. She was saying good-by to some of the men. She no longer wore the nurse's uniform. I knew she'd put it on just for me because I liked it. I waved at her. She wrinkled her eyes and waved back.

I went on out to the sunporch. This fellow was sitting in the wicker chair by the magazine rack. He put down a copy of the Reader's Digest and stood up as I entered.

"I'm Eric Garth. Somebody told me—"

"Well, sure. I'm from Decker's."

"Decker's?"

"Your car." He stood there a moment. He was about my height, six two, but maybe a little heavier in the middle. His yellow sport shirt bulged over his belt between the flaps of a tweed jacket. He was bright-eyed and smiling too much and his hair was combed too neatly. It was brown hair and it looked as if it had been cut directly into his skull with a very fine chisel, lacquered, then buffed to a sheen. He didn't quite know what to do with his hands. Then he seemed to remember and hauled a pad of paper from his coat pocket. "The Mercury convertible. Gun-metal color." He cleared his throat and smiled some more.

"What about it?"

"Why—" He flapped at the air with the pad but he didn't lose the smile. "It's down in the drive. Mr. Decker thought it would be fine to bring it out to you."

"Oh. I was coming in for it this afternoon."

"Yes. Certainly." His voice was all full of this smiling ha-ha. "Thought we'd save you the trip. Not really necessary. Just so Decker'll know I delivered it." He winked. "Not that he don't trust me, y'know."

I sighed. He pointed through the screen on the sun-porch, down at the parking lot in front of the hospital. "Right there, she is. Drives like a dream, too."

"Thanks." I didn't like the guy and I had kind of wanted to go pick it up myself. We shook hands. "Well, that's that, Mr. Garth."

I nodded. He swallowed, turned and left. As he passed through the doorway leading into the ward, Leda brushed by him. She looked at him, frowned, then came over to me.

She was an orgy of loveliness.

"Who's he?"

I told her. She wore a pale-green silk dress that had black streaks running through it, and it clung. Her au-burn hair set fire to that green and when she moved–which she did even when she didn't–I felt like that Roman of Nero's time at the feast where the naked princess stepped out of the pie with a snake in her teeth.

Leda moved over to the porch screen and looked down. "I've seen that fellow before. He's been hanging around out here, with someone else. Just lately."

"Probably delivers other cars, baby."

"Maybe."

I went over and stood beside her. The big fellow was just coming down the outside hospital steps. He joined a smaller man and they went on down and sat on a stone bench to wait for the bus. The smaller one had carrot-colored hair and even from this distance a sharp, bright-eyed face. He was pale and middle-aged.

"We've got the car," I told Leda. "There she is. Like it?"

She turned, slid her arms up around my neck. "Anything would do. I'll run along now. You can say good-by and meet me at my place this afternoon."

"All right."

"I love you so damned much," she said. "Because you're going to be a great sculptor and because you're just a little nutty. And, of course, you're going to be very, very rich." She hesitated. "Eric, why don't we get married here before we leave? Then we wouldn't have to hide...."

"We don't hide," I said. "You know that. Make believe. It's all right this way, for now. We'll be married as soon as we get home." I didn't tell her I couldn't take the chance until I knew more about myself. I wanted her as my wife but we'd have to wait for a while.

She poked the fingers of her right hand under my belt, twiddled them. "All right."

I laughed, pulled her close. For a moment she was quite still. "This way," I told her, "you'll be able to make sure I get all that dough."

Her body moved against me and she wasn't breathing. Then she did breathe. Right up against my throat. Hot breath and warm, damp lips. "Yes," she said. "Yes, that's right."

A psycho case back in the ward cursed monotonously, then screamed with laughter.

## Chapter 2

Leda was staying at a place in San Fernando Valley. She had lived in California for some time but only at the Veterans Hospital. She wanted a short chance to view the trade. She had it. She seemed not to care for it. A ranch-type hotel, catering to anyone who had a buck and a babe to spend it on. It also carried babes without bucks and lonesome bucks looking for babes. The Dark Mesa was just that. It overflowed with eucalyptus, green grass shaved so it just tickled your ankles like an expensive deep-napped carpet, and vine-covered, meandering, low-roofed, alley-wayed, muted rooms with all their views on the inside. It was trellised, fenced, scalloped, walled securely, and when you entered the front door into what was probably the lobby, you got a feeling.

I located Leda's hideout. She had two rooms and they were heavy like everything else at the Dark Mesa. It was built to appeal to the senses. The same way Leda was. I somehow distrusted her living here. But it hadn't been for long and I'd seen her most of the time. She was so completely frank about everything, there was probably no reason for my distrust. If Leda slept with any of the bell-hops she'd have told me. It was a rotten way to think, but that was her way.

"You took long enough, Eric. I'm all packed."

There were two suitcases by the door. I hadn't expected this.

"Packed?"

"Yeah." She stepped closer. She was wearing a lemon-yellow terry-cloth robe belted tight at the waist. Her auburn hair was thick and mussed and her eyes were oily, full of sleepy sunshine. Her skin was that way, too, and her lips melted. In a way I would always hate that, hate her–for being drawn to her the way I was. I didn't want to let her go from my arms. Her body was vibrant, lush beneath the robe and the warmth from her body reached me. I felt every full line of her pressed against me, through the robe. She pressed hard. She worked at it and sometimes it was as if she fought–like you'd mash two pieces of clay together, grinding them together.

"You like that," she said.

I squeezed her waist harder and harder. Her eyes fogged and she started breathing through her teeth, hissing her breath in and out, arching backward with the pain. "That's enough!" she said. "Stop, Eric!" Her voice was full of anxiety now.

I quit, swallowed, searched inside me for the patience every man is forced to be born with. I located enough to grin and take her hands.

"Why are you packed?"

Her shoulders still trembled with the ragged breathing. She cocked her head, tipped her lips nervously with her tongue.

"We said we'd stay here for a while."

"I want to leave," she answered.

"Mean find someplace else?"

"No. I mean let's head for home."

"Florida?"

She nodded. "Uh-huh."

It was quiet for a time. I couldn't think of what to say. We'd planned staying here for a time. The moments we'd snatched together on the hospital grounds were just that–moments. Hot and anxious in the shadows.

"Figured we'd stay on a bit."

She turned, walked away, whirled back again. "I want to go, Eric. Baby's been standing still too long." Her eyelids closed. "Can't explain it. I just want to go."

"Well, O. K." I took her in my arms. "You nervous or something?"

"No. I want to be with you–just with you." Her voice was way down in her throat someplace, almost a whisper. "If we stay here, we'll never get away. We'll stay and stay. You know we will."

"I see what you mean."

"Then we'll leave tonight." She smiled and I began to wonder if she had something on her mind. Something might be bothering her. Sometimes a woman will go so far with a fetching idea, then scare herself off. It's called seeing the light. They seldom realize they mentally manufacture that light themselves.

Leda hadn't been like that. She wasn't the kind to scare easily. She lounged on the arm of a chair and wrinkled up the corners of her eyes. "Did he scare you? Prescott, I mean?"

"No." I slumped in the chair and pulled her onto my lap. The robe fell apart over her long thighs. It hit me like always, that white flesh. The smell of her, the feel of her, full and urgent. She wriggled in my lap, fumbled the robe together.

"Prescott does that sometimes," she said. "When a man leaves the hospital. He thinks they'll remember better if they're scared."

"I doubt it." Her hair smelled good. I buried my face in it, kissed her throat. She made a noise of content, but her voice was a shade too loud.

"You aren't scared, are you, Eric?"

"About what?"

"I mean about–yourself."

Outside a car hissed up the gravel drive and white light reflected in diminishing convolutions through the heavily draped Venetian blinds.

"No."

"Doesn't it frighten you at all that you're going to see your brother? That you're free and on the outside again? Did you feel all right driving over here from the hospital?"

I didn't want to look at her. I couldn't hate her for asking these things, yet something twisted tightly inside me. It had always been that way with Leda. Drawn, yet repelled. I loved her. Yet in some ways I hated her. I hated her possibly for the same reasons I loved her. Something inside both of us met with sharp necessity, yet clashed. I wanted to tell her how crazy it all was. That I was as free of any cracked obsessions as she.

I could never actually hurt her physically, though sometimes it came close to that. But sometimes I was compelled to hurt her with words. I knew she wanted to marry, but I had to put it off until I was sure of myself. And once more I thought, We're a damned odd pair.

"That why you want to leave? Frightened of me?"

"Pooh!"

"Yeah. What's that supposed to mean?"

"I was wondering, that's all."

"Quit wondering."

It was funny. Things like that came out, and I know that sometimes I hurt her—just with words.

She took my face in both her hands and blinked at me. Her eyes were very large, concerned, her mouth slightly open. Her chin bunched. "Don't let's fight."

"Think I'm going to crown you?"

"With a wooden mallet?" She smiled.

"You've been talking with Prescott."

I was disgusted with myself for doing this but I couldn't stop. I was worried, plenty, and everything was jumbled in my mind.

"You told me all this, Eric."

"Did you talk with Prescott?" I heard the anger in my voice. I was ashamed of it, but it was there. It was what I felt. I couldn't rid myself of it. It would take time, like Prescott said. Only I half believed he had suggested eight-tenths of my worry to me. It was up to me to rid myself of it. Let it wear itself out. Or become conscious that it was never there in the first place. "Did you?"

"He called me in. Yes."

"Great. What'd he tell you to do?" I stood, dragged her up with me. I walked across the room, sat on the divan in front of the fireplace.

Somehow, touching her, being close to her, it was impossible to talk. She hadn't moved. She stood with her back to me, the long lines of her body showing even through the robe, somehow dissolving the cloth; the supple waist, the flare of hip, the broad curve of shoulder.

"He tell you to watch out?" I said. I realized what I was saying and I didn't like it. My voice went on just the same—harsh, filled with bitterness. "He tell you to get hold of him if I acted funny? Did he?"

She shook her head, not moving, with her back still toward me.

"He tell you I was dangerous, apt to do wild things? He warn you to stay away from me—or what?"

She whirled, came across the room, sat down beside me. I got a crazy thought. Maybe she was being paid to do this—part of her job. Maybe she was just seeing me home....

Excitement was in her voice. "No, Eric. Please don't. You're hurting me and you're hurting yourself. I simply talked with Prescott. He wanted to know more about your plans, our plans. You're so closemouthed."

"It's no business of his."

"He's concerned, Eric."

I nodded. "Concerned. Thinks I'll do some damn fool thing."

"You're acting like a child."

I kept silent.

"He has a right. So've I. We want you well."

"I am well."

"But, darling, you still dream those horrible dreams. Now, listen. We'll be married soon, and you know I love you."

"You want to be sure I won't kill my brother when I see him, don't you? You wouldn't want to be hooked up with a murderer. Damn it, Leda. Nothing's wrong with me."

"All right, darling." She came against me like a flame draws to your hand. "Now I'm going to dress. You're going to sit here and think. We're not going to be like this any more."

She rose, swung into her bedroom. She blew me a kiss as she closed the door. It was like she'd swung her hip against me. I heard her humming in there and I sat on the couch and knew how wrong I was to take off like that, blow up inside.

So much of what I thought was Leda could be my imagination. There was no evil in her. Not the kind of evil you'd think of, anyway. She was pent up. Her nature was like the heat that hesitates along the top of a blast furnace. Withering, hot, molten–anxious to consume. To consume was her nature. It was in her walk, in the way she moved her lips, in the motions of her hands–in fact, of her whole body. Yet it seemed unconscious on her part. I tried to read conscious movement into it. But when I thought about it, I knew it was nothing but instinct. Perhaps Leda was more like her mother than she thought.

I wondered plenty about myself, too. What was going to happen when I returned? There was the loan business my father had left. Frank was running that now. I wanted to get back and get some money. I needed money bad. Because with money I could go on with my sculptoring. That, and now Leda were the important things in my life. I wanted to do a nude of Leda in stone. Maybe then I'd have her– cold and warm at the same time.

And me. What about me? What was going to happen to me? Because there was always that void between sleep and waking. For

the long moments after I woke up, after dreaming, it seemed as real–
the wooden mallet, Frank, everything–as it seemed that blood-and-
thunder day back in Korea.

Leda and I had met close to a year ago. I was in bed all the time
then, unable to get around. I had a private room at the far end of the
ward and Leda was helping out at the library. She wheeled the cart
of books around, for bed patients.

There were trees out beyond my window and some hills, and if I
rolled and propped myself on my side I could see pretty well. The
room was small and out there it was small too, only in a different
way. It was a place composed of the region within my sight. It was
good to see it at all. The four walls of the room were bare except for a
religious painting at the head of the bed and that single window with
the sky blue, gray, white, pale, dark with rain or with the
unrebellious succession of days, and the green.

I was in a far wing of the hospital so there were no buildings in
sight, only the voluptuous unreality beyond the pane of glass; unreal
because I wondered then if I would ever be there again–where it
was. A kind of through-the-looking-glass thing, though not backward.
And between the myriad procession of hospital events, the time-
clocked meals, needles, blood-pressure and pulse counts; "We'll take
off the dressing. There, that wasn't so bad, was it?"; nights of dreams;
Prescott's first visits, "You don't dream?", the lies; "Ah, so you *do*
dream?", the truths at last, "A wooden mallet!"; the bedpans, the
changing of sheets, shave, wash, brush your teeth, the toenails
clipped, scar-tissue, haircut, the occasional scream of agonized
sound purling across the thick night, and worst of all the first
realization that that last scream was you–during the time between I
would look out the window. It was always fine and better than any
movie or play. It never became monotonous. Once in a while people
passed out there, though seldom, and I speculated as to what they
did in life; the fat, the slim, the quick, the weary. I speculated and
dreamed and thought intensely about my sculptoring and of how
much I needed it, how I wanted to return to it. Because thinking
about it grounded you somehow, made things real again. And I
watched the skies change and the clouds and the winds in the trees
out the window.

Then one day my door opened.

"Hi! How'd you like something to read?"

"Thanks. Never mind." I hadn't looked. That door had previously brought nothing to me but a minor or major agony. This could be nothing else.

"Well, have a look, anyway."

I heard the door swing wide and wheels running–one with a squeak–and crepe-soled shoes and the hiss of a nylon dress against what I suddenly saw was female flesh. The cart was piled high with books, with tabs sticking out of them, and magazines. That's what she'd meant for me to look at. I looked at her. She was something to watch.

There she was. My fate stood right there in the door with the books in the cart and looked at me out of still blue eyes. A fate that was going to be mixed up with death, murder, money, and hell. A lush red-lipped fate with thick auburn hair and long legs in a white dress which seemed to have been spun across her body.

Maybe I didn't think anything right then. Except that she was something real. You didn't have to look hard to see it.

"They say you haven't had any books," she said. "I thought you might like some." Her voice was soft, yet there was a rasping quality to it. An exciting voice. Her eyes were very steady.

I raised to my elbows, pushed back against the pillows. Something tore in my back and hurt like hell, but she was morphine.

It was a day in May, about three o'clock in the after-noon, and it began raining when she opened the door.

I hadn't said anything and she looked embarrassed. Her face colored up. When she started to turn the cart through the door, it caught on her skirt.

"Don't go," I said. "I might like something."

She was dubious now. But it was easier at that moment to let me see the books on the cart than to wheel the cart out the door. She half smiled and pressed her hair away from her face with both hands. It was a gesture I would often see and remember for the rest of my life. There was something in that gesture that made you want to sink your hands into that hair. As she moved closer to the bed I realized her eyes had changed from blue to gray. A cold gray, like wet black slate. Her mouth was broad, full-lipped, her body long and willowy with deep breasts, and she was very much alive. The blue returned to her eyes.

"What would you like to read?" Her voice was rusty. That was it.

"I don't know."

She smiled. "Lots of detective stories."

"That's good." I wasn't thinking. Not about books.

"Mysteries pass the time."

"Have you found that?"

"Well, sometimes I read them." She looked out the window. I saw that her eyelids were heavy. I thought then it was from overwork. It wasn't. I learned that later. It was natural with her. Her lids were dark. It wasn't eye shadow, either. It came from something inside her. Those heavy dark lids with the blue eyes were sure something.

Somebody opened the ward door down the hall and the draft caused my door to slam. She said, "Oh," and looked at the door. "I'm not supposed to be in here." She said it like she didn't give a damn.

"Yes."

There was a long silence. Maybe she was trying to be serious but there was always that twist at the corners of her lips.

"Are you hurt badly?"

"No. Are you a nurse here?"

"I've been here since before Korea."

"Why don't you sit down?"

"Oh, no." She had moved a scant inch toward the bed. "I've got to go."

"I'll think of some books I want."

"Do that. I'll come back tomorrow."

We looked at each other. "Let's cut this out," I said. "Let's relax."

"It's been a strain, hasn't it?"

We told each other our names. She knew mine. "The doctor told me. He also said you're interested in sculptoring."

"Yes." I didn't like to talk about that with anybody. It was the only thing I had, really. I wanted to keep it my own–all the way.

"Have you done any recently?"

"Hardly."

"Before you went away?"

"Commercial stuff, mostly. My home's in Florida. I have a place there where I work." I thought it over. "You could sit down. I haven't talked with a woman for a long time."

"Ah." She watched the rain out the window. It was darkening in the room now as the late afternoon slowly failed. "My father was an artist," she said. Her voice was touched with bitterness. "He hung himself. I found him that way, with the light cord twisted around his neck."

It startled me. They didn't talk like that around this part of the hospital.

"That why you're a nurse?"

"No." She stared at me, her eyes bright. "I planned it. I became a nurse so I could find some rich man, a helpless patient, and make him fall in love with me. Then I'd marry him for his money."

"Have you found him?"

Her dress hissed as she moved her leg. "No. I guess not." She told me her hitch would be up in less than a year. After she left I lay in bed and thought about her and knew she was going to get in bed with me. She had the look and that current was there between us. Then I decided I was off my nut and finally I went to sleep.

I awoke in a strait jacket.

It was the dream again. I had Frank up against the wall with one hand driving into his throat. The wooden mallet was in my other hand. I pounded at his head. He kept screaming. I heard him scream and scream as I woke up–only I was screaming.

I was in the hall outside my room. My fist was hurt bad from smacking it on the wall. They were tightening the straps.

"Look," Leda said one day. "You'll find out anyway. Dr. Prescott's made me a kind of special nurse to you. He thought it might do you good."

"It would."

She put the books down on the table by the head of the bed and stood there with her hands clasped in front of her. Her breasts thrust large and firm in a white lace brassiere. I glimpsed the shadow of flesh through the nylon uniform. Her eyes were deep blue and the light from the bed lamp shimmered in her hair. "We may as well learn to be frank and open with each other right away."

"It's a good way to be."

She looked at me sharply, then turned and sat in the chair by the window, crossing her legs. They were long gorgeous legs and the low-heeled crepe-soled shoes somehow enhanced them. In high heels her legs would be of the same impossibility of a Petty drawing. Only they'd be real. That would be something and she knew it.

"I know all about you," she said.

"That's not so good."

"Perhaps not."

"Come and sit beside me on the bed."

She uncrossed her legs and said, "I can't."

"Why?"

"Somebody might come." She made it sound like a caress. It was that unconscious trait of hers. Sometimes when she talked and moved she kissed you with her whole body. Maybe it was the tone of her voice. I wasn't sure.

"Come on," I said. "Be frank and open."

She glanced toward the door. It was very quiet. The staff would be eating and the room was dim, with only the bed light on. She came over and sat on the edge of the bed and said, "There."

It was suddenly very much more than I'd expected. When she was that near the true feeling of it struck me and I reached for her hand. I made it as much of a gesture of instinct as I could.

We sat there holding hands. It was abruptly ludicrous and I let go. She moved closer to me and said, "It's all right. I think I know how you feel." It was almost a whisper.

Leda was from a good family that had no money. They'd put her through the best schools on their name. She was a wild one and she showed it. A suppressed, combustible wildness. She was the type you might wonder about having a knife sheathed in the rim of her stocking. But you'd want to look, anyway. She seemed greatly interested in art, but had the idea people would kill art. They would kill the artist and he didn't have a chance. Through ignorance, through wanting something other than what the artist had to offer.

"I don't like persons like you," she said. "Because I saw it happen to father. All the fine things he did went into the furnace. They heated the front parlor."

"Forget it."

"You've got to have money."

Her father had hung himself, and her mother had gone to Germany before the war and joined the Nazi party for excitement. She'd been a fancy collaborator and had her own radio broadcast on a par with Axis Sally. She'd died in the explosion when the station was bombed. Leda rather lauded her mother.

"Really all right," Leda said. "Misplaced, that's all." So then she got her ideas about nursing and here she was, a First Lieutenant in the Army. That was her story.

"Help me fix the pillows so I can sit up."

"You feel strong tonight?" God, the way she said these things.

"Very."

She stood beside the bed and leaned over me to fix the pillows. I put my arms around her and drew her down and kissed her. I put a lot of pressure into that kiss, holding her down against me, and she started to let go. I knew that when she did let go, put herself into the kiss, it was going to be something. Her lips trembled and her breasts were against me and her hair formed a kind of tent over my face. We were in the tent together and it smelled good.

"Leda."

She fixed the pillows. I sat up against them.

"Leda."

"It was a trick," she said. "You shouldn't have done it." Her lids were still heavy. But beneath those lids the blue of her eyes had changed to gray. She walked over to the door. "Enjoy yourself."

"Leda–"

She went out. The door closed quietly and I heard her crepe-soled shoes whisking down the hall.

I lay there and thought about home with Leda all mixed up in it, her eyes, lips, and body drowning in the daydream. Because I was afraid of sleep–afraid of the real dream.

There was Lenny Conn. I wondered if he had changed; if he was still living on the bayou, fishing, and mowing lawns. Did he still live in that shack with the pictures on the walls? And the flat glass cases shelved in the mahogany cabinet he'd made. Like collecting butterflies. Only they weren't butterflies. And I wondered where that subtle perversion of his had led him. Women. Lenny Conn and his collection about which even the law could do nothing. Lenny. Not very old and not very smart, of backwoods heritage–but cruel. Cruel as the person who tears the wings off flies and watches them squirm is cruel. Lenny Conn, whom I had known most of my life, who had once been a conductor on a Pullman train, who loved women in the blind groping darkness of a fantastic wish, and who mowed our lawn and trimmed our hedges. Wily, at times inscrutable, clever and secret and laughable. Lenny along the shoals in a skiff with a gig in his hand, watching for flounder. Lenny, who was unable to comprehend why the Garths lived in a huge old pillared home with live oaks and drives and misery when he thirsted out his days in a scorpion-infested shack with his cryptic, startling collection.

Whenever I thought of home I had to push away the memory of another girl. Norma. My girl. It was like denying your name. I hadn't written her and she no longer wrote. I wondered if she still wanted to open a photography shop, if she still thought of me, if she would be there, when and if I returned. And thinking of Norma, the circle would flash around, completing itself with Leda. Invariably I would compare them–then think of Leda's breasts and thighs outlined beneath white nylon, in a savage effort to forget the girl who'd said she would wait. Because you do those things....

My light was out and it was past two in the morning. I heard the door open, the hiss of movement, and I smelled her bending over me. I felt her breath on my cheek.

"You're awake. Don't trick me again."

"Leda–"

"I'm sorry," she said softly. "It's just that they all try. I didn't want that from you."

"I'm special?" I needed her and knew it. She had become the something I had to have to endure, to flash back out of the hell I was in.

"I think you're special. I'm not sure yet."

"How long will it be before you're sure?"

I listened to her breathe and it was dark in the room. Her breathing was like her voice. It was very still and lonely and cool in the room with the wind outside the window and the shadows on the wall and her shadow beside the bed. It was always like that in the hospital at night; cool and lonely and very still and the room was longer, high-walled, and sometimes not secure.

I reached for her hand, found it, and she moved toward me. We kissed and this time it was all the way with her giving, then we parted, our breathing warm and nervous and shaking.

"Listen," she said. "We'll have to be careful."

"Don't go." I held her waist, felt the swell of her breasts, the fine line of her waist. I could see the outline of her long legs and how her hips flared. She put her hands over mine, pressing. "Please don't go, Leda."

"Good night."

"Leda—"

She went out softly and closed the door. But it was as if she were still in the room and I was sweating beneath the dressings.

She came often every day then. We would talk and occasionally she read to me. I didn't read any of the books.

"But it's all right, darling," she said. "I don't mind bringing you books. Maybe sometime you'll want to read them."

"With you? Who wants to read if he has you?"

It was getting so I couldn't stand it when she came close, or when we kissed. I needed her around, too, because it was worse now when she wasn't with me. I thought too much about Frank and what was the matter with me. I kept remembering Mother alone with Frank, unwell and unable. Normally she could handle Frank, anybody—but with her heart, I didn't know. And I never heard from her. I had ceased writing.

"You're big enough for a sculptor," Leda said. "Are you bold?"

"I don't know." Maybe she was the bold one.

"Have you ever loved anyone?"

"No." Norma's bright laughing face flashed across my mind. Why did I push her out?

"I'd be a liar if I told you I'd never loved anyone." It was in her eyes, like always.

"How do you feel today?"

"Mean as a snake."

"Any dreams?"

"Yes," I said. "You. A bad dream of you."

I reached for her and her lips were soft and warm and my hands were in her hair and it was wild and hot.

You're not well," she said, sitting up.

I pulled her down. "I'm all right."

"You're not sick, or anything?"

"No. I'm fine. Don't go away."

"Eric," she said. "I love you. I knew it would happen this way. I didn't want it to." The excitement in her voice was rich and impatient. The rustling of her uniform was maddened. "I'll have to be careful of your legs."

"Hell with my legs."

"Tell me you love me," she said.

"I do. I love you."

"Say my name with it."

"I love you, Leda." I could feel it all welling up inside me like damming the Mississippi river.

"Tighter. Eric!" She sat up, frowned.

God, I thought, I did something wrong.

She stood, glanced sharply at me, then walked toward the door. Her crepe soles whisked heartlessly.

"Leda," I said. "Don't go. Where're you going?"

She didn't answer. She closed the door and I heard her going down the hall. You damned fool, I told myself. You did something. What the hell did you do? You've ruined it. That's how you ruin it. I cursed and smashed the bed with my fist.

Then suddenly I knew I loved her. I was in love with her. It was no good, but that's the way it was.

The walls of the room eventually grew smaller with darkness and I fought sleep because to fight sleep was to win out over the dream.


Daily we grew closer and I became stronger but she wouldn't come to bed. Because someone might come into the room. I knew I had to get well.

There was little mail from home. None from Mother, and Frank's letters few and addressed to Prescott. Whatever news they held for me was brusque. He said he had run the loan business into some money. My father's crazy dream. All I saw was Frank running out of money. Mother was close to death, Frank said. Any light shock could take her away.

Frank ignored my questions. Sometimes I wondered a bit insanely if he was alive, if I hadn't killed him after all. Maybe that's why I was in the hospital. At these times I needed Leda.

And all the time, night and day, I fought the dream. I had to leave the hospital, get to work, get back to my sculptoring. I wanted to do Leda in stone. Inch by inch I learned her body by hand. Her mind. She had crawled into my mind. She was insidious and she kept me on a cliff of desire.

Then I was up and around. Stronger. Making my visits to Prescott's office alone now. I used canes. The dreams were bad and I told Leda all about them.

She spoke of Frank. "I can't see what you hold against him. Looks to me more like a go-getter than you. Looks like he'll have plenty of money."

"Wish you'd get money out of your head, baby."

"I like money."

"What else do you like?"

She looked at me. "Not like. Would like."

It was Sunday afternoon and we had planned to spend it on the hospital grounds together. She met me outside the building. I had looked forward to this for a long time. Being with her, alone, out of sight of people. But I hadn't looked forward to what I got.

I still used two canes. But I walked all right and felt fine. I felt as if I could tear down a brick wall.

I knew the moment I saw her....

She was wearing a dress. Not a nurse's uniform. It was a black dress with a zipper all the way down the front in a fold of white. Her eyes were foggy and heavy-lidded and she wore high-heeled shoes and sheer nylons and her hair was thick and blinding.

"We'll walk over there," she said. She was urgent, almost grim.

I couldn't speak right. My throat was thick. I was all bunged up inside and ready to burst. She brushed against me and we looked at each other. Her eyes were hot and her lips damp. We walked on down across the lawn, the green softness, until we were in a thick copse of fir and the walls of the hospital were shielded from view.

"Leda," I said. I held her and dropped the canes. She moved her body against me. "Let's sit down," I said, and the ground was soft and warm with the sun up there and the shadows.

She was suddenly mute. There was an expression of intense anxiousness on her face. She stood beside me, looked down at me, her eyes burning. She dampened her lips with her tongue, reached for the zipper on her dress. Her hands shook. The zipper screamed and the dress opened as she came down toward me.

There was nothing beneath the dress. She kept staring at me, peeling off the dress, staring with that mute, terrific anxiousness.

I cursed her. She was a complete savage, bursting with passion, lustful, wanton, wild. At first it was like drinking hot red wine. Then the whole world shuddered and rocked, with the trees thick and mingled with her hair and the smell of it with the sunny shade, a dark blinding explosion.

She was absolutely mine. The dream.

"You planned this. Your clothes, everything," I said finally. I held her close and quiet. She nodded against me.

"Yes. I've been crazy inside. You've made me crazy. Darling, make me sane again."

I did.


Prescott, the dream, the attempt to uncover the why of the dream, the mostly failure, the realization at last that the hospital was no more help. Leda and the long waiting and now we were going home. My home. And I would face the dream.

"I'll be right with you," Leda told me from the bedroom of the Dark Mesa. "Quit thinking the wrong way."

"Sure."

"Don't be afraid."

That was easy to say....

She came out of the bedroom looking wonderful in a gray dress trimmed with gold, carrying a short coat. She shone all over.

She put the yellow robe in a suitcase along with some other things, then faced me, smiling. "I'm ready," she said.

I didn't move from the couch. I was scared way down inside. I felt like hell. Because things were coming closer and closer.

"Eric," she said. "You'll be all right. It's the getting started. This is your first day away from the regime."

"Yeah."

"You'll be all right."

"O. K. I'll be fine." I rose, squeezed her hand. "You just want to start right now, without anything?"

"Without anything."

Her luggage wasn't heavy, and as we walked outside into the fine summer day, Leda was beautiful and laughing. The car was new and bright and I was free and going home. It was just too good, that's all. It was just too good.

## Chapter 3

That day in Alabama was sponsored by the devil and conceived in the blood-hot womb of hell. There was no way to recognize Leda's remote connection with its birth. It was her first-born of a brood of damnable days succeeding each other only in their hellishness.

And me—I just went along, like always.

Eight days after leaving the hospital in California, we reached Sordell, in southern Alabama, on a Tuesday evening. The trip had been fine, but my head rocked right now. So we picked out a tourist court called the Seven Pines. There were really countless pines, but maybe there had been seven in the beginning. There was a small pond called a lake.

The dream was persistent and with every mile nearer home I had more trouble quelling the desire to turn tail and run. It was like living in a vacuum of intense fear. Leda's hot nearness was the only antidote.

Our cabin, rustic, set up against the shore of the lake; surrounded by pines, was the last one in a semicircle of twenty.

"It's O.K.," Leda said. "You've been driving a lot. Let's stay here a couple days, rest up." She flashed a smile and looked sidewise out of her deep blue eyes. "We can play around a little, too. If you get what I mean. We don't want to be grabbing at each other like a couple of kids when we reach your home. From what you tell me of your brother, he might not like it."

"Hell with Frank! We'll stay, though. I feel like a sick dog– headache."

So we decided to leave on Thursday for the last stab to Cypress Landing, Florida. And I didn't feel sick just because of the headache. I was putting off the last of the trip. I felt like getting drunk, hauling Leda into bed, and staying there for the rest of time.

The owner of the Seven Pines, a portly, florid-faced, tobacco-chewing, overall-clad man named Woodruff, was pleased we were staying. Anybody would be pleased to have the likes of Leda around if only for scenery. She was wearing shorts. Leda did plenty for shorts. She had the solid, full, long shape it takes to fill them right. I'd told her so.

"You're just biased," she said. "And don't tell me it's the artist in you!"

Only two other cabins were occupied, and the owner lived in a combination house and lunchroom with his wife, Amelia. She was a long, thin, wrack of a woman, without hips or breasts, and with black hair combed flat to her skull like an Indian's. She didn't like Leda, but she tried to like her.

The convertible was parked in front of the cabin. I was tired and my head ached like hell. Leda felt fine. She always felt fine. She hadn't been out of shorts now for days now and in the cabin she thrust herself into a black play suit. It had green lizards climbing and cavorting on it. The shorts were very short, Leda's legs very long. Still she rolled the rims of the shorts high and tight.

"All I want's a shower and bed," I said.

"Better eat something. Your energy quotient's probably down."

"Quit playing the nurse."

"I never played much nurse with you, did I?" Her eyes were bright beneath those dark lids of hers and the tan she'd picked up on the trip looked good. In bed nights her body was warm and velvety. "Get that look out of your eyes," I said. "You feel so good, take the car and run into town. Pick up some tooth paste. I need some shaving cream and blades. Maybe I can grab a nap."

She came over and shoved herself against me. We kissed and it was good. I pushed her away, saying, "Go ahead, now."

It was already dark outside and through the open window the smell of rain yawned among crimson curtains.

Leda stuck her lower lip out, jammed her hands into her pockets. It only made the shorts more so. "O. K., stick-in-the-mud. I'll go have a cup of coffee in the lunchroom and tease the Woodruff's first. You can *rest!*"

She was like that. I grabbed her and she melted up against me, her mouth soft beneath the pressure of my lips. Her movements were frank, yet secret with desire—sly in a way that yielded a rich harvest of quick passion. That old feeling of choking urgency came over me and her eyes went smoky. Then she tickled me hard beneath my arms, whirled toward the door.

"I'll be back, lover-boy," she said. "Ta-ta!"

I jumped for her but she flung the door wide. Just outside, in the saffron glow of light from the cabin, she made a face at me and stuck out her tongue. I watched her hips as she went over to the car. They were something to watch and I never tired of it. The longer I was with Leda, the more I hated her and the more I loved her, wanted her.

The car drove off up the drive. I went inside, stripped, took a shower. The water was tepid, probably pumped from the lake. My head ached worse than before and I couldn't chase the big worry.

I slipped on a pair of shorts and stretched out on the bed. I wanted to sleep. But each time I dozed, I snapped myself awake again. It was the old grim taunt, the nemesis that haunted me every time I lay down, every night, every time I wished for sleep.

I feared sleep. Because with sleep came the dream.

We were nearing Florida and I knew we'd have to meet my brother. There was an actual fear in my heart. I didn't know what I'd do; I didn't know. I was scared to even think of it.

I envied Leda for the way she felt. Exuberant, full of zest. It was hard to believe she'd ever been a nurse. But then, remembering, it was hard to put my finger on any nurselike quality in Leda. Those long months at the hospital in California, after Korea, were jumbled, hazy.

I turned off the lights. The bed felt good. I tried to blank out my mind so I could sleep.

I must have finally succeeded.

The lights were on in the cabin. All of them. And bright. I woke up like that, with the door of the cabin open against the rain. A man stood in the door. His back was to me, but he wore a blue cop's uniform.

I sat up. Another man was in the corner of the room, also uniformed, and still another bent above the bed. He was in plain clothes.

"This Garth?" he said toward the door.

"I reckon so." It was Herb Woodruff's voice, from outside in the rain. "That's Mister Garth, leastways." The cop at the door stepped aside and Woodruff thrust his head inside, his jaws thrusting around a cud of tobacco. The shadow of his head loomed large and motionless for a brief moment against the wall. "These folks want to see you for a spell," he said.

"What for?"

The man in plain clothes beside the bed grunted. He wore a gray felt hat, freckled with raindrops, shoved back on his head and he had both hands in the pockets of his gray suit. He sported a dark red tie with a Windsor knot. There was a thick gold watch chain webbed across his bulging vest. I hadn't seen a vest in a long while.

I glanced at my watch on the night table. Eight-thirty. It was raining hard. Diamond drops of water glistened on the dark uniforms.

"My name is Redfern," the man in the gray suit said. He had a dry, papery voice. He had ageless eyes and they sneered at me. That's the way he looked at the world.

"Reckon you weren't really asleep, were you?" Redfern said. "Want to ask you some questions, Garth. You are Garth, aren't you?"

"What's this all about? That's my name." I was fogged with sleep and everything was a jumble. My head no longer ached but it felt thick, heavy, hard. "Sure, I was asleep."

Redfern motioned toward the cop in the corner. "This is Bill Hardy. Bill, when you sneaked in an' lit the lights did he 'pear to be sleeping?"

Hartly looked at me, snapped his eyes away quickly, shook his head. "No."

I couldn't recall dreaming. But I might have. I was damp with sweat.

I swung my feet to the floor. Redfern stepped back and leaned against the bureau. He folded his hands and leaned on one elbow. His eyes were wary, sneering.

Woodruff's face still hung in the doorway. The cop stepped outside, closed the door. I glimpsed Woodruff's face peering intently in the window as he walked by. The rain fell heavily on the lawn out there among the suddenly windy pines.

This Hartly was young, with a smooth, sunny face. He was trying very hard to look grim.

All I could think was, They've come for me. Where in God's name is Leda? My stomach burned and fear was like a thick clot of blood in my throat.

"Where's my wife?" My voice was shaky. I tried not to show anything. "What's happened?"

"You're a bit late with that one," Redfern said. "They usually get it in sooner."

"She went into town. Where is she?" They could have no way of knowing she wasn't my wife.

"You went into town, too, didn't you, Garth?"

"No."

"Sure," Redfern said. He released his hands and wiped his nose with a thick finger. His nails were dirty. The front of his vest was stained. But his eyes were still and cold with intelligence.

"His wife's over in the lunchroom," Hartly said. "I checked. I didn't bother her, didn't go inside."

"Naw. No use in that," Redfern said. "There was only one person in the car. A man. You, Garth."

It was getting me now. "All right," I said. "Tell me."

Redfern folded his hands and leaned against the bureau. "Suppose you tell me."

I started past Hartly, headed for the door. He grabbed my arm. I tore loose, whirled on Redfern. "Damn it! What's the matter?"

"Get some clothes on," he said. "It's cold and wet outside."

"I don't need any clothes!"

"Put some clothes on, like I say."

We looked at each other. I swore to myself, slipped into socks, shoes, pants, and a sweater.

"All right," Redfern said. "Come on."

"Where?"

"Get your coat."

"Haven't got one. It's packed."

He shrugged. "Well, just come on, then."

Hartly opened the door, looking very grim. Woodruff nudged me forward. We went on out the door and across the sodden lawn. It was dark; the rain shone in puddles on the drive and silvered the pines.

In the back of my mind the specter of the dream set up its everlasting haunt. It was a cheap ghost and I knew it. But it lurked in the crannies just the same, peering fiendishly forth, certain of my anxiety.

We went on to the far curve of the drive, then off the drive across the lawn between two cabins that were empty. My convertible was parked under some pines. I started on toward the front of the car, but Redfern gently held me back. "No. This way."

We stood behind the car in the rain. "Now, look, Garth. You going to tell me about it? Or you going to make it hard?" Redfern said. "Let's concede the facts. You're a dope and you know it."

I didn't say anything.

He sighed. "Were you in town today? Sordell? About an hour ago, say, maybe?"

"No. I've never seen Sordell, damn it."

Redfern sighed more loudly.

Hartly snatched a fingerful of water off the rear fender of the car, snapped it at the ground. "He's lying. Can't you see?" Hartly was very young. I felt like smacking him and remembered what Doc Prescott had said about that. But I hadn't smacked anybody in a long while. Blood came up into my shoulders and the back of my neck. The muscles across my stomach tightened, and there was a heavy, good stiffness in my fist as I closed it tight.

Redfern noticed. "Hang on, fella," he said. "Just hang on."

"Look," I said patiently. "Tell me who you are."

"I'm a detective with headquarters in Sordell. Police. This isn't routine, Garth."

"No," Hartly said. "Wise up, Garth. In a hit and run seems like somebody sees it most of the time. Only you're a dope, Garth. You run, but you quit too soon. It was a fast report. The tip was fast, and fast radio work. Slim Gullen down at the gas station even seen you turn in here. Wise up, for God's sake."

Hartly's words reached me through a fog. Hit and run? You didn't do those things. The wild craziness that used to grip me in the hospital took hold–inside.

I had to see Leda. If she was in the lunchroom, I had to see her. She'd had the car. She must know something.

"Let's look at your car," Redfern said. "We already looked, of course. Just want to show you."

We walked on around toward the front of the car. Hartly had a flashlight. I wondered where the other cop was.

Hartly lit the light.

In the hushed dripping of the rain Redfern held my arm. I was suddenly mad and I knew I could take him if I could get one swing at that bulging gut, that stained vest. I wrenched away from him, whirled.

My mouth opened and stayed that way. I spotted the left front fender of the car in the bright white light of Hartly's flash. Redfern hadn't moved.

"You aren't startled, are you, Garth?"

I was plenty startled and then I was scared. Hit and run is a bad thing. I was sure it hadn't been me. I'd been asleep. What about Leda?

The left front fender of the car was dented badly. The headlight was broken and part of the grille was bent.

"We already took some samples of blood," Redfern said. "Leastways, it looks like blood. There was so much of it the rain didn't even wash it away. Some hair, too. Red hair. Bet you didn't notice he had red hair when you hit him, did you?"

I just went on staring.

"Makes you think, hey, Garth?"

Then something snapped. Down inside me something let go; something that had been tied securely out at the hospital. It was like choking on water, spitting it out.

I looked at Redfern. He was looking at Hartly. I ducked low and swung with my right fist. There was no thought behind it, I just swung with all my might. The fist sank into Redfern's middle, I felt it sink, and he made a noise from his stomach. My head throbbed and all I could think was, Prescott said don't and if you feel like it, take a walk quickly.

I shoved Redfern before he struck the ground. I ran between the cabins, heading for the lunchroom. I had to find Leda.

"Pete!" Hartly yelled. "Samson!"

I ran on the wet grass, head down, my feet sliding.

A shadow burst from in front of a cabin. The other cop with his hand raised, holding something. I dove for the hand. My foot slid and I pulled a split.

The hand came down hard once, twice against my head, and then I was lying with my face pressed into the puddled gravel of the driveway and they talked over me. My head ached and bright white pains flashed into my middle like tracer bullets.

"My God, what a dope."

"Dope is right.'

"His fingers moved, he's coming around."

The rain was cool on the back of my head.

## Chapter 4

Sprawled in the muddy gravel drive I knew for sure it was all just too good. I had a bad head now, all right.

"He's got a hard head."

"The son-of-a-bitch, I should of cracked it."

"Come on, Garth," Redfern said. "Get up!" He grabbed my arm, helped yank me to my feet. The rain wasn't letting up and the night was as black as Amelia Woodruff's hair. "He just wants to play it the hard way," Red-fern said. "We get 'em lots of times like that. Reckon he'll loosen up, though."

I was dazed. Hartly had said Leda was in the lunchroom. I started to pull away from Redfern but he caught me up.

"Geez," Hartly said. "He still wants to run."

The other cop grunted and walked off toward my cabin.

"He's perturbed is all," Redfern said. "Anybody'd be perturbed. You'd be perturbed, Bill, if you done a thing like this. Reckon I'd even be perturbed."

"I want to see my wife."

"That's where we're going. Come on."

Redfern led me back down the drive and I saw a squad car with a spotlight mounted on the roof. The other cop was at the wheel. Hartly climbed in front. Redfern said, "I'll sit in back with *Mr.* Garth. You'll have to come back for his car."

We went around the drive and stopped in front of the lunchroom. I saw Leda seated inside at the counter, talking with Amelia Woodruff. Leda still wore the play suit with the green lizards climbing on it.

We went inside. Leda saw the cops, then me, and her eyes went wide. "Eric! What's happened?"

I stepped quickly over to the counter beside her, told her to be still. Redfern and Hartly stood behind me. Amelia Woodruff's eyes glazed and the long talons of her right hand fussed with a brooch which dangled from the bodice of her dress like a clock pendulum.

Just then Herb Woodruff came in from the kitchen. "Amelia," he said. "Amelia, get back here." He looked hard at me, then said, "Amelia," again.

She turned and looked at him.

Redfern said, "Yeah, Mrs. Woodruff. Better do like your husband says."

Amelia glanced at Leda, then me. She turned and stalked back into the kitchen. The spring door flapped like my grandmother's old palm-frond fan. The one with the Sherwin Funeral Parlors advertisement printed on it.

Neither Redfern nor Hartly said anything.

"Did you go into town?" I asked Leda.

"Sure." She looked at me anxiously. "I came back just a few minutes ago. What's the matter? You're all over mud."

"Never mind that. How'd the car get back to the cabin if you stopped here?"

"I didn't take the car, darling. I took one of those little buses that run into town." She shrugged. "I went to the drugstore, got the tooth paste and the other stuff you wanted." She moved her hand to the counter, flicked her finger against a paper bag. "I took the bus on around the town and back out here. The lights weren't on in the cabin so I figured you were asleep. Didn't want to wake you yet." Her eyes told me what no one else could see. But she kept looking at my mud-stained clothes. "What's the matter, Eric?"

"You sure you didn't take the car?"

"Certainly."

Redfern and Hartly said nothing. I felt hollow inside–hollow and dead. Then I seemed to wake up a little and knew I'd be able to explain it easily enough. It was all foolish.

I jerked my head at Redfern and Hartly. "They say I had the car in town. That I hit somebody, then drove back here."

Leda made a face. "For God's sake, that's silly."

Redfern grunted and wiped his finger across his nose. I looked at them both. They were as soaked with rain as I, but I got no satisfaction from it.

"This man's been very sick," Leda said. "He just left the hospital a few days ago. This sort of thing isn't good for him. I can vouch for him."

Redfern nodded. "Sure, sure."

The kitchen door flapped and Amelia Woodruff stalked into the room. She stood with both hands on the counter and looked at me. "Mr. Garth. We'd take it as a kindness if you and Mrs. Garth would leave right away." Her eyes narrowed, her black hair shone in the bright blue neon light that gleamed from bars along the ceiling. "We don't like your kind here. Please leave immediately."

"Amelia," Herb Woodruff called from the kitchen. "Get back here!"

"You hear me?" Amelia said to me.

"Amelia," Herb Woodruff called. "Get back here!"

She made a wry face and the brooch swung pendulously along her empty bosom. As her husband started through the door, she turned and went back into the kitchen. The door flapped. I could hear them talking out there.

"Darling, just tell these men that you were asleep in the cabin. That you didn't take the car." She turned to Red-fern. "He didn't drive into town. I'm telling you that. Ask Mr. Woodruff. He'd know if the car left here."

"We did," Redfern said. "Woodruff was on the other side of the lake digging night crawlers."

"Ah, it's an obvious tip," Hartly said. "Let's take him in."

Leda looked at me. "You didn't drive out with the car, did you, Eric?"

"Of course not."

"What's the matter?" Redfern said. "Can't you trust him?"

"She can trust me," I said. "You're not taking me any place."

Hardy made a face.

"Just what's so obvious about all this?" Leda said.

It was like having the doctors work on your wounds. You were off someplace, yet you were there, watching it. What they said didn't mean anything to you; it was of you, yet not for you. At the same time, it concerned you altogether.

There was something in Leda's eyes behind the smoke; something bright and what the hell. I didn't like it.

Hartly was talking. "The tip was phoned in and radioed to me. The license number and description of the car. Mercury convertible, gun-metal color. California plates. Probably the only Mercury convertible of that color with a California license in this county." He shrugged. "It was an anonymous tip."

"Where's this person I'm supposed to have hit?"

"The hospital," Redfern said. "He's not dead. Reckon you was scared of that."

I hadn't thought about death. Not this way.

"We'll go down to the station," Redfern said.

"Me, too?" Leda asked.

"Yeah, lady," Hartly said. "You, too."

"We'll stop by the hospital," Redfern said. "Maybe Allen got a look at Garth."

"I'll have to change," Leda said. She ran one hand across her shorts and all eyes followed the movement.

"You look all right, Mrs. Garth."

Riding into Sordell, no one spoke. The tires hissed on the wet pavement. Rain drummed on the car's roof.

Leda and I didn't speak to each other. Once when I glanced at her and she looked at me, I saw that her face was very pale. She drew close into the rear corner of the seat against the window.

The antiseptic odor, the stillness, the whisking, unruffled quiet reached me. A gray-haired, stout nurse sat at the hospital reception desk in the front hall.

"Hit and run? Oh, yes. Allen. Gerald Allen. In Two-Nineteen. Second floor. Just up those stairs right there, turn right. It's the second door on your left." She was big bosomed and she fussed with a pad of paper. "The doctor said if you all came you all could look in."

This was no dream. Maybe the dream was better. For some reason I thought of Norma, back home. She would have fought. She would have climbed all over Redfern and spat in Hartly's eye.

"Thanks, nurse." Redfern took my arm and the four of us paraded up the stairs.

Outside the door another nurse confronted us. Slim and too quiet, she spoke in whispers. She was impressed with her duty, probably a new nurse.

"I'm Sheriff Redfern."

"Oh, yes," the nurse said. "You can go right in, but you can only stay a minute. Dr. Morton said he can talk, but not to excite him. He's hurt pretty bad, you know."

Redfern's gaze swiveled to me. The nurse opened the door and we walked in.

The dimly shaded bed light above the white-painted hospital bed was the only light in the bare room. A white screen on rollers was to the right of the bed. The blinds were drawn and the man in the bed was detectable only as a hump beneath the tautly smooth white covers.

Bright-eyed, he watched us enter. He lay very still. Redfern drew me over beside the bed. The man's right arm lay in a cast and there were bandages on his chest and shoulder. There was tape on his jaw and dressings over his left ear.

"Mr. Allen," Redfern said. "We don't aim to bother you. So if you'll just say yes or no—Can you identify this man as the man who struck you with a car early this evening in Sordell?"

The man's gaze turned to me. He said nothing.

Then an odd feeling took hold of me. I turned to Leda, pressed her hand, started to say something, changed my mind. I stared hard at Gerald Allen.

I had seen him before. I was sure of it. Red hair. Not much of it but it was red, all right, and he was small, too. It was noticeable even in the bed. My mind went back to the hospital in California. Where a carrot-colored head of hair shone in sunlight and its owner stood on the hospital steps. Yes. Allen was the one–he had to be. But how could I prove a thing like that–and why?

"How about that, Mr. Allen," Redfern said. "You get a look at this guy?"

Allen shook his head slowly. "No." He closed his eyes. "I hurt. Leave me be."

I bent over the bed. "Allen," I said. "Allen, were you ever in California? Just lately? Were you?"

Leda pulled at my arm. "Eric, what's the matter?"

The door of the room opened. The nurse looked in. "Your minute's up," she said. "I'm sorry, you'll have to leave."

Was it sudden fright, then relief, that I noticed in Allen's eyes?

## Chapter 5

"I want to speak with my wife–alone."

We were starting down the hall toward the hospital stairs. Redfern frowned.

"All right," he said. "We'll wait on the stairs. You been co-operative. You didn't have to do this, y'know."

I just looked at him.

"Why d'they want to do that?" Hartly said.

"Maybe he wants to hold her hand," Redfern said. "Come on." They moved down to the first landing and stood there, talking quietly.

"Listen," I said to Leda. "Did you recognize Allen? Have you ever seen him before? Think hard, baby."

She looked at me. "Eric, what's all this about? Are you sure you didn't leave the cabin and go out with the car after I went into town?"

I felt anger and bitterness and I couldn't keep that out of my voice. "You know better than that. I'd tell you if I went into town. What's the matter with you?"

"Of course," she said. She looked at the floor, then at me. "What did you say about Allen?"

*"Have you seen him before?"*

She shook her head. "No, Eric. I've never seen the man."

I reminded her about the day at the hospital in California.

She recalled the men. "But I'm sure you're wrong, Eric. It couldn't possibly be."

I groaned inside. What use was it? It was like shouting, in a tornado. I might have known she'd see no resemblance. But it was there for me. I read it and it was there. "Listen," I said. "I don't know what's up, Leda. I didn't take the car out. The fender's dented and there was blood on it. If they type that blood with Allen's and find it's the same, they've got the car. I know I didn't do it. Why would anybody want to say I did?"

Leda's lips were damp and her eyes glistened, her lids heavy as always. Her hair was moist from the rain. She touched my arm. "Eric, whatever it is, it can be explained. I'm sure of that. I didn't have the car and neither did you. So there's nothing to worry about. I just keep wondering about—"

"What?"

"Nothing."

"It was the same man. I know it."

"Darling, you're excited and tired. Thinking of your dreams too much. You get back to the cabin, go to bed. You'll feel better in the morning."

I looked down the stairs toward Redfern and Hartly. Redfern motioned. "Come on, Garth."

I nodded at Leda. "Sure—home and bed. That's a long way off, baby, and I know it. You better learn it now. There's plenty of explaining to do. All I can see is I'm framed for something I had no hand in. It's more than just a mistake. Don't you see?" And somebody had moved that car—but I couldn't prove that, either.

She took my arm. "Come on, let's go," she said. "See if we can't find what it's all about."

We went down the stairs and joined Redfern.

"Look," Leda said. "My husband—" she glanced quickly at me, "isn't well. He's a war veteran. Just left a hospital in California. We're going to his home in Florida. He needs rest. This excitement is the worst possible thing that can happen to him."

"Doesn't look sick to me," Hardy said.

"Something the matter with him upstairs?" Redfern said.

I glanced at Leda. "Never mind." I didn't want her to start talking about that. Could be it would make things worse. This was bad enough.

Hartly watched the tight fleshy way of Leda's hips as she walked down the stairs ahead of us. I glared at him. He turned to me and winked.

Police headquarters was downstairs in the courthouse. The officer in charge of the desk, Lieutenant Morgan, was alone in the room of many sins. A row of lockers sloped against the far wall and there was a low bench at the back. The desk itself was on a small platform behind which a steel door with a small barred window shielded the cell block.

Hartly closed the door against the rain and we stood there dripping. The other cop had remained with the car. Leda seemed the least affected, but she was pale and her hands worked together.

Redfern said, "Here we are. A good night for a murder, too." He glanced at me shrewdly. "One thing I hate's a hit and run."

Lieutenant Morgan rested an elbow on the desk, planed fingers above his eyes, and stared at us. The fingers of his left hand drummed on the desk blotter. He had a long thin face with bad teeth and dark eyes beneath his blue cap. He took off the cap, laid it on the desk. He was bald save for a fringe of brown hair above his ears. His nose was bulbous and looked wormy.

Hartly stepped up, put one hand against the desk, and told Morgan the story. "This is Mrs. Garth," he finished. "She claims she was in town, too. She knows nothing of her husband's whereabouts at the time of the accident."

"I do," Leda said. "He was asleep in our cabin."

"Are you sure? Did you see your husband sleeping?" When Morgan spoke, he expelled a great deal of air with each word, like a dry whistle. "You really can't be sure of anything, Mrs. Garth. From what Officer Hartly says, you all were in the lunchroom after Hartly returned. You didn't go to the cabin as you didn't wish to disturb your husband."

"This is all rot," I said. "You know it's rot!"

"Is that right?" Morgan said. "Can *you* prove you were in the cabin?"

"I was there, that's all."

Morgan lifted a sheet of paper from his desk. Redfern slumped on the bench at the back of the room. I could hear him breathing.

Morgan said, "I have here a report from the hospital lab. Gerald Allen's blood type and the type of the blood found on the front of your car, Mr. Garth, correspond. It was human blood, and that alone is enough. Also, hair found with particles of human tissue on the bumper, headlights, and grille of your car, has definitely proved to be hair from the victim–Gerald Allen. Particles of glass from the headlights of your car were picked up at the scene of the accident. They'll doubtless be matched with what glass remains in the headlight of your car. Thus absolute verification seems to be the case, Mr. Garth. That in view of the fact that a witness, unknown but nevertheless a witness, gave us your license number and description of the car." He laid the paper down and folded his hands.

"I've seen the man before," I said. I told him of the California car delivery.

Lieutenant Morgan's gaze shifted to Leda: "What about that, Mrs. Garth?"

Leda chewed her lip, looked down, then up at Morgan. "I–I–"

"Leda," I said. "Leda, tell him!"

She turned to me. "Yes, Eric. I did see what you saw. But we really can't swear it's the same man."

Morgan carefully smoothed the sheet of paper with both hands. Redfern struck a match against the wall and lit a cigarette. He tossed the match to the floor, looked at me and shrugged. He blew a cloud of blue smoke at the ceiling.

Morgan watched Redfern over our heads. Redfern quietly inspected his cigarette.

Hardy kept rocking back and forth on his heels. His shoes squeaked. He made many faces.

"Leda. Can't you tell them anything?"

Her lips pressed tight as she shook her head. She made a vague gesture with her hand, looked appealingly at me.

Morgan said, "Sorry. We'll have to hold you." He reached in the desk drawer, came up with a bunch of keys, tossed them to Hartly. "Cell number three."

"I want a lawyer."

Nobody said anything. Hardy coughed twice.

"Would you be so kind as to see Mrs. Garth home?" Morgan said over our heads to Redfern.

Redfern stood, took a last drag on his cigarette, dropped the butt and tamped it out with the toe of his shoe. He talked around the smoke. "It'd be a pleasure." He nodded to me, frowned and said, "Come along, Mrs. Garth."

It was like swimming behind glass.

Leda turned to me, touched my arm. "Don't worry, Eric. It'll be all right. I'll be back as soon as I can. I'll think of something."

"Won't be able to see him till tomorrow," Morgan said. Hartly already held my arm. I could only stare at Leda. She winked at me and nodded slightly.

Redfern said, "Coming, Mrs. Garth?" He frowned at me again as if puzzled, shook his head.

Leda smiled reassuringly, touched her lips with her tongue, swung sharply about, and went through the door, followed by Redfern. Her quick footsteps were swallowed in the rainy night. It was like a movie scene.

"O. K., Garth," Hardy said. He shoved me gently toward the steel door. He unlocked the door.

We went down the row of shadowy cells. He didn't bother with the cell-block light. It was dim, with only a single bulb at the far end.

He unlocked the third cell from the end, motioned me in with a contemptuous grin. "Pleasant dreams." He locked the cell, went away, and I heard the steel door clang shut. Then their voices reached me from up there, a dull mumble.

The cell smelled sour. The walls were damp. Light from a street lamp through an outside window threw a pale glow on an iron cot which swung chained against the wall. I unhooked the chain, let the cot down. A ratty blanket covered steel slats which were supposed to pass as springs. I dropped the blanket on the floor, sat on the bare springs. To hell with that. I picked up the blanket, spread it on the cot, sat down again.

So there were bugs. Fleas. So what? There was nothing I could do about that.

I hadn't walked in my sleep. In the hospital I had walked from my room in sleep, slammed the walls with my fists, howled and carried on till I'd landed in a strait jacket. But I could never have blanked out, run the car to Sordell, hit a man in the street, returned to the Seven Pines.

Somebody had moved that car.

I was plenty tired. If I did get out of here tonight there'd be nothing I could do. The possibility of bail was there. I nearly called Morgan, but passed it up. This was as good a place as any to think.

Leda could turn herself on and off like a faucet. I remembered occasions at the hospital when she'd acted peculiarly. The way she'd acted tonight was something. It was as if she'd pulled a shade and run off with her true personality, leaving one behind that knew nothing about anything.

Once, at the hospital, she tripped a patient and he fell down two flights of stairs, breaking his arm in two places. Because he looked at her hips and waggled his eyebrows. But she told everyone she knew nothing about it. Even though some had seen her do it. She absolutely knew nothing, period.

Another time a nurse whom Leda disliked spilled some coffee on Leda's dress. It was an accident and the nurse apologized. But Leda knew a patient who was in love with the nurse, but too shy to come out with it.

One night when the nurse had late duty, Leda got some ethyl alcohol and fixed drinks for the patient until he was tight as a drum. Then she talked up the nurse's quality. Later in the night the patient rang for the nurse. She came to his room, unknowing. The man knocked her out with a caster from the bed, tore her clothes off, blocked the door with a chair.

It was four hours before she was missed. She came crawling down the corridor, naked, and was hospitalized for a month.

Although Leda had the keys to the storeroom, and others were sure of some of the facts, nothing could be proved.

"Yes," she told me. "I got the fool drunk. She'd have done the same to me if she had the chance. I think she liked it."

The next moment she would draw the shade. "What? It's terrible. Someone from the other wing must have accidentally left the storeroom door unlocked."

"But, Leda, you just told me–"

"Oh, that. I was only fooling, darling."

But I knew she'd done it. Funny thing was it didn't bother me as it should. Thinking about it when she wasn't around was bad, some. But when she was near me, the picture changed. She could act queer, but it was all right....

I sat there and pitied myself for a while. I'd heard how they could hold you in these backwater jails for God knows how long. I'd recently read in the paper about some guy who'd moldered in an iron flea-box for two years. Awaiting trial, while his case had long since been closed.

I stretched out on the bunk. The old fear about meeting Frank crept in and I thought of Leda, Mother, the business, the inheritance, my dead father, and they all got to swirling around viciously in my mind. There was a long, deep, yellow-and-black funnel like when they put the ether cup over your face and I went away spinning up the funnel into darkness.

"All right, Garth. Rise and shine."

I propped my eyes open against the dim glare of morning, stared at cell bars. It was Morgan. From the dirty windows above the basement wall, a hand of pale dawn palmed stagnant air.

"Somebody to see you," Morgan said. He unlocked the cell door. "Come on."

My mouth felt like the blanket I'd slept on. My eyes were sticky, my head ached. I was stiff in every joint. I swung my feet to the floor. Might better have been in the drunk tank. Company there, anyway.

Morgan was impatient. "Come on."

He stood there, jangled his keys, straight-faced. The long stretch of night duty had fingered blue-black circles beneath his eyes. His red bulb of a nose had paled to a gray mass.

"All right," I said. "Who's here?"

Morgan didn't answer. He left the cell door swinging open, clumped down the corridor ahead of me. He had a walk like a tired bull. We went on into the office and I stood there. My heart was quite still.

Leda was class this morning. She wore a crimson nylon suit. It was like tape across her body. A glistening black purse was slung from her arm. Her coppery hair shone richly. "Hello, Eric."

I couldn't speak. What stopped me was the man who lounged smiling at her side.

Frank.... My brother, Frank.

## Chapter 6

"Well, aren't you going to say something?" Leda said.

"Hello, Eric," Frank said. "How's the hero?" Big and false and sleek in a rich chocolate double-breasted suit, carrying a soft gray felt hat in his right hand. He stood there in the cigarette-smoky office beneath the dim lights with his contemptuous brown eyes, his nose wrinkled a little, and with that fine false smile I knew so well.

The shaking started in the pit of my stomach. It spread like water splashed on blotting paper. Spread down into my legs, up into my throat, my arms, my head. I stood there trembling, shaking. I knew I must be a fine god-damned picture. The whole long stretch of me, mud-covered, hair standing on end, bruised face. Eric Garth.

The dream drummed in my ears. I stared at Frank.

"Eric," Leda said nervously. "Say something."

I heard Morgan mount the platform behind the desk, rattle papers, cough dryly.

Frank grinned. Perspiration formed beneath my arms, trickled down my sides.

"Take me back to my cell," I said, turning to Morgan.

"Sorry."

I started toward the steel door.

"Eric," Leda said.

Frank cleared his throat.

"You aren't going back to your cell," Morgan said. "What's the matter with you, Garth?"

I looked at Frank again. Then my voice talked apart from me. Much too loud, hoarse and hollow.

"What brought you?"

The smile had dissolved on Frank's face. He looked overly concerned, worried. It was obviously false concern.

"I phoned him last night," Leda said. Her fingers drummed along the top of her purse. "He flew up. I met him at the airport. They've impounded the car, Eric. Frank has everything taken care of already. Don't worry about a thing."

Something clattered on the desk. I turned sharply. Morgan had emptied my belongings from the big brown envelope where he had put them the night before. "These are yours," he said. "Pick 'em up."

"Everything's fine, Eric, boy," Frank said.

It was like a knife.

"Leda and I had an early breakfast together," Frank said. "She told me all about everything."

I glanced at Leda. Her breasts heaved beneath the taut nylon, her eyes were veiled.

"Leda told me about this mess," Frank said. "I've made arrangements. Everything's taken care of."

"You said that."

"Don't worry, boy," Frank said. He was overgrand, more aggressive than I remembered. He was smoother and the cruelty that had always been in him showed on the surface now. The contempt was in his voice as well as his eyes. He was trying hard to be nice. Somehow I knew Leda liked the way he acted. "Saw Norma yesterday," Frank said. "She asked about you."

The shaking went out of me. I went cold and it scared me for a minute. I decided I'd better get out of here, and quickly. I started for the door.

"Better get your things," Leda said.

"You get 'em for me," I told her. I went on to the door. "You said you had it fixed, that I can go?"

"That's right," Frank said.

A door across the room slammed and Redfern came toward me. He looked as if he'd slept in his clothes, paid no attention to anyone, came directly up to me, guided me through the door into the morning.

"C'mon out to the car," he said.

"What's up, where we going?"

"Never mind."

"He go my bail, or what?"

"Something like that."

We went up a cement alley and across the courthouse lawn to a squad car parked by the curb. We stood there a moment, looking at each other. Redfern's eyes were fuzzy with sleeplessness, but the wary intelligence was there and the energy, too. I asked him for a cigarette and we both lit up.

A stocky, fresh-shaven, bright-eyed cop clipped down the courthouse steps, came across the lawn, nodded to Redfern, climbed behind the wheel of the squad car.

Then Leda and Frank came along. She laughed at something Frank said. As they neared, Frank fished in his pocket, brought out an expensive, foil-wrapped cigar, cut the end with a knife, and carefully lit the end.

Leda touched my hand. Frank watched her from behind his cigar. She was beautiful and she had pulled the shade.

"Let's go," Redfern said.

Leda, Redfern, and I sat in back. Frank crowded into the front seat, full of elegant movement.

As we drove off around the square I saw the loungers in overalls, chewing, talking, spitting on the lawn, or slumped in the sunny heat of the steps. We went on around the square past diagonally parked cars before colorful modernistic store fronts. Pretty soon we were on a blacktop road running beside a river.

"Where we going?" I said.

Frank turned flatly in the seat and his breath came hard as he looked at me. Redfern peered out the side window.

"Look, Eric," Frank said. "Reckon I had to do something. You're going to have to stay in Sordell till this hit-and-run business is taken care of. Made arrangements for you to live at a sort of, well, rest home for a spell. It's better than the jail."

I turned sharply to Leda. She covered a half-wild look with a sudden smile. But it wasn't quick enough. I didn't like any of it at all and the old crowded feeling that had been with me so long swept down again. The thing was I felt so helpless. I wasn't helpless. "Rest home?" My voice was quiet. "What do you mean?" I tried to hang on but I was falling apart inside. I wanted to reach out and grab Frank's face, tear it off. I forced my gaze to the rear of the front seat.

"The best thing," Frank said.

Redfern felt me tense, tapped my arm, whispered, "Take it easy, pal."

Leda's thigh was against me and I could smell her perfume. Her attitude was all wrong, somehow. I tried to convince myself I read it that way. Forcing myself to believe I suspected things that weren't here.

"After all, Eric–you've been sick, admit it," Frank said. "It's the best thing, I reckon. Only way it could be fixed."

We were suddenly riding faster and I watched the driver's red neck where it bulged over his collar. He had dandruff. And the sunny serenity of the morning was a mock. My mind was clotted with too much imagined wrong. I had to believe that. I felt secluded, wanted to talk with Prescott. I didn't want to see these people. They, even Leda, were foreign to me. Her leg and shoulder touching me, the soft perfume I knew–everything was becoming foreign. The sound of the car's tires whirring on the road. The still morning with the river....

Somehow the only reality was the turgid silence of Redfern who peered out the window. He smelled of sweat and stale tobacco, resting inert in the seat, a quiet lump of tired flesh. I had to shut up all the way.

Abruptly I was sick with the realization that I was repeating over and over, an old phrase that I'd repeated in my early boyhood. They can't kill me anyway. They can't kill me anyway....

It was a peaceful seeming place called the Riverview Sanitarium. A broad doorway sloped above white-painted cement steps beyond a curving sidewalk sided by immense green lawns and shady trees. The Riverview Sanitarium. There was an old man in a wheel chair out on the lawn in the blinding sunlight. A woman in a bathrobe walked with a nurse, talking and gesticulating. Two other men were mowing the lawn, far down beneath some trees, while a male nurse stood nearby. Over in the shadow of the sunporch on a long wing of the building, still another woman, very shapely, lay on the ground in a blue satin robe. A nurse sat in a chair, drowsing over a book. The woman half sat up, watched our car, then suddenly lifted her legs and drew the robe apart. She made motions with her hands, stuck her tongue out at the car. The nurse noticed and remonstrated with her. The woman cursed the nurse, flopped over on her stomach, and began pulling the grass with both hands.

There was a high hedge surrounding a good part of the grounds. The main building was set well back, and was sprawling and large. Other smaller buildings squatted in deeper shadow.

Leda tensed against me. Redfern climbed out of the car and walked around the other side.

"Here we are," Frank said. He was cheerful.

"Leda, what's this all about?"

"It's all right, I tell you," she whispered. "I talked it all over with Frank. It's the only thing to do. You'd be surprised how helpful he's been. Really, Eric, you've got your brother all wrong. I can't understand it."

"Sure, sure."

The young, freshly-shaven driver came around the car and opened the door. Outside I felt no less foreign. There was an aura of dead quiet around the place, just the whirring of the lawn mowers and the chirping of a bird in the vacuum-like silence.

I don't know why I went along with everything after that, but I did. Maybe I decided it was best to keep still.

There was a nurse at the desk who took our names. The nurse's name was Watkins. Then we went through a large sitting room. Another nurse sat at the far end. In an easy chair near the doorway a blonde lounged. She was dressed expensively in black dress trimmed with gold, and she was an amazingly beautiful woman, with dark red lips and hot brown eyes. She uncrossed long shapely legs as I passed her, and she nodded and smiled at me. Her teeth were very white. She rose, stretched like a cat, thrusting out her breasts, and said, "Oh, damn," at the ceiling. Then she walked to the other end of the room. Her walk was the most terrific thing I'd ever seen, without exaggeration.

We went on down a long hall, past another open room with tables and books and magazines, then another hall at the end of which was a room. My room. As I entered, I looked down the hall. A man teetered in the doorway of the room at the other end of the hall. He reeled around, and closed his door.

There was a bed, a bureau with a large mirror, a closet, and two windows with Venetian blinds. The bed was very neatly made with a brilliantly colored red-and-blue spread. It made me remember all the other hospitals.

Frank stood in the doorway of the room and Leda leaned against an armchair. Redfern came in, sat down on the bed. He hadn't taken off his hat and he breathed heavily. He cocked his head at me, pursed his lips, stood up abruptly and left the room.

I kept watching Frank. It didn't seem to be like the dream. Yet all the hate was there. I'd seen my brother and nothing had happened. I wanted to tell Prescott.

"How's Mother?" I said. My voice was flat, unfamiliar.

"Not so good." He shook his head. "Doctor says she may pass away any time, Eric."

"I've got to get home."

"Whoa, now. You've got to stay here. Wouldn't do Mother any good to see you."

"Why hasn't she written?"

"She can't write."

We looked at each other for a moment and he got how I felt. His eyes clouded. He turned, left the room. I heard him going down the hall.

"What's it going to be?" I said to Leda. She looked lush, impatient. My voice was still flat.

"You'll just stay here. A doctor's coming to see you."

"I don't need a doctor. What's the idea?" I stood.

Leda dropped her purse into the chair and moved toward me. "I'll tell you this. Somehow they've checked and found out about your record in California. They know you've been sick."

"There's nothing wrong with me now." Fear crawled around inside me.

Leda touched my shoulders. Her lips were damp. She held her hips against me, then her breasts. The coppery sheen of her hair came against my face. "You know I know best, Eric."

"Sure."

"There's nothing to worry about." She moved her hips.

"Why am I here?" I almost shouted it.

"It's best." She held tighter, moving her body in deliberate slow motion. "Frank's only thinking of your welfare. He's really quite nice."

I grabbed her, yanked her closer still. She breathed heavily. "I can walk out of here," I said.

"Don't try it. For my sake." She clung to me. "I could tell them not to disturb us for a while. Maybe you'd feel better...."

"Yeah!" I shoved her away. "Great God, Leda! What're you trying to do?"

"Calm you down." She was perfectly serious.

I went over and sat on the bed. Sure, I loved her just as always. I'd probably love her forever. Maybe in a way I wanted her right now, too. She was right. It might take some of this pent-up feeling out of me. But not now, damn it. She'd been at me ever since we'd been in the room. She'd shut me up like that—only I wouldn't let her.

I found myself thinking of the hate I felt for Leda again. That sense of being drawn, yet repelled. For the moment it looked as if I were stuck. The only person I had to bank on was Leda. I didn't know what she was thinking. I was fogged up too much to figure things out. And she was saying nothing.

I hated the smell of this place. Swift whisking footsteps came down the hall and a nurse entered. Hipless, without breasts, she seemed to have been born in the uniform she wore. The professional smile was no comfort. She had a button nose and unseeing eyes.

"I'm Miss Winney," she said. "Would you please get undressed and get in bed?"

"Look, Miss Winey. Please go away."

"Mr. Garth. Will you lie down?"

"I don't feel like lying down."

"I'll have to see Miss Watkins." She was very stern. "These are her orders."

"Go see her, then."

"Please–" She glanced toward Leda, tightened her lips, then whisked from the room.

Leda and I looked at each other. It was all there; all the months we'd had together. But right now it seemed to be fraying out like the end of a rope. I was sick with something I couldn't fasten onto.

"Eric," Leda said. "Will you do everything they say? Will you promise? We've got to get the hit-and-run charge straightened out."

I didn't say anything. Hit and Run. Allen.

"A doctor is coming to see you. It has to be this way." She paused. "Won't you be good, please? You know how much I love you." She moved close to me. "Frank's working everything out," she said. "No one knows you had nothing to do with that hit and run. It's the way the law works, Eric. You know that. Suppose Allen dies?" Her face was very serious.

"All right," I said. "I'll shut up. See what happens." I figured I could walk out of here if need be. I was worn out, ragged, didn't want to talk any more. Not even with Leda. I had to be alone. I had to think. Everything was building up into a grand mess. It was all going wrong inside, too—wrong with us. There had been too many well-made beds, like this one. Too many quiet feet down antiseptic hallways. And me sitting here in the same damned place, wondering what it was all about.

And then, looking straight into Leda's eyes, I knew something....

I hadn't met Frank. I'd met only the artificial counterpart he used when in company. It had to be alone—the two of us, face to face. I hadn't met my brother. I hadn't seen him at all. Only the shadow behind his eyes that always would be there. I hated him just as much as ever.

"I'm going now, Eric."

"Yes."

"I'm staying at a hotel. I left the Seven Pines."

"Would you tell Redfern I want to see him?"

"All right I'll be back some time this afternoon."

"I'll try and wait that long."

"Eric, do as they say!" Her voice was strained. For an instant she came against me and we kissed. The smooth, fresh roundness of her body was new and at the same time known and good. I had asked for none of this—neither of us deserved it. I knew Leda must be feeling rotten inside. Our plans were not only delayed, but the edge was dulled. It was like returning to the hellish, waiting months of not so long ago. Only this time patience had little skin.

Leda was being kind now, trying to help me feel all right.

"Don't feel bad," she said.

"Sure."

She squeezed my shoulder. Then she was gone down the hall. I heard someone talking out there, heard her laugh. Then it was quiet.

Pretty soon the nurse, Miss Winney, came into the room.

"Come on, now, Mr. Garth. Take your clothes off."

"To hell with it."

"You shouldn't talk like that."

I looked at her, went over and laid down on the bed. "This'll have to do."

Miss Winney pursed her lips. Then she came over, took my pulse and blood pressure. I felt like a damned fool, and knew I was just that. I didn't know what I was here for. I didn't know anything.

The doctor, Ralph Barton, wore steel-rimmed glasses and a brush cut. He sat in a chair across from the bed and said nothing.

"What's the story, Doc?" I knew better than to press him too far, or get mad. It wouldn't help. I knew these men.

He spread his hands, half smiled.

I thought it over. I really had nothing to fear. I couldn't go home because of the law. I had to stay in Sordell.

Dr. Barton grunted. He stood up, short and brisk in a short-sleeved tan shirt and gray trousers. He smiled blandly. "See you," he said. He nodded twice and left the room.

I went over and sat in the chair. Miss Winney came back, clung to the doorjamb and said, "We eat at eleven-thirty. Be ready." She fumbled her upper lips with a pale lower one. "You'll do better if you co-operate," she said. "Your brother said to tell you not to lose your head and walk out of here."

"Thanks."

She smiled and went away. A little later I went out into the hall, but Miss Winney appeared as if by magic. "You're to stay in your room, Mr. Garth."

I sat on the bed for three-quarters of an hour, hoping Redfern would show up. Finally I decided to try something.

At eleven-thirty a colored girl in a red dress and white plastic apron brought in my lunch tray and set it on the table. The lunch was meager.

"When does the staff eat?" I said.

The girl was in a hurry. "They's eatin' right now," she said, and went on down the hall.

I waited a bit, then went on down the hall into the sitting room. It was empty and nobody was at the desk. I took my time, went out the front door and started down the walk. The river was pale in the sunlight, flowing narrow and slow and peaceful.

The guy was as big as myself, which is pretty big. He was in good condition, dressed in white. He had large ears and needed a haircut.

"Where you going?"

"Taking a walk."

"Oh. Well, let's get back to your room, eh?"

"Who're you?"

"I'm Jim."

"Why can't I take a walk?"

"Now, look." His face reddened a bit. A heavy bunch of keys jangled at his belt, and his eyes were mean in the sunlight, squinting just a little with not much nose between them. "Come on, let's not be difficult."

"Suppose I don't want to go back?"

He didn't say anything. Just waited.

"Suppose I won't go back?"

He reached for my arm. I pulled away. He reached again and this time his fingers sank in hard and sure and his eyes grinned but his mouth didn't.

"I'm not going back to my room. I'm through with my room."

We stood very quietly, looking into each other's eyes.

"That so?" he said. He smiled with his mouth this time. It was a hell of a fine smile, like a laughing dog. It was a grand smile. "Let's cut this out, Mr. Garth. Let's just go back to your room."

"I told you."

He sighed. His shoulders slumped. He drew them back up with a strong gesture.

"They won't like this."

"To hell with them."

"Your attitude's all wrong, Mr. Garth."

"Hell with that, too." I looked at the river. "Hell with you for that matter." I whipped away from him, started down the walk.

He came after me like a bull. Breathing like one, too. But as soon as he reached me he was quiet again. He was perfect. I'd had this kind of handling plenty. It got me. I was a little mad now. I'd asked Leda to send for Redfern. Three hours had passed since she'd gone.

"Look, Mr. Garth," the man called Jim said rapidly. "I'm asking you once more. Go back to your room."

"No." I felt bull-headed. It was a good feeling because I hadn't been feeling any way at all for some time. "So your name's Jim?" I said. "That's a fine name."

He took my arm, tried to force it around behind my back. I went along with it and came up with my face close to his. "A good strong American name," I said. "Jim." I brought my left hand up and shoved it into his throat. Then I squeezed his Adam's apple. I felt it buckle in there and bright pain danced in his eyes. It sent him into action as I'd known it would.

He brought his right hand up, grabbed my forearm, came down with his left, and twisted. I went with him again.

"Jim," I said. "You'll have to do better than that."

He did, breathing good and loud now. I was out of condition. He cursed and said, "You guys!" Then he came at me with his head. I brought my knee up gently against his nose. He caught my leg and we landed on the sidewalk.

"That's it, Herbert," he said.

Something happened against the side of my head. Then it happened again and the lawn in front of the Riverview Sanitarium tipped up with the buildings way up there above me and I started sliding toward the river.

## Chapter 7

The steel legs of the cot were bolted to the floor. The floor was cement. There was a smell in the room. Lysol, maybe. The smell was damp, cool, vinegarish. But the room wasn't cool. It was hot and an arm of sunshine elbowed me in the face. It was yellow and it was barred. There were two windows, barred. The door was thick wood, with a small barred opening. It was whitewashed as were the cement walls. I rolled over on the cot, touched the wall nearest me. It was damp and flakes of warm-wet paint and whitewash came away, dusting onto the mattress I lay on.

Somewhere a woman sang in a hoarse, laughing voice, "...right in the corner, where you are."

My head didn't ache, but I felt lethargic. I felt like more sleep. I knew I'd been given a hypo, a sedative of some kind. As I lay there, my mind came more awake.

Somebody walked by the door, stopped. More footsteps.

"He's come around."

I recognized Jim's voice. The man I'd fought with out on the front sidewalk. I swung myself to a sitting position on the cot. A face moved away from the small barred opening at the door.

"Think he'll eat?" somebody else said. It was a woman.

"God knows," Jim said.

"He should eat. It's been three hours. He didn't eat lunch. You going in there?"

"I dunno. He hasn't messed the place up any."

I sat there, listening. I stared at the floor, not the door, and let them talk.

"You better check the commode," the woman said.

"Yeah. Later," Jim said.

"He don't look–that way. He looks sane as you."

"Ever see any of 'em didn't?"

"Well, Isaac. He scared me plenty."

"Hell, I could scare the pants off you, Janie."

Giggles. Sounds of stiff cloth rustling and fast breathing, then a sharp, lingering, feminine, meaningless, "No!"

"Ah-h-h," Jim said. There was a loud smack of hand against flesh, then an elastic snap. More rustling and fast breathing. "So you do today," Jim said. "Afraid you'll catch cold?"

"Shut up. Don't! He might–"

"Nobody'd believe him," Jim said. "C'mon over here."

"Not now!"

"Why not now?"

The other woman with the hoarse voice sang again, "Nearer my God to the-e-e-e-e-e!"

"Oh, Jim, you made me lose a button."

"You're in good company. C'mon, Janie."

"Tonight."

Jim grumbled. "That's right. We both work tonight," he said more lightheartedly.

"Yes, and I'm dead already."

"You'll be dead, you rascal, you!" the woman with the hoarse voice sang.

"A lot she knows," Janie said.

"She knows," Jim said. "She told me. She tried to get me yesterday. Said she'd fallen in love with me."

"Oh, hell. I can't find that button."

"Let it hang open."

"Are you going to give him that tray? I'll be darned if I'll give him this needle. You'll have to. Watkins said you'd have to if he looked queer."

"I gave him a helluva shot before."

"What's the matter with him, really?" She gasped. "Stop it, Jim. Can't you wait till tonight?" She whispered, "My God, they'll tell Watkins."

"He's tough, is all," Jim said. "Thinks he wants to kill somebody, or something." They both laughed. There was a beating on the door.

"He looks all right," Janie whispered. "Just tired."

"Hey, Eric," Jim said. He was using my first name now. That was nice.

"Hurry up," Janie whispered. "I want to get home. Two hours and we have to come back here. Damn Lucy. Why'd she take sick?"

"You hungry, Eric?" Jim said.

I looked at him. "Come on in," I said.

His face went away from the small barred window.

"Better put it through the slot," Janie said. "He looked at you awful funny."

"Hey, Eric," Jim said. "You scheming?"

There was a small square opening, closed with a hinged door just below the barred opening of the window. This must be the slot they'd referred to. It would be for passing things through in case a patient was violent.

It was a fine thing, all right. Everything was so suddenly messed up that I didn't really feel any way at all. That would come later.

"Why don't you come on in?" I said. "Jim."

"You want to kill me?" Jim said. Janie gave a short laugh and said, "Stop it. You always tease them."

God, I thought. I'm insane, now. A hit-and-run driver who has gone insane.

"They always say that," Jim said. "I'll kill you, I'll kill you!"

"Stop it, Jim."

"Eric, d'you feel that way?"

"Have you seen my wife?" I said. "Has she been here?"

"Yes, she's been here. Your brother was here, too."

I didn't say anything. There was a small white bureau bolted to the wall and a commode in the corner of the room. Leda had been.

"Where is she?" I said.

"She had to go," Jim said. "But she'll be back, Eric. She said to tell you she'd be back tonight sometime. After you felt better. After you eat something. Hungry?"

"What time tonight?"

"Go ahead," Janie whispered.

A lock scraped and the door swung open. Jim was carrying a tray with some tin dishes on it and he still needed a haircut.

"Why don't you see a barber?" I said.

He ignored that. "Time to eat," he said. He put the tray down beside me on the cot. I glanced toward the open door. A girl, Janie, stood there, with half of her showing through the opening. She had jet-black hair and a build that crowded her white dress to the bursting point. Her red lips were formed into an inquisitive, expectant O. Her dark eyes matched her mouth. Her breasts showed through the material of brassiere and dress, and at the end of her torso a button was missing from the dress, which gaped open. Her right hand passed diffidently back and forth over this bit of temptation. Her belly heaved and she carried a cotton-wrapped hypodermic needle in her left hand.

"Hello, Janie," I said. She was certainly prepared. For anything.

She smiled and held it, trying to avoid my eyes.

"You hungry?" Jim said. "You still want to fight?"

"Why am I in here?"

"You wouldn't go back to your room. Remember?"

"Yeah, but why here?" I stood up, faced him. He backed away one step and his gaze flicked toward Janie. She didn't move.

"You've got to co-operate, Eric," Jim said. "You want to feel right, don't you?"

"I feel right."

"Sure. Well, you'll feel better. You'll just be here a little while, like that."

We looked at each other. His eyes were trying to smile but they were mean and there was nothing intelligent about them. He was still a big guy and in better condition than myself.

"I asked to see a detective Redfern. He been around?"

Jim shook his head. "No. You won't be able to see anybody but maybe your wife, that's all. For now, anyway." He cleared his throat. "Why don't you eat something?"

Two days later, when Leda came to see me, I was still in the locked room. It had been plenty bad and was getting worse, what with Doc Barton's silence and this locked room. I'd seen or heard nothing of Leda until she came to the door that day.

Jim let her in and closed the door on us. I hadn't caused any trouble and they were growing lax.

Leda looked hot and tired. "I'm sorry, Eric. There've been so many things I had to do."

"Sure." I was mad all the way, now. The dream rode me and I wondered incessantly what people knew that I didn't.

Leda's eyes were smoky, like they always got when she wanted me. She was wearing shorts again. Yellow shorts, as tight a fit as possible, and a thin fuzzy white sweater, which stretched like rubber over her breasts. She wasn't wearing a brassiere. Her coppery hair was thick and I was mad, so when she squeezed in close I grabbed her tightly.

She breathed out hard and I smelled whisky. Her lips sought mine, searching almost frantically. She pressed against me, leaning on me, pulling me toward the cot in the bare room.

"What the hell's up?" I said, holding her off.

"Don't," she said, "I haven't seen you for two days."

"That's your fault."

"Tell me later. There's nobody outside, darling."

It had been lonely. It wasn't lonely now. There'd been a lot of things I'd wanted to tell her. I had wanted to give her hell.

Now it was different, because Leda affected me that way. I still wanted to give her hell. But that would be different, too.

"Why haven't you been around?"

"I'm here, Eric. For God's sake, bawl me out later."

We were on the cot, sitting, and she pulled me down. We lay on the cot pressed tight together and she was breathing like nothing I'd ever heard.

"What gets you this way?" I said.

"Anticipation. I told that man to leave us alone. There's nobody around. Quit making me anticipate." She found my lips and kissed me with her whole body and the shorts were so tight they felt like skin.

She arched her body and screamed way down in her throat; an almost silent screeching.

I heard somebody whistling in the distance. Then I didn't hear anything but the thunder of blood.

Leda wasn't a bit tired.

"What got into you?" We were lying on the cot. Leda sat up, looked at herself and laughed.

It was over now. She had been wonderful, but I was alone again. Somehow even with her here, I was alone. The whistling came by outside the building, nearing.

"Get out of sight. Over there," I said, motioning her beside the door. A moment later Jim's face appeared at the small barred panel in the door.

"Everything all right?" He couldn't see Leda and his eyes weren't smiling. They were a little harried.

"Fine," Leda said.

He tried to see her, but couldn't. She was a picture, with the white sweater rolled up half over her breasts. "Would you send that nurse I was talking to in the office down here?" Leda said to Jim. "Right away?"

Jim frowned. "O. K. That's Janie, Mrs. Garth."

I wondered if Janie'd found her button. I hadn't inquired. Jim went away and I looked at Leda standing there, lurking sultry and warm with her still smoky eyes and her belly moving softly as she breathed.

"I–I couldn't get here any sooner," she said.

"For God's sake, put something on," I told her. She managed to wriggle into what was left of the shorts. They made her look like something highly delectable out of Dogpatch. With one hand she held the tears together. Moving slowly, she came over and sat on the cot beside me.

"Where's Frank?"

"He's gone home," she told me. "He couldn't stay on."

"But I stay on just fine."

"There's a mix-up, Eric. You shouldn't have fought with the nurse, like that. What with your background and everything."

She was thinking of something else. It was pretty obvious. "I suppose you know I've been drinking," she said. "I had to. I couldn't bear thinking of you in here."

I didn't say anything. It was all cockeyed. Her coming here today as she had. It was as if she'd come to repair her watch, or something. And now that everything was in running order, she wanted to go. It was in the way she acted and talked.

Then I asked her the question I hadn't wanted to ask.

"What are they going to do with me here?"

And she said, "I don't know." She said it to the floor, staring at her feet.

"What about the hit and run?"

"Nothing new."

I could feel the blood pounding again. She wouldn't tell me anything. Maybe she didn't know anything, but she could try to relieve me. I grabbed her wrist. "Damn it!" I said. "What's going on?" I kept my voice down, speaking soft and hard, right at her. "They can't hold me here, you know that. I'll break out."

She watched me, moistened her lips, looked vague.

I threw her hand into her lap. It bounced limply. "I asked you to tell Redfern to stop in and see me."

"He's very busy," she said.

I wanted to hit her. Maybe there was something wrong with me. Barton would come and sit and watch me. Jim never said anything. The other nurses brought me pills I refused to take. And they hadn't stuck me with another needle.

We sat there for another hour, talking about nothing, while I verged on actual madness. Because no matter what I said, Leda persisted in her vague, half-nervous manner.

Janie came down and Leda borrowed a needle and thread from her to sew up the rips in the shorts. So she sat sewing while I tried to get her to talk.

"I'm leaving with you," I said finally.

"You can't, Eric!" For the first time she showed interest. "You can't do that."

"Why?"

"Because they'd come after you. They'd get you. This'll only be for a little while, darling. Then everything'll be all right again." She had finished sewing up the shorts. She put them on again. They fit so tight she had to mince steps when she walked. It was something. "They—Redfern, there, must have a lead on the accident, or something. I'm sure it won't be long, now."

"He tell you that?"

She stared at me. "No, not exactly."

I cursed, sprawled back on the cot, and turned to the wall. Pretty soon her lips touched the side of my face.

"I've got to go," she said. "I'll see you tonight."

"All right." I didn't give a damn.

"See you tonight, then." I listened as she went to the door. Jim came along presently and let her out and locked the door again. They were talking, and I heard her laugh as they walked off across the grounds. Then the woman with the hoarse voice began singing a spiritual.

Leda never came back that night....

A slow monotony of days and nights passed with the sun for a few hours and the blackness for the rest and then the sun again. And the dear old procession of event-less events. Only now it was different.

It worked on me. It worked like a ferment inside with each hour, building and building until something was going to give. Because nobody told me anything.

"There'll be time when you co-operate," Doc Barton said from behind his steel-rimmed glasses with his short-sleeved shirts and neatly creased trousers. "We don't like to keep you locked up like this."

"Damn you!"

He spread his hands. "You see?" Already he was on his feet, edging toward the door. Not exactly showing me how he felt, but trying not to show me.

"How can you keep me here?"

A smile of sympathy. I wasn't supposed to be able to detect smiles of sympathy.

"Where's my wife?"

"We haven't been able to locate Mrs. Garth," Barton said. "Now that's something else, Eric," he went on. He was standing by the door, and it had been two weeks with me ready for fighting now. "I've been playing along with you, waiting for you to tell me. But now I have to press you a bit. Why do you persist in calling this woman your wife? It's one of the things that–"

"Get the hell out of here!"

"We know damned well she's not your wife! She was with your brother all the time around town, Eric. Seems to me they were rather close. Wouldn't surprise me if–Listen, you've got to snap out of it."

I came at him. Jim was on the other side of the door and the door swung open. Barton stood his ground. "C'mon, Doc!" Jim said. "Can't you see?"

"No," Barton said. "Tell me that, Eric. Why do you insist she's your wife? If you'd get that much straight we'd have taken a step forward."

"Damn you! Get out of here!"

Barton sighed and went out through the door. Jim looked at me. He'd got his hair cut. Now it was much too short. Almost shaved. He looked like a very thick-headed hick. "That's right, what Doc told you about her," he said.

"You, too," I snapped. "Get!"

"Sure, Eric," Jim said. "I'll get. But I'll be back. My bed's right out here now. I live in the next room. I'm your neighbor now, Eric. Just take it easy."

I moved for him. He closed the door and shot the bolt.

My breath was hot in my throat. I paced the room like a caged cat. I tried to calm down and couldn't. Because I would not believe what was already in my head. Leda had gone off with Frank. She'd been with Frank. It was torture. I forced myself to think differently. She had vanished; she'd gone away to do something. But always the words returned–with Frank. Barton was merely trying to shock me, startle me–for some reason of his own.

This was how the trapped felt when they knew they were trapped and when they had sense enough to wonder why.

Not the truly sick. They didn't always know, or they didn't care. I cared, plenty, and wondered why. I sat there trying to calm down, trying to think it all out and–Bang! I'd be out on the floor, standing, ready to smash anybody who entered the room.

A couple of days later I realized I was being watched.

Jim slept just outside my door now. I could see his bed. My bureau with a small mirror above it, cemented to the wall, was faced on the opposite wall where Jim was with another bureau and mirror.

I found out about those mirrors and it made me sick.

One day I was staring at myself in the mirror, seeing what this was doing to me. I looked wild and I felt wild. My thoughts were of Leda with Frank, because Frank had money and I was locked up. I was through. Frank had it and Leda wanted it. Even while thinking like that I tried to close my mind, certain I saw things cockeyed. I condemned myself for thinking of Leda that way.

I heard Jim cough. So far as I knew, he wasn't in the building.

It struck me all at once. I forgot Leda, Frank, everything. I moved with the cough, fast for the door, and looked through the slot. I'd caught him and I wanted to tear the door down.

"Eric!" Jim said. He was closing a small cabinet, or maybe a panel that made up the mirror on his side. I could just see him, by pressing my face against the cold bars on the door.

I went screwy. The top on the bureau came off like you'd lift the lid on a kettle, screws, nuts, bolts, and all. I smashed it at the mirror on my side. It shattered and I was looking into the excited, worried face of Jim.

A mirror, hell. A window where they could watch whoever was in this room.

"Eric!"

"Hell." I dropped the top of the bureau, went over and flopped on my cot.

Leda wasn't real any more. Nothing was real. They were actually driving me insane. Outside, Jim was calling for help.

Pretty soon Dr. Barton came along. He didn't enter the room, but stood outside the door, talking to me while a carpenter patched up the hole where the mirror had been.

Barton talked on and on, but I didn't talk at all.

"You've got to learn to co-operate, Eric."

I remembered Leda. Her glinting eyes and her long flawlessly curved white body tense with breasts gleaming in soft light. Her back, the full firm contours of her hips, and the ache inside me didn't change. I'd always love her—wild bodied and cryptic, quick to cleave and hot willed. I hadn't wanted to love her. But I did and nothing would ever change that. Everything would work out right.

And I would remember she had vanished. She was gone....

The way she'd look at me, then squeeze her thick hair with it bunching between her fingers, alive and coppery, a sable downpour about her face.

It was like I was bunged up inside, not alone with all the crazy trouble. Leda was right here, yet she was gone. I couldn't catch hold of it; the thing wouldn't form like it should. I could smell her and feel her and she was here with me, inside my head. So what do you do? You say to hell with it. Only the words don't have any meaning.

I hung on for two months like that. They kept me in that room and they told me nothing. Even Doc Barton was acting puzzled and he didn't come so often.

"You've had no mail, Eric?"

"None. Never mind."

He would frown but he wouldn't tell me anything. I think he really tried to locate Leda. But he didn't have any luck. I tried hard not to think of her. I didn't have much luck, either. Because she was inside me and it was bad. And every time I thought of her close to me, Norma got in there somehow, blonde and smiling....

"Well, you're going outside today," Jim said.

"Oh."

"Going to rake the lawn."

"Great."

"Sure."

"I love raking lawns."

"Wish you wouldn't hold things against me, Eric. Things go right, maybe you'll get back to the main building again. You ain't caused much trouble lately."

"Good."

We went on outside. I had a pair of overalls now, and this was the first I'd been outside since the day they'd locked me up. The sun was blinding and, staring at my hands, I realized I was white as a sheet.

"A half hour, you got," Jim said. He walked alongside of me. "Make the most of it."

I thought it over. "Could I make a phone call?"

He thought that over. "I don't know. C'mon up to the office." They were trusting me all over the place now. It was a wrong move on their part. But even I didn't know that yet.

"He wants to use the phone," Jim told Miss Watkins.

Miss Watkins thought about it for a while. She was seated at the desk and she had very big breasts. They flowed around inside her uniform like very soft dough or mashed potatoes. Her eyes were small and her mouth matched her eyes with a single, small red pout.

"Whom do you wish to call?"

"You'll be right here," I said. The phone was at her dimpled elbow.

"Is it a long-distance call?"

"No. Local."

"I guess it'll be all right." She eyed Jim, and he nodded assurance that he'd stand by with folded arms. Janie went by through the sitting room, rolling her hips, with a hypodermic needle in one hand. Jim winked at her and she bridled slightly. Miss Watkins saw it and fussed with a pencil. Janie vanished, rolling her hips fine.

I got Redfern on the line.

"Hello. This is Garth."

"Ah."

"They don't tell me anything about the accident," I said. "I want to know what's up about that hit and run. They don't say anything."

"Where are you, Garth?"

"You know where I am."

"You mean you're still out there? At the San?" He was politely incredulous.

"Yeah, that's right." .

"Good God." His manner changed subtly. Not much, but just enough to be noticed. "Well, well. Did you get your car all right?"

"What? Listen. What about that hit-and-run business?"

"Why, hell, Garth. That's what I mean about the car. They should have told you. Allen withdrew all charges. Said he wasn't sure about anything. When they won't place charges, we can't do anything."

I stood there hanging onto the phone as if it were a piece of dead wood. My insides turned over and I felt dizzy. Then my head began to clear.

Redfern said, "We turned the car over to that there girl. *The one you called your wife, only she wasn't.* Turned the car over to her and your brother. Say, did she go away, Garth?"

It burned down inside. I seemed to sense a smile in his voice. I swallowed what I wanted to say. "Yeah," I said instead. "You turned the car over to them. They're no charges, like you say?"

"Like I say."

I glanced toward Jim. He was over in the sitting room talking with Janie. Miss Watkins had her back turned to me and was busily sharpening pencils.

Redfern said, "Is there anything–," and I laid the phone down carefully on the desk and walked quietly out the front door into the blazing sunlight.

Then I ran like hell.

## Chapter 8

I knew that if they caught me now, chances were I'd be kept in that locked room forever. A man who was suspected of being out of his mind, as I was, didn't stand a chance. There'd be no way of my explaining how I felt. I could say over and over again, somebody's doing this to me. I'm all right. There's nothing wrong with me. I know that. And they'd just sit and listen and walk away and make motions at their temples to their friends.

It was a mean fix. So I ran hard, down the walk to the street. The river was over there and for a brief instant I thought of diving in, trying to swim away. But those things were only done in the backwoods, not here, where they'd just go around the block and pick me up when I came out dripping and exhausted.

I spotted a car at the curb. It was an old Ford coupé with a smashed fender.

"Eric!"

It was Jim, coming hell-bent down the walk after me. Miss Watkins was yelling at the door. I made for the coupé, yanked the door open and dived inside. The keys were there. Luck was changing. Maybe.

I got the car started as Jim landed on the side and pulled at the door. I cut a sharp left fist and caught his forearm. He let go, running beside the car as I drove off.

"That's my car, Eric! Man, don't do it!"

His face bobbed red and mad beside the car, his eyes not pleading but mad, too, and his mouth a dark yelling hole in his head, as he ran along, leaping hedges and staggering on the curb.

I ripped the wheel left, not caring now, and Jim dived for it. I didn't hit him, but he hit the dirt, hard. As I whipped around the corner I glanced in the rear-view mirror. Jim was kneeling half up, still yelling at me. Then all I could hear was the roar of the motor and the rattle bang of the smashed fender as I headed for the main road.

The car ran smoothly. It was a hot afternoon. The sun was white.

They'd be after me. I had to ditch the car. I was wearing overalls. I had no money. So far as I knew I was judged a mental case. That would bring out a posse in this country; maybe a mob with shotguns, muzzle-loaders, and what-have-you, all yelling and ready to get the madman who had escaped from the Riverview Sanitarium.

I knew something else. Something I had refused to admit to myself and something no one had been willing to answer.

Why was I being held at the sanitarium? Because somebody'd had me committed. Otherwise I'd have been free to go and they would have been able to tell me. All they'd told me was I was there for a rest and not to worry, that everything would be all right. They hadn't even acted that way when I'd entered the hospital in California, really sick.

But what stuck in the back of my mind, scaring the blood down into my throat, was the thought that perhaps they were right. Maybe I was nuts. Maybe I was going home to kill my brother.

Because I was going home. Nothing would stop me.

As I gunned the Ford coupé down the blacktop road, hoping I'd hit a main highway soon, Leda sat beside me. Her ghost was there and she was naked, carrying yellow shorts in one hand. Leda. Leda was gone. Leda had disappeared. Vanished.


The one you called your wife, only she wasn't.

Neat. Like that. I had to get home. Find out what I could and see Frank face to face. Once that was out of my system, I'd be clean.

Then I could spend the rest of my life hunting Leda. I knew I'd find her because the world isn't big enough to hide in. Not for Leda it wouldn't be big enough. I told myself she wasn't with Frank, hadn't been.

I tried to tell myself I'd find her because she'd run out on me when I needed her most. When I had to have her support. I didn't know where she'd gone. She had weakened and run out on me. Alone, I told myself. Alone!

Because I loved her. She was in me. She was a part of me and no other woman–not even Norma–could ever take her place. There was only one, Leda, and it had to stay that way. It would stay that way.

The blacktop road ended and I hit a stretch of bouncy tar-ribbed cement, which sent the Ford leaping like a stricken sparrow.

When I got home I knew I'd see Norma. She'd be there, as she'd always been. And maybe she'd always be my girl. But there could only be one Leda....

Trees, low hills, shallow gutters, sunny-sided fields sloped past the car with speed, blurred in my vision, dusty through the windshield.

I held the pedal to the floor. It was like flying low. Sunlight jerked in unrhythmic splashes on the road, the car, and across my face. The engine spat and roared with that same unattainable and terrific savagery seen in the myriad and untame noises a hen makes when being chased by a rooster with a one-track mind.

Cars that passed, and cars I passed drew out of the way with a slow-motion illusion that was confounding. I knew I was wild, I knew the exertion of the past few moments was telling. But I also knew the old glands were pumping adrenalin and so long as I utilized it, they'd keep pumping.

Stay excited until it's all over. That's what I told myself. Make it a blur. And then I got the idea.

Get drunk. Back there in my mind Prescott babbled about how I should stay away from the bottle. But if I did, I'd get calm again. I couldn't afford to get calm now. I had nearly a thousand miles to cover and it had to be done fast. Once it was done, things wouldn't matter.

All right. Clothes. Money. Ditch the car. A bottle. And home. How home? Plane. That was the fastest.

How to get them?

The second-hand car lot on the edge of town flashed by with a red-and-white sign reading: "CANNE'S CARS." I rode the brakes without half realizing what I was doing. ,The car fishtailed. I made a sharp U turn and beat it straight for Canne's place. The Ford whirred like an over-revved plane in a spin as I bounced up the gravel drive leading between flashing new cars into the lot.

"Well, two hundred, mebbe. No more. And that's going pretty high, too." Canne was freckle-faced, heavy jowled, and dressed sleekly in a tan sport suit. It was obvious to Canne. He was beating a poor hick.

"All right. It's a deal. I need the cash."

"Haven't I seen that car before?"

"You may have. I came to town a week ago, been working here since then. Probably saw it around town."

"Sure. I've seen that there car before." His eyes were big and I wondered that he didn't get them full of dust. There were purple veins strung in a webbed shield across his nose.

When he'd paid me and I'd signed the car over in Jim Phelby's name, I said, "Can I use your phone?"

He was reading the registration I'd found in the glove compartment. As I stood there in my worn overalls, jittery, impatient, a police car wound past outside with siren wailing and moaning like the passionate shepherd. It may have been a fire. It could be the police were going to a ball. But I was certain all that hurry was for me.

"Sure, go on, use the phone," Canne said. He wiped his nose, folded the registration, tossed it into a desk drawer among odds and ends of papers.

I called the airport, which was only ten miles away. Their next flight to Tampa, Florida, would be in a half hour. Could I make a reservation? Certainly, no need, really, plenty of space. Reserve me a seat, anyway. All right.

Next call: Western Union, charge Albert Canne. Is this all right, Mr. Canne?

NORMA MEET ME DREW FIELD TWO O'CLOCK THIS
AFTERNOON
ERIC

Yes, honey, it's all right.

Next call: Send a cab right over to Canne's cars. What's the address here, Mr. Canne? Two-ten Lee Street. That's right, right away.

Next call: Is this the Riverview Sanitarium? Yes, Miss Watkins, speaking. She was excited, breathing hard, and I could see, in my mind's eye, her mashed-potato breasts heaving beneath her uniform. Miss Watkins, would you tell Jim Phelby his car is at Canne's car lot? Tell him that—wait a minute, Miss Watkins—tell him Eric Garth says he'll see that two hundred dollars plus expenses are wired to him by tomorrow morning. Yes, thank you. I'm sorry, Miss Watkins, good-by. She was having a time.

"Aren't you James Phelby?" Mister Canne said. The papers and pencils in his shirt pocket weighted it down badly.

"Certainly."

"Oh."

I went out front to the walk. Pretty soon the cab came along and I directed the driver to the airport. "And step it up, will you?"

"Sure thing."

"Stop right there, will you?" I said three minutes later. "By that clothing store."

The cab braked to a stop. "Only a minute," I said, climbing out. The driver yawned and scratched his neck. "Listen," I said, handing him a twenty-dollar bill, "while I'm in here, go some place and buy me a fifth of whisky."

"What kind?"

"Rye. Any kind."

"Done."

I went on into the clothing store. We were on the main business street in Sordell. As I entered the store, I wondered vaguely what Leda had done with my car. It had been a nice car for eight days. It had been a new car. Well, there were lots of new cars, but if I'd had it, I could have had more money from Canne, and there wouldn't have been any possibility of Watkins tipping the police where I'd been.

Because they'd trace the call, I was only hoping for one thing. Jim would be with the police, hunting for me, and Watkins wouldn't be able to say I'd phoned. They wouldn't be able to trace me to Canne's car lot until I was on the plane for Tampa. Or maybe even in Tampa. That would be the thing I had to hope for. Radio could stop me at Tampa plenty quick. I'd march off the plane into the arms of Florida police. An escaped lunatic.

I bought a cheap pair of pants with the cuffs on, because I couldn't wait for them to be altered. "I'll need a jacket," I said. "A shirt, too."

"Yes, sir."

They wondered why I was in a hurry. I didn't tell them. I bought a hat, too, something I'd never worn as a civilian. Altogether, I looked exactly like somebody who was running away from a sanitarium after I'd put the clothes on.

"You can keep the overalls and shirt," I said.

The clerk's hair was marcelled, perfumed, and he didn't want to soil his fingers touching the overalls.

"Really," he said. "We don't want them."

"That's a shame," I said. "Because you're stuck with 'em."

"But what ever will I do with them?"

I told him an impolite way to rid himself of them. He blushed madly and I went on outside in my new duds.

I climbed aboard the plane with the fifth of whisky under one arm. I felt like an escaped convict. Then I knew that's what I was, for real.

The stewardess came down the aisle with some orange juice. It made a fine surreptitious orange-juice cocktail with the whisky added. I had to share it with my seat companion, a psychiatrist headed for Miami.

"I'm going down to take a cure," he said.

"Oh."

"But this won't hurt. I've been on the stuff for five years. My wife insists it's too long."

"Think it'll do you any good down there?"

He smiled tiredly, stirred his orange-juice highball with a well-manicured little finger. "Does it ever?"

## Chapter 9

His name was Hatchell and the pretty stewardess and I had a difficult time pouring him off the plane. He knew he had to catch another plane in two hours for Miami.

"Think you can take it?" I said.

Hatchell groped blindly into the afternoon, winked obscenely at the stewardess, and said, "Most assuredly." There wasn't much left of the fifth. Hatchell had a tremendous capacity. "No difference," he argued. "Fi'teen minutes I could diagnose your case."

"Am I a case?"

"We all are," Hatchell said. I left him standing quite straight and stern and neurotic on the front steps of the building in front of the parking lot.

He was headed for a fine place to take the cure.

Then it was afternoon. A lonely afternoon. And I suddenly knew it had been a fool gesture, wiring Norma to meet me at the airport. She wouldn't be here.

Suddenly, through the tightening fumes of what whisky I'd been able to steal from Hatchell, California and the hospital became the peace I wanted. Home was an abrupt, ludicrous return to hell.

I moved on across the sunny street to where the cars were parked. Out on the field a transport's engine bellowed.

"Eric!"

It was something like fear. Maybe that's what it was. They hadn't radioed to hold me at the airport, or they'd have been here long before this. It was something else. Something from before the bad time I'd had at Sordell. Norma's voice and the part of the country you'd grown up in, and knew, that was unknown now.

She hadn't changed much. She came across the street, walking fast as always, her tawny blonde hair all over the place. Then she started running. She wore a tight blue skirt, white blouse, and loafers.

"Eric! My God, you came. You really came back." She stopped running about six feet from me, stood there breathing hard. She took another step toward me, smiling, then not smiling.

"Sure. Told you I would." We stared at each other. Probably there were a lot of things that went unsaid insofar as a passer-by might notice. But plenty was said in the way we looked at each other.

"I thought you were kidding," she said.

"No time for that."

"Oh." She nodded, swallowed. "I took a chance, anyway. Thought maybe you were just blinded by an Alabama moon."

I took off my hat, scaled it at an ash can. I missed. Home was like that....

The transport bellowed plenty as it turned on the runway. I wondered how Hatchell was doing. Norma had put on some weight. It looked fine in exactly the right places as an adjunct to what she'd had some years ago. It had been fine then too.

"Are we just going to stand here?" I said.

"No." She watched me intently. "No, of course not. My car's right over here."

"Good." I followed her over to a dust-covered black Chevvy sedan. The left front fender was crumpled and I recalled another crumpled fender. But this was different.

"Still heading for other cars' lights at night?"

"Uh-huh. Habit now. Get in. Sure seems funny, Eric. It's been a long time." She gave me another intent, quick glance.

We got in. She drove away from the airport. I saw the way she watched me. Trying not to let me see all the questions, with her eyes big and brown and her teeth gnawing her lower lip. Hell. She'd been my girl. Only now she was more woman than girl. It came to me she might be married even, maybe with kids, too. It could happen.

I'd been through a war, gone crazy, been tied up in straight jackets, fallen in love with a woman who walked out on me the first rough time we had, and I was still hanging onto a dream. That Norma Dean was still my girl.

And there was another wild dream, too–the wild one that cropped up that day in Korea all full of blood and dark damnation. So go on home to the old home where your mother's dying and see for sure if you want to kill your brother. See if you're going to kill him now. Go ahead, find out....

And Allen had withdrawn the charges. So there may as well not have been any hit and run that wasn't me, anyway. Why? Why had the man, Allen, withdrawn charges after being hospitalized? Why had I been tossed into the booby hatch? Why had Leda gone away?

Leda. It was like having warm sirup poured over your head, hot down your sides, flowing along the veins. Outside and inside, too. Leda. Leda and Norma–two very dissimilar women. Only maybe not. I no longer knew Norma Dean. Once I'd known her very well.

"We won't talk much for a while, will we?" Norma said.

"No."

"I decided that would be best. We just'll sit here and not talk."

"Yeah."

"O. K."

"Sure."

She drove for a time and I didn't think about anything except how dirty she let her car get–how she didn't care about things like that. She only cared about people and trying to do what's right. Norma.

"You've been gone a long time," she said.

We turned onto the main highway toward Tampa, then took a cutoff that headed toward the coast down below St. Petersburg.

"I wasn't sure you'd show up," I said.

"Neither was I."

"But you did."

"I did."

Her blue skirt was hiked up above her knees. She wore nylons, and her legs were round and good to see. She had a nice body, better now than when I knew it last. Her breasts were fuller and they had more round firmness. Her thighs were thick and solid, but trim, and she had very slim, neat ankles. Her body was perfectly proportioned with a solidness not often seen. Her arms were like her legs and she had a seductive throat. I used to kid her about that. I always told her that her throat was like her thighs and sometimes it got you that way. There was nothing soft about her; nothing pale. But her skin never acquired the dark tan some persons achieve. Her skin was an olive, maybe, an off tan that was rich and when you touched her skin it made you hold your breath. Because you didn't know for sure what you were touching. Her hands were like that, too. Norma was quite a girl.

Leda was quite a girl. Quite.

"Were you hurt badly–in the war?"

"All how you look at it."

"You seem a little more–well, sober, maybe."

I took the fifth of whisky from its paper bag and held it up for her to see. "Have one?"

"Maybe."

The whisky had blurred everything as I'd hoped it would, but somehow things suddenly needed more blurring. I uncapped the bottle and handed it to Norma. She turned, winked at me, and took a long, healthy slug. She handed the bottle back, I took one, put the bottle between my feet on the floor.

We began to pass familiar landscape, though we were some distance from Cypress Landing. Norma drove fast, with her chin stuck out a little.

"Seems funny, coming home," I said. It was more frightening than funny, but I couldn't tell Norma that.

"Does it?"

"It's been a long time."

"Give me some more of that." She motioned toward the bottle on the floor.

After she drank and I drank, I said, "You seem to like it better than you used to."

"I'm a professional drinker now. I've got my photography shop. Drinking helps me not to see the old biddies I have to photograph. They never want to look what they are."

"Good for you."

"No."

"All right. No, then."

We drove on in silence for a while. Norma and I had gone to school together. We had played together when it was too early for anything else. Then we'd fished together when it wasn't too early, only we didn't know yet. Then we got to know and we only pretended to go fishing. You can't fish on a blanket in a field of clover beneath a live oak's shade. It was fun pretending to go fishing.

"I suppose you met lots of women?" Norma said.

"Sure, hundreds. I didn't go fishing with any of them though," I lied.

She motioned toward the bottle. I handed it to her. We drove quietly on through the afternoon with the sun splashing in patches or brilliant white lakes on the highway. The bottle tilted three times.

"I haven't been fishing either, damn you," she said.

"All right." The whisky was touching her. "Why did you come?"

"Goddamn you."

"All right." We drove on for a while. It had been a long time not to go fishing and it was hard to believe. Only Norma was like that.

The bottle tilted again and flew out the window. It shattered on the highway. Norma wiped her mouth with the back of her hand, glanced at me quickly, then away.

"You punk," she said. "You didn't even write. You didn't answer one of my letters. There, now I've said that. I've acted like any dumb bitch and it's out of my system. It's all right now."

"Don't be vulgar," I said. "You didn't have to come."

"Don't I know it."

"I'm sorry I wired you."

"Don't be sorry."

We drove on for a while. Even through the whisky the dream pursued me. Close to home. It became worse. I didn't know my way around any more. I was a pioneer. A slightly tight pioneer who was scared; who had too many things for one man to worry about. Much too many.

And Leda was right there in the car with us. Between us, like a hot brick wall....

The sign read: "POP'S LIQUOR STORE."

Norma stopped the car. "Go ahead," she said. "Get another one."

"Bottle?"

"Shut up and go ahead."

I went on in and bought a fifth and came back to the car and we drove off toward Cypress Landing. Pretty soon we were in the country again.

Norma's skirt was riding higher now. We were both riding higher. She had started in on the new bottle, taking small nips.

"How was she? What did she look like?"

"Who?"

"Hell." She reached over and touched my arm, then put her hand on the wheel again. Her hair was sunny and she looked clean and good there in the car.

Maybe if I get real drunk, I thought. Maybe then I can forget there ever was a Leda. Maybe forget that my life's been going to hell fast with all the dreams breaking up, too. I knew I couldn't forget any of it.

I was hungry for Leda and I was going all off inside without knowing what to do about it. I was wound up tight.

This girl beside you. She was your girl. What do you think she feels now? Why do you think she drove to the airport and met you? Why?

The car swerved a little on the road. Norma pulled it back, glanced at me, hiked her skirt up to her stocking tops. "Are my legs as good as those women's you were with?"

"Better," I said truthfully. "Better than ever."

Norma wouldn't be like this without the whisky and somehow I knew she wouldn't be like this with anybody else. I began to feel rotten about Norma now. As though I didn't have enough to feel rotten about. I wished quietly it was just the feeling rotten and not something else, too.

"Do you feel anything for me any more?" She twisted in the seat and looked straight at me. "Damn it, I'm drunk. I want to know things. We've been talking like a couple of fools, Eric. We've known each other all our lives and did things and you wired for me to meet you like that and now...."

"Sure," I said. I patted her knee. It was warm and solid and the nylon was slick beneath my hand. My hand touched the warm flesh and Norma drove faster.

Then I began saying, damn, damn, damn, in the back of my head. Are you trying to be true to anything at all? Leda, Leda, but my hand remained on Norma's knee and she held her lower lip between her teeth.

I took a long drink and the sky and horizon blended, then sharpened, then blended. I was drunk. There was a lake off there to our left and the car suddenly bumped over a dirt road. Spanish moss flopped heavily against the top of the car and pieces flew in the window while Norma and I jounced together, and she smelled good and was warm with my arm around her when the car stopped by the lake shielded by bushes and trees and moss with the engine dead, and Norma's face next to mine was lazy wild with her eyes half open and her mouth redly damp through all the tears.

"Eric. God, Eric." She began crying, not harsh outside, but inside there, stricken with it, choking on it. "Make it business, then," she said.

Her lips weren't tender, they weren't savage, they were Norma with Leda lurking off in the shadows with the yellow shorts in her hand.

I drew away slightly and Norma's arms were taut and warm around me. Then I held her close because her breasts were good and her body was warm and more demanding than yielding.

She breathed hard now, with her face hard, and she wasn't crying at all that you could see, only way inside she wept and screamed with it, with her eyes dry and hot like a flame.

"Yes, damn you," she said, breathing it out with her eyes hot and dry and wide open.

The open door of the sedan flapped gently in a soft gentle wind which came breathing along over the lake among the trees, with warm Florida smells of humid dampness between the singing shadows that swooped black and blinding and full of harsh and bitter pain. The open door of the sedan swung gently and all the red yelling of the blood cleaved through the shadows. The open door of the sedan swung gently, to and fro. Wild and with unseen tears in the sunny afternoon.

I hadn't been near Cypress Landing in a good while. It had grown some, changed. The main street glittered with chrome and plate-glass windows, fresh sidewalks, and newly laid road. People on the streets looked more browned by the sun and they wore more white than I recalled. The cars seemed longer and shinier and they traveled faster.

Modernity was settling in and I realized there were a lot of tourists. Even in summer. It hadn't been that way. We passed the sheriff's office and I supposed Clyde Burkette still lounged behind the scarred desk in that room of many smells. Clyde had never liked me much, though he did like my brother Frank. The whole town knew how Frank and I hated each other. I wondered if Frank would be at home with Mother now.

Norma and I had quit the bottle. But we still felt the liquor. I certainly did and she'd hit it harder than I had. She motioned out the window. "Look."

On the right hand side of the street a sand-colored building façade of planes, angles, and plate glass supported a sign of heroic dimensions reading: "FRANKLIN GARTH."

The sign said nothing else.

"He's gone great guns."

I nodded. "Yeah." Nothing else. Just Franklin Garth. He was that well known and the building had cost money. I tried not to think of that.

Leaving the business section, small and tidy, the smoldering lethargy of oldness set in. The streets were relaxed and quiet as they had always been; the houses crouched and heat flaked beneath spreading shade trees and supple palms awaiting God knows what without impatience but maybe with a kind of careless scorn.

Then that changed as we struck the beaches. New developments again. White and green and mauve and pink and tan cement-block cubicles baked in an ashlike wasteland of sand, breasting the Gulf of Mexico. Trees had been uprooted. New palms withering and sparse and crippled, rooted like dead men with one arm raised, fingers clawing at the sky, burned out, hellish and forlorn. The mark of civilization–like fly specks in an erratic line across the sticky side of a postage stamp.

Here and there the richer places, beautifully landscaped, carefully kept, but sided by sand and somehow sad.

"I want to go to my place," I said. "The barn. Remember the barn?"

Norma had wept afterward at the lake and we hadn't talked since. I hadn't wanted to talk because of Leda; she was like an iron clamp on my mind.

"Yes, I remember the barn. It's a mess, Eric. Needs cleaning. I used to go there sometimes and sit."

"Oh."

"Don't worry. I'm all right now. Nobody else ever went near the place, unless maybe that man–Lenny. He went there sometimes." She paused. "I saw him looking in the window once. Looking at that statue you made of a modern Venus."

"How is Lenny?"

"He's come up in the world some. Nobody knows how. Still lives in the same place, only rebuilt. He drives a car and dresses real sharp."

"I told you about his collection. You ever see it?"

"You kidding?"

"Sure."

"My God, I wouldn't touch him with gloves on."

She turned off the main highway and pretty soon we reached the barn. It was badly in need of paint and the grass was waist-high.

"I just used to walk down and look around, see that nobody had broken in, sort of," Norma said.

"Thanks."

She looked at me, trying not to let me see the pain in her eyes. "Forget it." She sat there a minute. "You going inside?"

"Not now."

"Look," she said. "You take my car. Go on home like you want. I'll clean the place up." She looked away.

I didn't say anything.

"Go ahead," she said. "You take the car, anyway. My shop's just up the road. A beach shop. Get more trade that way. I can walk easily. I walked over here lots."

"Oh."

"You go ahead." She got out of the car. "I'll kind of clean it up inside."

I looked at her. "You know where the keys are?"

"The same old place," she said. She patted the purse she took from behind the driver's seat. "I put 'em here. So nobody could get 'em."

"All right."

"You go on, then."

She turned and stared at the barn. It had a skylight but that was covered over, and the cypress plank sides made it look like a sun-bleached backwoods shack. But I knew it wasn't too bad inside.

"You didn't have any luggage, or anything?"

"No. All right. I'll borrow your car."

"Yes."

I left her standing there like that. I turned the car around and headed for the main road. I was going home.

## Chapter 10

Here and there, but not very often now, the old, old places could be seen, set well back on the inland side of the road, or reached only through ageless growths of banyan, cypress, and gum, by sand or clay roads hewed clean by Negro slaves a hundred years ago. And kept clean by Negro men today.

The Garth home was such a place.

Backed by a small, key-dotted bayou, joined to the Gulf by a length of man-made, cement-walled canal in which the hulls of two sailboats rotted, the house hovered hugely above a front lawn a quarter mile in length.

But it was freshly painted. The front gallery no longer leaned and the white columns were new and straight.

There's money here, thought the viewer. What else?

There were two cars in the long U driveway. I parked Norma's sedan behind a shiny black Lincoln, got out, and started up the gallery steps. The door opened and there stood my brother Frank.

He looked as if he'd been struck with a board across the face when he saw me. His eyes widened, his face went deep red, then he calmed. It was an abrupt calm, fought down, leashed.

There was no greeting. "I knew it," he said. "Somehow I knew it." His voice was as loud as ever and very Southern. Dressed in a milky Palm Beach suit with a brilliant hand-painted tie of orange and purple, he looked even more assured than when I'd seen him in Alabama.

His brightly brown impatient eyes roved quickly over me and dismissed me. And the contempt was in his voice. "I thought you were–"

"How's Mother?"

He stood with his back to the doorway and said, "We haven't heard from you, as usual. How–Never mind." Again the contempt, the restless eyes.

"How in hell could you hear from me? How's Mother?"

"She's dying, Eric." His hands were nervous now. "She's not at all well."

"Why didn't you let me know?" I said. I was seeing my brother now. All right, what are you going to do about it, Garth? You're looking at him and it's Frank. How about that? Did you kill him once or a million times?

"Look," I said. "Why didn't you write, do something? I had to break out of that place. Is that funny?"

His lips paled slightly. He shook his head. "She's dying, Eric. Hanging on just like Father. The doc says any time at all." He cleared his throat, and his eyes danced around, searching, searching. It was almost as if he were looking for some place to run. "I'm not glad to see you. I couldn't tell you that then. I want you to know that. Up there in Alabama, it was different."

"Mutual feeling," I said with a nod.

"Mother's been asking for you a lot."

I didn't say anything. I knew Frank, and he was plenty disconcerted about something. His eyebrows were hiked with a slow amazement.

"Where's your luggage?" He smiled. Another habit modified, but not broken. Prompted by fear, possibly, he had always laughed to take the edge off scorn.

"Haven't any. I told you I broke out of there."

"Wandering rooster come home to roost, with only the shirt on his back. A cheap shirt, too." He was groping for something. I eyed him, then shoved by him into the cool shadows of the front hall.

His voice was nervous, filled with rapid noise. "The doctor's with her now. You won't be able to see her, Eric. He'll be with her, and he's left orders. Nothing must disturb her, Eric–"

I kept walking, up the long stairway, down the hall toward the large front bedroom where she would be. Frank was right behind me. I paused, looked at him. There was stark cold fright in his eyes, the most horrible example of naked fear I'd ever seen. "You can't see her, Eric. She's sick, dying."

"All right."

He pulled at my arm. His touch made me furious and I flung his hand down, started for the large front room.

His voice was tired, resigned. "She's not in there."

"How come?"

He shrugged, motioned toward a partly open doorway across the hall. This was what had once been a guest room, one of the guest rooms.

A slim, white-haired man in a gray suit, with a stethoscope around his neck and twirling gold-framed glasses in his hand, stepped into the hall. He blinked at me, then moved lightly up to Frank.

"How is she?" I asked.

The doctor ignored me. "She keeps asking for Eric," he told Frank. "Talking about him, as always."

"This is Eric," Frank said. His voice sounded peculiar. "Dr. Bantram."

The doctor put on his glasses, nodded as he looked at me. "Then it's all right now." He shook his head at me. "There's nothing I can do. A matter of time and not much of that. The slightest shock–" He snapped his fingers. "Her heart's like a crippled butterfly wing." He nodded. "Anyway, maybe she'll feel better now with you here. No more pretense, eh, Frank?"

"No." Frank's voice was hollow.

"What do you mean?" I said.

The doctor nodded at me, patted Frank's arms, and walked swiftly down the stairs. At the first landing he turned, called back softly. "Going over to the hospital. You can reach me there. I'll be back around seven this evening." He went on downstairs.

Frank shoved his hands into his pockets. "You came at an opportune time," he said.

I stared at him. He slowly dropped his gaze.

For a long moment she was not recognizable to me. The blinds were drawn and she lay in the pale saffron shade of the old four-poster, canopied bed. She lay in the exact center, her nearly shoulderless body and gray head propped by three huge pillows. Suddenly she was terribly old, much older than she should have been. Her thin white face, strong-browed, resigned, was utterly without expression. Only her eyes, agatelike, proved the old hard strength. Her hands were folded over the smooth white counterpane.

"Here's Eric, mother," Frank said.

"I can see, Franklin," she said. Her voice was kind, smooth, alert, but filled with a nervousness. And death squatted patiently on that bed with an obviousness that was disturbing. "They were all right," she said. "They told me at first, then they didn't tell me any more. You're alive and well."

I went over beside the bed table laden with medications and took her hand. "Hello, Mother. Of course, I'm all right."

Without moving her head, she looked at me from the corners of her eyes. Her cool, thin hand pressed mine lightly, then unfolded like a leaf.

"You weren't one to write," she said. "Like your father. But you probably couldn't write. Were you in a prison camp?" She paused while I groped blindly for an answer. "I wrote you often, had Frank mail the letters. Did you get any of them? Up until the time you disappeared?"

"Disappeared?"

Her face went serious with slight pain. Characteristically, she was holding whatever she felt inside her, not showing it, not letting it out. She was a strong woman.

"I'm sorry I didn't come sooner," I said. "What do you mean I disappeared?" In the back of my mind I thought about the letters she had written and knew Frank had never mailed them. I had ceased writing, but it hadn't made any difference. What did she mean, now?

"Yeah," Frank said. "Sure, sure. Reckon he was worried just sick. Let you believe all that stuff." He stood at the foot of the bed, leaning against a post, and nervously bit the end off a slim cigar.

Her eyes blinked his way. Then she folded her hands and stared at them. "You may not even know," she said. Her hands twitched and her mouth jerked up into a short sharp grimace of pain. "We received a telegram from the government. It said you were missing in action during the line of duty. We thought you were dead, Eric."

I stood there. I didn't look at Frank and I didn't see anything for a red flashing moment. Missing in action. She was out of her mind. Frank was right. I shouldn't have come into the room. It had jarred her badly.

"Who knew about this telegram?" I said quietly.

"Why, everybody. I told everybody, and they thought it was terrible, Eric. When you walked into the room, just now, I felt like I– Well, I nearly screamed, son."

"Well, it's all right now," Frank said. He spoke rapidly. "He's back. Was all a mistake. Those things happen. Once I knew a man–"

I looked at him and he ceased. "Did you bring her the telegram?" I asked Frank.

Mother said, "Sure, he did, Eric. He's taken good care of me." Her eyes shot toward Frank, alert, then back to me. "Now everything's all right. They tell me I can't get excited, Eric. If I do, I may die. I have to stay calm."

I knew I had to break this off. She was becoming plenty excited. Disturbed, too.

"It was all a mistake, yes," I said. "They made a mistake. I've been in a hospital. But I'm all right now."

"Certainly." She chuckled. "Have you done any work?"

"None since before the war in Chicago. Just before I went overseas. A bas-relief wall panorama in a hotel in Chicago. Made quite a stir for a while." I wasn't thinking about what I said. My mind was on other things.

"Until the city fathers stepped in and tore it down," she said. "Right? They called it obscene."

"Yes."

"You got paid?"

"They had to pay. The contract was filled. The hotel owner liked it. He had no choice. He has it at home now."

"I read about it, Eric. Wish I could have seen it."

Frank snorted. "I've heard it doesn't pay much."

Mother had seen a telegram saying I was missing in action. Those things happened. From the government. Her voice grew noticeably weaker.

"What about you?" I said. "You look fine."

"Don't lie, Eric. I'm dying and you know it. They've told you. Feel better now, though. Kind of a shock, you coming home like this, but I feel better. We thought you were dead, for sure. Missing in action usually means that. They put your name on the honor roll in the park, Frank says. Doesn't mean anything. But it's there, anyhow." She chuckled. "Now you can take it off, eh?" She tried to poke me in the ribs but it was a futile gesture which fell short. There wasn't much strength left in her.

I began to feel a hate for Frank that was incomparable to anything. I watched him light his cigar. Pale azure smoke mingled with the saffron shade. The house was quiet save for the loud shrieking of a jay outside the window.

Frank moved to the other side of the bed and sat in an arm chair. He seemed preoccupied with a loose bit of leaf on his cigar.

"I do wish you could have let me know how you were," she said. "But, of course, that's your business." She was speaking with an effort now. Her head moved restlessly from side to side.

"Maybe we'd better talk later. You should rest."

"I've been resting too long already."

I sat on the edge of the bed. She stared at her folded hands. The jay shrieked. Frank cleared his throat.

"If you had money," she said. "You could go ahead with your sculptoring now without worry. Right?"

"It would help. It's a long road to recognition."

"You remember your father's business, how it was to be left to you and Frank?"

"Certainly."

"You know how your father left it? So you and Frank would have it together? It should have been done long ago."

"Yes."

"Well, I couldn't handle it. I was too much like your father. But the business wasn't to go to you and Frank until I die. Your father left it in terrible shape. I needed someone to help."

"Frank volunteered," I said.

"Yes. He not only put it on its feet, but you'll both be rich. What with everything else, too."

I waited.

"He made certain conditions and that's what I've wanted to see you about. Only I thought you were dead, Eric!" Tears formed in her eyes and her lips trembled. I could actually see her try to get hold of herself, fighting with herself. Because the doctor had told her she mustn't excite herself and that's just what she was doing. She glanced toward Frank. "I've been too ill to pay any attention to the business. Frank took it over under a condition."

I looked at my brother. His head rested back on the chair and he blew smoke into the shadows. He deliberately avoided my eyes. My palms grew damp and I dried them on my trousers. She apparently knew nothing of how Frank was operating. But there was something else here. I could feel it, and I didn't like it, not even understanding completely what it was.

She said, "I want it all settled now. Today."

"Reckon we can?" Frank said.

She seemed not to hear him. "Frank had me sign the entire business over to him. It was the only condition under which he'd work. That was before we received the telegram about you, of course. Then after that it was all right, anyway."

The jay ceased its wild shrieking.

"Everything's signed over to Frank, now. I agreed. He said when he had it running smoothly, we'd tear up his papers and the both of you could sign new ones–share and share alike. But, of course, that was before...."

"I really don't–" I didn't know what to say. My life was a grand mess.

She raised her hand. It trembled weakly, fell back to the bed. "Isn't that right, Frank?" she said.

"Yes, that's what I said then." He eyed his cigar. He was no longer nervous; he was almost bold.

"But now things are fine," she said. "You're really alive, after all. I want everything in order today. As your father wished."

I said nothing.

"Frank has gone through with his promise to make the business good." As she spoke I saw a faint film of perspiration spring out across her forehead.

"Mother," I said, remembering what the doctor had said. "We can put this off a while. Perhaps you should rest."

"Yes," Frank said. "I agree." He didn't move.

"No," she said. "Now. It can't be put off. Frank," she turned her head, "have you that paper? You can tear it up now. I have all the other papers here." She reached and opened a drawer on the table, took out some papers folded neatly and tied with a blue ribbon. The exertion tired her. "Lawyer Algren. Phone him, Frank. Tell him to come immediately."

Frank rose slowly, placed his cigar in an ash tray. "No. I've been thinking. I've changed plans."

"Changed?"

"Yes."

I stood. Mother's fingers twitched on the papers in her hand. "What do you mean, Frank? I was going to have half interest in the business signed over to Eric before we received that telegram, whether I died or not. That doesn't change anything, because he's alive, now. And the other will has to be altered again now." Her head lifted from the pillow. I pressed it back. She said, "Have you the paper you signed, Frank?"

"It's in my safe-deposit box at the bank." He smiled. "Now, take it easy," he said. His eyes flicked over to me, brown and bright. "Let's not rush into this."

Mother's head nodded up and down jerkily. What color there was in her face drained away. "I want those papers signed today," she said. "Lawyer Algren will come right away if you call. It has to be today, Frank." She turned to me. "Eric, go phone Algren."

She was afraid. I was afraid, too, because I didn't want to look at Frank.

"That won't be necessary," Frank said. He placed both hands on the foot of the bed and leaned toward her. "Listen. Do you think for one minute I'm going to go into partnership with a bum? A good-for-nothing? After I've worked like hell to build this loan business into something, after I've given everything I had to make it go? And the other–the will–why should that be changed?" He paused.

"Frank," I said. "Save it."

"It won't save." His voice was filled with contempt. He faced me, then looked back at her. "It won't save at all. You may as well know that right now. I'm not going to tear up that contract. The business is mine. I made it and I intend to keep it. It's state-wide. And the rest of the money's going to be mine, too. Who's taken care of you? Who's sacrificed his youth, his time and effort, just to keep you happy? Eric? No. He's been off to the wars." He was talking levelly. It would have been easier on her if he had shouted.

"Frank...." Her voice was dry. She strained forward and, with an effort, sat up in bed. I reached to guide her back, but she knocked my hand away.

Frank said quietly, "You may as well know this, too. When I made that proposition, had you sign the business over to me, I had no intention of ever going through with our bargain. I did it to save you whatever heartbreak–"

She was trying to say something but it wouldn't come. Her face was gray, pale and tortured. "Your father–" she managed. "Eric, call Algren!"

"No," Frank said. He remained cool, leaning over the bed, but his eyes shone and the vein in his temple pulsed bluely. "The contract can't be broken. It's solid. I made sure of that." He straightened. "Eric's like father was. Lazy, shiftless, good-for-nothing. Face it. In a year there'd be no business, no money. And he'd run through the rest of the inheritance buying whisky and women. I can smell the whisky on him now. He reeks of the stuff. Look at him, a tramp, a bum."

Mother trembled and her breathing was rapid. "Frank," I said, "shut up!"

"I won't. I won't shut up. I won't. I don't reckon you can make me shut up, either. Coming home high and mighty to clean up, but I know and you know I know. Mother's too soft-hearted. You're all the same. I'm the only one in this family with any business sense. You know why? Not because I inherited it from a strange member of the family who had some pride, some intelligence, no, not that. Because there never was a Garth in this damned country with enough brains to do anything better than bait a fishhook, or swill corn whisky, or paw at the maid's leg. Yes. Because I'm a Garth in name only, thank God." He glanced at me. "You. The beloved, no-good son. You reckoned I was proud of the name Garth? Well, I reckon I'll take what I deserve. Nobody's done anything for mother but me. I'm the only one. I've stuck by, and I don't reckon anybody'll take what's due me, by God." He was breathing hard. "I worked for it," he said. "Some intelligence, by God."

"Eric," mother said weakly. "Don't let any of this talk bother you. I never–Frank promised, he promised so many things." Her breathing was a rapid flutter. Her chin quivered helplessly, the papers fell to the floor. She grabbed for them, but missed. "You lied," she gasped, pointing at Frank. "You lied to me! No son, no son at all!"

"Now, Mother, you must rest," Frank said. "You'll see it's all for the best. Think it over."

"Frank," I whispered. "Get away. Get out of here."

She was shaking and could no longer speak. She mouthed soundless words, her eyes voiding helpless agony.

"We'd lose everything," Frank said. "Father was wrong, that's all. You're wrong. I won't do it." He spoke with a calmness that cut like a knife.

She reached for her breast, her fingers clawing, and fell back in the bed. Her eyes closed, wrinkled with pain.

Outside the jay screamed again and again.

I whirled toward Frank. "Call the doctor, hurry! Hurry up, you fool!"

"She'll be all right, Eric," he said. He stared at her for a moment. Then something touched his face; something reached him, warned him, as she gasped. His features dissolved with fright.

I shoved him toward the door. "The doctor–get him!"

"Yes, yes. All right." His voice wavered. "She'll be all right." He hurried from the room, his feet pounded along the hall.

At her side, I didn't know what to do. But inside–I was crazy. If Prescott could have had a look into my mind just then, he'd have slapped me in a strait jacket. I didn't know what to do.

"Your father," she said. Her voice was very faint. "Frank–" she said.

"Lie still," I told her. "It's all right now."

Her eyes came open. She gazed startled about the room. She tried to breathe, through the white pain that showed in her eyes, for a long while without success.

The jay screamed five more hellish times and ceased.

## Chapter 11

I walked slowly out of the room, down the hall, until I reached the head of the stairs. I stood there and watched Frank come up from below. His flagrant hand-painted tie streamed over his shoulder. He held a fresh unlit cigar in one hand.

"Is she all right?" he said. "I got Bantram. He'll be right over."

Something inside me began to expand. Blood pulsed and pounded in the back of my head.

Nearing me, Frank thrust his face out, brown eyes glittering. "You did this," he said. His voice was hoarse. "It's your fault, coming home this way. Why didn't you stay up there? We don't want you here."

Then I saw it. He was scared. Fighting to attain a dominance over things that had long since left him. The big brother who wasn't a brother at all, but still trying to wish himself off as a god, preparing the ritual in his mind so you could see the cogs working. Scared way down to the soles of his feet, his eyes all sick with sudden belligerent hope. Because he knew I knew plenty. And he had to play his hand out, fast, before the man on the other side of the table opened his eyes any further. But it was too slow.

"All right, all right," he said. His voice was strained, fast, and pleading. He tried to fight the pleading down and attained an abrupt brass. "So I faked the telegram. Who's to know? Who can change it? What difference? Why not?"

"Why not?" I said.

"I told them she'd had illusions, dreamt it. Told them to agree with her as I agreed when with her in their presence. Nobody doubted. Told them no telegram had come. It was no harm, because you won't have the money. It's not yours. You've done nothing but whore around all your life." He was talking so fast the words stuck together head and tail. He knew he was going to get hurt and he didn't like the idea. "So I faked the telegram. What you going to do about it? Nothing. You can't do a thing." He was wild with it, wild with the thought that he could succeed. "And all the rest, too. Think you're so damned smart. By God, I'll show you what's smart." He was almost crying because the walls of his majestically foolish scheme were crumbling so fast he couldn't escape getting hit by a few bricks. Maybe a whole wall. He wasn't sure. It wasn't nice to watch.

"So you faked a telegram?" I said. "And all the rest?"

He hesitated, paling. "Yes."

I lifted my fist from the floor. Everything I had was behind that blow. It connected flush with the side of his jaw. His cigar flew in a savage spiral. I hadn't known whether I would strike. Now I wanted to hurt him.

His feet left the stairs in wild groundless running. He crashed against the banister, scrabbled cursing onto the first landing. On his knees, he faced me. Then, standing, he started up toward me, red-faced, enraged, and hoping he wouldn't lose face.

I started down. "She's dead, Frank."

"Dead," he said. "Dead...."

"Yes. That's what happens to people. Are you afraid of the word? Would you rather I coated it with sugar so you could swallow it without choking?" None of this was any good. It would cure nothing. It could never save Mother. But I had to do it and at the same time all the fear that was inside me welled up to the surface. The pain in my fist was far from agony–it was sweet.

"She's dead," he whispered. "You've killed her."

He stood there/ saying that and I hit him again. Again he sprawled down to the first landing. This time he came at me like a dazed but furious bull.

We stood face to face on the landing. He was breathing hard. He started to say something, then swung. I caught the blow on my left forearm and got in a straight, hard right. He went over the banister, clinging, and pawed himself back onto the stairs. "She's dead up there!" he shouted. "This is sacrilege."

His face was twisted now, his bright eyes blinking. He stood there hunched over, licking off his lips. The whites of his eyes slowly turned pink. This was what I wanted. I wanted him as mad as he could get.

"Your pretty suit's getting bloody," I said.

He glanced down. I kicked for the point of his chin. He nailed my leg and twisted. He had weight and he was in a hell of a lot of better condition than I'd figured. Pain spun into my belly and we took the rest of the stairs fighting.

I wanted to break him like I'd break rock. Change that contemptuous face–tear that smile away.

We crashed into the hallway with him on top. He bubbled at the mouth and sobbed a little as he slammed at me.

"You aren't fit to live, Frank," I said. I got one hand up between his arms and grabbed his throat. You handle rock, your hands get hard, your fingers very strong. Like Norma said one time, you kind of catch the hardness from the rock. I squeezed his throat as if I closed my fingers on the handle of a maul.

He grabbed for my hand. I swung up my left and brought the heel down hard on the bridge of his nose. It cracked. He let out a yell. Blood pumped into my eyes.

He rolled off, making noises in his throat. My fingers snared the back of his coat collar. The coat ripped like a zipper.

Then we were on our feet. He cursed me in a concerned calm manner that was almost comical. Something–the shock of mother's death, the way he'd acted in the bedroom–somehow prevented him from really fighting. And I found that I wasn't sure whether I wanted to kill him or not. I thought about the wooden mallet and the battle-field in Korea and the wooden mallet hanging on the rack in the barn with Norma there and then Leda screamed into my mind like some wanton image of lost hope.

"You're no good, Frank. You're rotten."

He came at me. I feinted with a left, leaned with all I had behind my right. It caught him in the gut.

He bowed slowly, stared at the floor, gagged.

"Oh, God, God, God," he said.

"You've got what you want."

"Get out of this house."

"I'll go for a while. But only because I don't like looking at you."

I walked down the hall and out the front door. I left the door open and stood on the gallery a moment. Then I went on down into the driveway and over toward the side of the house where a length of hose lay coiled like a snake on the fresh green lawn.

I turned on the hose and let the warm stale water run out until it was cool and fresh and smelling faintly of rubber. I drank and rinsed Frank's blood off my face and hands. Then I took off my jacket, tie and shirt, left the shirt and tie on the lawn and put my jacket back on. The shirt wasn't bloody. I combed my hair and went out back and stood there watching the sun shimmer on the water.

I felt wrong inside. I wished I hadn't started anything with Frank. But I had and I felt wrong inside about it. It had been kind of good in a way, though. Some of his affectation had left him. But there was no real satisfaction anyplace. I didn't know any more really about myself than I had back there in California. Except that I hadn't killed him. But maybe that was because there wasn't a wooden mallet handy. I knew my mind was working like a sick mind, sometimes. Anyway, if I knew Frank at all his affectation would return quickly enough. Fake telegram or not. There was no point in wondering about it.

Frank would be lost without his front. But that front was only paper now, not even a good grade of cardboard. It had become more than a mere front. It was his nature. He probably didn't even realize it was false any more. I wasn't sure I'd broken his nose although the cartilage had made a good noise. I hoped I'd broken his nose. I hoped that.

He didn't know what fear was.

I glanced up at the rear bedroom window where she, would be lying up there in bed. The black arm of a pine limb reached almost to the window ledge with a spiked clump of green leaf on the tip and three cones. That's where the jay had been.

At the foot of the pine was a wooden bench. I went over and sat down. I hated Frank as I had hated no one in the world, and I tried to reason. Don't rationalize, Prescott had said. View it all objectively. Hell. There was nothing but hate, white and hot. Yet I knew death alone wasn't a thing you blamed anybody for, exactly, and not this kind of death for sure. Mother had been a good woman and she'd lived, but not much, only she hadn't known of any other way to live. Maybe that was wrong, too. Because you never did know what went on in another person's mind–the little things that went to make up the dream. Leda and Frank and Norma and Lenny and you and me.

We all did a little carving, trying to shape that silver image into something closer to reality, or what we wanted as our reality. Only the knife was dull always, because the one true image remained. And it died with you if you didn't allow it to walk out of your head. If you tried to change the silver into gold, or alter color, or shape, or poise, you weren't you, really. Because the one image remained. And that was you. Bastard, king, warrior, bum, or just the guy who shoves molded dough into an oven and brings out bread.

A small boat with an outboard motor went *phut-phut-phuttle-phut* by close to shore. A man balanced with both feet, one on either gunwale, holding a gig. Somebody had told them flounder would be along here. But not in the afternoon they should have said. At night. And the tide was wrong. The one operating the motor waved to me, then the one with the gig, and I waved. The sound of the motor went echoing across the tiny keys of snarled mangroves.

I heard a car coming along the drive pretty fast. I went around front. It was Dr. Bantram in a hurry up the front step of the gallery. He saw me, paused, blinking behind his glasses with his black bag hanging.

I turned off the hose and went up to him. We climbed the steps and stood by the front door.

"How is she?"

"She's gone," I said. "She was gone before Frank called you. He didn't know. Will you take over?"

"Yes. I'm sorry, Eric. It had to happen. It was due, any time." But there was that look in his eyes of complete unconcern about death with slight wonder about me because I was the town bum once. He went back to his car and dropped the black bag into the front seat, then returned to the open front door where I waited.

"Her heart was never strong. She survived three bad attacks somehow, so it had to be this time."

At the end of the hall Frank was coming down the stairs.

"Does Mrs. Garth know?"

"Mrs. Garth?"

"Yes. Your brother's wife."

So here it was. Not sharp—dull realization and finality. Almost relief, maybe. The sudden sickness was almost nepenthe. Leda and certainty.

"Here she is now," the doctor said.

A yellow convertible was speeding up the drive, flashing through patches of sunlight and shade like the revolving blades of an electric fan. A woman was at the wheel.

The car stopped behind the doctor's. The woman stepped from the car and my heart rocked then. She wore white shorts and a fuzzy white short-sleeved sweater.

Frank was in the doorway. He didn't look at me, but he had washed up and he had on a clean shirt. The mess he'd made in the front hall was gone. Frank's face was badly bruised and his lip was cut and swollen.

"Frank!" she said, seeing his face. "Frank. What's going on?"

Sunlight streamed on her as she came up the steps. Everything went out of me, even knowing. I hadn't believed. It hadn't been what it was, even knowing. Knowing all these months. Sure of something like this, yet denying it.

Inside I turned to mush, swearing all the time that it wasn't so and knowing it was. Leda.

She paused. I hadn't moved, the muscles in the backs of my legs went so rigid they ached. She paused for only a second, not smiling, just seeing me and telling me to shut up, be still, with her eyes gray and abrupt. It was like looking into burned-out twilight—seeing the night back there. Her auburn hair glowed and sparked from the sunlight behind her. Then she brushed past me.

Leda....

She was more beautiful than ever. Her long legs, her lithe, full-breasted body. A white light came on behind my eyes and stayed there. Everything went foggy. I heard Frank speaking as I moved away.

"Leda," he said. "Leda, Mother died. You see who's come home? It's Eric." He glanced toward me, his voice scornful. "You remember Eric, don't you?"

"Frank," she said. "Darling."

I walked across the gallery through the crazy impossible dream. The dream I had tried to deny. I was tired and sick. I didn't look back.

"Mother's dead," Frank said. Bantram cleared his throat.

I went down the steps into the crazy but calm sunlight that bit like white ice through the shade.

Leda Thayer was not alone. I had found her. She hadn't just vanished–hadn't just run off. She was my brother's wife–wife to wealth.

I wanted to run. It was all I could do to walk through the silent afternoon.

## Chapter 12

I walked straight on across the lawn until I reached the main beach road. I didn't look back. There was every reason why I should have remained at the house. I couldn't. I hated Frank's guts for what he'd done to Mother. There was no point in saying, "If–" because the deed was done.

I turned back off the beach road and went to the car. It was like walking through smoke. And I couldn't face Frank. Not with Leda. God, I thought, Leda is here. She didn't vanish. She just came home. She's right here. It was like seeing the back of your head in a mirror.

Leda. Frank's wife. It was unbelievable, yet true. She hadn't really even recognized me. It was taking a long time to sink in. She had married Franklin Garth. She had married half million dollars and my brother, who wasn't even my brother, after all.

"Leda, you see who's come home? It's Eric."

Yes, she remembered, all right.

But that one look at her had turned the trick. I wanted her....

Breaking into a run I tried to push the afternoon's events out of my mind. It was impossible. I wanted to leave Cypress Landing right away. I knew I wouldn't.

As I climbed into the car, it was like finding the home ground they talk about; it was like grabbing hold of God's beard and saying, "Maybe I don't rate, but give me a chance, just for the hell of it, will you?"

Leda. Why? Leda, why?

There was one large room in the barn extending clear beyond the rafters to the large skylight. The other two rooms were more or less catchalls, though one was used as a kitchen and the other had a bed in it.

The windows–large ones I had put in myself years ago–had all been shuttered, but now the shutters were open and entering the back door into the kitchen, I smelled meat frying.

Norma was nowhere in sight. There were chops in the frying pan on the wood stove. There was also a pan of German raw fries.

"Anybody home?" I called.

Norma came through the door leading into the studio. "Hi," she said. "You were gone a long time."

She was a mess. She'd changed to dungarees and one of my T shirts, resurrected from a box of old clothes. She was dirt and dust from head to toe. She dangled a filthy rag in one hand and a ragged broom in the other. Her face was smudged with black streaks and cobwebs spun in silvered clots from her bright blonde hair.

"Gorgeous," I said. "Absolutely gorgeous."

She smiled and wiped her face with the dustcloth. It had a startling effect.

"I figured the place might need cleaning up some."

"I don't mind," she said. "The pussycats get me. I never saw so many in my life." She paused, slightly excited, waved the broom toward the studio. She had sobered up. "You should see 'em," she said. "Pussycats all over the place. Thousands." She beamed happily and my insides snarled up. "I got most of 'em, though."

"Wait," I said. "What do you mean, pussycats? We got a menagerie?" All I could think of was hundreds of cats running around the barn. "What'd you do with 'em?"

She started to laugh, waved the cloth, choked on the dust, then said, "You don't understand. Come here."

I followed her into the studio cluttered with modeling stands, racked tools, chisels, mallets, completed and half-completed statues, statuettes, and other forgotten odds and ends. Also there were crates and boxes of stuff I'd sent home for storage here.

"Well," I said to Norma. "Show me." I felt fine, all right. Just fine. And this kid had gone ahead believing things possible even in the face of disbelief. Leda. Wait until Norma saw Leda. Lots of people put imaginary guns against their heads. I'd pulled the trigger six times in the last few minutes. Then I realized that wasn't the way. I threw the gun out the window.

Norma bent behind a battered, frazzled upholster couch, came up with a large puff of dust and cobwebs which clung together.

"There," she said. "See? Pussycats."

I didn't say anything.

"There aren't many left," she told me. "But it was fun while it lasted."

"All right," I said. "You'd make a good wife."

She swallowed. "How's your mother?"

I tried to explain what had happened without making it sound too terrible.

Her sympathy was genuine. "I'm sorry," she said. "You came back at a bad time. I'm really sorry, Eric."

"Yes. Everything's happened at once."

"Oh?"

I walked across the studio, unwound a rope from a wall bracket and let down the trap that covered the skylight. Turning, I said, "There was a woman, Norma. You were right."

"Oh."

"She vanished for a while. I didn't know where she was."

"I see."

"She's married my brother."

Norma dropped her pussycat, leaned the broom against the wall, hung the dustcloth over it. "Think I'd better watch those chops for supper," she said. She moved quickly into the kitchen.

I followed her. "Did you hear what I said? This woman, she's my brother's wife. She's living right there."

"Don't you think I'm good, though?" Norma said. "I went down the road to the store and bought all this for supper. So we can eat, you know? You wouldn't have anything to eat here, if I hadn't–restaurants are probably–"

"O. K. Forget it."

She didn't answer. She made a great clattering at the stove. Then she turned quickly and looked at me. "Eric. I'm sorry. About everything. Especially about your mother."

I went back into the studio and closed the door. The homecoming of Eric Garth, I thought quietly.

It was easy enough to say Mother would have died anyway, that the doctor was sure she couldn't last much longer, that her heart was barely beating. Only I found myself blaming myself for that, too. If I hadn't come, it might not have happened. The old magnificent "if."

Don't be stupid. It would have happened anyway.

Frank should have kept his mouth closed. But that was his way. Anything to grandstand.

So he had the business, the money, the house, the woman. I picked up a dried-out, half-finished image of a clay woman clinging to an old armature and hurled it base and all across the room. It shattered against a post. I felt all the hate boiling up inside me and I wished I'd really broken Frank like that piece of clay. I could do it.

I had to see Leda....

"That Lenny Conn is here."

I turned, breathing hard, trying to control myself. Norma stood in the doorway. She watched me for a moment, frowning. "He's been drinking. I wouldn't let him in."

"You wouldn't–good. Don't, damn it. No–go ahead." I ceased. Lenny Conn pushed by Norma and strode grinning into the room.

He had a white face that looked slick. It should have been tanned because most of the years I knew of his life had been spent in the sun. But slugs don't tan, even though they sometimes crawl from under their logs into the sunlight.

"Eric, by God. Had to get over. Heard you was back from the wars." His mouth dangled open and his wily pale eyes searched the area just above my left shoulder. He never looked you in the eye. He whirled sharply, stuck a long pale thumb into Norma's ribs. "Ol' gal, here, still beatin' the shady's for you, hey?" He jerked away, saying to Norma, "Don't get me wrong, now."

"Hello, Lenny."

Norma went back into the kitchen.

"I swow, you been a heller, ain't you?"

"Not much. I see you've turned a leaf."

He looked down at himself, stretched an arm out and half-drunkenly inspected the sleeve of his fawn-colored tropical worsted suit. He wore a nylon shirt which was soaking wet with sweat–disproving their coolness–and which was buttoned, without tie, at the throat. The wings on the collar of the shirt were about a hand and a half long. One wrinkled outside his jacket collar, the other crumbled in a wad beneath. The shirt was pink.

Lenny was built like a bear and he wore clothes like a bear might. His hair was a scraggled mass of yellow curls and his pale-lipped smile revealed a string of even gray teeth, which lapped slightly like shingles on the roof of an old barn. They may or may not have had moss along their edges. He hadn't changed except for the clothes and a new flaunting air.

"I done fair," he said.

"How?"

He winked. When he winked he showed you the shingle teeth and lifted one shoulder. He covered the wink quickly, though. "Ain't so shiftless no more. Hit's only right a man should make his way in this here world. I fished and gigged my way into the upper brackets, Eric. Bought a car an' hired me a Negro to run the boat an' do the work. I just sit." His laugh was wind with phlegm in it.

"How's the collection? Any new specimens?"

He glanced with terrific furtiveness toward the kitchen doorway, took a sidewise step toward me. "A few new pippens!"

"Good."

"One would get you right," he said. "The lady's in the papers ever day. Whyn't you come over an' have a peek?"

I had no intention of going to Lenny's place to see his collection of nude pictures and statues, even though some of them were of extremely prominent women, actresses and the like, who had used Pullman trains when Lenny was around.

"Sorry, I'm busy," I said.

He was downhearted. But only for a moment. Lenny's emotions were of short duration.

"Heered yo' maw died."

"Yeah. Look, Lenny, I'm busy." He had heard quickly.

"That's all right. I reckon we all busy." He stood there, looking quite drunk and utterly lost. "See Frank an' his new one right often."

"Did you want anything, Lenny? I'm really busy."

"Now you bring it up, reckon I do." He moved across the room, padding quietly, halted before an old statue of a woman's torso done in a fashion I'd once thought powerful. It was the one of Venus that Norma said she'd seen Lenny watching through the window.

"Like this here thing," Lenny said. "What you asking for hit?"

I sighed. "What'll you offer?"

He tightened his lips. It was a job. "Fi' dollars."

I tightened mine. "It's yours."

Between the two of us we got the statue into Lenny's car, with Lenny bubbling slightly in his throat over his new prize. The car was a Packard, a couple of years old, convertible, painted a bright and unblemished scarlet.

He started to get in, then said, "Oh, most forgot."

"Yes?"

"Miss Leda—she asted me to tell you something."

I didn't say anything. So he knew Leda.

"I an' Miss Leda's good friends."

"Fine."

"She says to tell you she wants to see you. Says, 'Lenny, tell Eric I'm miserable.' Says, 'Tell Eric I got to see him right away.'" Lenny paused, rubbed his nose sharply upward with the heel of his hand. "Leda's right nice, now, ain't she?"

I thanked him and watched him drive off. Venus sat beside him, mute and quite unconcerned over any fate which might be in store for her.

I suddenly felt like a camel drinking water after he'd crossed the Sahara. Word of Leda did that to me. I stood there watching the smoking dust of Lenny's car whirl down the roadway and vanish on the main road.

Another car's engine starting, whirled me around. I was just in time to see Norma's steady face as she drove by. She said nothing and she drove fast. Likely she'd overheard the conversation.

I went on inside and walked to the studio. I looked up at the skylight. The glass was as fogged as the inside of my head. My chest felt, as though it was in a vise with somebody slowly turning the handle so my breath came shorter and shorter until I might not be able to breathe at all.

Leda. I could feel her skin against my palms, see her eyes spinning down there in the darkness, hear her heart beating and smell the wild uprush of memory.

I stood there for quite a time, listening to myself think. Finally I walked back through the kitchen and out the rear door. Just as I closed the door a car rumbled swiftly down the sand road leading to the barn.

This time it was another convertible, with the top down. It was Leda at the wheel, her auburn hair gleaming in the myriad-hued sunset in the western sky above the Gulf. The car slid to a stop and she sat there watching me as I slowly walked toward her.

"Hello, Eric," she said. "I came as quickly as I could."

## Chapter 13

This was fine. Now that I had her here within reach there was nothing I could think of to say. Or whatever I did think, I couldn't say. She wasn't long on talk at that moment, either.

"Eric," she said.

I looked at the car, the sky, the long stretch of sand road and browned waist-high grass, the trees, and beyond them the faint line of bayou showing between patches of Spanish moss. But my gaze always came back to her. She wore the same white shorts and halter, her hair was windblown, her wide, full-lipped mouth damp and red, her eyes bright and impatient. She smiled, her teeth gleaming strong and white. "Why don't you say something, Eric?"

"Sure," I said. "Let's wear that record out."

The smile went away, she moved her legs, undid the top button on the halter. The shorts were very short, her legs very long, and there were only two buttons on the halter.

"Get in the car," she said. "We'll go some place."

I couldn't tear my eyes away. The lush, graceful lines of her body beneath her tight clothing shaped up inside me. My hands began to tremble; I rammed them into my pockets.

Her eyes were troubled now. She brushed soft thick hair away from her forehead, flicked her tongue across her lips, took a deep breath. That did it. I was half-afraid now, then slow anger knotted inside me.

"I'm humble," she said. "I've come to you." She looked straight into my eyes, and her own softened as she shook her head. "I've made a terrible mistake." She lowered her voice. "I thought I was being smart, selling your car, pulling a stunt like this. I was afraid maybe, too. Only more just being smart. Only I've hurt myself early. Your brother went overboard all the way up there in Alabama, Eric. But I only hurt myself. I can't stand it, Eric." Her tone went slightly shrill. "I need you, I've needed you ever since I left. I was insane, not you. You've got to help me." She paused, her hands gripping the steering wheel. "That last day with you, at the sanitarium. Oh, God, I was mad. I'd just left your brother. That's why I was like that, so I couldn't–"

"You're my brother's wife."

"You love me, Eric. I know you do. And I love you. Our plans. You've got to help. I don't know what to do."

"I don't want to talk about it. And your friend Lenny told me your story. Said you wanted to see me. But you're married, and that's that. Did Lenny show you his collection?"

She ignored it, but her eyes flashed. "Frank won't divorce me, won't let me do a thing. I've tried everything. Can't even get it annulled, because...."

"You've got what you wanted." I suddenly wanted to hurt her as she had hurt me, make her cry for it, and then not give in to her. "I don't want to talk about it."

"You've got to help me." Excitement came into her voice now and her eyes began to burn. She spoke rapidly, leaning toward me now, and I could smell her perfume, and the excitement and the memories crowded in. "Listen, Eric. I lay awake thinking, remembering. It can't have been so short a time, all this has happened. He's not like you, nobody's like you. I've got to–" She bit her lower lip, then went on. "I've got to be with you. I'm not going to hold back, damn it, Eric. We know each other too well for that. I go crazy every time I think of you."

"You've made your bed," I told her.

"Darling, it's no bed. I'm alone in it. Good Lord, Eric. Can't you see? Can't a person make a mistake?"

I thought of her walking out and leaving me in that place in Alabama, behind bars, and said, "Yeah, sure."

"You made one today," she said. "A bad one. Bantram knows you beat up Frank. You broke his nose, did you know that? It'll be all over town. Horace Bantram may be a doctor, but he's an old lady–a gossip. Of course, nobody knows what's been going on with you, you and your dreams, and all—out there in California." She waited, breathing hard. "I know what they think of you in Cypress Landing, and they're going to think worse. Frank's telling it around already that your coming home killed your mother. I'm sorry, Eric. But being sorry doesn't help."

I didn't say anything, but I damned Frank under my breath. That was just the kind of move he'd make. Not that it made any difference how people felt. And the dream. She would stick that in.

Suddenly she said, "I've got to get back. He'll wonder where I am. What with everything the way it is." She tried to smile. "I'll be back."

"There's no reason," I said. "Nothing to say."

Her temper changed and abruptly the old energy returned as she lowered her voice. "All right," she said. "We'll play it that way, then. You'll take me back, and I'll see you later. I'll see you a lot. I don't care what people think. I know you want me. And by the way, I notified the sanitarium that you were home, and all right. I signed your brother's name, because he'd never do it."

"All this is no use, Leda."

She smiled, watched me slyly. "No?"

"I won't see you. We can't—"

She interrupted bitingly. "I'll haunt you, darling. This isn't a game of new love, remember? I know what you like and how you like it. I know how you feel about me. Don't forget that. And I know something about that other one, too. Norma?" She started the car's engine. "But she's out of it, and you know it. I'll be back and I'll find you. I'm not going to beg, but you'll see, Eric."

The car roared into reverse and as she backed swiftly toward the main road I realized the abrupt change that had come over her. I tried to tell myself she couldn't come back, she wouldn't—but I knew she would and I knew what would happen.

On the main road, she gunned the car viciously and rapped twice on the horn. I stood there and thought I knew what had to happen, and never realized I had no idea at all....

## Chapter 14

Without returning to the barn, I hiked it back to the main road
and caught the beach bus into town. There was still time before the
stores closed and I wanted to buy a second-hand car. As I walked
down the main street I knew the smartest move would be to leave
Cypress Land-ins. But I knew I wouldn't leave.

A gray Stetson swayed up the street with a florid, toothy face
beneath it. Clyde Burkette, Sheriff. He was a big man, big and broad,
with black-button eyes and overlarge hands and one of the
drawlingest backwoods drawls I'd ever heard.

"Eric, Lord, yes. Eric Garth. Bless my soul."

"Hello, Clyde." We shook hands. Mine was lost in his immense
grip and I have a large hand. He never smiled, he grimaced, showing
his teeth, which he picked continuously with his right thumbnail. It
made a sharp clicking sound and the louder he clicked the madder
he was becoming.

"You've lost weight," Burkette said.

"Have I?"

He nodded. "What brings you back here?"

I shrugged. I got to thinking how bad it would have been with him
on my tail if Leda hadn't notified the sanitarium. He would have
enjoyed plucking me up.

"Yeah. I reckon so. I knew you was in town, all right. Word gets
around fast. You know that, too, hey?"

"Yes."

"Sorry about your mother, Eric. A good woman." His eyes
narrowed and he started to say something, but thought better of it.
"Word gets around mighty fast."

"It's been good seeing you," I said.

"Sure. Your brother's doing great, isn't he?"

"Looks like it."

"Sure. He married up with a fine girl, there. She's sure a looker. I
keep telling Frank he should watch his step, though. Playing a mite
too close to his vest for real comfort. The Hewitt boys–you
remember the Hewitts?"

I nodded. We were standing in front of the First National Bank.
Down the street a block on the other side the huge neon sign spelled

out the name FRANKLIN GARTH in red letters against a white-and-blue background–literally spelled the name out, then flashed it all once, then spelled it again. The sign seemed to monitor the whole street.

"Old man Hewitt died a couple months ago. The boys are down on Frank. Airy one of 'em wouldn't check himself to crack down on Frank with a Winchester."

"Oh?"

Burkette began to pick at a front tooth. "'At's right. They say Frank sold 'em short. They lost their farm. Your brother owns it now. Legal. Frank sure's no Garth from the neck up. I mean–" he hastened to add, "so far's business is concerned. Plumb legal. A smart one. He better stay off the back roads, though." Burkette grimaced.

"Probably no real danger," I said.

"Probably." His black-button eyes snapped. "You bust his nose today, Eric?"

"It's been good seeing you, Clyde." I shoved on by. He stood there nodding and picking his teeth.

Word did get around fast and Burkette didn't like me. It still made no difference. I went on around the corner and crossed the street to a second-hand car lot.

The owner was just locking up as I walked in. I didn't care much what kind of a car it was so long as it ran. My top price was low. But I needed the car.

I came away twenty minutes later driving a beat-up Ford. When the owner realized who I was he wanted to sell me the whole lot. But that would've been trading on Frank's name. The car's engine had been souped up so there was plenty of speed, but I figured one more rattle and it'd fall apart in the street.

So it was all over town that I'd come home and caused my mother to die of a heart attack, then broken my brother's nose. By now there were doubtless many additions to this tale. Among them Frank's word that he had managed to deal his rummy brother out of the business he'd built up. I could visualize Frank exclaiming how I'd returned to collect now that he'd put the business on its feet.

It smelled.

The barn was dark when I drove the car up behind it. I'd had the feeling Norma might relent and return. She'd gone off in a huff and I didn't like it. Maybe she wasn't alone. Maybe today had cracked the case in more ways than one.

I went into the kitchen, remembered that I'd forgotten to check with the light company about turning on the electricity. I had used to work here all the time, hardly ever going near the house toward the end. I found a candle and lit that, took it with me into the studio. I stood the candle on an empty stand and heard a sound from the old couch.

"Hello, darling. I told you I'd be back."

Leda was lying on the battered couch, her eyes shining in the candlelight and she wore a dress now, bright green with a sheen and black, high-heeled pumps. Prepared for the execution. She had her legs on the couch with her head propped beneath her arms. She was smiling.

"Did you see Lenny again?" I said.

"Lenny? No. I've been here about twenty minutes. He wasn't around here, darling."

I didn't ask about Norma. If Norma had seen Leda come here there was no telling if she'd ever speak again. Norma had a dark and specific imagination.

"Did you drive?" I said.

"My car's parked over in the bushes."

It was all twisted up inside me. I hadn't been able to straighten any of my thinking yet. Too many things had happened. Because of my mother's death I hated to admit it even to myself, but all I could think of was Leda.

"You can't hang around here," I said. It amazed me to be able to say these things, act this way, when I wanted her more than anything in the world. When one look at her set the blood pounding with memory because I was hungry for her; impatient for the fierce unrestrained loving I knew now was mine. "You can't stay," I said again.

"Can't I?" She lifted her arms, ran her palms down over the thrusting mounds of her breasts, softly down across her hips and thighs. "Afraid of your brother? Afraid to take what's yours?"

I couldn't answer. The dress fitted her like a tight filmy sheath and desire was in her eyes.

"If you aren't afraid of your brother, you should be. He's concocting some fine stories, just fine." She paused, and I hated Frank just a little more. "Come here, Eric. I've waited and waited–" Two women today had waited, but this one was fire. She went on, "I can't stand it. I won't stand it any longer, I wasn't made to." She sat up, swung her feet to the floor. The tight, thin skirt hissed up over her knees and her smile was warm and sly. She rose slowly and started toward me. As she passed the stand with the candle on it, she blew out the light. For a moment the room seemed dark, then bright stars and moonlight came down through the skylight and she was against me, her body warm, pliant, her breath loud.

Inadvertently my arms went around her, there was nothing I could do, and her body pushed against me almost angrily. She wore nothing beneath that dress and the expensive weave of the cloth slid softly against her warm curves. Her breasts were full against me, and her mouth sought mine.

Everything went mad. All the pent-up longing of both of us was drowned in a fury of caresses.

Feeling her was like touching a living flame.

It was wild crazy loving and she said things only I would ever hear and half recall as we tumbled headlong and viciously up through blackness into the star-studded night.

"It's funny, now, isn't it, Eric?" she said. "All that to-do? I told you I'd be back."

We were still lying on the couch, staring up through the skylight at the night and I wouldn't see anything funny. She was still my brother's wife, even if she was my woman. And I was helpless with her around; I couldn't fight, couldn't do anything save what she wanted.

And Leda had changed. Here within the past few hours I'd seen a side of her I'd never seen before. She had changed, or she had been holding out on a part of her personality before. This new part was a bit wrong, a little cockeyed, somehow.

"I love you so much it makes me nuts inside," she told me. "I haven't known what to do."

"You did well enough." She had swung everything her way again. She had me hanging there again, like always, and there was nothing I could do about it. Maybe nothing I wanted to do. But I knew I did have to do something because it couldn't go on this way.

Up against the wall by the doorway leading into the kitchen was a rack of different sized wooden mallets. I wondered when I'd ever get to use them, then felt a stab of anxiousness because that was the rack where the wooden mallet came from. The one....

Leda saw where I was looking and answered a thought.

"You can do me in stone," she said. "In marble. You always said you would." She was excited. Sitting up, she leaned over me, watching my face. "You will, won't you? Look," she said. "It would be a good excuse."

"For what?"

"For my being here, damn it. Can't you see? Nobody could say anything, then. After all, you *are* Frank's brother, and all."

"That helps a lot."

"Well, so people talk. So what?"

"So, nothing. I'll see."

"Say you will!" There was something desperate in her voice.

"Why don't you get a divorce? Then we could–"

She interrupted, ignoring what I'd said. "Would you do me in clay first?"

I watched her, not speaking.

She grabbed my face with both hands. "Would you? Answer me."

"Yes. All right."

She sighed. "I knew you would, darling. It's perfect. You can start right now."

"It isn't that easy. You know that, Leda. There's a lot of preparatory work." She had most certainly changed. Too, something of her old self was gone. "Besides," I said. "The marble would have to wait a long while."

"Why, silly? I have money. I'll get the marble."

That shut me up again. She was taking all of this as a joke and I didn't know how to take anything, any more. I felt ill at ease and sick inside.

She was a beautiful, demanding woman. Maybe too demanding. She was blind to everything but her own selfish desires, as the old

Leda hadn't always been. Yet I loved her and wanted her for my own. Again I realized what a lousy mixed-up life mine was, how uneasy my mind was, and how peace seemed to be leaving me forever.

I should have been happy as you are after you've been with the woman you really love and peace should have been there with us and there should have been no feeling of aloneness. But there was no peace and the antagonism was there because something was missing. But what? I didn't know.

I kept remembering, too, the hit and run; the accident that had been called off. And there had been none, not with me involved. Yet, my name had been used. A description had been given of my car...too many things had happened.

Then I got to thinking about Leda again. How maybe if I did model her in clay and finally in stone, maybe then I'd find what I was looking for. Maybe it would solve some of the riddle. Peace might be there, waiting, because the work was inside me, too, aching to come out. It hadn't come out for a long while. Maybe that's what was the matter.

"Kiss me," Leda said.

I did and it didn't solve a thing. I had started to dress when the door opened.

"Eric? You in there?"

Norma stood in the doorway. I know now that if I'd stayed on the couch she might not have seen us, I might have been able to silence Leda in time. But as it was, Norma looked straight at me and Leda said, "What is this?"

Norma stared at Leda in the half darkness. Leda didn't move her position on the couch. The whole thing was sickeningly obvious. Norma wore a black bathing suit and carried a towel over her shoulder.

"Get out of here!" Leda said loudly. She sat up on the couch, looked at me. "Eric, get her out of here!"

"I'm sorry," Norma said. I couldn't see her expression very well. Maybe it was a good thing. She left hurriedly, slammed the door.

Leda was on her feet. "And that's Norma."

"Yes. So what?"

"My, God, Eric. Do I have to slit her throat?"

"Don't speak so loud."

"I'll shout if I like," she said. "What was she doing here?" She came toward me, her naked body gleaming in the moonlight, her hair in wild disarray. "This is fine," she went on. "Just fine."

I tried to take her in my arms. She twisted free.

"Stop it," I told her. "You said you knew about her. Probably just stopped in. Probably."

She seemed to calm down, then, and commenced dressing. But she didn't talk much after that and although she kissed me good-by with fervor, I thought she acted a bit peculiar.

Which wasn't, after all, very odd.


"Well, it's really done, now, isn't it?" Norma was standing in the kitchen as I re-entered the barn. She'd lit two candles and stuck them on a shelf up beside the stove. The cold chops were still in the pan on the stove. Norma was still in the black bathing suit and she was a striking-looking woman, but the expression on her face was sad.

"Nothing's done," I said. "What do you mean?"

"You know what I mean." She walked over to a chair and sat down, crossing her legs. The night was quite warm and there were sparkles of water in her blonde hair. She'd been swimming.

"I thought I'd be mad," she said. "But I'm not, really. Somehow I'm just sorry for you."

"Well, don't be sorry for me. What reason have you to be sorry for me? And if you mean Leda, never mind getting your back up. She's–"

"That's what I said." She lifted the towel off the back of the chair and drew it around her shoulders. "I'll be leaving," she went on. "Today was a sort of big good-by, wasn't it?"

"Damn it, Norma!" Things were reaching the stage where I wasn't even sure of a move from one moment to the next.

"O. K.," she said. "Damn it." She rose, went into the other room, then came back to the kitchen and walked to the door. She looked at me for a long moment. "You're a good guy, basically," she said. "But the breaks are against you." She opened the door. "I'll be seeing you," she said, and the door slammed.

"Norma!" I called. "For God's sake!"

The door opened again. She stood there quietly, with the towel over her shoulders. "It was a long wait. I was a fool to have been sure of some things. Good-by, Eric," she said. "Thanks for the ride."

## Chapter 15

I saw nothing of Frank until the day of the funeral. Quite a few townspeople were at the cemetery and though they spoke to Frank with the usual undertones and whispers, they did little else than nod to me. I didn't mind that, either. I was thinking of Mother and how she had come to her grave. I tried not to think Frank's blundering had caused her death, but I couldn't keep the thought from my mind. Several people stared at me openly and whispered behind handkerchiefs, or wrists.

After the service, I started toward the car. Quick footsteps approached behind me. Frank called, "Wait up, Eric."

I turned. He wore a dark suit, black tie, black shoes. His eyes were puffy and there was adhesive over his nose. But the contempt was in his eyes...

"Get in your car," he said. "I want a word with you."

"Let's skip it," I said. I climbed behind the wheel and slammed the door. He fastened his hands on the door, and stared at me. He was breathing sharply.

"I didn't think you'd come," he said. "Didn't think it meant that much to you."

"Let's drop that tack."

He cleared his throat. "That isn't what I wanted to talk about."

I waited. Some people walked by the car. It was a large cemetery, shaded by towering palms, live oaks drooping with Spanish moss. I didn't feel in the mood for talk about anything, especially with Frank. I watched Leda get in their car parked ahead of me on the drive. She also was in black, with a veil. She looked anything but in mourning; the dress was tight and glistened in patches of sunlight.

"I want to speak about my wife," Frank said. "For three days she hasn't been home. Half the night she's away." His face reddened up, now, and his hands clenched nervously on the door. He spoke louder. "I want you to leave her alone. You hear? You may have known her once. But that's changed. You hear?"

"Fine."

Several people standing on the grass beside the drive turned and stared. Frank didn't seem to notice.

"Can't you take care of your own wife?" I said.

"She tells me where she's been," he said. "I won't have it. I told her so. It's to stop as of now." Again he cleared his throat, he was highly nervous. I had to hold myself in, talking to him, because I wanted to hit him. I wanted to break his nose so he wouldn't have any. The dream didn't frighten me any more, much, and all I wanted to do was hurt the man. Not in a dream, either.

He said, "She's been with you all that time. She hasn't been near the house. I hardly see her. I won't have it!"

I shrugged and started the engine.

"Shut that off," he said.

I let it run.

"She's posing for you. Naked, you hear? My wife. People will talk."

"They sure will with you bellowing."

He tried to calm down, but his voice was full of emotion and it carried through the silence of the grounds.

"She's paying me for the work," I said. "I need the money. Don't be so damned shallow."

"You heard me, Eric. I want it stopped. I don't care what she's told you. She's–she's highly emotional, excitable." He stared at me for a long moment, his face working, his eyes very bright. "That's all," he said. "And don't come around the house. I don't want to see you. Just remember that–and what I've said."

I noticed Leda coming toward us from their car. She was smiling and her every movement was provocative in the early afternoon sunlight.

Frank turned his back on me and walked rapidly up to her. He took her arm and I heard him say, "Come along, dear." They went to their car. Quite a few people had watched the little episode and I guessed not a few had heard some of what Frank said.

I went on back to the barn.

Leda had been with me for three days. She came early in the morning and remained. We swam together, and I was doing a large work of her in clay, full-figure. The pose was full, feet spread slightly apart, hands clasped behind her back, head thrown back with that wealth of auburn hair tossed and tumbled by a wind. It would be very beautiful, but not so beautiful as she. I was so much in love with her, wanted her so badly, that nothing Frank could say bothered me. Nothing anybody could say. She was mine and that's the way it was.

It seemed we could never still the hot flame that had grown during the time of separation. We tried. The posing was difficult, the work difficult–because one or the other of us could only stand it for a short time before we weakened and took to the couch.

Those three days had been an orgy and they gave promise of an endless procession to come. And the work came, too, it felt good to work. And I didn't dream. Leda mentioned the dream a lot, but we didn't dwell on it.

I hadn't known she'd told my brother all that she had. But thinking about it, I saw it was the best way.

She'd always been open about everything. Perhaps a little too much so.

There was a place not too far from the barn on the main road called the Sea Breeze Drive-in. I stopped there for coffee and a hamburger once in a while. Norma's photography shop was nearby and it was necessary that we should eventually meet.

We did. Me with my coffee and Norma at the end of the line in her car, with a milk shake. She came over.

"Hi, Eric. You're still alive."

"Cut it out. I've been meaning to get around and see if you–"

"You can cut that out. Anyway, Lenny stops by. He's told me all about everything. Gay old time, eh, Eric? Don't let a chisel slip, will you?" She watched me. "You look pale, Eric." When she walked away her hips flirted with the soft wind which came in over the Gulf.

Driving back to the barn, Lenny drove up and stopped me as I was turning into the sand road.

He was drunk, in his ubiquitous pink shirt.

"Going to town," he said. He winked and showed me the shingles, hitched one shoulder. "Wanta thank you for that there statue. Hit shore is a beaut. Got 'er in my bedroom, now."

"Fine. Keep it up. It'll get you someplace."

"Whyn't you come on over sometimes? Ain't seen my new place, Eric. Hit's different."

"I'll bet."

He gunned the motor on his crimson fireball. "Well, gotta get goin'." He winked again and went on off down the road.

Back at the barn I felt somehow flat, empty, washed out.

I walked into the studio and looked at the statue I was doing of Leda. It was taking a lot of clay, but she wanted it that way. "Of, me, Eric. All the way–the way you feel it!" So she could see what I felt and what she'd really look like when I got around to working in the marble. Because usually they were smaller. It was a damned fine piece of work. I'd caught something of her force in the pose, her carelessness–her wantonness.

She'd probably be around soon. Suddenly I didn't want to see her for a while. Thoughts of the funeral had lowered my spirits.

I went and got my swimming shorts, put them on, grabbed a towel, and headed for the Gulf. Maybe some salt water and sunshine would bring me around. God knows, something had to.

I walked on down the sand road and on over to the beach.

## Chapter 16

It was dark by the time I returned to the barn. Coming down the sand road, I noticed a light lit in the studio and a large sedan parked in the road beside the barn. At first I didn't recognize it, then I recalled seeing the same car parked in Frank's drive when I first came home. His car. Must be Leda had come over and was waiting for me. It was likely she'd had a long wait. I'd spent the rest of the afternoon until now on the beach, thinking. The only conclusion I'd reached was that something had to be done.

Either I left Cypress Landing, or Leda managed a divorce. One or the other. I preferred the latter but had about made up my mind to the former. Except that I had decided to fight. Half of the money from the family, half of the business, was mine. I had to have it because I needed it, was entitled to it. There were ways and I chose to find them. I'd been too easy going, I'd let things slide already, because of Leda. This was going to cease. Maybe it was hazy in my mind, but it was something to work on.

Entering the kitchen, I called, "Hello?"

No answer. Still in my swimming shorts, I tossed the towel over a chair. I was foggy. I'd fallen asleep out on the beach and slept for a long while. I pushed open the door leading into the studio.

It was very bright in there. I'd arranged electric fixtures so I could work at night. They were all turned on. What I saw wasn't nice. But I only saw part of it at first.

The clay figure of Leda was smashed to a pulp. It had literally been torn down and trampled into a flattened mass on the floor. It was covered with a man's footprints. Wires and wood jutted from the mangled clay. There wasn't a solitary feature left.

Then my breath left me. On the floor by the couch was Frank, sprawled out. Beside him was the largest of the wooden mallets from the rack on the wall.

I didn't breathe with the loud pumping of my heart. I went over and looked at Frank.

You didn't need to look far to see he was dead. His head was smashed almost as badly as the clay. Blood covered him, the floor, the couch. Tufts of hair and blood clung to the wooden mallet.

For a long while my brain screamed nameless things. My ears rang from the blood in my head. I bent down, looked at Frank, stood, weaved around the floor.

He'd been wearing a white suit and he had been my brother for all my life up until the other day. So he was still my brother, really. I had hated him enough to kill him. But now I knew he'd still been my brother.

I went back, felt his hand. It was cold. The lights glared. But nothing sank in and it was crazy. Yet, it was true. My brother dead– murdered.

Like in the dream with the wooden mallet. Smashed. And if there was relief inside me, it was rapidly supplanted by a sharp, terrible fear. Days at the hospital rushed back, with Prescott seated at his desk, trying with all his might to tell me something I couldn't believe. And now–what would Prescott say, do?

Frank's eyes were half closed and he still wore the remains of the adhesive across his nose. But his nose had been flattened for sure, now.

I held my hands out, stared at the trembling. I inspected them, not wanting to tell myself even what I searched for.

Then, slowly, it began growing inside me. It was very still in the barn. Outside the wind softly buffeted the roof and walls and if you listened hard enough you could hear the cars passing on the main road and between the sound of the cars the faraway hiss of the Gulf against the beach.

Frank was murdered. It hadn't happened just recently, either. He'd been dead for some time.

I tried to tell myself somebody had done it, maybe to frame me. Who had I seen since the funeral besides Norma, Leda, Lenny?

Nobody. I'd gone to a remote spot on the beach and stayed there till I'd returned. I'd seen nobody. And I had slept. I couldn't remember dreaming. Maybe you didn't remember dreaming when you really didn't dream.

Stop it! It wasn't pretty at all, this picture.... The husband comes to the sculptor's studio, grows insanely jealous because of the nude statue of his wife who's been seeing the sculptor regularly. He smashes the clay image and the brothers fight. During the fight the husband is killed with a wooden mallet, pounded to death, his head smashed to a pulp.

And I could almost hear a voice saying, "Yes, Eric Garth was a patient here. Yes, he dreamed all the time that he killed his brother with a wooden mallet."

And all Cypress Landing knew how Frank and I felt toward each other; the fight we'd had on the eve of Mother's funeral.

I heard the car coming down the road.

For an instant panic took hold. Then I realized I had to stay calm until I could think it out. That was a laugh. Think it out was a laugh. I grabbed for the wall switch and cut the lights, went into the kitchen and out the back door. I grabbed my towel from the chair in the kitchen as I passed.

It was Leda in the yellow convertible. Convertibles were in season. Death was in season. Death bloomed dark in the dooryard. Black petals.

Leda was out of the car and approaching me before I could reach her.

"Hello, darling. Give us a kiss."

I kissed her. It was like kissing the trunk of a tree.

"What's the matter, Eric? You all right?"

"Nothing. Been working. Thought I'd take a swim." Then I cursed myself. That was the wrong thing to say. That could mean I'd been at the barn. "I've been walking for a while. Figured maybe the water'd do me good."

"I know something that'll do you more good."

"Oh."

"I came over earlier this afternoon. You weren't here. Frank sure put up a row," she said with a laugh. "I told him off. Told him I'd come over here whenever I chose. Hell with him."

"Sure." My throat was thick and my heart pounded like fury.

"Come on, let's go inside. I want to look at myself." She chuckled. "I mean what you're doing, of course."

"Don't you want to come for a swim?"

"It's getting cold," she said.

"We could take a walk."

"What's the matter with you, anyway?" She cocked her head and looked at me, frowning. Then she let go and started for the barn. She wore a light coat over her dress and it bellowed with the wind.

You don't know what to do at a time like that. You stand there and you can't act. She paused halfway to the door and stared at my car parked on the other side of the barn. "Say," she said. "I thought that was your car over there." She pointed toward Frank's sedan. She strolled toward it, hands thrust deeply into her coat pockets. Then she paused, turned, looked at me. "Frank's here," she said. "That's his car."

I couldn't speak.

"Is he here now?"

"I don't know. No. He's not. I don't know."

She hurried to the kitchen door, flung it open. It was dark. She switched on the kitchen light by the door.

"Don't go in there," I said. "Come on, Leda!" I ran toward her. She went on through the kitchen into the studio. I reached her side just as she flicked on the switch. The studio was abruptly brilliant and she screamed.

She stood there looking down at Frank, or what was left of him, and screamed.

She turned to me, grabbed me, buried her face against my chest. "My God, Eric," she said. "You've gone and done it. You've killed him!"

"Don't say that!"

"Oh, my God!"

"Shut up." I shook her. She was trembling. I shook her some more. Her eyes were large and round, the pupils jet-black.

"The dream. That crazy dream." Her breath came in little sharp gasps. "You've got to tell me. Don't try to hide it from me. Did you kill him, Eric?"

"No."

She looked down at the body, twisted quickly back to me. "Murder," she said. "It's murder."

She didn't have to tell me that. Any hope I'd had of peace exploded and I knew what I was in for.

"The Hewitts," she said. "Sure." She looked at me. "Oh, Geez, murder." She pulled me toward the kitchen door. "Quick, let's get out of this room. I can't stand it."

"What about the Hewitts?"

"They had it in for Frank."

I recalled what Clyde Burkette had said.

"They're a backwoods family," she said. "Frank gave them a big loan, then when they couldn't keep the payments up, he settled for their land and home."

"Has he done this before? To anyone else?"

She nodded. "Yes. But it's all legal."

"Sure." I could feel the body lying there on the floor. Death was legal, too. Frank had found out just how legal. I couldn't have done this. But Leda—what did she believe? Could I have done it? Or had somebody like the Hewitts?

We went into the kitchen. I turned off the lights in the studio and we stood there in the kitchen looking at each other. She was very pale and though I tried to think, my mind was a rushing blank. There were so many things that could be done, that had to be done—and quick. But I didn't know what to do.

"You've got to run," she said simply.

"Run? Are you crazy? That'd be admitting the worst. You know that." I paced up and down the kitchen floor. If my world had been crashing around me before, it was nothing compared to how I felt now. More and more it did dawn on me how well I was implicated in this. And the more time I wasted the worse it became for me.

Because had I done it? I didn't think so, but the dream had been a strong thing.

"Yes," she said. "But you don't have to admit. It's obvious what's happened, Eric. It would be to anybody. All right, say I believe you didn't do this." Suddenly she grew paler still and sank into a chair. Her lips were dry. I went to the cupboard and reached for the whisky bottle. Back there by an old can of coffee was a forty-five automatic I'd treasured for years before the war. Only the other day I'd had it out, cleaned it, fired a few rounds down by the bayou. I knew the clip was full. The pistol's black shape stood quietly in my mind as I closed the cupboard door.

I poured us each a drink, handed her one. She gulped it solemnly.

"I'm going to call the sheriff," I said. "You coming?"

"The sheriff?" She rose, faced me. "Don't be a fool, Eric. That's the worst thing you can do. They'll pin this thing on you."

I didn't listen. Inside I cursed myself for feeling any relief over Frank's death. But it was there, wrong or not wrong, and somehow I knew the dream was finished. But even with the dream gone, as I somehow knew it had to be with death, the real part of the dream was here with me now. I wondered how I'd get through it. Frank was dead now, and I knew it. So there could be no more dream. Only I knew the right thing to do, and I had to do it.

"Are you coming?" I said. There was no phone in the barn, the nearest being at a gas station out on the main road. "Don't forget," I said. "If I'm in this, you are, too."

"How can you say that?"

"Just want you to know. We're in it, Leda. And it's bad. It's the worst of them all." I stepped over to the door. "Come on," I said. "We've wasted enough time already."

"You can say you just came in, just found the body. We've got to think, Eric. You can't go off without a plan. We've got to think."

"I have." I opened the door. "If you want to stay here, all right."

She came with me.

I didn't tell Burkette what it was all about, just said something had happened and I had to see him right away. I told him to come alone. Maybe he was the wrong one to call, but I knew him better than the police.

"Be right out, Eric. Couldn't you tell me what's up?"

"You'll know soon enough." I hung up and Leda and I went back to the barn.

"What're you going to tell him?" she asked.

"I don't know."

We stood outside, waiting. The sky was overcast and the wind had come up some, fingering the palms against the dark-drenched sky.

I tried to keep my mind away from the body lying in there on the studio floor, away from all the crazy things that had happened, and could happen.

I thought of the big neon sign downtown in Cypress Landing and of how it blinked and flashed the name of a dead man who, in some people's minds, had got what he deserved. I wished I had gone and talked to the Hewitts.

"You still love me, Eric." Leda moved against me. She seemed tiny against the background of murder, but as her fingers touched my face I knew I would always feel the same about her. No matter what happened.

"Yes," I told her. "Nothing'll change that."

She sighed. We didn't kiss, we just stood there, waiting, like two pawns in the hands of the gods.

The sheriff's gray sedan rolled down the sand road about twenty minutes from the time we called. Two men climbed from the car. One was Clyde Burkette, his pale Stetson gleaming in the car's lights as he walked toward us. The other was a deputy, quite young, and very grim.

"Hello, Clyde. Come inside a moment."

He nodded, glanced at Leda, shrugged his eyebrows, but didn't say anything. The grim-faced deputy, who somehow reminded me of Hartly up in Alabama, looking neither right nor left, opened the door himself, preceded us inside. I lit the lights.

"Thought you were coming alone," I said.

Burkette shoved his hat on the back of his head and picked at a front tooth with his thumb nail. "Gallagher came along for the ride."

Leda went over and sat by the kitchen table. She still wore her coat and she looked very tired around the eyes. Her lips were tense and she kept her hands clasped on the table. Suddenly she leaped to her feet, ran out the kitchen door. I heard her gagging outside.

"What the hell is this?" Burkette said.

"Yeah," Gallagher said. "What is this?" He was very grim, very professional. His gray shirt and trousers were creased immaculately, his sparse hair was combed flat without a single strand astray, and his eyes were very steady.

Leda stepped back into the kitchen. She was even paler than before. Her eyes were watering and she clutched a handkerchief to her lips and swallowed with regularity. It seemed odd, seeing a nurse sick to her stomach. But I guess it can happen.

"In here," I said. I opened the door to the studio, lit the lights, and motioned Burkette ahead of me. Gallagher crowded right behind him. As they entered the room I couldn't tear my eyes off the butts of their revolvers, holstered high on their left sides.

Deputy Gallagher saw the body right away. He went over and knelt beside it. Burkette clicked loudly at his front teeth with his thumbnail, then turned to me. His eyes were squinted.

"Your brother."

"Yes."

He looked at Leda, who stood partially in the doorway, then turned to me again. "You got around to it, finally, eh?"

I'd expected something like that.

"I didn't do this. Why in hell would I kill my own brother?" The wooden mallet and the dream, you fool, my mind said.

"We'll let that pass."

Gallagher stood. "Been dead quite a while," he said. "Geez, look at his head."

There was no excitement in them while I kept burning out inside; burning out like a candle. Burkette kept watching me all the time.

"So this is Garth," Gallagher said. "This is the guy you told me about?"

Burkette nodded. "Reckon so. Listen, Eric. I been expecting this. What's your side?"

I told him exactly what had happened. That I was modeling Leda, I told him that, too.

He kept looking at Leda and then me with those infernal black-button eyes of his. I felt everything shredding out, tightening up, weakening. Everything I said had a hollow ring to it.

"What about the Hewitts?" I said.

"What about 'em?" Burkette said. He went over by the body and frowned at it for a while. "A fine job. Wasn't your mother buried today?"

"Yes."

"What were you arguing with Frank about out at the cemetery? Heard about that. He was making quite a ruckus about something out there."

Word got around fast. Burkett had told me that.

"Nothing," I said. "It was just—nothing."

Leda hadn't said a word. She leaned against the doorjamb, not looking anywhere, just standing there with her eyes blank and unseeing.

"What you got to say, Mrs. Garth?" Burkette said. "Looks like you led Frank a merry chase."

"Leave her out of it," I said. "She just happened by. I found him, like I said. She came along just before I called you."

Gallagher edged over until he was by the kitchen door. He stood with his hands on his hips. We all stared at each other. The room was very still and outside I could hear the wind moaning against the barn.

Burkette clicked his teeth. "How about that, Mrs. Garth? I asked you a question. You don't have to answer. Neither of you have to answer, I reckon, you don't want to. You'll answer later, anyways."

"I don't like it," Gallagher said.

Leda shifted in the doorway. "I–I don't know," she said softly. She was still very pale, with the handkerchief in her hand. She avoided looking at the body, she avoided looking at anybody, even me. "I–it's just as Eric, Mr. Garth–Eric said."

"Eric'll do, I reckon," Burkette said.

"For God's sake, Clyde!" I stepped over to him. "Act decent, will you? We've known each other a long while. You've got to help me."

"You'll need help, all right. Where's your other dame, Eric?"

Gallagher looked very grim.

"Sure," Burkette said. "Sure."

Death was so commonplace to them. Burkette eyed the body some more and said. "Reckon we'll run to town. Me an' you, an' the girl. Gallagher, you stay here."

Now it really began to get me. "Listen, Clyde. We're wasting time. Whoever did this is laughing someplace. Can't you see it's a frame? I'm it?" I had to believe that, or I'd take a mallet to my own head.

He nodded. "You're it, all right. But I don't see any frame, Eric. None whatever. It's right pat, I'd say." He cleared his throat. "We'll have to hold you."

"I'm not going anyplace."

Gallagher grinned.

Leda said, "You'd better do like they say, Eric."

God, now her! Like back in Alabama. A cold deadly repetition. I looked at her and realized right away she was all I had in the world. She smiled at me. It was something to have somebody, let me tell you. Because the world all went apart around me. I couldn't understand it. Why in hell should I be framed for murder, and by whom? It had to be that. It had to.

"Shall we go?" Burkette said. He glanced at the deputy. "Just sit tight here, till I get back. Don't touch anything."

He guided me toward the doorway. Leda moved ahead of us into the kitchen and right then I knew I wasn't going anyplace with Burkette, for sure. Everything was working too smoothly and I was it without any trouble at all.

There's a moment that comes in every man's life when he's got to act. If the moment slips by, he's a goner for sure, and it's unlikely he'll get the chance to act again. Anyway, he either acts or he doesn't and sometimes his life can hang on that instant of decision. It isn't even decision, it's instinct.

I knew if I walked out that door with Burkette life might not be very sweet, or very long. Somehow things were mapped out for me, had been ever since I'd left California. I had to find out who did this myself, and I had to do it quickly. But before that, I had to get by myself and start.

So instinct led me by the cupboard door just as Burkette paused to look in the other room beyond the kitchen. Leda was at the outside door and the deputy was in the studio. His footsteps came toward the kitchen, and my hand moved toward the forty-five on the cupboard shelf by the coffee can.

Leda saw what I was doing and her eyes opened wide.

I grabbed the gun, snaked it down, and Burkette turned as I rode the slide. He didn't move. But somehow I wasn't as worried about him as I was about Gallagher who had just entered the kitchen.

He pulled his gun. I didn't want to fire, but I did, and the forty-five bucked and thundered. The slug tore into the wall next to the young deputy and his gun clattered to the floor.

"Get over next to him!" I told Burkette.

Burkette grimaced at Gallagher. "You fool!" he snapped. "You goddamned fool! Why didn't you fire?"

Gallagher didn't say anything. He stared at his gun on the floor.

"Kick it over here," I said. "Hurry up!"

"Eric," Leda said. "Don't do this–Can't you see it's wrong, Eric?"

"Quiet," I said. "Start Frank's car. Frank's. Mine's no good and your heap's too light. Pull up by the door."

I looked at Gallagher. "Take the gun out of Burkette's holster and drop it. Drop it right away quick."

Burkette was very plain. "Now, damn you," he said over his shoulder to Gallagher. "Here's your chance. Take it, you fool! You've got as much chance as he has. You'll have a gun in your hand."

Gallagher hesitated. Burkette was right and I'd never given him credit for that kind of courage. He goaded Gallagher on.

"Go on," he said. "You yellow-bellied son-of-a-bitch! You'll have a gun right in your hand. All you got to do is shoot!" He lowered his voice, pointed with meaning. "If you don't shoot, by God I'll break you clean back into diapers. Get me?" He paused. Still Gallagher waited, sweat glistened on his face and all the grimness was gone now. He looked like a lost kid, worried to death, scared stiff.

I knew this was the only way, now. If I tried to get that gun from Burkette, he'd pull something. I knew he would. He was mad clear through, and busting out all over. His face was dark red, his eyes snapping.

Gallagher looked at me and his hand moved toward Burkette's left hip.

"If you do," I said, "I'll kill you."

The words seemed to hang there in the room. Gallagher drew the gun from the holster very slowly. "Now!" Burkette yelled. "Get 'im!" He dropped to his knees.

Gallagher stood there a moment with the gun dangling in his hand. It was his moment, just as it had been mine.

He started to shake all over. The gun clattered to the floor. He looked as if somebody had hit him with a hammer right behind the ear. I thought he was going to bawl.

"Now, get back in that other room, both of you!"

Burkette stood. He didn't say a word. He didn't look at Gallagher or me. Turning, he walked into the studio, brushing by the deputy as if he were so much lumber stacked against the wall.

I wondered if the deputy would ever get another chance? He would certainly have reason to look grim now.

"Clyde," Gallagher said. "Clyde, you saw him with the gun, there. Damn it, you know I couldn't–he'd have killed me–maybe killed us both. Clyde, can't you–"

Burkette ignored him as completely as if he weren't even in the room.

"Oh, Geez," Gallagher said.

Leda came through the kitchen. "Car's ready," she said.

"Don't do it," Burkette said to her. "Don't go with him. I'm just telling you. Don't."

"Oh, God," Gallagher moaned.

Kneeling carefully, I kept the forty-five squarely on Burkette and picked up the other two guns. I stuck them in the waistband of my shorts.

Gallagher sat on the couch, slouched over, and stared at his feet. His smooth hair was tousled now. His moment to act was gone and he knew it.

Over my shoulder, I said, "Go get in the car, Leda."

"Don't do it," Burkette said.

I heard her move behind me. "Eric, I–"

"Get in the car and start the engine. I'll drive."

"All right." Her voice was a pale whisper.

Burkette didn't speak. I heard her go out and right away the smooth roar of the big car's engine sloughed through the night, parrying with the moan of the wind.

"I didn't do this," I said, nodding toward the body on the floor. "Sorry you won't believe me. It'd make things much easier."

"Well–Maybe I do, now," Burkette said.

"Never mind that," I said. He knew there was no use attempting wiliness now. Anything went. "I'm going to see what I can find out. Somehow. I'm going to lock this door and the other door. If you come out of here before we've gone, well–" I shrugged.

Burkette turned his back. I went on out. There was no way to lock the inside door. From the kitchen, Burkette called to me.

"We'll get you, Eric. Just remember that. You won't get away."

"We'll get you," Gallagher called. He was trying to come back into the good graces of his superior.

"Shut up, you fool!" Burkette said.

I went on out, locked the door, and leaped for the car. Leda was huddled in the front seat.

I gunned the sedan around the barn, through a field, and over onto the sand road. We were doing fifty by the time we approached the main highway.

"Somebody's coming," Leda said. "Look out."

It was a girl in red shorts, walking on the side of the road. Then I saw it was Norma. She was on my side, and as the car flashed by, we looked straight at each other. She recognized me.

"Eric!" she yelled. "Eric...." But the rest of her words were lost as the tires screamed on the smooth, broad blacktop road.

## Chapter 17

Clouds of driving rain like gusts of steam broke across the front of the car. The tires whined on the water-flushed highway as we droned ahead at a steady eighty-five. It was a sweet car to drive and we could very easily need all that power before long.

"Where we going?" Leda said with a tense note of fear. "You've got to run, Eric. Run fast and far."

"Got to find the Hewitts," I said.

"But why? What good will that do?"

"I don't know."

"Then forget them, for God's sake, Eric."

"Do you know where they live?"

"Darling, this is no time to think about the Hewitts. You've got to think about us. They'll be looking for you."

I glanced at her. She strained her white face toward me and I cursed silently. I didn't want her to go to pieces; it wouldn't be like her to do that. I hoped to hell she would hold up. She had to hold up.

I had turned away from Cypress Landing but I knew I'd have to find a back road in order to cut around the town and inland. It was a good thing this country–once I'd been familiar with every trail, cow path, and woods road in the section. But it would be bad on a night like this. The swamps and the jungle threatened the shoulders of those roads wherever you went and this rain wouldn't help matters.

"Maybe the Hewitts had nothing to do with this," I said. "But maybe they'll know something. They're my only lead."

"You're going to play detective."

"You can call it that." I looked over at her. She was a beautiful, white-faced, frightened woman; so beautiful that for a flashing instant I wondered if I wasn't glad all this had happened. We were together again, all the way, clean. But I swore at myself for that, too. She was curled up with her back to the door, her coat thrown wide, her skirt in her lap. Long legs with the sheen of gold sloped into the shadows below the dashboard, gleaming palm's widths of soft thigh winked above the tops of sheer hose. With glistening red lips, full and warm, and with eyes that could burn with passion, I loved her. I loved the wildness inside her, the strands of fury that cut through her soul, the urgent need that powered her being.

"Watch the road, Eric."

"I am."

"O. K." She was thinking. "Listen, Eric. They'll be after you, we've got to hide someplace. For a while, at least. Someplace where we can think." She moved closer to me and her breast brushed my arm.

"Yeah, you're right. But where? Anyway, I've got to see the Hewitts."

"All right, all right." She hauled the two guns from the waistband of my swimming shorts and put them in the glove compartment. They'd been gouging my middle. "But then we can go to Frank's cabin."

I didn't know about that, didn't know he had one, or where it was.

"Nobody'll ever find us there," she said. "He had it built quite a while ago. It's way in the jungle. On a river. Nobody else lives anywhere around, and it's reached only by an old trail off a dirt road." She described where it was. I remembered the section and it was hellish. It'd be a good place to hide out, all right. The country would be flooded out there tonight.

"You sure nobody knows about where that place is?"

She gripped my leg with her hand. "No. Nobody. I–I went out there with Frank a couple of times."

"Don't tell me." I swerved the car sharply to avoid a sinkhole, then spotted the road I wanted back toward the town, cutting off to our left. The rear end ripped around on the rain-sluiced pavement as we took the turn. The road was dirt but well-packed and not too bad as yet. I opened the engine as far as she'd go.

"We'll see," I said. "I want to talk with that family first. They've got to know something. People who are skinned by a man stick together. Anyway, they're apt to hold council."

"You sound like a senator." She placed her hands beneath the waistband of my swimming trunks.

"Don't," I said.

"I'm just warming my hands." She wriggled her fingers. "Don't you like it?" She squirmed closer. "You've got to get some pants, Eric. I'd lend you mine, but...."

I heaved an inward sigh of relief. So long as she stayed like that, it was all right. It could be plenty bad with a hysterical woman on my hands. "Didn't know you wore any," I said, and swung the car off on another road that would take us past Cypress Landing. We were in pine country now.

I had placed the forty-five on the seat beside me. Leda pulled it up from beneath her. "Some gat," she said. "Or do you call it a rod?"

"I want you to tell me where the Hewitts live."

"Right where they did before. They just moved over the line of their land after Frank took it away from them. They built a shack."

I knew where it was, beyond Cypress Landing about five miles in more pine country. It wouldn't take us long to get there.

This thing had to work itself out. Fast. If the Hewitts seemed O. K. and knew nothing, then we'd have to head for Frank's cabin. Until I thought of something better. And until I could rid myself of the prompting in the back of my head, saying, "The dream, remember, Eric? You were asleep out there on the beach. Did you dream?"

I remembered Norma's flashing legs in the headlights of the car as we'd come out of the sand road. What had she wanted? Probably just calling my name. She would think the worst when she heard what had happened. I couldn't blame her for that. She'd had a raw deal.

We came out on a stretch of main road.

"Going to have to run on this for about a mile," I said. "And we'd better get some gas at the first station."

Her fingers tightened on my arm. "Should we take the chance? They may be broadcasting descriptions."

"We've got to take the chance." I pointed to the gauge. It showed empty, the needle wavering. We were probably running on aroma.

I got to thinking about Burkette. By now he was after us, trailing like the bloodhound he was, and cursing himself and everybody else. If I knew this country well, he knew it equally well, or better. He'd hunted every inch of the land for miles in all directions, and he was a backwoodsman at heart. A dead shot with any kind of gun, hard man on the trail, he spared quarter to no man and least of all himself. I knew what I was dealing with. He was mad clear through by now, and chances were he'd shoot on sight if he glimpsed me.

I didn't want to kill anybody. All I wanted was freedom now, freedom and the rest of my life with Leda. I'd straighten that life out now, too. For rights.

"There's a gas station up ahead," Leda said. "I'll make a dash for the ladies' room while you fill up."

"All right. But be sure it's a dash."

It was a small place, with two pumps. Rain silvered the scene and I imagined the guy running it would howl plenty when we drove up. It was a wonder it was open.

As I drew up beside the pumps, Leda swung her door open and ran for the side of the station itself. She leaped puddles through the rain with her hair showing copper in the lights. I knew what must be going on inside her, knew how she must feel, yet she was holding up. Because she knew about the dream, too. She had the stuff, all right. There hadn't been a whimper.

The round-faced attendant came to the car with a slicker pulled to his ears. He was soaked.

"What'll it be?"

I told him to fill it up, then remembered I was broke. I didn't say anything. Leda had to have some money.

"That'll be five and a half," he said. He peered in the window and thrust out a dripping hand.

"Wife's got the money," I said. "She'll be right along."

He stood there in the rain. I knew he was swearing under his breath. Still she didn't come.

Finally, after what seemed an hour, she appeared, running toward the car. She got in, slammed the door.

"Money," I said. "Quickly!"

"Money?" She looked at me, her eyes wide. "Oh, Lord."

Something went bang inside me. Then she started fishing in her coat pockets. She came up with a five and three ones in a crumpled wad.

"Here." I gave the man six dollars and gunned the car out of there. He would remember us, that was sure.

"Darling," Leda said. "Sorry to be so long. But I got you something. Look!"

She pulled a crumpled bundle of something from beneath her coat. "A pair of overalls," she said. "They were hanging on a nail in the men's room."

"What were you doing in there?"

"I just peeked in. Stop the car and put 'em on."

I did. It was getting plenty cold. They were grease-stained and I was certain they were the attendant's overalls. This would mark us for sure. But it couldn't matter now. I felt better with them on.

Fifteen minutes later we crawled along the muddy road opposite the Hewitts' land, or what once had been their land. Through the vicious streams of rain ahead I glimpsed a lighted window.

"This is it," Leda said. "Just a shack. See, that's where they used to live."

"Yeah." We passed a dark house, thrust against the pouring landscape, and I slowed down by the shack just beyond a fence. There was a driveway. I turned in, then slammed on the brakes. A big man in a Stetson ran toward us.

"Burkette!"

"Garth! Damn it! That's him!" Burkette bellowed.

"Get out of here," Leda said. Her voice was tense.

Burkette was running from the shack toward us, then he veered over to his large gray sedan parked ahead of our car in the drive. He yelled something else but his voice was drowned in the sound of wind, rain, and my car's abruptly snarling engine. A spotlight swiveled around to us, blinding me for an instant. I saw Burkette raise his arm and a gun spat flame into the streaming night.

I shoved the gas pedal to the floor and cramped the car across a short expanse of lawn, back to the dirt road. Again the gun blasted, once, twice, three times. But we weren't hit.

For the first time I really understood the jam I was in. I was it for murder. It hadn't been clear in my mind until now. It hadn't been real, but a snarl of panic coiled inside me as I shouted, "You all right?"

"Yes, yes. Get going–that's all, Eric!" She was twisted in the seat, looking back toward the shack. "They're coming."

"Got it to the floor. Can't see a damned thing."

"You got to! They're shooting again."

The car lurched and skidded over the road in the mud-slimed ruts.

"They're closing in, Eric." She moved next to me in the seat. "You've got to go faster. You've got to lose them." There was a sob in her voice, then she began to swear. The things she called Clyde Burkette reached beyond obscenity, beyond my imagination. She pounded the dashboard with her fists. "You've got to lose them!"

Burkette had figured this was where I'd head for first. I'd proved myself a dope all over again.

Leda's voice was shrill. "Eric, suppose they shoot our tires."

I wheeled the car off the road at the first turn. For an instant I thought it was all over with. Grass sprung in the middle of the road and I saw it was nothing more than a wagon trail, one of those which spider-web parts of Florida like Martian canals. I recalled it as a detour to a main road leading away from Cypress Landing. If we could make that road we might be able to lose Burkette long enough to lose ourselves in the backwoods and head for Frank's cabin.

I tramped on the gas and prayed.

"They missed the turn," Leda said. "They missed it!"

## Chapter 18

Burkette may have missed the turn that first time, but it didn't take him long to swing the car around. Only moments, and that spotlight gleamed like the leaping white eye of a dragon in the rear-view mirror. I gave the car all she had. The wheels thundered over the rough road.

Leda's voice was quieter now, but there was an edge to it I'd never heard before. "What if they get us, Eric? What'll you do?"

"I don't know. They won't get us."

"Sure, but what if they do?"

I didn't answer. What use was there? A file of car headlights spat their meager illumination through the blinding rain ahead on the main road. I cut directly into the traffic and started passing.

There was barely room for two cars abreast, but I let it ride, cutting between oncoming autos down the middle of the highway.

"There's no point my saying be careful," Leda said.

"No. Just sit tight."

"I wish to hell I was tight."

By the main route I knew it was about fifty miles to Frank's cabin if I judged right. But we couldn't take the main route. It would mean staying on this road too long. We could only use this road long enough to lose Burkette, if that was possible.

It was almost blind driving. All I had to depend on was the natural instinct of the other fellow to get out of the way. To them I was a drunk and they did get out of the way.

"I can't see anything of them following us," Leda said. "But it's hard to say."

Fifteen minutes of that and we were clear of traffic. The road was just pouring night as far in both directions as we could see.

On either side of us now lay jungle and swampland. An occasional water-filled cutoff glistened in the car's lights, pushed into that tangle of throbbing vegetation. Tall cypress trees flanked us, their skeletal arms trembled with the weight of wind-smashed Spanish moss.

I knew we'd have to turn off soon into that. I knew what it could mean, but it was our one chance. Unless I wanted to trust luck on an upstate run.

The thought barely struck me when I pushed the brakes and wheeled the car around.

Just ahead on a curve in the road two squad cars hovered, with slicker-tented men patroling patiently. I didn't think they'd seen us, but I couldn't be sure.

"Road block," Leda said.

"Yeah. This is really it. We've got to start into that." There wasn't much else to say. I hoped to select the lesser evil of the many rain-washed and insecure roads.

"But–but this isn't the way Frank took me up there," Leda said.

"Sure. I'll find it, though. We're headed right, and I know this country."

"God. We'll get stuck, sure."

"Maybe not." I swung in to the left through a running ditch of water nearly hub-cap deep. It fanned out in a muddy shower beyond the slope of the hood, then backfired onto the windshield.

I wrestled the car straight.

"Keep an eye on our tail."

Not that it would do much good. If they'd seen us at the road block, and tailed us, we'd have to stick to this road anyway, because I knew it didn't turn off save for cow paths into nowhere.

Now came the fun. The road was swamped with water. We sloughed from one side to the other in running ruts, leaped over unseen roots. Rubber shrieked and screamed against the fenders and I thanked my dead brother for buying the best. Rain drummed all over the car in increasing and diminishing thunder–hood, top, windshield, side–like a reefer-drunk drummer on different kettles.

Off in the rain-shrouded night jungle life let loose their agony in high-pitched sound that rose even above the motor's howl and the driving rain.

I kept the pedal on the floor. I knew the road was straight for a good long time. Then gradually the road rose and we came up out of that swamped mud. The tires hummed on what was once hard-packed ground. It was softer now, like glass mushed over with oatmeal, but a hell of a lot better than back there.

"We're going it now," Leda said. "We're O.K. now, aren't we, Eric?"

I chanced my first look at her for quite a time. She had both hands on the dash, her head thrust forward, bright eyes searching the wild night ahead.

"You're a trooper," I said. "A real one. I'm sorry I got you into all this, baby. But I'll get you out."

She glanced at me and smiled. Her lips were a bit tight and the smile went cockeyed. "I know you will, darling."

Then I saw the yellow gleam of two cat's eyes ahead. It was another car approaching. I didn't decrease speed.

"There's a bridge!" Leda said.

But I saw that too late. The other car and I started across the narrow bridge at the same time. Wood planks rippled in a staccato roar, loose, and our rear end bucked and swung straight at the oncoming car's lights.

I tried to wrench it back. We were going too fast.

At the instant we hit, I knew it was a truck. An old truck.

Leda screamed and we rocked off into the night, smashed through the wooden guardrail. For a time there was no sound save the wild whine of the motor and the monotonous thump, and crash as metal and glass gave way, as young trees snapped. I held to the wheel and watched us dive down an embankment of withered pines, straight at the rain-mottled, gleaming surface of water.

We struck hard, head on, and water geysered into the air. I heard a sharp clunk beside me, and Leda sprawled across the wheel. She'd smacked her head. She groaned, and the car settled a bit to one side and was still.

A small cloud of steam hissed above the water and vanished. The engine creaked, we settled again, then it was very silent. For a moment.

"Hey, down there!" A cracker voice yelled through the rain from up on the bridge. It was the voice of an old man. "Y'all right, down there? Hey, y'all right?"

## Chapter 19

"Leda, Leda!" I shook her, tried to straighten her in the seat. She moaned. Up on the bridge the old man yelled something again. "Are you hurt, Leda?"

She moved against me, then slowly pulled herself around in the seat. We sat with our feet braced against the dashboard, looking down at the windshield, the hood of the car, water and darkness.

"I'm–I'm all right," she said. "Hurt my head."

"Quick," I said. "Out your side of the car. We're in water, but it isn't deep. Just climb out and start away from the car. Think you can do it?"

"Yes, but–"

"Never mind the buts. We can't let that guy up there get sight of us. C'mon." I opened the door against mud on her side. It would only open partway. "Squeeze through," I told her.

She lifted herself through the door. "I'm dizzy."

"Yeah." I searched around on the floor for the Colt automatic. It was down between the clutch and brake pedal. I shoved it in my pocket and climbed out after Leda into the water and the raining dark.

Up on the bridge the man was shouting. Then I saw something else. Chickens were on the bridge, squawking, fluttering around. A dead chicken floated in the water next to our wrecked car. Three more flapped and clucked wildly in the small stream.

"Ye won't talk," the man on the bridge said. "Damn it all to hell anyways. Truck busted to nothing an' all my chickens loosed, airy a one ain't kilt or loosed. Damn an' goddamn! Is anybody down there?" His voice echoed for a brief instant, then was muted by the rain. "They dead sure hell, I reckon."

"Keep going," I whispered to Leda. "Head for dry land, over there." I shoved her through the water, which was up to our knees. "Be as quiet as you can." It was then I knew I'd struck my leg on something. The one that'd been wounded in Korea. It was painful.

We made higher ground. I found a tall cypress on a hummock with knee-high grass soaked, but soft, around its base.

"Sit down–never mind the mud," I said. "We'll wait till he goes."

Leda sank to the ground, leaned against the tree. I hunkered beside her and watched. It was very dark, but the lights from the truck on the bridge threw an eerie yellow glow over the landscape with the rain coming down in a steadied fall.

"How's your head?" I looked and saw she'd cut it pretty badly above the right eye. It was best to let the rain wash it.

"Geez," Leda said. "What a mess! Eric, what'll–"

"Hang on." I motioned her quiet. The old man on the bridge was coming down the far side, just beyond where our car went through the railing. Our luck, smash into a truck loaded with chickens. I tried to reckon how much farther we'd have to go to reach the cabin. I knew precisely where we were, and according to my guess we'd have a rotten sight of miles before we found the place. If we found it....

"Dead, sure as Blue's a hound an' Bessie's belly's swelled like a melon." The man waded through water to the car. I couldn't see him clearly, but he cursed plenty about the chickens. "I didn't do nothin'," the man said. "I didn't do a thing, no-siree. Seen 'em comin' like faar thu a tin hawn. Them lights a-comin' jes like faar thu a tin hawn. Din't do nothin', damn an' goddamn." He reached the car. "Dead," he said. "Dead as hell." He looked in the driver's side. "Airy a soul!" He thrashed around the other side and stood by the open door. He stood there for a long while staring inside the car. He didn't say anything.

Finally he started away from the car, then stopped. "They gone," he said. "They done taken off. Mebbe floatin' in the river." He started to cry, great racking sobs which cracked through the rain. He blew his nose with his thumb and sobbed some more. "Gone," he said. "Reckon I'm done fer. Ain't airy one chick lef'. Truck dead as hell." Abruptly he cursed into the night and thrashed back toward the bridge. He didn't say anything else. Then I saw him cross the top of the bridge, silhouetted in the lights from his truck. His shoulders were bowed and he shuffled. He picked a chicken off the guard rail and threw it with all his might in the direction of the truck. It screamed and clucked. Then he was gone.

"We've got to move on," I told Leda.

"All right."

I helped her up. She looked at me. Blood was running down the side of her face. "Which way?" she said. Her tone was resigned at first, then she seemed to summon courage and strength from somewhere. "Let's go, Eric. Let's go, we've got to get to the cabin."

"Sure." We had to get to the cabin. She was certainly determined about that.

"It'll be dry there. We can build a fire," she said.

The rain didn't seem to be coming down so heavily now. Up on the bridge there was no sound, but the dimming headlights of the old truck still gleamed in shallow saffron.

"Do we follow the road?" she asked.

I shook my head. "We'd never get there that way. Take all night. Got to cut cross country. Think you can do it?" I didn't believe I could myself. Yet I knew I had to. Because ever-blossoming in the back of my mind was the reminder of murder. I pointed down the narrow stream away from the bridge. "That way."

"All right, darling," she said. "I'm game."

She was game for anything.

We hadn't gone a half mile when I knew what we were up against for real. The rain had settled down to a fine dripping drizzle. The rain didn't matter. We were soaked through, mud-caked, and my leg was plenty stiff.

We kept to the mud-choked bank of the stream. It would bring us out on the Oklatoochee River and Frank's cabin should be about a mile upstream. I knew we'd have to cross this small tributary, but I didn't want to chance it now. The water would be black, deep, and treacherous. Clots of sodden moss brushed us as we pushed on.

"Look out!" Leda cried, falling back on me. A bird—probably a white heron—thundered up from directly before us. Leda breathed harshly, clung to me. Her dress was torn in the front and she clutched her coat across her breasts, looking as wild and untame as a jungle cat.

"Best thing is to move fast," I said.

"Oh, sure."

"If we stop, it'll only be that much longer."

"Can't we just rest a while?" She paused, her eyes flicking around the night. "No. No, we can't. You're right. We'd better get going."

At a small bend in the stream an uprooted slash pine bridged the moldering banks. Its trunk thrust itself away into darkness on the other side, but I knew we had to cross here. An obscene grunting and thrashing on our side of the stream in the underbrush decided the move quickly.

Leda went first and I guided her with my hands on her hips. We made the other side and I took a look at the sky. A couple of stars winked fitfully between ragged wisps of dirty storm clouds. The rain was decreasing more and more, the storm was breaking. High overhead among the drenched clutter of oak and cypress a monotonous wind moaned.

Still we clung to the bank of the stream.

During the past few months plenty had happened to me. Right now my work seemed empty and foolish; the elements could do that to a man. Mother dead because of Frank's blind, selfish witlessness. Frank murdered by somebody who had it in for me, or who used me as an easy mark to frame. I'd been with two fine women, one lost with me now, chancing death because I'd been a fool. The other kind and good in every respect, hurt deeply because I couldn't see as she saw, couldn't return her love. For love it was. I knew that now. Norma had never disguised it, but I'd never been able to believe it.

And behind me somewhere Clyde Burkette clicked his teeth with his thumbnail and snapped his black button eyes.

With me always the haunting shadow of the dream....

Frank, dead on the floor, with a wooden mallet beside him. The very implement I'd always used to kill him in the dream. But I couldn't make myself believe such a thing was true. Dream, yes—actuality, no. And I knew I wasn't nuts, then; death had proved it to me.

The cabin was our only home, now, escape was really cut off. No transportation. The only thing I could think of was finding a boat someplace around the cabin. With a boat of some kind, we could go down the Oklatoochee, to the Gulf of Mexico.

The rain ceased. But where the trees had seemed to shelter us some before, now they rained from their water-laden branches.

Bleak gray dawn paled the eastern sky as we broke through the undergrowth and found the broader, deeper, blacker Oklatoochee.

Leda was excited for all her tiredness. "I remember this," she said. "Frank and I hiked down this far once. I remember it!"

"Good," I said. Then I hadn't been wrong. The cabin wouldn't be far off, because Frank was no man for the woods. He wouldn't go far from the cabin.

"It's up this way," Leda said.

I looked at her. She was a mess, but even so, with the cut over her eye, her water-slimed clothes, her matted hair, she was somehow wildly beautiful. Her face was pale, but there was bright excitement in her eyes. She seemed to have more energy than I.

"Don't know what keeps you going," I said.

"You do, Eric. You do."

"Thanks. But it can't be just me."

"Is, though. What you do to me, too."

We stood there looking at each other, trying to smile, weaving with fatigue.

"You're a rich woman now, Leda. Damned rich."

"Does that matter?" She came against me and touched her lips to mine. "C'mon, Eric. Let's get to the cabin. I'm about knocked out."

We reached the cabin after locating the dirt road. The road was muddy, a mess, but we slogged along it and found the cabin up against the river bank beneath the mammoth spread of a banyan.

The excitement of reaching the place stirred Leda. I noticed the change. Whatever tiredness had been in her seemed to disperse. She walked faster, striding. The soft water of the rain had dried out in her hair now, and the auburn hues sparked even without sunlight. The sky was overcast again and the air was chill.

It was a four-room cypress-plank affair, built solid and weather-tight.

"Well," she said. "We're here." She stood at the door and looked back into the roadway, across at the tight growth of jungle that pushed against the horizon. Out back the Oklatoochee wound like a black snake, its mirrored surface tingling with mystery.

The door was open. We went in. It was furnished comfortably, in heavy leather, deep-napped rugs, and with a large fireplace in the front room.

Then I noticed how really tired I was. Leda went through the house hurriedly, her heels thudding on the rugs. She returned to where I was throwing newspapers and small chunks of dry wood on the hearth. I lit the papers and in a few moments warmth began creeping out.

"Any signs of life?" I said.

"What do you mean?"

"Anybody been around?"

"Oh. Certainly not." She draped her coat over the mantel and looked down at herself. Her dress was torn across the breasts and there was a slit in her skirt clear to the waist. The thin material clung to her form like adhesive. Then she eyed me quietly.

I bent down, poked the fire, laid some heavier wood on the irons. Resinous pine caught instantly and the cold morning warmed.

"We made it all right," Leda said.

"Yeah. Now we're here," I said.

She smiled, turned and walked into the other room.

I sat on the floor feeling the heat from the fire and feeling suddenly drowsy as the room warmed. We were here, and now what? We couldn't stay long, because they'd find us eventually. We'd have to move on, someplace. I saw us forever on the move, then, forever looking back, forever chased. It was no good. I had to find an answer because there was an answer. Someplace.

The only way I could find that was to return to Cypress Landing and start snooping. But how could I do that? Inside I was empty and sick and the more I thought about it, the worse I felt.

It didn't seem to strike Leda so badly. She took things more in her stride than I was able to. I could see the papers hitting the street this morning. I could see the body of Frank with its head smashed lying on my studio floor. The clay image of Leda. The blood-covered mallet.

I'd been poking through life like the average guy, dreaming of murder more than the average, but still never realizing it could get so close. And when it is close, when it happens like this, you don't understand it at first. Shock, sure, but only because it's so close to you. Because you've seen dead men before. But your brother, even if he was a louse, was still your brother. Even half-brother.

Then you see you're the guy who's nailed to the cross. You're the guy they're after. But even that doesn't hit you until you comprehend the fact that you didn't do it. And that somebody; probably somebody you know did it. And they framed you for it.

"Darling."

I turned around, blinked my eyes. Leda stood beside me with a blanket wrapped around her. She knelt down and the blanket fell open. She'd brushed her hair to a coppery sheen and her lips were damp. There was only a slight bump over her eye now and the cut hardly showed. I was drowsy, tired, and she looked good.

"Why don't you undress?" she said. "You'll catch cold."

"Sure." I slipped off my swimming shorts and she rolled up next to me, opening the blanket.

"We'll stay here," she breathed. She kissed my throat, her teeth nibbling as she moved against me. "We'll just stay here together."

"We can't for too long."

Her pressure tightened. "Yes. Yes, we can! Oh, Eric! Excitement gets me this way and when I'm tired–"

We were lying in front of the fire. We were warm and comfortable with the fire and I felt worse every minute.

"We'll see if we can't dig up something to eat," I said. "Then we'll pull out of here."

"Pull out?" She sat up, squeezed her hair away from her face with both hands. "We'll stay right here," she said. "Listen, Eric. Where would we go?"

She had me there. But I wasn't going to sit here and wait for nothing to happen. I had to make things happen. What good was life if you couldn't live it all the way? What was the real murderer thinking? How did he feel? He was free, roaming someplace, laughing up his sleeve. But who in hell was he? And why had I been framed?

She snuggled close. "Why don't we go to sleep for a while?"

I ignored that. "Has Frank got a boat?"

She hesitated. "No," she told me. "Not that I know of. No, he hasn't got a boat up here. Why?"

"We could run down to the Gulf."

"Oh, Eric. Forget it, will you?"

"Forget murder?"

"We're safe enough."

"For how long?"

She shook her head. "Don't you see? We're together, Eric. Why– Why, look. You could forget all about it, darling. I could go back, say I'd escaped from you. I'd have the money. I could meet you again. We'll stay here a few days, then I can do that. You could change your name. We could go to South America."

"But I didn't murder Frank!"

She shrugged. "What difference does it make?"

"For God's sake, Leda! What difference...."

"Take a drink," she said. "Don't you like it here with me?"

"That's not the point."

She laughed. Her eyes were bright now. She stretched lazily, lay flat on the floor beside me on the blanket. "I'm staying right here," she said. "It's safe here. Where would you go? What could you do? Nothing. You know that, Eric."

"I can't stay here, knowing all the time I didn't do it. That whoever did is free."

She raised herself on one elbow. "Bosh. They'll never find you here."

"They would eventually. It'd get out somehow, it always does. You've got to keep on the move." I felt tortured inside because nothing was clear to me. "I love you," I told her. "I've brought you into hell. I've got to clear myself."

She shook her head. "If you go, darling, you go alone. I'm staying. I'm tired. I don't think I feel so well. Last night was pretty bad."

"You look damn fine to me."

She patted my face lightly. "Because you're blinded by love, silly."

I grabbed her wrist. "Damn it," I said. "Anybody'd think you don't want me to find out who killed my brother!"

Leda's mouth went slack and she tried to draw her wrist away from my grasp.

The man's voice from behind me in the kitchen doorway snaked into my guts. It was a familiar voice and I whirled sharply.

"'At's exactly right, Eric," he said. "Just exactly. Leda don't want you to know a durn thing. Only now it don't matter. Ain't that right, kid?"

It was Lenny Conn. He lounged soaking wet and muddy against the doorjamb. In his fist was a blued-steel revolver and the muzzle was pointed at my bare middle. He let his mouth hang, and he looked very tired in his ruined tan suit and pink shirt.

Leda stood slowly. I saw her start trembling all over, and she cupped her palms over her breasts. "God!" she said. "I thought you'd never come!"

## Chapter 20

Leda laughed.

She stood there and laughed. At first her stomach moved with secret mirth, then she gasped. Her laughter rang in the room, coarse, loud, and she actually staggered with it. It was wild, hysterical laughter and it cut down into me. She doubled up with it. She looked at me, laughing hoarsely, and her gray eyes filled with tears, her mouth gaped like a raw wound and her body rocked. "Oh, God, God, God," she whispered. She was unable to speak aloud.

"What the hell's carried you off?" Lenny said. He didn't move from the doorway.

I stood up, grabbed my swimming shorts.

"Nature boy," Lenny said. "Take it easy, nature boy."

I put on the shorts. Leda continued her racking laughter. She lurched over to one of the large, leather-covered easy chairs and sprawled into it. She was sobbing now, trying to talk. "I can't help it," she said. "I can't. It's been too much."

"Yeah," Lenny said. He eyed her. "Too much is right."

She sobbed convulsively now, her shoulders shaking, eyes streaming. Her face was twisted and I didn't know this Leda. I didn't know her at all. But I was beginning to see things, terrible things that I didn't want to believe. It was like a new kind of fear–something you were deadly afraid of. You knew what was coming, almost, you knew it. You wanted to shove it away, turn your back on it, not believe. But it was true....

"It's been so goddamned long," Leda cried. "Oh, Lenny. I couldn't have stood it another minute. Nerves are shot. Last night was mad–mad! Where've you been–where?" She shook all over, trying to hold herself with her arms. "He's so damned dumb, Lenny–so damned dumb. Oh, thank God it's over. Thank God." She subsided a bit in the chair, weeping softly. Every now and then her shoulders trembled but she didn't make much noise now. "Didn't think I'd make it," she said. She sprawled back into the chair, with her head flung back and her eyes on me. But she didn't laugh now, and she abruptly moved her gaze.

"What's it about?" I looked at Lenny. All the pent-up swinelike rottenness was staring out of his eyes.

"Ain't 'bout nothin'," Lenny said. He cracked a sloppy grin. "You just got yourself all messed up's all."

"How do you mean?"

"Is he dumb, or is he dumb?" Leda stood, watching.

Well, at last I knew. "You killed Frank," I said to Lenny, "didn't you? You killed him. And–" I turned to Leda, "you–you knew it. You knew it all the time. Not only knew, but...."

"Knew it?" she said. "Listen to him, Lenny."

"How'd you find this place?"

Lenny snorted. "She done brought you here, Eric. Leda brought you here. You been framed for murder. Don't you see yet we done it? Us?" He grinned, gawking at Leda. "Always liked you, too, Eric. But, well–" He watched Leda again.

I watched her, too. Saw her eyes, her red lips, her body and knew her for what she was. In a matter of moments my whole life had done another complete wingover. I had loved this woman.

Now I hated her. I hated her guts. In that instant I knew real hate and it stuck. My brain reeled and recovered itself and I knew I would get them. Get them right. This was no meager hate; this was the real thing.

Leda started talking. Her beautiful body bared in the room, her eyes bright again now, her full lips half smiling. "I actually had trouble with you," she said. "I almost fell for you."

"Yeah," Lenny said. "You know what you tol' me. I wonder about you sometimes. Mebbe I wouldn't trust you far's I could throw my skiff." He meant it.

"Lenny killed Frank, sure. It was a good setup. We planned it, just lately, Eric." She licked her lips and greed showed in her eyes. The wildness I had liked in her was not what I had supposed at all. It was something else, something much worse. "I got onto the way you think in the hospital. Figured I'd hook you then, and I did. But you got messed up in that hit and run and Frank was there, all clear. He liked it, too–well enough to marry me quick." She laughed. "You dumb ox. Frank schemed that hit and run, Eric. Didn't know that, did you?"

I stood there, listening. Those men who delivered the car....

"The man, Allen," she said. "He and the other fellow you saw at the hospital had been bought by Frank to pull the hit and run. I didn't know then, of course. But I got it out of him afterward. He was plenty scared about it. He had faked the telegram so he'd be sure of your mother's money when she died. Then he heard you were coming home. He had to do something, he was desperate. It wasn't too sharp, but it fooled you. And it's fooled lots of people who don't know a guy will do about anything for dough. Like Allen. He let his friend beat the hell out of him, and they framed you for the hit and run. It cost plenty, too."

Frank had had more nerve than I supposed.

"Then when he got you cooped up in Alabama, he had Allen withdraw the charges, and paid them off. Figured you'd be stuck for a good long time behind bars. He told some dandy stories to the psychiatrist there." She paused. "I got it all out of him. He'd do anything for me." She eyed Lenny. "So would you, wouldn't you?"

"We'll see," Lenny said.

Leda bit her lip. "Anyway, you know about that now. Frank was trying to keep you away from home until your mother died. He never did know about that crazy dream of yours. Lenny and I decided we'd scare you good on that, having Frank–Frank lying there with the wooden mallet." She stroked her thighs quickly, leaned toward me. "You'll never even have that little blonde thing now. You won't have anything." She smiled, she knew what I was thinking. "Worked it pretty good, didn't I? I played hard enough, God knows."

"Yeah," Lenny said. "I seen you. Too hard, sometimes."

She whirled. "What's the matter with you? You're nothing but a punk. Didn't have to work hard on you."

"Shut up!"

"I won't shut up!" She tossed her head, her hair swirled about her shoulders, and I believed all those things I'd heard at the hospital about Leda Thayer. "I've got you, Eric. I've got all that money Frank sweated for, too." She laughed, watching me, watching what was going on inside me. "You're mad, aren't you? Too bad–too damned bad for you, brother. Oh, boy, I had a time getting you here, didn't I? Not much trouble making you stay long enough, though–eh?" She moved her hip once, very slightly and I hated her just a little bit more. "Yes, Eric. I planned it, with Lenny. Gave him a little money, too, so he could have some clothes for a change. Gave him a lot of things–didn't I, Lenny?"

Lenny's eyes were shining like wet Christmas tree bulbs.

"Frank was no good. She's professional, Eric. You didn't have a chance."

She glanced at him, her eyes sly. "Don't you wish you had a chance, though? You couldn't buy it, Lenny. I gave you lots of mementos, but not the big one. Did I Lenny?"

I could see the fury mount in Lenny's eyes. I wondered if she saw it. A dumb, harassed, knifelike fury.

She threw him a look from cold gray eyes and I watched her lips. They were very tight and there was a tiny rim of white around them. I wondered how such a beautiful woman could be so rotten inside. She sighed. "I had a hard time acting right with you, Eric. Plenty hard, but I came through."

"You came through," I said. "So you've got the money, Frank's home, everything. You cleaned up and your hands are clean, I suppose?"

"Lenny killed Frank. He smashed his—his head." She paused, and her face went a little pale. I knew she was remembering. "Yeah," she said. "I got sick. That was legit. Lenny would have cut up the body for what I promised him."

I waited, hoping. I knew that in the pocket of those overalls tossed across the back of a chair by the fireplace was my automatic. If I could reach it. But would I get a chance to use it? My eyes flicked just once toward the overalls. Leda caught the look and grinned.

"Oh," she said. She moved lithely over to the chair, picked them up, tossed them over her shoulder. "I'm going to put something on," she said, and went on into the bedroom. Her body looked as perfect as ever.

Lenny and I watched each other.

"I didn't like doin' that," he said. "But hell, Eric. You didn't like your brother, anyways."

"He was a human being. You don't just go around killing them, Lenny."

The gun in his hand hadn't moved an inch from my middle. I could feel the sweat dripping from my armpits. Lenny looked a little sad, but his eyes were harder now. Leda drifted back into the room. She wore a maroon corduroy man's bathrobe and she had her hands jammed deep into the pockets. She stood over by the fireplace. There was about them both a look of expectancy.

"You see," Leda said. "With Frank dead and you framed for the murder, I get the money."

"We–" Lenny said. His lips jerked loosely.

She ignored him. "I had to be sure you'd go for me. But I wasn't much worried. I've done the work." She looked at Lenny. "You know that of course, Lenny. I sat outside that damned barn till he came home from swimming last night and found Frank, too. While you were drinking."

"Sho. But who done it?" Lenny said.

She didn't answer. They watched each other.

"So, now what?" I said. I wanted it all.

Lenny spoke. "This here wasn't in the cards for sure," he said. "An' it's gonna be hard."

Leda wouldn't look at me. She watched Lenny.

She said, "We only planned this part in case you took it into your head to investigate who'd done the murder. The law's certain you did it. I've got the business, and I'll sell. I've got the inheritance, all of it." She paused, took a deep breath. "We also get the credit for catching you. Only you can't tell about it, see? Because you'll be dead, Eric, when we bring Burkette out here."

"Who figured that one?" I tried to stay calm, to think, but that gun muzzle was steady.

"We did," Leda said.

"She means," Lenny said, "that she thought it up. She thinks of everything. She's a smart one, I done told her she was."

"Yes," Leda said. "I'm a smart one. And I'm thinking right now, too."

Lenny giggled. "I know what you think with, Leda. You told me."

I had noticed plenty of antagonism between them. It kept getting stronger as the minutes passed.

"Well," I said. "It's a lot of money, nearly a million. But split two ways it's not so much." Perspiration covered me now. My palms were clammy and I was in the room with death.

"We're stuck with it," Lenny said. "Leda ain't so bad. We'll make out."

"How do you know I'm not so bad?" she said. "You couldn't know. I wouldn't let you know."

"You will, honey. You will, because that's what we schemed up. Birds of a feather, baby, an' all that there stuff. Remember? We'll step out in the world, like we ought."

"You're one bird that's molting before my very eyes," Leda said.

Lenny looked a question.

"I don't need you any more, you pig," Leda said. "I had a husband once. He's dead, so I can do it all right. I know I can do it and stand it."

They had forgotten me. But still that gun muzzle did not stray and Lenny's eyes were quick now. I was caught cold, flat.

"You don't need me no more?" Lenny said.

She shook her head. "I've got the money and I'm in the clear. Eric forced me to come here, you see?"

"Forced you to come here?" Lenny said. He snorted. "Don't kid me!" He laughed outright. "That sure is a hot one, ain't it?"

"Yes," Leda said. She took a single step forward, her long white thigh parting the folds of the bathrobe. Just once her tongue flicked across her lips. "And here's another hot one–just for you."

Lenny stood with the gun in his hand one minute. The next instant he bowled backward into the kitchen. Three explosions slammed inside the cabin.

Leda's hand was in the pocket of that bathrobe and flame spat through the pocket. Three solid bucking times.

Lenny clutched his stomach with his left hand and sat down hard. He brought his gun up carefully, struggling. He was gasping with the effort and the pain inside him. There was a look of absolute stricken wonder on his face. He fought with that gun, trying to get it up.

"Did you hear that hot one?" Leda asked. Her voice was a bright whisper and there was something of hot satisfaction in it, of unpleasant, wild relief. "Did you feel it, Lenny? No more pouring over the collection now, no more additions–And no me, ever!"

Lenny fought with the revolver. He was dying and he knew it. It was all over for him. Only one thing was left and he wanted very much to do that one thing. She could have ended it there, but she didn't. I watched her face and it was taut. She began breathing faster and faster, her lips parted, her breasts thrusting almost convulsively.

Lenny fought with the gun. Then he squeezed the trigger, just once. The lead slug tore through his foot and into the floor. He fell back dead.

Leda shuddered and relaxed. She breathed deeply. "Geez," she said. "That did something to me."

I couldn't look at her sagging lips. Leda was no longer sane, something had gone bang inside her, now. Her eyes were glassy.

"You see, Eric," she said. "I could never split the money. And–and I couldn't let him–"

"It's funny," I said. "But they never seem able to split the money."

She swallowed, glanced at Lenny, then turned her gray eyes toward me again. I kept trying to tell myself that here all pride and defiance were gone. That only emptiness remained, emptiness behind a shell of beauty. A clay shell. I tried to tell myself that was all she was–nothing but clay and clay could be smashed. Lenny had smashed clay. I tried to tell myself that. But I had loved this woman and even now–after thinking the things I had, after seeing the things I'd seen her do and heard her say, after I had watched the vicious turbulence within her–I couldn't help wanting her still.

I was as bad as she. Worse, perhaps. She was all wickedness combined; all the dirt of many gutters–a murderess and one who could not love. But had she loved? I still wanted her–I knew I could not have her....

Her voice was soft now. "There's one more thing I've got to do." She was pulling herself together after discovering that killing Lenny hadn't been the easiest thing in the world to do after all. But Leda was Leda, my Leda, and she did pull herself together. "I've got to kill you," she said. She drew the forty-five from the pocket of her bathrobe and it looked terribly large in her white hand. The pocket was burned.

And I knew the weaknesses of man. I didn't want to die. That was one weakness. I still wanted this woman. And that was the other weakness.

Death was big but it was also final.

I leaped for her. The automatic bucked in her hand once again and the cabin rocked with explosion. But she had missed and the gun was empty. I was on my hands and knees.

"Leda!"

She whirled, ran for the kitchen. The rear door slammed. I went after her, stubbed my foot on Lenny's body and sprawled across the floor.

Lenny's revolver was caught under my chest. I scrambled up with the gun in my hand and headed out the back door after her.

In the shallow gray light of morning I glimpsed her flashing legs, the auburn hair, and that maroon bathrobe flapping along the river bank.

"Leda!" I shouted. From in front of the cabin I heard the abrupt sound of a car's engine, the quick slew and rumble of tires gripping the muddy road. I paid no attention, ran on toward the spot where Leda had vanished.

## Chapter 21

Wet grass along the steep crumbling bank of the river showed me her path. I followed, running, knowing I had to reach her. Then I saw her.

"Leda!"

She turned, looked at me. She was standing on the river bank, grasping a low long waving branch of a live oak. Moss tumbled over her shoulders as she half crouched watching first me, then the rushing waters below. Site stood half naked, the maroon bathrobe falling away, watching me approach, and she was so beautiful it almost stopped me.

"Leda–"

Her eyes were filled with fear and they fastened on the gun in my hand. Once she quickly turned her head, flashed a glance at the black, sirupy, swirling river again where it thrust like an animal against the cliffed mud bank below. Taut fear showed in the sudden grimace she showed me and her eyes were insane. She let go the branch and the maroon bathrobe fell from her body.

"Eric," she said, and I rushed her.

For a long moment we tangled on the bank's crumbling lip. She fought wildly, passionately. The gun fell from my fingers as I grasped her arms. Her smooth white body was lush, savage, but not with love–never with love.

With fear, now.

"I loved you," I said. "Did you ever love me?"

Her right hand raked red-tipped nails across the side of my face and her teeth gleamed white between her lips. I held her to me, felt all the lithe tortured length of her body and again her nails raked me. Across my neck, my shoulders. She writhed, cursed.

"I don't love you now. Hear me, Leda? Hear?"

She cringed back, bending, her lips parted, her eyes black-pupiled and afraid.

"But I want you! Hear me?"

I heard my own voice, shouting, harsh.

I had to hurt her. Nothing mattered but that. I had to hurt her for real just as she had so perfectly wrecked me.

Her lips were parted as I grabbed for her. All the hell-hate in her snapped across her eyes. For a second, as I moved, she crouched, wild-eyed. Then she leaped.

She struck at me, then turned and ran stumbling along the bank away toward denser woods.

I sprawled on the ground, half over the bank, knowing the sure fate that lay in the swollen mad river beneath me. Scrabbling back, I found the gun and went after her.

The bank rose on a gentle incline, walled with twisted roots.

"Leda!" Her naked body flashed against the morning. I fired the gun twice into the soggy earth. She whirled, her mouth wide and soundless. Then she screamed.

Her long nakedness thrashed for a brief instant as the bank crumbled beneath her feet. She vanished into the black waters of the river.

It was much swifter than it looked. As I came up to where she'd fallen something swirled in a rush against the surface, already far downstream. Her face, maybe, then an arm, a leg, very white and small and moving away.

I stood on the bank, watching, while mudclots broke off beneath my feet and splashed in the wild water. I couldn't move.

And that was all. Quickly gone. I saw no more of her and the river was the same. Leda Thayer was gone. She had found escape through death. No one could live where she was now.

I walked back to where we had fought. Trampled into the wet grass at my feet was the maroon bathrobe. I dropped the gun into the folds of blood-colored cloth.

"Eric."

I glanced around. Coming through the grass toward me was Norma. She still wore the red shorts and the white sweater and her hair was very golden. Clyde Burkette stalked behind her with two other men. One of them was Gallagher.

"Hello," I said to Norma. All right. They were here and it was over and I was it. Leda's scream still echoed in my mind. But Leda was gone.

Norma stood facing me as Burkette, Gallagher, and the other man came up.

Norma and I stared at each other. Yes, I was it.

"We saw it," Norma said. "Most of it. We found Lenny, Eric."

I could never explain Lenny's death.

Burkette shoved past Norma and strode up to me. His face was haggard, his gray Stetson grimed with mud.

"We been trying to catch you," he said. "We trailed you from your car, last night. Old man with the load of chickens on his truck reported the accident, Eric." He glanced down at his mud-caked shoes. If it hadn't been for Burkette's knowledge of the trail, his being a born backwoodsman, he might never have found me. He did not pick his teeth. Somehow his attitude had changed. "Soon as I realized where you were headed, I sent Gallagher back to town. He brought another man and the car up the back road. Met us down yonder a piece." He waved his arm vaguely.

Gallagher and the other man stood in the grass. Gallagher didn't look very grim any more.

I didn't feel anything. Just tired, now—tired and empty. I didn't want anything any more, not anything.

Burkette cleared his throat. "You been through a heap, I reckon. Reckon mebbe I had you wrong, Eric."

I didn't say anything.

"Eric, the girl—Norma, there. She saw it—saw him back there—" he gestured toward the cabin beyond the tangled undergrowth, "when he killed Frank. She come to the barn and saw it through the window. Didn't know what to do, I reckon. Excited. Finally made up her mind to tell you. But she missed you. Listen," he said. "We been chasing you ever since. Trying to tell you. You was jamming yourself up, Eric." He coughed, swallowed. "Owe you an apology, Eric." His gaze dropped. "You'll be a big man in these parts from now on."

I'd heard it all. It didn't make sense, yet it had to be true. I looked over at Norma. For a second her face was rigid, then slowly she smiled and there was something in her eyes that was very different from something in another pair of eyes I remembered so well. She nodded, stepped toward me.

"That's right, Eric. I was with the sheriff at the Hewitts when you drove in."

"But you fired at me...."

Burkette shook his head. "In the air, figured it'd maybe stop you."

"Then you know I didn't kill my brother?"

"Knowed it for hours." He shoved his hat back. "The one in the cabin," he said. His hand flicked toward the river. "She did that?"

I nodded.

He started to turn, paused. "Body'll snag at the bend. Best we get on down there." He glanced at Gallagher and the other man. "Least the body'll make the bend if the river says so. I wouldn't want to swim in there." The three of them waded through the grass.

Norma was tired. But she smiled again. The river moved sluggish and certain toward the bend. I couldn't smile right then.

Norma kept watching me. I wanted her to go away, to leave me alone. I was sick right now, but someday it would be all right.

"It's all right, Eric," Norma said. "I know what it is to be lonely."

We stood that way for some time. Both of us knew what the other thought. And it was my turn to understand.

## THE END

# 77 RUE PARADIS
## by Gil Brewer

## Chapter One

THE SENSUOUS SCARLET GLOW from the floor lamp in the cheaply furnished room seeped under the partially closed lids of Baron's eyes, and he lay rigidly on the bed, thinking it all through one more time with a kind of fevered relentlessness. He tried to shut his mind against the harsh sounds of Elene's quick movements as she crossed and recrossed the room. He heard her hesitate before the dresser and her skirt lifted, a garter snapped against flesh, the skirt was lowered, smoothed. She cleared her throat, recommenced the nervous stalking from the wall to the scantily curtained windows overlooking the Rue Paradis and that strange, hour-lingering yellow twilight of late afternoon in Marseilles. Back and forth she stalked, to and fro, and Baron actually held his breath as he drove deep again into tight remembering. He recalled the chronologically ordered moments of the past two and a half years, perspiring and slowly thinking his way straight to this empty-handed present–to this cheap room with this cheap cocotte who somehow still possessed her soul. And to what was left of himself, Frank Baron. Even seeing it clearly, he would never admit defeat. There was too much hate for that–too much of everything.

You don't trace and seek a man for endless months, across continents, through endless cities, beyond mountains and plains, and then suddenly drop it. The insane part of it was that he really searched for a man's existence. Because he had never seen the man. A human being that existed. Somewhere....

Yes, he thought. He destroyed me. He destroyed my life. Somewhere I'll find him–someday.

Like bright black moments on a stark white screen, the tragic elements of the remembering sprang tauntingly awake, and he experienced the usual torture. Those frenzied weeks before the trials. The waiting and the cruelly patient days during which he lost his wife and his daughter, Bette. Losing Patricia, knowing she had left him, he could stand that–but Bette was something else again. The headlines, screaming, "Traitor!" The closed factories he had once been so proud of, and the closed bank accounts, too. All gone. Finished, like so much sand washed along a smooth curb into the sewer. Because all the time there had been inside him this howling cry, yelling at them that they were wrong. None heard. Not even that day on the witness stand, when the cry burst past his lips.

Ruined, destroyed, shattered by a lie.

It had taken more than one hand to accomplish everything, he knew. But he also knew that a single mind had conceived the major plan. With meagerly rationed money from a single secret bank account that his understanding lawyer had arranged for him, he began the search without a clue. He had only his oath, sworn passionately to himself, of vengeance. He did not like the word itself, because it somehow cheapened the quest. But cheap or not, that's what it was. So from the environs of the closed airplane factories, from the Midwest cities, he pursued a nebulous trail of talk. And very gradually he discovered the faint, elusive, but telltale aura of a *modus operandi*. A careful rationalization of this alone led him from New York to Chicago to San Francisco, then to Mexico City and Panama and Tokyo and down through Brazil and back to New Orleans and Kansas City, tracing the dim trail of that mind's existence. Questioning everywhere. To Capetown, to Italy, then back home. To Rome and Paris and home again, with the money dwindling fast now. But with the trail sometimes brightening, almost as if that mind paused to laugh, just around the corner, allowing Baron to hear the laughter. But faintly. Then, suddenly bright, it had led him to Paris– and now Marseilles. The money was all gone now, everything he owned pawned or sold, and the trail was absolutely ended.

There was nothing left to go on. It was like carrying a pail brimming with precious water for miles, only to discover suddenly that the pail had no bottom. That there had never been any water.

There had never been a name. Only a method.

Baron twisted on the bed, keeping his eyes closed and fiercely closing his mind to remembering. He did not want to remember now, only to rush skimming along the surface of things. To remember the details of each interim clearly was to go on through torture that would leave him spent, exhausted.

"*Chéri?*"

Elene. He had forgotten her. She meant a great deal to him and he wondered momentarily what would eventually happen to them. And as he wondered, the memories slipped away, and he began to be himself again, slowly. He relaxed, with only the ghosts haunting him. The newspapers had followed his journey quite well, but they termed it debauch. Frank Baron's death fling. Well, let them think it. To hell with everything but *him*.

"Frank, *mon cher,*" she said.

"Yes?" He looked at her and she smiled at him with that quick motion of the head and shoulders that helped to reveal the self-conscious boldness he admired.

"I am hungry," she said.

He said nothing, watching her. He knew she didn't like being watched. It made her move her head and shoulders still more and he liked seeing this. Scarlet touched her cheeks and her dark eyes sparkled and he wished they could go someplace far beyond far mountains. He knew he would never find a better companion, a more understanding lover. Since they had met that night in the café, she refused to leave him. She liked his nose. *She* refused to speak of any other reason for remaining with him. "It is your nose," she told him. "It is a great, defiant nose. A strong block of a nose. A nose with character. Many persons have noses that are entertaining," she told him. "But none is so interesting as your nose, *chéri*. Let it go at that, then. I am in love with your nose."

For his own part, he had never imagined a prostitute could be anything like Elene. He had heard the stories, but he had never met one. Not like Elene. For many days now he had refused to admit to himself that she had any calling other than their own life together. He couldn't understand why she stayed with him. He knew he was boresome. They had not eaten regularly. They were behind in their rent. Looking at her now, he wished they could always be together. If peace might ever be found, then surely Elene had helped to show him a way.

"Well?" she said. She was wearing a soft dark blue skirt and it was tight, sheathing her fine hips. A loose white blouse fresh from her private iron lay smoothly beneath the golden-brown flush of hair that coiled and clung to her shoulders. Her breasts moved vigorously against the blouse and Elene was very much alive. But hungry, he thought. Yes.

"You wish to be free of me?" he said.

Her scowl was dark, her gaze threatening. "No."

"What will we do?"

"I will work."

He grinned at her. About everything she was coldly frank. Her life had taught her that was the easier way. Now she pouted slightly.

"But I am hungry."

"You know I've got that money."

She nodded. "You went out to the Château d'If this morning."

They looked at each other for a time and he thought about the five hundred francs in his pocket. It was the most money he'd had at one time in weeks. He had helped a Frenchman take a boatload of tourists out to the Château d'If. He had rowed one boat and the Frenchman the other. They had insisted on going out in rowboats. There were all kinds of excursion boats that left the *Vieux Port* on regular runs to the island Dumas had made famous with his adventurous Count of Monte Cristo.

Elene came over to the bed and sat beside him. She touched his forehead, whistled silently. "Fever," she said.

He clawed into his pants pocket, brought out the single paper bill, quickly thrust it in the open flaring throat of her blouse, down between the warm breasts.

"I won't be long," she said. "We will eat, *chéri.*"

"No appetite, Elene."

She smiled, leaned and kissed him, and he felt the vague stirrings of desire as her damp lips pressed his. For a moment she leaned hard against him, her body and her hands moving with that same frank, bold approach he had enjoyed during all their days together. Abruptly she moved away and smiled at him once again. She waved a warning finger.

"Later," she said. "We must eat first." She paused and he wished she would go away. He needed her much too much. "Frank," she said, "I'm going to buy cognac, too. You need the brandy." She paused, turned away, and slow agitation showed in the stiffening of her shoulders. "For three hours," she said. "For three hours you have not spoken. I will return quickly, and we will talk."

"We owe money here," he said.

"Pooh!"

"All right. See that you don't open the brandy before you get here. See you don't forget to come home."

She grinned wickedly and winked. "When I get back, you'll tell me everything," she said. "I love your nose, but I think a nose is not enough. You are holding it inside you, *chéri*. This is bad. If I thought it could be a woman, I would laugh. It would be to laugh at. But it is not a woman. It is something else and you must tell me."

"You think I'd be all right then?"

"*Certainement!*"

She went away and he heard her heels clicking on the stairs. The street door slammed and again he heard her heels down there on Paradis, clicking on the pavement. Then nothing, and he lay there wondering how he could ever explain it to her. She knew nothing and up to now she had not questioned him. He began to know he had to leave her. Yet the very thought of being away from her frightened him, because for this first time he understood what it was like to be alone.

He sat up on the bed, swung his feet to the floor, and stared across the room through the scarlet lamp glow.

Elene had come from Normandy. As a very young girl she had sold herself to the Boches during World War II, when her home had been destroyed. She nursed her father through sickness this way. They lived in a ruined cellar and she fed him, buying food with money earned in the only manner possible. When he died, she walked and flirted her way to Paris on the Red Ball Highway, then eventually came to Marseilles. She was frantically alone when he found her that night in the café. She was sorry for nothing, refused to discuss it after the first explanation. She was one of many.

He sat on the bed and realized that he was straining to hear her returning footsteps. She didn't have far to go, only to the corner and back, and he waited. Time slipped by and there was no sound from the street. The yellow twilight progressed into further yellow twilight, darkening faintly, but not yet dusk.

He blanked out his mind. He thought of the brandy. They would forget for this one night, and tomorrow he would start fresh. He would begin again, because there had to be a renewal of the trail.

Only she did not come. He refused to think she might have slipped away with the money for a night of her own. Yet he could not keep the thought from his mind. She was human, all too human. And he was anything but fun for her.

He began to pace the room. He looked down on the street. It was solemnly empty and the room with its scarlet lamp glowing was suddenly a torture. He knew he had to stop thinking this way. He knew it was not alone Elene's going with the money that bothered him. It was everything. He needed that brandy and a moment later he was on the street himself.

He would tell her how foolish he had acted. She would meet him on the sidewalk.

But she did not. Elene wasn't in the café where they bought their wine. The bakery was closed. He moved down Paradis to the Cannebière and headed toward the harbor. If she had decided to make it a night of her own, that was the direction she would take. It was where he had found her and it was where she would be....

Then finally the twilight had become a yellow dusk. He hurried now up from the *Vieux Port* along the Cannebière, heading for the next tourist café. He had tried the ones along the harbor; she hadn't been there. Understanding and anxiety had given way to anger now. If he could get his hands on her and at least some small remaining part of his five hundred francs he would be happy. Also lucky.

He decided to warm her bottom. Yet how could he expect her to act differently?

Then somehow he knew she was gone. There were a few more spots he might try, but he felt it, a washing away of faith. Because he had so little faith in anything. He tried to tell himself that Elene was not the type to run off. Wasn't she? He laughed to himself, walking swiftly now.

The small gray German Opel sedan stopped directly before him as he stepped down from the curb into the street. The rear door came open and he saw the gun.

"Get in," a man said.

There was nothing else to do. It was that simple. He had no time to think and it was like a revelation of the ending he had been coming to. The door, in opening, brushed his sleeve. One step and he was in the car. A man in the front seat beside the driver put a hat on his sleekly combed head. *"Alors."*

The Opel sped up the street. The door slammed, and Baron waited with a kind of empty patience.

## Chapter Two

THEY HAD WORKED VERY FAST and with professional skill. A slow tension began to build inside Baron as he realized this. Somehow, the dreamlike way the car had appeared, and the way he found himself here on the rear seat, became a truth among a life of hazy lies.

The man in the front seat partially turned his head.

"Monsieur Baron? Frank Baron?"

"Yes."

"Please, monsieur. Say nothing. No one will speak to you. *Voilà.* It would be a waste."

Baron sat stiffly now on the edge of the small rear seat. He saw the man up there tap the driver on the shoulder, point to the left.

They came onto the Rue Vacon and turned right on Paradis, and by the time they passed the building where he had his room–or where Elene had hers–they were doing an easy sixty. On Paradis this was an interesting speed. They lurched on the old tracks, narrowly missed taking a wheel off a horse-driven cart, swung back into the right lane, bumping across the worn bricks.

He had seen none of them before. The driver was young, he wore a cap, and though it was dusk now and rapidly darkening, Baron made out a very red face. The man beside him was in command.

He glanced across at his neighbor in the rear seat. The heavy gun barrel clunked just once, sharply, across his kneecap.

"Look," he said. "This is foolish. What the hell is this?"

The Opel's engine was in good shape. He could feel that much. It sounded as if it were winding up, like a spring-wound toy car just before it exhausts itself. Only this engine was not tired.

They turned left again, passed the prefecture, came on along until they struck the broad, tree-lined Prado. Now the driver really opened it up. It was plain they weren't going to stop for a while.

He stopped himself from looking once more toward the man beside him. The kneecap pained badly. For another moment or two he remained on the edge of the seat. He no longer thought about being hungry. He had forgotten Elene and the five hundred francs. He had absolutely no idea of what it was all about. He sat there, frightened. Then gradually the fright went away. There was nothing to hinge it on. No reason to be afraid.

"You've made a mistake," he said. "I have no money, not a franc. I'm completely broke."

Nobody spoke.

They knew him. The hell with it. He had been trying to say the hell with it in Marseilles for three months now. He could afford to go on saying it. He got a smile out of that and relaxed in the seat. There was nothing else to say. For three months he had been at a standstill. It didn't matter what was happening, so long as it was something. His life no longer mattered. It traveled a course, that was all. He had to recover volition and one way was as good as another.

They drove for some time. He quit trying to place where they were going. It was much too dark now, and they traveled too fast. Besides, it was tiresome. Whatever it was they wanted, he would soon find out.

He kept himself somehow in this frame of mind until the car turned abruptly into an alley and stopped. All he knew was that they were somewhere north of St. Charles' Station. They had wound in and out all over Marseilles.

"Get out."

The man from the front seat held the door open for him. His friend in the rear prodded him tightly with the gun barrel. He got out and looked at the man from the front seat.

"All right," the driver said. He had unlocked a door in the brick wall of the alley. They went into darkness.

He began not to like it again. The fright began to work up into him again. He tried to push it away, to retain the feeling he had manufactured in the car. He could not do it. He remembered Elene and suddenly felt that those few moments before she left the room had been moments of peace. Because now his personal tortures were sinking into a background of memory only. He found he did not like this at all.

They went along a damp, musty-smelling stone hallway. Their heels chunked hollowly on big stone flags. The young driver lit a flashlight and Baron had an impression of brick walls, well worn. They turned down a corridor to the right and went through a curlicued wrought-iron gate into the usual garden. As they crossed the garden on more flags under a star-freckled sky, Baron saw that it was not the usual garden. Flowers bloomed in the night and buds swung from an enormous vine, like giant teardrops. There was the heavy, suffocating odor of night-blooming jasmine. A miniature fountain sprayed weakly from a plump, doll-like stone nymph's head into a circular cement dish in the center of the garden. They went past some twisted trees that looked like weary old ladies flapping lace shawls over their heads. They entered another door by way of another wrought-iron gate and went down another corridor.

The flashlight in the driver's hand stopped, played on a door and latch. He knocked. He turned, grunted at the man with the hat.

"Again," the man with the hat said. "*Encore.*"

The driver knocked again.

"Yes. Enter," a woman said.

The flashlight went out. But not before Baron saw the driver smile brightly at the man in the hat. The gun poked. The door opened.

Inside it was warmer, but the smell was still present. It was an odor he had often met with in Marseilles; a presence of damp stone and gray, tired centuries.

"Yes, Lili?"

The woman was seated at a table across the room, with her back to them. She rose. She turned and glanced at the man in the hat without looking at anybody else. It was quite a feat, Baron decided. She wore a red artist's smock and held a long slim paintbrush in one hand. She had been painting designs on pottery and china plates. Some of the plates, showing carefully intricate work, were racked against the wall above the table where she worked. She was quite tall and slim. The smock somehow managed to reveal the slimness and at the same time give promise of a fine young body beneath it. Her legs were straight, her shoes black, high-heeled, dainty. Her hair was raven black, not too long, and there was something sly about her. Right away Baron liked the slyness.

"Yes," she said. "One moment."

She disappeared behind an immense Chinese screen with a scene of red and green dragons and a white pagoda by a turquoise lake painted on the black cloth.

A man's voice reached them, but the words were unintelligible. Baron heard the door open behind him then, He glanced around and the driver and the man with the gun were just leaving.

"Quietly," the man in the hat said. He had the gun now, holding it in a hand sheathed in a gray cloth glove.

They waited.

The room was very quiet, as though they were deep underground. Baron could smell linseed oil now, and turpentine and paint.

The girl spoke softly from the other room and again the man's voice reached them.

Baron looked at the man in the hat. He did not like what he saw. Everything fitted too well. The man looked quite human, no different from anyone else. He was a man of medium build in a gray suit, wearing a gray topcoat of thin smooth material and a gray Homburg. His shoes were shiny, but not too shiny. His eyes looked quite honest, unsuspicious. He wore an inconspicuous blue tie and his shirt collar was clean. It was too perfect. There was nothing particular about the face. Two eyes, a nose, and a mouth. But the gloves. Baron was immediately suspicious of any man who wore one glove with the back turned down and carried the other in his bare hand.

Too, there was the gun.

"Come," the girl said.

She waited by the corner of the screen and looked at the floor as they walked past her. Baron got a whiff of good perfume, very faint, elusive. The jasmine out there in the garden should give up, he thought. It wouldn't stand a chance.

He kept trying to bolster his courage in this way. He frankly admitted to himself now that he was scared.

"He is here," the man in the hat said.

A huge bull of a man stood looking at them from behind a desk as big as a barn door. He drummed fingers like miniature baseball bats on the desk top.

"Lili," he said, "close and lock both doors. Thanks."

He looked at Baron and sighed.

## Chapter Three

BARON WAITED. On top of what was happening, he realized he had a bad toothache. He wondered that he had not felt it before. Recently the filling had come out of a large cavity and now the tooth really ached.

"Arnold," the big man behind the desk said, "will you sit over there by the door? Thanks."

Baron decided Arnold was a good name for the man in the gray hat. Damn the tooth! He watched as Arnold found a straight-backed chair, pulled it over beside the door, and sat. He still held the gun. He took his hat off now and laid it carefully on his lap. His hair was something out of an old-fashioned pomade advertisement, parted exactly in the middle.

"Frank Baron," the big man said.

Baron said nothing. He stood about four paces from the enormous desk and watched the enormous man and cursed his tooth.

"I am Hugo Gorssmann."

Baron nodded. He began to feel uncomfortable, standing there. This Gorssmann watched him with a pair of very small eyes that were like lively black bugs waiting to pounce on something good.

Gorssmann sighed again. It was a sigh that took place somewhere behind the buttoned, cream-colored vest. Truly, Gorssmann was the largest man Baron had ever seen outside of a circus. He was not fat. It was meat. He wore dark-blue trousers, pleated and without a wrinkle, the cream-colored vest, a French-cuffed blue-and-white striped shirt, a dull maroon tie. The shirt sleeves were partially rolled back over hairless, freckled arms that looked like heavily inflated tire tubes. His mouth was lipless, like a clamp; a straight slash above the jaw, which went down without a neck to the knot in the maroon tie. He was bald, his skull knobby and liver-blotched, with a fringe of disconcerting kinky red hair above each ear. Gorssmann was quite a picture.

"I shall speak to you in English, Monsieur Baron," Gorssmann said. "You prefer this?" When he spoke it seemed that no part of his face moved. The lips separated somewhat and the words came out. That was all. With each word Gorssmann hissed faintly.

"It doesn't matter," Baron said.

"Correct," Gorssmann said. "It doesn't matter in the least. You speak French, German, Italian, and halfway decent Spanish. But you cannot write Spanish, can you? And when you write Italian, it is truly a mess."

Baron blinked at him.

"Was there any trouble, Arnold?" Gorssmann said.

"No trouble."

"You may put the gun away, Arnold."

"You think—"

Gorssmann nodded. He raised his eyebrows slightly at Baron, sighed again, and sank into an overlarge chair behind the desk. The chair vanished.

"Sit, of course, Baron. There." Gorssmann moved one finger toward an armchair beside the desk.

Baron decided to hell with it again. He went over and sat down. He was conscious that he looked quite ratty. His suit, a brown sharkskin, was filthy. There was a three-cornered tear in the left trouser leg. He wore no tie, no coat. He had sold his hat for twenty-five francs in a café weeks ago. He was badly in need of a haircut. The tooth ached worse all the time. He touched the cavity with his tongue, and winced.

The only thing Baron knew so far was that Gorssmann spoke French with a fine Parisian accent.

"I don't know exactly how to approach the subject," Gorssmann said. He drummed on the desk with his baseball bats, glanced carefully at his fingertips, looked once again at Baron.

"It's simple," Baron said. "You've made a mistake. Somewhere you've got your wires crossed. It's obvious to me. I haven't got a cent."

"Precisely." Gorssmann turned his head a scant inch and said to Arnold, "He hasn't got a cent."

"Then what do you want?" For the first time a touch of real anger took hold of him.

Gorssmann clucked his tongue, shook his head. He could not turn his head well because of the amount of meat that stood in the way.

"I have a proposition," Gorssmann said.

"Oh, great."

"Your attitude is not good, Baron. Not good at all."

"Have you got a cigarette?"

"That's better. Believe me, I was sure of you from the start. You aren't the kind–Here." Gorssmann leaned like a derrick and handed Baron a mahogany box of English Ovals. There was a lighter in the box beside the cigarettes. Baron put the box back on the desk, lit up, waited some more.

"You did not find the girl, did you, Baron?"

"What girl?" Something bad touched him lightly and went away.

"Elene Cordon. You were looking for her, were you not?"

Baron watched him. This was just fine.

Gorssmann moved his shoulders. Possibly he shrugged someplace, but it was only bare movement by the time it reached the outside. "We have the girl, Baron. You would never have found her."

"But why?"

"Ah. Now we begin to get someplace. Your attitude changes, Baron." He turned slightly toward the man in the chair. "Arnold. Did he talk coming here?"

"No."

"No excitement? Fright? Fear?"

Arnold shook his head, ran a palm carefully across the hair at the back of his head, looked at his palm, sniffed it. "No," he said. "Nothing."

"Bold, then."

"I would say yes," Arnold said. "Bold, unworried. I would say he did not care." He paused, then said, "Of course, this could be an act."

Gorssmann nodded, looked again at Baron.

"You *will* care, Baron. Seriously."

"If you're trying to worry me," Baron said, "you're succeeding. Is that what you're trying to do?"

"A peculiar man," Gorssmann said. He stared at the top of the desk. He seemed to be debating about something. He frowned and the meat humped into a small mountain on his forehead.

Baron was just a little bit more scared now than before. His life had never, from the first, been channeled in this direction, and he kept realizing the fact more and more as time went by. He would be distinctly more at home in an American back yard, cultivating shrubbery and a fine lawn. For the first time he allowed doubt to enter his mind, or perhaps doubt simply won itself through the wall, and he wondered how he had survived all this time, running up and down the world, chasing someone he didn't even know. He swallowed and recognized embarrassment. Then the embarrassment changed into something else and he recognized this, too. It was fear. Plain, simple, direct fear.

"What did you bring me here for?" Baron said.

"I'm getting to that. As I say, I don't know just how to approach it. You're much the man I expected, of course. But there are certain facets." He stopped, stared again at the desk.

"What about Elene?"

"The girl. I had forgotten. Neither here nor there." Gorssmann paused on a long inward breath, scratched his throat meatily. "You've come a long way, Baron. Both up and down. How would you like to go up again?"

"I'm afraid I don't understand."

Gorssmann leaned to the right, opened the bottom drawer on the desk, withdrew a polished brown leather brief case. He held his breath, found a key in a pocket of his vest, unlocked the brief case, put the key back. He lifted the brief case upside down over the desk and a sheaf of papers tumbled out. "*You*, Baron," he said, pointing to the sheaf of papers with his other hand.

Baron said nothing. He remembered the cigarette, took a last drag, dropped it on the floor, and ground it out with his foot. There was a good rug on the floor, deep nap, green. Gorssmann watched distastefully as he did the job on the cigarette.

"Suppose you tell me about yourself, Baron," Gorssmann said. He clasped his hands across his front, like stacked fence posts, and stared glumly at the papers on the desk.

"I'm not going to tell you anything."

"Why?"

"Because I'm damn well thoroughly mad and I see no reason to tell you anything. That's why."

"I see. Would seeing the girl help?"

Baron stood. He made a move toward the desk. Gorssmann sat back a little and Arnold stood up, holding the hat in both hands. Gorssmann chuckled, lifted the brief case from the desk, and slammed it against his legs.

Baron sat down again.

"Haven't you grown tired of this life?" Gorssmann said. "Aren't you rather ill from doing the things you have been doing all this while?"

"All what while?"

"Please, Baron. Let us be honest with each other. I mean since the beginning of the end. You are a broken man, Baron. You must know that. Does this please you? The memory of what you were, the knowledge of what you are? Living with a common street girl, allowing her to perhaps even work for–"

He came up fast, took one step, slammed his hand down on the desk in front of Gorssmann. "Just don't say that," he said. His voice was tight and he looked into the bug-like black eyes, seeing nothing. "Don't ever say that."

"Ah-ha," Gorssmann said. "Sit down, Baron. You mean there are still ideals?" He turned with a light flick of his head toward Arnold. "Perhaps we have swooped down too soon. Perhaps we should have waited a little longer. Could it be, Arnold, that we have mistaken the proper time to strike?"

Arnold did not answer. Baron looked at the man and watched him sitting there. He was carefully cleaning a steel comb with a matchstick, digging fine particles of pomade and lint and dirt from between the teeth and wiping them on the rung of his chair.

"No," Gorssmann said. "If we had waited any longer, you might have come to something else. Perhaps even done away with yourself. Because you are hurt, deeply hurt, aren't you, Baron? Confess." He leaned toward Baron, hissing quietly. "This horrible business in your country. It has affected you deeply, is not so?"

Baron looked down at him.

"Please, sit. Thanks."

Baron sat down again. He crossed his legs and looked at Gorssmann, beginning, to feel tight all over and giddy in the head. He wanted to swallow, but when he tried, his throat was perfectly dry.

"Yes," the big man said. "You are deeply affected." He straightened in the chair, flapped the brief case back up on the desk. "But we know these things."

"What do you propose to do?"

He watched as Gorssmann shrugged and wondered how he was able to sit here like that, waiting the way he did. The only word for it was ominous. Gorssmann was obviously sadistically inclined, and whatever was going to happen would be revealed slowly. Possibly painfully. He could sense this. He felt that every question was richly baited, like a secret trap.

Baron heard the words stumbling from his lips. They sounded all right. He wished he had more control, but he realized now that he had never prepared himself for any finality. For a long time he had pursued; his every waking hour—and a good share of his dreamtime—had been spent in a melodramatic portrayal of The Chase. He had not counted on anything like this.

"Say what you have to say," he told Gorssmann. "Get it over with. I want to leave. If you have the girl, let her go. There's no reason to hold her for anything. Whatever this is, there's no reason. She doesn't even know who I am."

"She does now, Baron."

"It changes nothing."

"All right," Gorssmann said. "We have bantered enough. We have wasted words and energy. I had to do this, though. Now we begin."

Baron watched him and he did not feel at all well. He felt worse than ever before in his life. It seemed that he was suddenly being allowed certain revelations, a kind of insight, or hindsight, into his living and himself that had been withheld. He did not belong here. He was out of place. It was disconcerting and fear seemed to weep on the walls, tenderly anxious in the shadows. He belonged back home, in the States. At the same time, he knew he had to brave it out, whatever it was. Only don't be too brave, he thought. Because then it can turn into something else. And you need some of that bravery yet a while. Because remember, he thought, you have to go on until you find *him*.

And thinking this he stared at Gorssmann. He knew what he had felt all along, but refused to admit. These were the type of people. My God, could it be that Gorssmann was the very man he was after? This was, he had to admit, almost the way he had imagined it would be. Though he had always pictured the final scene with himself in Gorssmann's place. Suppose ...

And it snickered in his brain, like that. The thrill of it went bright white along his shoulders and up the back of his neck.

Gorssmann continued to watch him, his face immobile.

The chance that this was the end of his trail was anything but pleasant. There was plenty wrong about it and he wanted to get up and run.

"You are ill?" Gorssmann said.

Baron shook his head. He would have to wait and see. Gorssmann continued to observe him, the black eyes snapping and crawling like bugs. They revolved in the sockets and Baron closed his mind again, frightened now of the remembering and of the present both. He knew now that he was quite ordinary, that he did not belong here, that he was, as Elene would say, "to laugh at."

"Three years ago," Gorssmann said quietly, "you were a big man in the United States, Baron. Before the war in Korea you were left a large automobile factory by your father. It was a new car in your country–new as compared with other familiar makes, such as Buick, Chrysler, Ford, Willys...." He waved his hand, like a Zeppelin straining at its mooring tower.

Baron waited. He tried to fight off the waves of sickness that rushed upon him. The certainty was being revealed.

"The make was taking hold, was it not? Yes, it was. It sold. It was a going thing, as they say. It was a good car. I know, I have owned one. Here nor there." He waved his arm again. "Your father died and you were left with the business. You were a smart young man." He shook his head and looked sorrowful.

"Meaning what?" Baron said. He knew he was speaking only to keep up his courage. These things Gorssmann was telling him could have been culled from newspapers.

"You don't feel so well?" Gorssmann said. He shrugged. "It is regretful. To continue, then. You were a very smart young man. Clean-cut. Intelligent, almost. I say almost, because at that time it was true. I am not yet certain of the present, even though intelligence is inherent. Here nor there." He flagged his arm again. "Yes. You wanted to do right by your father's memory. It was hard, at first, because you were, by your country's standards, rather average. It would take effort. You had never really thought of entering your father's business. It was overlarge for your thinking. But, anyway, you took over and you were soon making money. Lots of money. You were married. You had two homes. One in Florida, one back by the factories—your business. Now it was the business you loved and you had begun to learn it. Everything was good, smiling. And then the war. The Korean war."

Baron listened, his memories pulsing in time with the throbbing ache of his tooth.

"Was she pretty? Baron?"

"Who?"

"The wife. Remember?"

"Who are you?"

"Not now, Baron. Was she beautiful? Patricia?"

Baron was tense in the chair. He leaned forward. "Who are you?" he said again.

"Not now. After, Baron—after. Answer me. Was your wife, Patricia, beautiful?"

Baron looked at him and Gorssmann's eyes did not blink. Gorssmann turned away, fished momentarily among the papers on the desk, came up with a large photograph. He held it by one corner, waving it in front of Baron.

He felt the knot twist a little inside him, twist and wrench and then go away. He recognized the picture. It was a snapshot, blown up. A picture of Patricia that summer in Maine when she had worn the Bikini for the first and last time, wearing it that once out there on the rocks, while they swam. She had large breasts. She had been unable to control them. Yes, just for him. He had taken the picture and there had been only the one. He had not been able to remember where it was himself. How could these people have that picture?

It was blown up as far as it would go without distortion.

"I will answer for you. She was a beautiful woman. And your daughter, Bette, is a beautiful young girl, too, Baron."

Gorssmann looked at him and waited.

Baron did nothing, thought nothing. This was becoming evil.

"You're thirty-eight now," Gorssmann resumed. "You married early—at twenty, to be exact. Your first and only child, Bette, was born in the first year. That would make her seventeen? Close enough. Ah—well, so. Of course, Bette is with her mother?"

"Yes." The single word came from his lips inadvertently.

"Of course. Just now Patricia is in Bermuda. With a Spaniard. She admires the dark texture of his skin and he thinks the very world and all of the white texture of hers. You recall, of course, she did not believe in sunbathing for its own sake? Consequently, she remained natural. She is no longer quite so natural. A bit worn around the edges, Baron. But"–he shrugged, waved his hand–"aren't we all? Aren't you, Baron?"

Gorssmann laid the picture back on top of the sheaf of papers. Baron sat there staring at the light glinting across the photograph, an oblong of reflected light, nothing more.

"You love your daughter, very much, don't you?"

He did not look toward Gorssmann. He stared at the floor.

"A year–over a year–since you have seen Bette?"

Something cold and cruel began to cut him up inside. He closed his eyes against it. What was Gorssmann trying to do? It *had* been a little over a year since he'd seen Bette. She was a wonderful kid. It had hurt him plenty to leave her with Patricia, but that was the way of things.

"Ach, so. The war. You did the right thing then, too."

"About my daughter. What are you trying to say about my daughter?" There was a touch of anxiousness in his voice now; it only seemed to make things slightly worse.

"Later, Baron–perhaps."

"Damn you!"

Gorssmann raised his eyebrows slightly. "You contracted to build airplanes for the war. Bombers. You did well there, too. Your father had done well during World War Two. I imagine you recalled your father often. Perhaps summoning up his ghost now and again, to sit in judgment on one thing and another. Am I correct?"

Baron sat there, floating in misery now.

"Yes, eh? Deeply affected, troubled waters, Arnold. We were right from the very start, of course. So! You went along that way, Baron, working for the war–building airplanes. You learned much. You were a student. You met people; people from all over the world. Your contacts are enviable, believe me. You went to Washington. You sat in on conferences. In other words, you became *somebody,* so to speak. You were happy. You imagined your wife too was happy. You did not know that she dreamed of dark Latins with gold earrings, did you? Here nor there." He leaned back in the chair and the chair creaked, the sound driven into the very foundation of the building.

Arnold coughed three times, into his hat.

Gorssmann came forward again. He held his black gaze on Baron, picked up the leather brief case. "And then, Baron—what?"

Baron didn't speak. He felt like the cobra watching the little tinkling silver bells.

"Then *calamity!*"

Gorssmann swung the shiny brief case up and down hard. He smashed it into the sheaf of papers on the desk. Papers flew wildly into the air, fluttered around the desk to the floor. Gorssmann brutally flung the brief case at the desk. It skidded across the top and slipped to the floor.

Gorssmann was breathing hard. "As I said before," he went on, "those papers are you, Baron. *You!*" He straightened, glanced over at Arnold by the door.

"Arnold," he said, "pick those papers up and arrange them in their proper order. *Merci.*"

## Chapter Four

ARNOLD PICKED UP THE PAPERS, arranged them, thumbed through them. He stacked them neatly on the desk in front of Gorssmann. He retrieved the brief case, lined it up with the papers, and returned to his chair.

"Thinking?" Hugo Gorssmann said.

He could not speak, could not bring himself to say the words.

"Not now, Baron. I know well enough what you are thinking."

Baron reached nervously for the cigarette box. He noted the way his hand trembled, tried to still it, failed. He lit another cigarette, sat back in the chair, waited. He wondered foggily where Elene was. He hoped she was all right. He wanted to avoid thinking in circles. He knew he might as well face it. These boys were playing a game and it was not cards or even marbles.

Bette. Just now he did not even want the thought of her in his head. It was a worry, sharp and clear. Patricia did not matter. It had been a wrong marriage from the start, held together only for the child's sake. It had taken the sharp jar of financial jeopardy and scandal to take Patricia away—when he needed her most, for the first time in his life.

He looked over at Arnold. Arnold returned the look without smiling, or even blinking.

"Am I permitted to leave here?" he asked Gorssmann.

"Baron, dear Baron—have I underestimated you?"

"Then I'll leave."

Gorssmann changed his face slightly. This was a smile.

The big man said, "Calamity. Very bad, a shame, indeed, awful. Considering what I know of you, I can understand the shock. It must have been a tragic moment when you learned that over in Korea planes were beginning to fall apart. It must have been much worse when you learned that only the planes coming from your plants fell apart. This was a bad thing."

Arnold coughed. "The light," he said. "All right if I turn off that light and you light the desk lamp?"

Gorssmann nodded. Arnold touched a wall switch and the overhead light went out. A desk lamp came on and Gorssmann's features were tinged with watered blue. The desk lamp poured a broad lake of the watered blue light all around the desk. Baron sat there bathing his feet in the light.

"In my eyes," Arnold said. He coughed again.

"Some even fell apart before they got there," Hugo Gorssmann said. "There was great confusion after a time. It took time, too. Committees had to be formed. There was voting and more confusion, inspections, discussions—red tape. Clerks worked overtime with second endorsements, and third and fourth endorsements. Delegates were appointed. And all the time the planes continued to fall apart. A pity. Because"—he blinked—"when the planes were inspected they looked all right. Just like any other planes. Then, after many deaths and a great deal of confused running hither and thither, it was discovered that you were to blame, Baron."

He sat there with the remembered echo of the verdict rising anew in his ears, suffering the sharp pain in his chest, the confusion once again a part of him.

"Inferior grades of material and so forth. Here nor there. But you knew it was not your fault. You purchased the very best of materials.

Everything underwent rigid inspections. Then *what?* Sabotage, Monsieur Baron. Sabotage."

The cigarette burned between his fingers. He looked at Gorssmann.

"Go ahead, on the floor. It's good we picked this time, instead of waiting any longer. Your manners are disintegrating. The rug must be cleaned anyway."

He ground it into the rug with his foot. He did not know what move to make. All he knew was that he should make some move.

"You knew you were not at fault," Gorssmann said. "But they found you at fault and you lost everything you had. Your wife, your homes, your money, your business. You very nearly lost your life. They ripped you apart. They destroyed you. You screamed sabotage. Certain people high up believed that to be true, that you knew nothing. But they were high up in the wrong way. They could not help you. You managed to stay out of prison, but you had little left. At the first hint, your wife left you. To many you are a murderer of valiant men who went to war in planes that fell apart." Gorssmann chuckled. "They said you were careless. You were money-mad, living on blood. Ah, politics!"

Baron did not move now. He could not. It stunned him. He felt certain of what he was faced with. He did not know what to do.

"So we come to the interesting part now–don't we, Baron?"

Baron looked at Gorssmann. The big man was grinning. It was a kind of all-knowing, hateful grin that embraced the world, and it was heartless.

"You see," Gorssmann said, "I know what you're thinking. Shall we wait? All right, the newspapers, then. They say you have gone to hell. You did have a small bit of money that nobody knew of. A year ago you saw your daughter for the last time, and of late you've been in Europe, finishing your debauch. So the papers say. But the money ran out."

Gorssmann took a series of long breaths. He fished a blue silk handkerchief from his side trouser pocket and blew his nose with a kind of fiendish gusto.

"Of course, Baron," he said through the handkerchief, "it was sabotage. You know it, I know it." He blew harshly. He shrugged. He wiped his nose carefully, stuffed the handkerchief away. "Instead of working toward the right end, opening their minds to sabotage, sifting it out, they went crazy. They would rather pick on a businessman with a great deal of money, a success, and wring him dry, destroy him. Yes, even during the war when they needed you, Baron. You know the business, you have studied, you are smart enough. You have a good mind. But you were vulnerable because you were rich, you see? Scandal. People love scandal. They thrive on it. Would eat it instead of thick steak or chicken three times a day. Gossip. The same thing. They would not listen. They finished you. Almost." Gorssmann chuckled.

"Are you through?"

Gorssmann clucked his tongue. "Baron, Baron," he said.

"What is it you want?"

"They destroyed you, Baron, remember that. No more planes came from your factories afterward. They were turned into other hands, but nothing was accomplished. They cut their own throats painstakingly, because your plants supplied plenty of planes. It could have continued, if they had listened to you."

"And you?" Baron spoke softly.

"All right. You think I am the one, don't you?"

Baron heard the words, and he was prepared for them. It was a shock, just the same.

"For months," Gorssmann said without changing his expression, "you have continued to make a fool of yourself." His voice rose slightly. "You think we are all idiots? No, Baron, I'm not the man you're after. You are not even close, Baron. Listen." He leaned forward, the chair creaking. "For nearly a year we have led you around by the nose, while we readied matters. Just sit quietly and listen. Don't strain so! We knew what you were doing when you began your silly questioning, your quest." Gorssmann wiped his nose with the back of his hand and belched faintly. "You've been sitting here, thinking more and more that I am the man you've been trailing all this time. Baron, you are in many way a king among fools. We let you spend your money. We sent a man out to leave a trail for you to follow. A trail that would end in Marseilles–*here!*" Gorssmann paused, seemed to hesitate in his thoughts. "All right. I will tell you this: The man you seek lives. But he is so big you could never touch him, Baron. All you have done is to aid him toward the largest enterprise of his career." Gorssmann went sober. "And of mine, too, I might add."

Baron listened and felt the walls of panic grow around him. He had read of how they worked. Now he was experiencing it. Using all his will, he controlled himself, fought down the wildness that seethed inside him. For a brief time he thought he would go mad. He wanted to stand and lash out, fight against Gorssmann. Gorssmann represented days and endless days and nights and weeks and months and, yes, years of sworn endeavor. Yet Baron found he could sit here and look at Gorssmann and nod and agree and listen. He wondered if perhaps his subconscious was working for him. Really working, the way it was supposed to. He needed time. Time to think, time to sort out the devilish cunning of these people. For he was completely trapped and he knew it.

"What do you want?" he said softly.

"First, you must cease, as of now, to continue throwing your life away. Consider that you have wasted over two years of your life in a vain search for something that can never exist for you."

Baron did not speak. He waited. The shock of knowledge was so far out of hand as to be almost bearable. He wanted to laugh abruptly. But he did not laugh.

"You will work for us, Baron. You know aeronautics well. You are on friendly terms with many great people who are in the airplane industry. Steven Lang, for instance–the American. Gustav Stroyer, Lewis Strickland. But the one we are concerned with is your very old and dear friend Paul Chevard. The Frenchman. You remember Chevard?" Gorssmann smiled now.

It was all unbelievable, yet horribly true. Baron's mind seemed to dash off in every direction. How could you fight a thing like this? How could you even stand against such a quiet, insidious worming out of fact?

"Certainly you remember Chevard. He has been a close friend of yours for years. Odd that you haven't looked him up, Baron. He is right here in Marseilles. He will appreciate seeing you once again."

The room was still. The blue lake of light caked like blue ice. The shadows became a threat. Gorssmann seemed to become grotesque in his hugeness.

Baron stared at Gorssmann. He could only stare. He could not speak. He could not move.

Gorssmann stood abruptly. He began to curse. His swearing filled the room like burning rocks hurled across weeping mourners' heads in a funeral hall. He swore and slammed the desk with both fists, thundering, his face turning crimson, then flat white. He was like some monstrous fat baby, screaming in its crib.

"Arnold!" he yelled. "Arnold, get Joseph. Get him, bring him. Get him!"

Arnold rose from his chair, tendering the brim of his hat. "But Hugo—you said there would be no need."

Gorssmann swung on Baron. The big man's face was like mountainous terrain in the midst of an earthquake.

"He is still the fool! He sits there! I can tell what he is thinking. His attitude is still bad. Still not *what it must be!*" Gorssmann was panting heavily, his breath hissing like a nest of snakes. He sat down, stared stupidly at the desktop. His voice bubbled wetly from between his lips now and there was a purple tinge to his lips. "Get Joseph, thanks. Get him, Arnold."

Arnold rapped on the door. Soon it was unlocked and he left the room and Baron still stared.

"This thing. It is yet funny, eh?" Gorssmann said.

"No. No, not that."

"You will change, Baron. This to think about while you are in the other room with Joseph. Listen carefully, Baron." Gorssmann was obviously controlling himself with strong effort. His eyes were glazed with whatever flamed inside him. "Several hours ago in America, your daughter went boating on a lake in Florida. She was not with your wife, see? She went boating with a friend. It is in the papers now, of course." Gorssmann paused, still panting rapidly. "You will read it, perhaps. The friend drowned, the boat tipped over, see? According to the news, to what you will hear, your daughter also drowned and they have not found her body. They never will, Baron. *Never.* She is already on her way to France. We have her. Understand that? Let it sink into your thick skull, Baron. We will keep her. Think deeply about this." He stopped abruptly, stood up again, hissing faintly. He was like some enormous animal in clothes. "Here is

Joseph. Arnold, explain to Joseph that he is to take this man into the other room and show him how to change his attitude."

"Wait!" Baron said. He moved toward the desk. "There's no need of this." He heard his small voice beating like a small single wave against a cliff. "What have you said? What's this insane business about Bette?"

"Ah, but there is need," Gorssmann said. He swallowed forcefully, still hissing, breathing rapidly, trying to regain the lost breaths. "It is the core that counts. I waited to tell you about your daughter, to see how you would react to the other. The barest hint and you went sly, Baron. I saw it in your eyes, in the way you listened. So now–Joseph."

New doubt and fear welled up within him.

"But I'm willing to listen!"

"Of course," Gorssmann said. He spoke calmly now and as calmly sat down in the overlarge chair. He breathed slowly again and was obviously pleased. "But not a few moments ago. Listen. When you return to this room you will have made up your mind. One way or the other." He paused. "There are only two ways, Baron–only two."

## Chapter Five

"THIS IS JOSEPH," Gorssmann said.

Baron turned to face a kindly-looking man of about six feet, with heavy shoulders. The man wore a gray knitted crew-necked sweater and dark trousers. He was somewhere in his late twenties.

"No use trying to talk with him," Gorssmann said. "He is a deaf-mute. A good enough fellow. There is nothing else wrong with him. Only that he makes his money in a rather violent way." He gestured broadly with his arm.

Baron felt his own arm gripped brutally and he was sent spinning across the room into darkness. He came up against a wall, looked back. The man Joseph was coming toward him slowly with the light from the desk gleaming over his shoulders, putting his figure in silhouette.

Baron knew already that he could do nothing with this man. It seemed futile to him. Everything seemed futile, yet he heard the sound of his voice yet again; he heard its meagerness and there was the sound of futility here, too. "There's no need of this," he said.

"Perhaps not," Gorssmann said.

Arnold came across the room and opened another door leading into darkness. He reached around the jamb and snapped on a light. The room was bare and Baron went spinning into it–into a field of bright white light. The door slammed and Joseph stood with his back against it, watching him.

Baron saw only the brilliant white of the walls, the cement floor. The walls were like silver, like mirrors that reflected only light, not images. The glare was achingly intense. High on the walls, all around the room, were racked the bright white floodlights that shone downward, and he could feel their heat.

He turned again to Joseph. The man started walking toward him. Baron opened his mouth to say something, then closed it, remembering what Gorssmann had said.

Joseph reached for him.

Baron dived. He wanted to get inside those hands, grapple, fight. Rage took him, rebellion, and he struck out, not against the man before him, but against an utter and complete helplessness that overwhelmed him.

He picked himself up off the floor. He did not even recall being struck. Then his head began to pain as if it were being slowly crushed. He looked for windows. There were no windows. The door was closed.

Joseph walked across the room and leaned against the wall, watching him. The man looked ordinary. Bigger than average, but there was nothing in his face to explain this. He did not smile. At the same time he did not grimace. He was breathing normally.

Baron rose to his feet. He looked at the man, wondering.

Joseph stepped quickly up to him.

There was confusion in Baron's mind, and fear. Not being able to reach this man, knowing he could not hear, could not speak, was somehow agonizing.

Joseph sighed shortly and his lips tightened very slightly. He closed in rapidly. Baron tried to outguess him, tried to reach him, fighting. It was useless. The man was trained completely and flawlessly.

He was rocked with a terrible blow to the head, another from the opposite side. Then he was kicked in the stomach. He sprawled backward on the floor. His head struck the cement and he lay there looking up at the man.

Joseph stepped in close to him and kicked him in the side of the face. He slammed his foot against his head, kicked him in the side, stepped upon him with his full weight, went across the room and leaned against the wall. He stared at the floor, not at Baron.

It was mad.

An agony of pain swept over him, then gradually diminished in falling waves of color through his mind. He lay there in this dying, breathing pain on the cold cement.

Then he came quickly to his feet, made for the door, tried the knob. It was locked. He turned and Joseph was still leaning against the wall, watching.

His life had weakened him. He had not eaten properly in weeks, months. He realized for the first time in a year, and cared, what a physical wreck he was. All of this was senseless. What was it Gorssmann wanted him to do? What had he said about Bette? It could not be true!

He had to get away from here. The man he sought was alive. Gorssmann knew who he was. That was the single thought. He must reach the police–somebody.

Joseph walked toward him.

Now he fought.

He fought as never before in his life. Half laughing with the pain of memory, he saw in a flash that he had never been forced to fight anything before. His battle had all been inside, all this while, all these months. Physically, he was a mess. He felt old, useless, overwhelmed. It took him less than a minute to see how futile it was to fight back. He could not even touch the man. Joseph was beating him with a steady, calm completeness that was terrifying. Hardly a part of his body was left unbruised.

Finally he could not rise from the floor. He tried hard, but nothing moved. Then he lost consciousness.

He was seated in the chair by Gorssmann's desk. The big man himself held a glass of brandy to his lips. Arnold helped hold him in the chair and he came to that way.

He wrenched, choked on the brandy. Gorssmann stepped back, looked at him, put the glass on the desk. He went around the desk, walking smoothly, effortlessly, and sat down.

"Arnold. Let him go."

Baron heard the voice through the ringing in his ears. He knew the hands that were supporting him went away. He knew he was falling, but he could not prevent it. He sprawled from the chair and landed on the green rug with his head under the huge desk. He was bleeding. His mouth was filled with blood.

He lay there for some time. Finally he worked himself back to the chair, pulled himself up, and sat down. His head was loose on his shoulders and he had difficulty in keeping his eyes focused. There was a peculiar buzzing in his head.

Joseph was gone.

"Unpleasant," Gorssmann said. "More brandy?"

He shook his head. He said nothing. It was a kind of wild blathering of sound. He tried again. The same thing happened. He nearly wept and fought and tried still again.

"No more brandy. No, thanks."

He laughed. The laughter changed to a fit of coughing and he coughed blood in a vicious spray, bending down with his head between his knees, laughing and choking and coughing.

He sat up again, looked at Gorssmann. Gorssmann was sitting cockeyed in his chair. The desk was cockeyed, on a slant. Then it straightened and at the same moment something cracked inside his head and all was perfectly clear and normal again, though painful.

"Odd," Gorssmann said. "I'll bet you don't know how close to death you came, Baron. Really, now. The human mind can't believe that, because it suspects a great deal more pain and agony to come before death. Actually that's not the case at all. You can go along like that and die, never even realizing. Here nor there. Enough. Now, what do you think?"

"Is Bette all right?"

"She is all right. She is alive. You will even see her, probably."

"What is it you want me to do?"

"Tell you some now, some later. Please, here–Arnold! Take Monsieur Baron to the washroom. Help him clean up."

"You're a Red–a Communist."

"No," Gorssmann said. "Naturally you would think that. I hate them as much as you. Or do you?" Gorssmann chuckled. "You were prepared not to hate them, eh? No, we are not Communists. I am not."

"Come, monsieur," Arnold said.

Baron staggered to his feet. When he walked it felt as if he were wading.

The washroom was at the back of the big room in which they had been seated. When he looked in the mirror, he did not seem nearly so battered as he had imagined. At least, this was so once he washed the blood away.

Arnold proved to be no help whatever. Arnold had discovered that his fingernails were dirty.

"Yes," Gorssmann said. "On the road to Cassis. You know Cassis?"

Baron nodded. "I've been there—swimming."

"Well, this is on the road. It is secret, of course. We know it is an airplane factory, that much we know. France is working hard, Baron, very hard, behind those walls."

"Walls?"

"Fences, really."

"But what do you want me to—"

"You will know soon enough. For the time being you will go home, gather yourself together. I will give you some money." Gorssmann paused, watching him. "Did that bother you much? My telling you I will give you some money? Does it trouble you deeply?"

He shook his head. He knew enough now to admit nothing.

"It does not matter," he told Gorssmann.

"A spoken truth, though still a lie, is sometimes as good as the real thing," Gorssmann said. He chuckled. "We all have to go through this time. It is—difficult. For some it is *very* difficult. You will have this money. Buy clothes, eat some steak, plenty. Do not drink so much. But I need not tell you these things because you are thinking about Elene—and Bette—and yourself. You are concerned now, Baron. You are concerned with the same things we are, even though obliquely. *N'est-ce pas?*"

Baron said nothing.

"Certainly. We must think of our loved ones and of ourselves." Gorssmann grinned. "You see how it works?"

"Yes. I'm afraid I do."

"For example, you hate me, but"–he raised his eyebrows–"it doesn't hurt me and we accomplish great things together. Eh?"

"If you say so."

"That is better. You are regaining your humor. You had too much humor a while ago. But, then, humor is a precious thing. Without it a man is doomed from the start."

"Yes. What is it you want me to do?" His voice was solemn and, hearing it, he felt the faint faraway toll of doom. He was startled that his mind worked this way. He knew he was beat down. He knew he must not let Gorssmann see too much of how he felt.

"You are a good friend of Paul Chevard's. French aeronautics. The Air Ministry. He is a big part of this. It is a plane, Baron–a jet-powered plane. I know little of this, only what is necessary for my part of the enterprise. It is enough to say that no other country has achieved what they have at the plant near Cassis. You know something of this thing called 'thrust'?"

Baron nodded.

"What seems to be the most accepted high standard of pound thrust in the very best of jet-engined airplanes?"

Baron sighed, thinking back, then covering the three empty years since he had been in the industry. "Possibly ten thousand pounds," he said.

"You know how necessary this is to the capacity performance of advanced jet engines?"

Baron nodded.

"Then imagine performance at double that. Twenty thousand pounds thrust, perhaps more–surely more, from the rumors. No country has approached it."

Baron watched tensely as Gorssmann leaned forward. The big man's face went slightly red again.

"Do you know what this will mean to whatever country has it? The country that can develop this thing? I will tell you. The air industry has to combat a single terrible enemy. During wartime, because of intensified production, this enemy is doubly bad. The enemy is time, Baron. A powerful new plane is built. Millions of dollars are spent on design and models. Yet, in a matter of months, sometimes weeks, the machine is obsolete because of ceaseless innovation." He paused, watching, waiting.

Baron was far ahead of him now, his mind catapulting through this story.

"The country that has this thing is a good ten years beyond every other country. See? You can answer the rest for yourself. I do not lie about this."

"And Chevard?"

"We must work by different means. All countries use various means. This time you are the means, Baron. We have known of you, waited patiently for the proper time, and–here it is." He hesitated, coughed lightly. "When you began your foolish questioning, after the collapse of your business, one of us came up with the idea. Things were not yet ready. So we let you work yourself to the bottom, both physically and mentally. Now you are ready, and we are ready." Gorssmann shrugged.

It was like standing in the middle of a treacherous swamp, having tried for untold time to find solid ground. Then someone explains quietly that there is no solid ground. There is only swamp, forever and ever.

"You know these people. You are friends of theirs. Chevard likes you, we know. They believe in you. You will approach them and explain that you are–on the road back. Yes. You wish to start life anew, build yourself up again. Eventually prove yourself innocent of the foolish charges laid against you by your own country. They will understand. What better than to take you into their confidence? You will take a job of some kind in the plant over by Cassis."

"It will never work."

"Ah, but it will. If it wouldn't, you would not be here, or in France, and your daughter would be in Florida–or possibly even with you someplace in America. Now." He stood, overwhelming the desk, his huge meaty face smiling in its own fashion. "I will tell you this much: The tremendous capacity of this plane is accomplished by what we know of as a 'breather.' It is a simple enough invention, possibly. But there is only the one, you see? Anyone can equal the building of the engine. But the breather, no. It is so secret it even makes me perspire to speak its name. Can you guess what your job will be?"

Baron watched Gorssmann. He could say nothing. He could not trust his voice.

Gorssmann shrugged. "It is just as well. I will talk with you again, and explain. For now, then, here...." He opened a drawer in the desk, took out a bundle of franc notes with a rubber band around them, and handed them to Baron. "Take this and get yourself in order. We will contact you. Do not move from your present address."

"Suppose I fail?"

"You will not fail." Gorssmann came around the desk, pressed him to his feet, guided him toward the door. Arnold stood up and looked at them. "You are the only man who can do this job. There is no such thing as failure. Every move is blueprinted, Baron. And, Baron–I can never tell you how important this is. You are the man. You go home now. Rest, become a person again."

He felt dizzy, sick, his body ached. It all had to be a dream.

"Lili," Gorssmann called, opening the door. "Show Arnold and Monsieur Baron out. Thanks."

Arnold preceded him through the door. He turned away from the door, looked again at Gorssmann.

"When will I see my daughter?" he said. He could not keep the anxiousness from his voice. "You're certain she's all right?"

Gorssmann grinned. "In time you will see her. She is perfectly safe." He closed the door in Baron's face.

Baron turned and Lili rose from the table where she was painting. She laid down her brush and stepped up to them, where they stood beside the Chinese screen. She was a very pretty girl, her black hair gleaming in the subdued lighting of the room. She smiled faintly at Baron, held out her hand.

He took it, felt a warm pressure.

"Welcome, monsieur," she said.

Arnold grunted impatiently beside him. Suddenly Baron was startled and he stared hard at the girl Lili. Her face was expressionless now. He wondered if he could have been wrong. Then it happened again. Lili, holding his hand, quickly but obviously scratched the center of his palm with her index finger in a universally accepted gesture. Just as quickly, then, she released his hand and turned away.

"*Alors,*" Arnold said. "Quickly. Come, we go."

Baron stared at Lili's back. But already she had settled herself at the table and was again dipping her brush into the paint on a colorfully neat pallet.

## Chapter Six

HE STOOD ON THE CANNEBIERE and watched the Opel vanish up the street, the taillight winking redly. It was the exact spot where he had been standing hours ago, when the car stopped before him.

He started on along the street. His body pained him in every muscle as he moved. He was bewildered. He did not know what to do, what was happening to him.

A girl stepped toward him from a doorway. "Monsieur!"

"What?" He turned to her.

"Ah, *Américain!*" she gushed, came up next to him. Her breath reeked of cognac and her eyes were blackly wicked. "Sailor, eh? Dronk, eh? Zigzag, eh, babee?"

"Go away."

"Babee, listen. Babee!" She grabbed his arm, slung her plump hip against him. She showed him her teeth and they were not good. "Me plenty good," she said, her black eyes whirling, glittering like twin pots of sin.

"Please," he said.

"Too much dronk?"

"No."

"You sick?"

He tried to pull away from her.

"I no sick, babee. Hot like hell. Babee, you come weez me, eh? Me good for you, babee. Zigzig, plenty good. Zigzig, babee!"

He yanked away from her. "You missed the boat," he said. He walked on up the street, limping slightly, bewildered.

"*Cochon!*" she screeched after him. "Peeg, peeg, feelthy peeg! Dronk! *Cochon!*"

He heard her heels clatter wildly toward him on the pavement. Then they stopped. He glanced back. She was beneath a street light, watching him. Her face was flat white. Lipstick was smeared all over her mouth, down on her chin. She turned, walking slowly in the other direction, reeling slightly. Her purse, hanging from one hand, scraped the sidewalk as she moved away toward the harbor.

He went on, reached the Rue Paradis, and turned to the right.

Gorssmann. Hugo Gorssmann. All in one night. He could not believe it, and thinking of Bette in Gorssmann's hands made him ill all over again. And Elene, what about Elene? Good Lord, what was he to do?

He had to go to the police.

That *was* a laugh.

The street was not busy. The city seemed calm. An occasional legionnaire hurried along, apparently sober. They drew hardly enough pay to get drunk. Music slammed from some of the cafés; other cafés were absolutely empty and looked like old-fashioned drugstores back home, with the cold enamel, the zinc bar, and the twisted wire chairs.

He entered one he knew and ordered cognac.

The bartender, Pierre, was very thin, gray-faced, with a long lock of hair hanging down the side of his face. He stared at Baron, frowned.

"You sick?" he said.

"No. The cognac, Pierre."

"*Bon.*"

He paid the man, yanked one of the notes from the bundle. It was a five-hundred-franc note. Pierre stared at it, then stared at him.

"What you owe?"

"Sure, take it out."

Pierre rang it up, gave him back ten francs, and smiled broadly.

He drank the cognac. It was like water. He looked at the glass.

"Pierre. Did you see Elene tonight?"

"Elene? No. She was in early, not late. She came in, bought cigarettes, and went away. That was all."

He turned and left. He moved on up the street, walking in a kind of vacuum. He turned in at Number 77, went up the long flight of black stairs lighted only by the dim saffron glow from the downstairs hallway. The stairs creaked. The house smelled of old cognac, old wine, old fish, old bread, old years, and old love.

His door was open. He had not locked it. He went in, pulled the tasseled cord on the 1927 lamp with the wild-angled shade. It glowed once again with that scarlet light. Elene's idea. "Better for the eyes, *chéri,*" she had said.

The bed was unmade. It was sway-backed, a double bed that smelled like an old double bed. He limped across the room and stared at himself in the big, mottled mirror over the dresser. He leaned on the dresser with both hands, looking at himself.

He was a mess and he certainly did look sick. Joseph had spared his face, though. There were no cuts on his face, only large swellings along either jawline and beside each eye by the temples. It changed his appearance considerably. He looked as though he had his cheeks full of cake. His eyes were muddy and harried.

He returned to the bed, slumped down on it. He stared at the threadbare, colorless carpet on the floor. The sagging, faded curtains on the window fluttered in a small wind. Somebody out on the street shouted at somebody else and a girl laughed high on the scale, cutting it off sharply.

He lay down on the bed and stared at the ceiling, at the stretches of peeling paint he and Elene had often counted. Twenty-seven spots, there were. Five spots had appeared since he had lived in the room. You never saw them come; they appeared as if by magic.

He had to go to the police. He knew this. He knew that no matter how long he remained here on the bed, he would eventually get up and go to the police.

He began to perspire, just lying there.

He could not stay on the bed. It had become already a kind of cell, a method of imprisonment, because of his strong sense of being so completely trapped. He was surrounded with a bulwark so strong and so neatly rigged that there was no possibility of a loophole.

He knew Gorssmann and the rest of his clan would allow no loophole. Since they had spent months arranging things, they certainly had overlooked nothing.

He came to his feet from the edge of the bed in a rush. He limped to the dresser, fumbled in a cluttered ash tray for a decent-sized cigarette butt, lit it, and began to pace the room. He paced consciously. He tried to keep on the move, attempting in some way to find enough nerve to take action. Nerve, that was it.

He had never thought of himself as a courageous man. He would stand up to whatever he had to, but, too, he had never clearly expected to find himself in a position such as this. How could he have been such a fool as to spend the past two and a half years and every bit of his money trying to locate somebody he didn't even know? He must have been mad.

Did he still want to find this man, this person, this existence? He asked himself the question, standing in the center of the room, staring at the small cigarette butt. Yes. The answer was there, all right, waiting.

He had come this far, he would not stop now. He went over and sat on the edge of the bed and stared at the scarlet lamp shade. But how? How was he to find a way? He dropped the cigarette on the floor and ground it out with his foot in a light fury of exasperation.

They were more than clever. And he was more than absurd.

He had to treat it all logically and very slowly. And he must hang onto whatever presence of mind he possessed.

This thought brought laughter to his lips. But the laughter vanished when he suddenly recalled what Gorssmann had said about Bette. How was it possible than men could weave such a perfect web about another man? It was done, he believed Gorssmann. Bette was in their hands. What should he do? What could he do?

He remembered that afternoon in Atlanta when he had last seen Bette. She had been with her mother at Patricia's father's home and Patricia had been out.

He remembered how Bette had looked, there on the big old gallery. The honeysuckle was in bloom, and her eyes were glowing with freshness and happiness at seeing him.

"Don't you want to see her?" Bette said. "She'll be back shortly."

"Not if I can help it, honey."

"I understand."

"I'm glad you do. I'm going to Europe. I wish you could come with me. It's been six months since I've seen you." And he tried to discover how she lived and what boys she was going with, what she did for fun, how Patricia treated her, without asking it outright. And all the time his mind had been clouded with the thoughts of his trailing.

And he had learned little or nothing from her. Just that she was healthy and young and vital, and that she wanted to be with him.

"Aren't there some arrangements you can make?" she asked. "Can't you do something?"

"You know what your mother would do."

"Yes."

She was sitting in the hammock, lying back against the pillows, swinging idly. He watched from his perch on the gallery railing, where he could see the drive, in case Patricia should return unexpectedly. Bette was truly a beautiful creature, and he felt a father's pride and it wrenched him some inside, knowing he could not enjoy time with her. Blue-eyed, blonde, fresh, and vitally young. Talking with her made him feel old, stale. He knew that if he could be with her more often this feeling would vanish.

"I read the papers," she said. "You're a heller, aren't you? Frank Baron's prolonged bat. Where does he get the money? You know what they say, Dad? They say you should have been shot." She paused. "But it's dying out, lately. If you only wouldn't get yourself into the newspapers like you do."

"Sophistication doesn't become the young," he told her.

"Phooey," she said. "Don't you worry about me."

"I mean the way you talk, Bette."

"I have to be sophisticated," she said. "You should see the circles we travel in. Mamma is a dear."

"A dear what?"

"That's a good question."

"Do you believe what you read in the papers?"

"Certainly not. I know what you're doing."

"What does your mother say?"

"Good riddance."

He watched her, drinking her in, because he had no idea when he would see her again. She was growing up so suddenly. The last time he'd been with her, she had not talked this way. She had been a little girl then. She was greatly changed and it had seemed to happen overnight. There were so many things he wanted to know about her and he wasn't finding out anything. He supposed other fathers had been through the same situation.

The one thing he was happy about, that had troubled him more than anything else before seeing her, was that she somehow had not grown away from him. If anything, they were closer than before. She was a wonderful girl, soon to be a woman, and he was proud of her. He was proud of her beauty and of her mind and—well, of her. He wondered how she had managed to miss Patricia's stamp. He had worried about that, too.

"You know," she said, "you arrived here a little over an hour ago, and you'll be leaving soon. I don't like it."

He shrugged. He wanted to talk, to get really close to her. But there seemed no way. Right now was as close as they would ever get.

She had gone very serious just then. The expression on her face changed and her eyes had become inquisitive and sober. She stopped rocking back and forth in the hammock and the skirt of her brightly flowered dress was stilled and he could smell the honeysuckle.

"You're not letting what they did get you, are you, Dad?"

He shook his head.

"Really, why are you traveling all over like you do? Why do the newspapers print what they do?"

Again he shrugged. There was no way of explaining. So long as she knew the stories weren't so, that was enough. He could not tell her what the truth was. It would be too laborious.

"Are you trying to rectify it?" she asked.

He said nothing.

"You are, aren't you?"

"What makes you think that?" he said.

"Because that's what I would do. I'm darned if I'd let them lie the way they do. Mother believes it all, you know. But I don't. I want you to know that." She smiled. "It gave me a hard shell."

He laughed and she laughed and he went on staring and smelling the honeysuckle, wondering in the back of his mind if Patricia would return. Maybe he even wanted to see Patricia. See what she looked like. Know what Bette was up against, because he knew Patricia now.

"It's almost like that story, 'The Man without a Country.' People believe it that way."

"It's nobody's fault," he said. "These things happen, and let's forget them. Someday it'll be all cleared up."

"I hope so. But I've never had a chance to talk with you about it."

"We haven't had a chance to talk at all." And then he had gone over there and placed his hand on her head. "Maybe someday soon," he said, and she looked up at him, smiling, and then the smile vanished.

"Here's Mother," she said.

He turned. Patricia was driving into the yard. Bette leaned up quickly and hugged him and he kissed her good-by and left by the back door. He cut through the alley. And when he reached the street across the block, he looked back and Bette was standing there by the garden gate at the corner of the alley and she waved to him.

He remembered how the afternoon slant of sunlight had struck her hair, and fire seemed to shoot out of it, and he had wanted to go back there and get her.

Walking on around the corner of the block, to where his taxi waited, he realized they had said nothing to each other. The moments were gone and he hadn't asked the questions he had scrawled on the back of the envelope in his pocket, as a reminder. He had found out nothing.

And then, climbing into the taxi, he knew he had found out something. Bette was still his daughter and she was a fine girl and she had not forgotten him.

He returned to his hotel and wrote her a long letter explaining everything in detail; all that he was doing, all his hopes for her. He called for a messenger and had the letter delivered to her hand only. He did not wait for a reply, because his plane would leave in thirty minutes.

Sitting here on the edge of the bed, thinking about it, he could still smell the honeysuckle and hear the gentle creaking of the rope on the hammock.

He rose and stared at himself once again in the mirror, remembering everything. Elene, and she made him ache some inside too, and what kind of effort should he make? He knew he must go to the police.

He grabbed a towel, went down the hall, and washed. He brushed his suit as best he could, hunted up a pin of Elene's in the dresser, and fixed the tear in his trousers. He still looked raveled around the edges and swollen in the face. But they wouldn't think he was a drunk staggering in from the gutter.

After turning out the lamp, he stood for a few moments in the darkness of the room. A cosmic breather, he thought. That will mean atomic power as sure as hell. Maybe Gorssmann has the name twisted. He must.

Standing by the window, he carefully drew the curtains and looked down on the street. He felt melodramatic, yet he knew he had to convince himself thoroughly that every move he made would be serious. They had allowed him freedom on the streets because they knew he was hemmed in, that he could do nothing. They had not reckoned with how he felt. It was the culmination of all events that did it. He would take the chance, go to the police, there was no other way. He needed help–now.

He knew Gorssmann would have somebody watching him. It had to be, that was all. There wasn't even a question of doubt about this fact.

Funny about that girl Lili. Why had she done that? She certainly couldn't expect … But maybe she did. He stared at his palm in the gray darkness, remembering.

Searching the street through the window, he saw nothing unusual. Not too busy, but moving with nighttime traffic. There were always loiterers on Paradis. A girl here, another there, waiting for the nothing they always waited for. A couple pressed into a doorway beside a café.

He left the room, went down to the street He was unable to breathe evenly. It was an effort to keep the wrong thoughts from his mind; the thoughts that would prevent him from going through with this. He turned to the right, walking up Paradis toward the Cours. He would pass the Palais de Justice, one block over. He tried to see if anybody followed him when he moved, but saw nothing.

This was the beginning. Because they needed him, they would not kill him immediately. But he had no illusions. They could make it uncomfortable and in the end there would be no chance for recovery of mistakes.

His palms were sweating and consciousness of the aching tooth began to return in sharp, painful waves. He couldn't seem to walk smoothly. He was much too tense, too watchful. Face it, he thought. You're scared stiff.

He wished he had a revolver. A gun of some kind. That was one thing he had to have. Just having a gun in your pocket helped.

He turned abruptly, crossed the street, and his breath lifted into his throat and caught. He saw the man. It was no one he had ever seen, but he knew the man was following him. As he turned to cross the street the man had stopped suddenly, wheeled, and faced the gray-glaring window of the closed bakery.

Baron paused in the middle of the street and looked at the man. The man kept his back turned, then suddenly sneaked a look at Baron over his left shoulder.

## Chapter Seven

BARON TURNED AWAY HURRIEDLY, forced himself to walk slowly toward the opposite curb. He reached the curb, and for a moment stood there in the grip of indecision. He broke into a nervous sweat, wanting to be as unobtrusive as possible and having no idea how. He suddenly felt that he needed more courage than he had.

Without actually staring at the man across the street, he moved on the sidewalk over into the doorway of a tobacco shop. It was closed, but a dim light burned at the rear of the store, the naked bulb dangling over a black steel safe. He turned his back to the man and peered into the tobacco shop, staring at the old safe. He knew very well that as soon as his back was turned, the man was watching him. He decided to go on up the street. Turning quickly, he tripped over a wooden box beside the shop doorway and nearly fell. His heels scraped and clattered on the sidewalk as he windmilled, seeking balance.

He stood absolutely still then, cursing quietly to himself. Then, turning, he stared at the man across the street. The man was gone.

Baron began walking. Immediately he saw the man again. This time the fellow was directly opposite him, on the far corner, leaning against a building.

A street girl came along on the sidewalk over there, and accosted the man.

Baron broke into a run, abruptly cut it off sharply, and walked into a café. He ordered a double brandy and drank it at a gulp. He left the café and started up the street again. He began to feel better. The brandy was a good thing. He knew he would have to lose the man who followed him, but lose him in a matter-of-fact way. It must not appear that he wanted to lose him. Because it shouldn't matter to him if the man followed him.

Baron turned his mind off completely, or thought he did. He was perspiring heavily now. His hair was matted on his head, and his belt was too tight, and his trousers were soaked with perspiration. His shoes hurt, and there was a hole in the toe of his left sock. With every step he took he could feel his toe rubbing against the damp, rough leather of the shoe.

He had to reach the police. He had started it now and he would finish it. What would he tell them? He had no idea. Yes. He would tell them everything. The truth. They would simply have to understand and come to his aid.

There seemed to be no relief. He turned left on the next street, walked fast, cut across the street, and entered an alley. He ran silently through the alley, very conscious of the toe in the shoe now, and came out on the small square before the prefecture. He ran across the square and around behind the building and turned right, still running, along Sylvabelle. There was no sign of the man. He cut across Sylvabelle and ran into another alley. He leaped breathlessly into the air, almost stomping on a man and a woman loving on the cobbled alley floor. The man swore and the woman groaned, her voice rising in monotonic waves, beating against the walls of the alley, following Baron as he ran. Reaching the end of the alley, he thought how odd it was that as he jumped over the couple back there, he had smelled the strong odor of tobacco.

Then he saw the taxi. He hailed it, rushing into the middle of the Rue Saint Jacques. The driver blasted the horn several times, the sound lifting merrily, wildly into the night. The taxi stopped. Baron hurried inside and sank back against the seat.

"*Commissariat de police,*" he said. "*Vite, pour l'amour de Dieu!*"

"*Très bien, monsieur.*"

As they moved away and cut through a dark alley, the horn blatting viciously, he watched for the man. He saw no sign of him.

So this is how it is, he thought. This is how it is when you're trying to get away, when somebody's after you. He lay back against the seat, with his head by the window, watching, trying to get his breath and still the frightened thudding of his heart.

A young man, an *agent de police*, met Baron as he entered the bare waiting room outside the office of the *commissaire*. The waiting room both looked and smelled like Baron's old grammar-school rooms. The floors were worn boards, well oiled, and there were benches around the walls, well polished by many impatient behinds. The benches were knife-nicked along their edges, and here and there Baron saw black initials and dates carved into the old oak. There were three brass spittoons at three corners of the room, beside the benches. In the very center of the room, in line with the pebbled glass door signifying the office of the *commissaire,* was a straight-backed, cane-bottomed chair. The *agent de police* stood leaning behind this chair, a hand on either side of the back. He regarded Baron coldly and with the self-conscious, penetrating, supercilious stare of a young, new officer.

"I must see the *commissaire,*" Baron said.

The *agent* said nothing. Baron gave him a long look, decided the man was half asleep, and brushed past him toward the door.

"What is your business?" the man said. He had taken Baron's arm as he walked by.

Baron looked at him again.

"Important," he said. "Urgent. International."

The *agent* did not change expression. He wore no hat. His cap was hanging on the inside doorknob of the door Baron had just entered. He had yellow hair, parted far down on the left side, just above the tip of his ear. The hair was combed flatly across his skull, toward the other side. It gave Baron the impression that the man looked out at him through a curved opening in a length of yellow pipe.

"*Américain?*"

"*Oui. Vite, s'il vous plaît.*"

The *agent* released Baron's arm. "It is late," he said.

Baron said nothing.

The man shrugged. "Wait," he said. He lounged across the room and creaked through the door into the office. The door closed.

Baron stood by the chair. He walked around the room. He looked up at the cold glass windows that circled the walls of the room, revealing nothing but water pipes. The room was not near an outside wall, and the windows were dark beyond the elbows and joints and sockets of water pipes. The pipes ran all around the room behind the windows. He waited a long time, perhaps five minutes.

Abruptly he stalked toward the office door. His first step in that direction brought the door open. The young *agent* returned, closed the door carefully, lounged over to the chair, and put either hand on its back once again. He did not look at Baron.

"Come back tomorrow," he said. "It is late."

A plain-clothes man came out of the office, rapidly closed the door, looked at neither of them, put his hat on, and left the waiting room. He was trying to shove a sheaf of papers into his right-hand coat pocket and they would not fit.

Baron stepped quickly over to the office door, opened it, and entered. Behind him the *agent* said, "Very well," and did not move. Baron closed the door.

The office was empty. There was a large desk cluttered with papers, and a black cheroot burned in a clean ash tray beneath a green-shaded desk lamp. Behind the desk large windows opened into an alley. The limb of a tree waved slowly behind the windows. On the left wall of the room was an open door and Baron heard somebody snorting in water in there. Then whoever it was coughed and spat and grunted.

Behind him the door opened and another uniformed officer entered. He walked quickly to the desk, put down an envelope, picked up another envelope, and left.

The *commissaire* came out of the washroom, drying his hands on a towel, still coughing. He stared at Baron, finished drying his hands, wiped the back of his neck under the open tunic, tossed the towel inside the washroom on the floor.

"What?" the *commissaire* said.

Baron started to say something, attempted something else, then stopped and said nothing.

The *commissaire* was bald. He was a stocky, red-faced man, with clear blue eyes, rather merry, Baron thought, and a wrinkled uniform. Under his eyes the flesh sagged in wrinkles, which went along with his dress. He moved decisively. He went to the desk, picked up the cheroot, poked at the envelope the other officer had left, coughed, and stuck the cigar in his mouth and chewed on it.

Finally he drew a great puff of smoke, breathed it out, stepped up to Baron. He stared into Baron's eyes and waited.

Baron opened his mouth and everything came out like water from a faucet. He told the *commissaire* the entire story, sparing nothing. Once it got going, he was not able to stop it for a moment. It rushed from him. Every word was a kind of pleasant relief and he drove toward the end, breathing hard, wanting to get it all out of him, onto somebody else's shoulders. As he talked he imagined himself somewhere peacefully resting, on a bed perhaps, with no troubles in the world, with nothing to bother him, with only peace and contentment just outside his door. It was a feeling that grew and grew as he talked, and by the time he finished he was smiling and the perspiration had begun to dry on his hands and face. His palms had been so damp they were uncomfortably dry now. He wiped them against his trousers.

"It is very serious," he told the *commissaire*. "You know of this Gorssmann? You know of Cassis?"

The *commissaire* nodded. He turned his back on Baron, went around his desk, and sat down in the large, high-backed, leather-upholstered chair. "Yes," he said. "I know of you, too, monsieur."

The *commissaire* stared at his desk and smoked his cheroot. Baron felt it becoming warm in this room again. His palms began to perspire again and something was starting all over again, down inside him. The moment of respite had been brief.

The chair creaked as the *commissaire* leaned back, smoking. He leaned forward, brushed the ash from the cheroot, rested it carefully on the tray, and leaned back again, creaking.

"Don't you understand?" Baron said.

"Let me see your identification."

Baron fumbled for his wallet in his jacket pocket, flung it on the desk in front of the *commissaire*.

The *commissaire* picked up a pencil and poked at the wallet. "Just your papers, please." He poked the wallet across the desk, past the ash tray, beyond the cluttered papers on the desk.

Baron showed him his papers. The *commissaire* nodded, handed them back.

"Who are you?" the *commissaire* said.

Baron stared at him.

"Please," the *commissaire* said.

Baron began to experience the same sensations he'd had when listening to Hugo Gorssmann. It was a feeling of complete enclosure and the sudden outrage down inside him sought for a way out, his mind instinctively feeling there was no way out.

"Why did you come here?" the *commissaire* said. "Providing you are Frank Baron, what can you want with us?"

"Don't you understand?"

The *commissaire* looked at him, rocked slightly in his chair, creaking. He leaned far back in the chair and looked at Baron. "Have you your passport?"

Baron swallowed whatever he'd planned to say. He found his passport, flipped it across the desk to the *commissaire*. He watched as the officer glanced quickly through the passport, compared the picture with the man before him, and grunted. "I see," the *commissaire* said. He handed the passport back to Baron.

"Obviously," Baron said. "You've got to do something."

"What are you doing in France?"

"Nothing in particular. Don't you see? Until now—"

The *commissaire* pursed his lips. He rapped his knuckles on the desk and shouted, "Henri!"

The office door behind Baron opened and the blond *agent* entered. He closed the door and raised his eyebrows at the *commissaire*.

"I warn you," Baron said, "you're losing time."

The *commissaire* looked at him and said to the young *agent de police*, "You will draw your pistol, Henri, and search this man."

Baron stood still and waited as Henri searched him and discovered nothing but the roll of franc notes. Henri tossed the franc notes on the desk, trying not to watch them too closely.

"What are you trying to do?" Baron said.

"Security measures," the *commissaire* told him.

"You doubt what I say is true?"

"It may very well be true."

"Then for God's sake, stop acting this way!"

"Anyway you look at it," the *commissaire* said, "it is bad." He picked up the cheroot, relit it from a greenish brass desk lighter, puffed, laid it in the ash tray, and leaned back in the chair. He scratched the back of his hand, swallowed, pursed his lips. "Your papers are not in order," he said.

"You're joking."

"I assure you, monsieur."

Baron turned all the way around, performing a kind of pirouette, then leaned across the desk. The perspiration had really started again. He could not seem to reach the *commissaire* and he was beginning to understand that there is nothing so disconcerting as not being able to reach somebody in time of real need. He had to convince the *commissaire*, but just looking at the man, he knew it was futile. The *commissaire* had made up his mind about something.

"You expect me to believe this tale?" the *commissaire* said.

"You've got to believe it."

"Henri," the *commissaire* said. He nodded toward a door on the other side of the office. Henri nodded back and Baron caught the look of pleasure in the man's eyes.

"We will have to detain you," the *commissaire* said.

"Oh, no," Baron said. "No, you don't!"

"Please," Henri said, nudging Baron with the barrel of his revolver toward the door on the other side of the room.

Baron shrugged him away, went around the desk belligerently.

"Arrest at attention," Henri said, "or I am forced."

"Go to hell."

"It is to warn."

Baron bent over the *commissaire*, grabbed his arm, held his face close to the man. His voice was even louder than he'd thought of making it. "You've got to do something," he said. "You can't just sit here. The Republic is in danger, *monsieur le commissaire*. Don't be a fool."

"He calls you the fool," Henri said. "Release or I am forced."

The *commissaire* looked at Baron, and nodded toward Henri. Baron understood what he meant. Henri would, in another moment, obey the impulse.

"How did you find out about Cassis?" the *commissaire* said.

"I told you," Baron said.

"Laughing," Henri said.

"Do so," the *commissaire* said to Henri. Henri came over and took Baron's arm, held the gun just under his elbow, and began to guide him across the room toward the door.

"My apologies, monsieur," the *commissaire* said from behind them, and the chair creaked. He heard the *commissaire* leave the office and the door slammed.

It was the detention room. Henri thrust him aside, closed and locked the door. There had been no need to tell him not to try to escape. There was no way out. There were no windows. Only one door led from the room and it was a solid oak door. He heard Henri on the other side of the door, pacing the office floor.

There were several chairs in the detention room and a single golden oak table about eight feet long. There were two dry inkwells on the table and three broken-nibbed pens. A single sheet of paper was by one inkwell somebody had doodled on it. There was a steam radiator, stained with rust where it leaked at one end, and the air in the room was very close.

A key scraped in the lock of the door, the door opened partially, and the *commissaire* leaned around the jamb, looking at Baron. "We cannot at this time allow you the usual," he said. "You understand this? It demands the utmost. Security is vital. I am sorry, monsieur."

Baron made for the door. The door closed and the key grated and clicked.

"Truly," the *commissaire* said from the other side of door. "Wait a little." Baron heard him walk away.

Somewhere in the building a telephone began to ring.

Baron tried to tell himself that at least he was safe. It was a conclusion reached very deviously and it did not help at all. It only seemed to make matters worse, and for the space of a moment he lost his head. He went over to the door and banged on it with both fists as the precariousness of his position became clear. Finally he quit that and went over and sat in one of the chairs by the large table. Nobody had answered when he banged on the door.

Gorssmann would never suspect for a moment that he had come to the police. No sane man would have done this. It placed not only himself, but Bette and Elene, in horrible danger. How could he have been such a fool? If Gorssmann somehow got wind of this, it would be all over. He tried to discover the true motive for his coming to the law, but his mind drew a blank. He was here. It had seemed the right thing to do. Now he knew he must somehow get away.

Again he left his chair, with Bette's name flashing on and off in his mind like a red light. He went to the door and began banging on it again. They could not hold him like this. He had to get away, find somebody who would listen, and act.

He began to see how things really were more and more clearly and he knew he had to get hold of himself. Gorssmann might, at this instant, be trying to reach him. The man who had been following him had probably by now reported his disappearance.

He pounded still harder on the door. He could hear the frantic thunder of his own knocking. It reverberated through the nighttime emptiness of the old building, and above the knocking, like an old woman's intermittent screams, the telephone rang and rang.

### Chapter Eight

ABOUT A HALF HOUR PASSED and Baron felt himself slipping toward a very real despair. There had been no answer to his knocking on the door and the telephone finally stopped ringing. His own mental condition was a trap now. There were pitfalls he had to avoid. It was a battle to stay clear, of them. The one thought that tortured him most was the memory of what Gorssmann had said about Bette. He could find no way of forgiving himself for coming to the police. He called himself every name he could think of as he paced the worn board floor of the detention room. Nothing helped.

He did not hear the door open.

"Monsieur?"

He whirled as the *commissaire* spoke loudly.

"Someone to see you, monsieur," the *commissaire* said. He stepped aside in the doorway, brandishing a newly lighted cheroot, and a tall cadaverous man strode past him. The man came on into the detention room and stood looking at Baron across the large expanse of table.

"This is Louis Follet," the *commissaire* said.

For a long moment nobody spoke. The *commissaire* sighed abruptly, took another frantic puff on his cheroot, turned his back, and closed the door. Baron heard the distinct sound of the key in the lock, the click as the bolt shot into place..

Baron was slightly disconcerted about Follet. He did not know who he was, but he was of that type seen hanging around water-front bars. His clothes were wrinkled, baggy, the gray suit well worn, the stringy tie raveled on one side. He carried a soft felt hat partially crushed in one hand. He was very thin, but large-boned, his cheeks sunken in a gray face that did not smile. The only lively thing about Follet was the probing look in his eyes.

"Yes?" Baron said.

Follet said nothing. He kept watching Baron with those bright-blue eyes that seemed to burn in his head like the blue flame on an alcohol lamp. The eyes did not waver. The eyes simply watched and watched and Baron began to feel the perspiration again.

Follet placed his hat beneath the elbow of his left arm, probed his pockets until he found tobacco and cigarette papers. Standing there, watching, he rolled himself a fat cigarette with long curling shreds of tobacco. The shreds hung from the end of the cigarette as he lit it. From the time he lit the cigarette until it burned out close to his lips, Follet never took it from his mouth..

"I am from the *Sûreté Générale*, Department of Air Intelligence," Follet said at last. The cigarette jiggled between his lips as he spoke. Otherwise he did not move.

Baron quit looking at the man. He went and slumped into a chair by the table, folded his hands on the table, and looked at them. He listened to Follet breathe and decided the man was consumptive.

"You are now in the hands of the secret police," Follet said.

"Must we talk in code?"

"You are bitter?"

Baron started to explode, managed to stifle it. He heard Follet's quiet chuckle, glanced up. Follet's face hadn't changed. The chuckle worked its way around the cigarette.

"Would you mind very much telling me everything you told the *commissaire?* The *commissaire* is a good man, but prone to excitement, monsieur. It would help if I heard this extravaganza from your own lips."

Baron said nothing.

"Please, monsieur," Follet said. "I promise to listen carefully."

Baron looked at Follet again. He decided to hell with it. He might as well tell him. They would keep him here anyway, and Follet somehow did not seem like the *commissaire.*

"All right," Baron said. He went through it all once more. He told Follet as thoroughly as he could, everything. He did not want to have to tell it again. Even thinking about it made him ill. When he finished, he was so worked up he could no longer sit in the chair. Again he began to pace the room. "I came here thinking I could get some help," Baron finished. "Now I find nobody believes me."

"Pitiful, isn't it?" Follet said. He moved over to a chair by the table, stuffed his hat in his jacket pocket, and, folding himself carefully, almost mechanically, he sat down, leaned his head back, and watched Baron. "May I see your passport, monsieur?"

Baron found his passport, flung it across the table. Follet's hand snatched it up. He glanced quickly through the passport. "You say you are Frank Baron?"

"Yes," Baron said. "I am Frank Baron. Can't you read?"

"Monsieur, please," Follet said. He picked a shred of tobacco from his lip, wiped it on the edge of the table, breathed smoke, and handed Baron his passport. "It is true, the picture there is of you. A good, clear picture, too, I might add. No doubt at all about that. But see for yourself. Your name is Longwell–Herbert Longwell, of Richmond, Virginia." Follet breathed some more smoke as Baron flipped incredulously through the passport. "Can you blame the *commissaire?*"

"But–I *am* Frank Baron!"

"*Certainement!*"

"Are you ridiculing–"

"But no, monsieur. I know for a fact that you are Frank Baron. I know all about you." Follet waved his hand across his face, dropped the hand into his lap. The cigarette jiggled between his lips. "You are in trouble, monsieur."

Something like a cloud of relief spread through Baron. His hand was trembling as he held the passport. In the back of his mind he realized that somehow Gorssmann had substituted this faked identification for his real papers, but more than that, he sensed in Follet's voice the thing he had been looking for: understanding.

"Well?" Follet said.

Baron looked at him. "What do you mean?"

Follet shrugged, puffed rapidly at his cigarette. There were tiny tinges of red high on his cheeks and his eyes burned brightly. He coughed mildly around the cigarette.

"I am satisfied you are telling the truth," Follet said. "But truly, monsieur, you are in a terrible position. I have no way of telling you how terrible." He paused. "I have no right to tell you how terrible."

"I don't understand."

"You will, monsieur. But what is it you want me to do?"

Baron began to feel the slow mounting wonder all over again. Was he never to find a shadow of peace?

"You did right in coming here," Follet said. "In one way, that is. In another way, it is the worst possible thing you could do. I mean, regarding your daughter, monsieur. I take it she means much to you?"

Baron nodded.

Follet shrugged again, the bony shoulders moving beneath the tent of his suit jacket. "And this—this girl, Elene Cordon? You are concerned about her, too?"

Again Baron nodded, turned away. He got what Follet was trying to say.

"Isn't there something you can do?"

Follet glanced away. The cigarette had gone out between his lips. He leaned over, spat it out on the floor, stepped on it, proceeded to roll himself another. Baron watched the long dangling shreds of tobacco fry and sizzle as Follet lit the new cigarette. It bobbled precariously between his lips.

"We know of Hugo Gorssmann," Follet said. "I have even met the man. Over ten years ago, monsieur, I allowed Gorssmann to slip between my fingers." Follet cursed obscenely. "He is a go-between; a very smooth operator. We would like to have him, monsieur. I would personally like to—But never mind. Gorssmann makes his contacts, arranges certain deals. He is of no country. He sells his merchandise to the highest bidder. Here in Europe, things are different from where you live, monsieur. There is much middle dealing. Small trifles are planned and carried out with magnificent energy and scheming. This is no small trifle. Gorssmann will stand, as he told you, to make enough to retire on it." Follet paused, smoking. "It is obvious what he wishes you to do."

"Yes?"

"To steal this thing that is so important. We know of Cassis, the plant, Baron. What Gorssmann says is true."

Baron began to pace again. Follet seemed to be avoiding the issue.

"You know, of course," Follet said, "that when you complete the job for Gorssmann, there is but one thing?"

Baron paused, turned, looked at Follet.

"Death, monsieur," Follet said. "Hugo Gorssmann was lying in his teeth. I don't wish to alarm you, but your daughter, monsieur—"

"Don't say it!" The words rushed from Baron's lips.

Follet shrugged again. He was completely calm, composed. "You must face these things, or not face them—as you choose."

Baron sat in a chair at the table, rose and paced, then returned to the chair and sat again. All the time he was very conscious of Follet's eyes following his every move. He knew Follet watched him, trying to discover something. He wondered what it was. One kind of light burned in Follet's eyes—the light of question.

"We know who Gorssmann is dealing with now, too," Follet said. "But where the fellow is is something else again. It is a reincarnation of the Nazi movement in Germany, monsieur. The head of this movement is the man we want. There would be no sense in trying to stop Gorssmann. "

The words hung there in the air.

"What are you trying to say?" Baron asked.

Follet shrugged. "Simply this, monsieur. We cannot intervene."

Baron just sat there. He was stunned. He was unable to comprehend what Follet kept pressing at him.

"You mean you'll do nothing?"

"Precisely."

"What about me?"

"What about you?"

They looked at each other for a long moment. Baron felt lost. He tried, in his mind, to find some solid ground to rest on for a moment, but everything seemed to be disintegrating chip by chip. The more he pursued this thing, the worse it became.

"You're going to hold me here?" Baron asked.

"But no, monsieur. That would be asinine. No. You are the guinea pig, monsieur."

Baron could not move. He kept on staring at Follet.

The building was very silent. All Baron could hear was the slow, contained breathing of Follet and the occasional whoosh as Follet dispelled smoke into the already stale, ancient air of the detention room.

"The plant at Cassis," Follet said. "We cannot touch it. It is a separate thing, monsieur. It has its own police, its own government. This is the only way for total security. If some actuality occurs, then we may step in. Until then–" Follet shrugged, puffed at his cigarette.

"But the French government," Baron said. His voice was loud and the anxiousness was in it very strong now and he recognized the fear, too. "I should think this would be important–vitally important."

"Believe me, it is. It is the most important thing in the Republic today, monsieur. There is nothing to equal it. If it goes awry, France loses a vital step toward regeneration." Follet paused, smoking quietly now. He slapped his hand on the table edge several times. Baron expected him to continue. Follet did not continue. He stopped slapping his hand on the table edge, raised his eyes, and looked at Baron. The eyes were quietly steady.

"But I came here because–"

"Because you desired aid, monsieur. Aid that we cannot give you." Follet's voice rose slightly now and there was a new note of seriousness here. "We want to help you, monsieur. It would give me great pleasure to act. But we cannot. We are always prepared for something of this kind. Do you know you have been under continual surveillance since you've been in France? Because we knew you were after the person who sabotaged your factories during the Korean war. It was becoming obvious to many, monsieur. We wanted you to lead us to this fellow." Follet shrugged. "Now I discover that Gorssmann is in on it. He has, as he told you, been leading you around by the nose. Monsieur, this is a tired world, a sick world. Europe writhes on a bed of fever, the sickest of all. We all play against each other. We gamble and we wait, we pray and we hope."

"And what are you trying to say?"

"That you are free. The door is no longer locked." Follet nodded toward the door of the detention room.

Baron stared at the door.

"Freedom is a peculiar thing," Follet said. "Isn't it? You can have it, and at the same time not have it."

Baron was unable to speak and Follet continued to smoke and wait. It was very obvious and Baron knew he was trapped beyond escape.

## Chapter Nine

FOLLET MOVED SLIGHTLY on his chair and cleared his throat.

"If we helped you now," he said, "if we stepped in and prevented this, we would stand to lose everything, monsieur. We would lose Gorssmann, surely. We would lose the one man who may mean more to Europe's destiny than even Hitler thought he might mean. This is the very man you would like to meet, monsieur. It is the man who will buy from Gorssmann. We cannot afford this."

Baron wanted to say something. He still could not speak.

"This has happened quickly, I admit," Follet said. "But we are used to this. One acts when one can, not before—usually after, when it is too late." He stopped speaking abruptly, watching Baron closely now.

"You mean you want me to continue with Gorssmann? Just as though I never came to you?"

"It's up to you," Follet said. But Baron saw the obvious relief in the man's eyes. "Entirely up to you. You will leave here, just as you came in. Free and not free. We will never bother you, perhaps. Remember this, monsieur. From the time you leave this building, we do not even know you exist beyond what anyone knows from the newspapers. We know of no Herbert Longwell. We know *nothing!*"

"I see."

"I hope so. And this remember: We cannot help you in *any* way. No matter what happens to you, it is not our concern, unless you tread on us—as anybody might. It is completely up to you. We will be forced to treat you the same as we would treat Gorssmann, if it comes to that. You must understand this. From the moment you leave here, we don't know you, until you cross our path. It must be this way. If at any time you wish to speak with me, it will be arranged. We will be around, perhaps. You'll never know. But you will be treated as though we were not around. You, monsieur, as of right now, are an enemy agent–a spy in the pay of an international spy ring." Follet clawed in the breast pocket of his suit, tossed the bundle of franc notes on the table. "You know what happens to spies?"

Baron frowned.

"It can easily happen to you, monsieur. Like that!" Follet snapped his fingers loudly. He stood up, withdrew his smashed felt hat from his pocket, began straightening it. "If you do ever wish to reach me, come to the Café Demoiselle on the Prado, near the Place Castellane. Speak to the madame, ask for Room Two. You will remember?"

Baron's mind was in a whirl. He nodded. He experienced the sudden desire to run, to run someplace, anyplace at all, and hide.

"You can do nothing?" Baron said. "Nothing at all?"

Follet took the cigarette from his mouth, dropped it on the floor, stepped on it. He smiled at Baron. He rapped Baron lightly on the shoulder. "*C'est la vie,* eh?"

Baron wished he did not feel as ill as he did.

"Come," Follet said. "I wish to show you something. We will take a small ride together, then I will leave you."

Baron walked dazedly toward the door. Follet opened it and they went into the office of the *commissaire*. The *commissaire* was not there. They went on through, across the waiting room. The *agent's* hat still hung on the doorknob. Baron walked with one hand in his pocket, his fingers clenched around the bundle of franc notes.

"We will use the back way," Follet said.

They walked through the silent, dark building, out into a still darker alley. A car was waiting. They climbed into the rear seat and a driver in plain clothes started the engine.

"It won't take long, monsieur," Follet said.

Baron sat silently in the midst of despair.


They entered a small driveway behind a gate, shielded by tall shrubbery. After the car stopped, Follet guided Baron through a shadowed doorway and into a broad hall lit with dim bulbs along its ceiling.

"Through this door, please," Follet said.

Baron did not even wonder what was coming. As they went down a flight of stairs and into a fairly large room, cement-walled, cool, and approached a desk, he could think only of the many things Follet had told him. And his mind mused on the impolite edge of fear. He heard Follet speaking with a man at the desk, but he paid them no attention. Follet again took his arm, guided him down the length of the room. They stopped by a table covered by a sheet. Baron's heart rocked abruptly and the fear mushroomed.

The man who talked with Follet was a squat, middle-aged fellow with a sober red face. He wore a gray apron. He leaned forward and whipped the sheet back off the table, and Baron looked down into the half-closed, horrorshot eyes of Elene. Her body was stretched out on the table beneath the turned-down sheet. She still wore the same clothes he had last seen her in and her arms were tight against her sides.

"Well?" Follet said, watching Baron. "Is this the girl?"

Baron could not tear his gaze away. It was bad. It was very bad. Elene's throat had been sliced from ear to ear. Her head lolled backward, mouth gaping, partially off the table's edge. Whoever had done this job had taken three separate strokes with a sharp instrument. On one of the cuts, the killer had sawed with the blade. There was no sign of blood. The clothes were damp.

The sudden sensation of death came into Baron.

"She was found on the edge of the canal, not an hour ago," Follet said. "Her name is Elene Cordon. Is she the same?"

"Yes," Baron said. "She is the same."

Baron hesitated, then reached out quickly. He lightly pulled back the front of Elene's blouse, probed between the cold breasts. He withdrew the five-hundred-franc note, stood there staring at it in his hand. It was wet and one side of it was stained darkly with her blood.

Baron turned away, still holding the note.

"You begin to see?" Follet asked.

"Yes," Baron said. "I begin to see."

"Is there anything you wish to tell me?"

Baron looked at Follet, suddenly now overwhelmed with the knowledge that Elene was dead, that he would not be able to tell her of the many things he had wished to. She had been a very fine woman and they had murdered her, cut her off when she might have pulled herself up to a plane worthy of herself.

"Yes," Baron told Follet. "I'm going to do whatever I can–whatever I possibly can."

Follet said nothing. He stood there looking very gaunt and gray and he probed for his tobacco, rolled himself a cigarette. He took several large drags, settled his battered hat on his head. His face was quite expressionless.

"You will find your own way out, then," Follet said. His eyes brightened momentarily. "*Au revoir,* monsieur."

Baron watched Follet's rigid back vanish across the room and through the door. Turning, Baron went over to the table. The other man waited beside the table, but stared at the floor and did not speak. Baron placed the five-hundred-franc note beside the body on the table. He did not look at her now. He turned away and left the building.

Once again on the street, he began walking toward the Rue Paradis. There was a small clean wind. He was tired. The night was kind.

## Chapter Ten

BARON SLOWLY CLIMBED THE STAIRS and opened the door to his room. He went inside and reached for the cord on the lamp.

"Do not turn the light on, thanks."

"Gorssmann!"

"Yes, Baron, it is I."

Baron was very glad the lights weren't on. Gorssmann would surely have noticed how he looked, and he did not look well. He'd had no idea that Gorssmann would be waiting here for him and it was a considerable shock. He knew he should have been prepared for this. Hereafter he would be ready for anything.

The pale light from the street lights suffused the room, blending with the shadows, and Baron made out the enormous hulk of Gorssmann, seated on the bed. His round face shone in the darkness, lighter against the darkness of the wall.

"You have been out?" Gorssmann said.

Baron said nothing, listening to the hissing of escaping air as Gorssmann spoke.

"Well?"

"What does it look like?"

"I see."

"I don't like being followed, either," Baron said.

"Yes. He was clumsy, wasn't he? I'm afraid we can't use that fellow any more. He was new, I was trying him out. He failed miserably."

"I'm tired. What is it you want?"

"Frankly, you worried me. Where have you been?"

"Walking. I was walking and thinking."

"Excellent. Very good."

"There's no reason for you to check up on me," Baron said. "You ought to know I'll go through with this."

"Ah, but I do know. Certainly, Baron. Forgive me my curiosity. I like to take particular care of–well, of persons in your position." Gorssmann coughed lightly, then chuckled. "Also, I have decided to tell you your job, Baron. There's no point in putting it off any longer. Then, while you get yourself in order, you can be planning the attack." Gorssmann paused, then spoke just as Baron was about to speak. "We let you plan your own method of attack, you see?"

"Swell of you."

"Watch the humor, Baron. Sarcastic humor is good in its place. Just now we must be serious."

Baron said nothing. He went over and let himself down into a chair by the windows fronting the Rue Paradis. He could hear somebody walking slowly up the street. It was growing late now, and with the night, the streets seemed to become lonely and reverberant. The footfalls echoed almost nostalgically. Baron listened, waiting, and was conscious that he ached more and more as time went on. His joints were stiffening and he knew tomorrow would bring plenty of pain. Joseph had done a thorough job. For a time he had forgotten his tooth, and without thinking, he touched his tongue to the cavity now. Pain lanced his jaw, brought sweat out on his face.

"By now you must know you are to take the plans for the cosmic breather from the plant near Cassis." Gorssmann sighed. "This, Baron, is your job. Simple? Certainly. Chevard will know where these plans are kept. They will not be at his home here in Marseilles. They will be at the plant, probably under guard, I imagine in his office. We know this much. There is one set of plans. The breather has not yet been built. They have been studying the plans. Now, further. We have reason to believe that a miniature model of the breather has been built." Gorssmann hesitated, breathing rapidly, and Baron saw him withdraw his handkerchief from a side pocket and mop his face. "This model, wherever it is, must be destroyed. You see, there were other models, other plans. But they have all been destroyed. Only one set, only one model. That was their security measure. It was also their mistake. The mistake of underestimation."

Baron waited, trying to keep the air from the cavity in his tooth. It ached horribly now.

"You follow me?"

"Yes, yes."

"Well, that's it. You commence by going to Chevard. He and his family are in Marseilles. It should be easy." Gorssmann stood, coming off the bed in a powerful lunge. For a moment he stood there, breathing rapidly, the breath hissing like air escaping from a punctured balloon.

"What about Elene?" Baron said. "Are you going to continue to hold her?"

Gorssmann moved silently toward the door of the room, turned, and stared through the darkness at Baron. Finally he said, "We will see."

You son-of-a-bitch, Baron thought. You vile son of a killing murderous son-of-a-bitch.

"Arnold!" Gorssmann called.

Arnold stepped in through the door from the hallway.

"Good-by, Baron," Gorssmann said. "I'll keep in touch with you. Don't rush things, but also, don't waste time." Gorssmann turned toward the door, then back to Baron again. "By the way, Baron. Your daughter, Bette, has arrived in France."

Baron came out of his chair. He started to speak, shaken with sudden anxiousness. Gorssmann stood for a moment by the doorway, then turned and left the room. Baron listened to Arnold and Gorssmann descend the stairs. Then he heard the street door open and close.

Bette was in France. He wondered if he could believe Gorssmann. If she were in France, very likely she was in Marseilles. He began to pace the room, but stopped abruptly. He had to stop acting the way he did. He went over and lit the lamp, the scarlet glow burning in the shadows, and with his hand still on the cord he remembered Elene's face there on the table in the morgue. He wanted to cry out. Because there was so little he could do. There was nothing to bring against the conflict that surrounded him; nothing but himself. There was no way to fight back. Every move he made was watched probably by both the secret police and Hugo Gorssmann. Either party could annihilate him. His life was an open book to all concerned; they knew everything of his personal life. He no longer had a personal life. His room might even be wired; how could he tell?

This thought stirred him into action. He canvassed the room, turned it inside out, and found nothing. He flung himself on the bed and he was truly sick inside.

Elene dead, because of him. And Bette in their hands. Follet had been right, of course. When all of this was done, Gorssmann would see to it that no traces were left. *He* would be the single element that must be destroyed because he would not alone be useless, he would be dangerous.

Sitting up on the bed, he stripped off his jacket, then his shirt. He drew his undershirt over his head and frowned down at his arms and chest. He was covered with bruises, cuts, freshly forming scabs. He was a mess. He rose, stripped, found his bathrobe, took a towel, and padded down the hall to the shower. It was some shower. It was more like a piece of very old pipe, possibly early Roman, with a leak in it. He stood beneath the trickle, soaped himself, rinsed off, dried with the towel, and returned to his room.

He hurled the towel at the dresser mirror, flung himself on the bed. Almost immediately there came a timid knock on his door. He rose carefully, his body smarting from the soap and water, and went to the door and opened it.

The girl Lili gave him a single quick, sly look, then hurried past him into the room.

"Quickly," she said. "Close the door, monsieur!"

He did so, turned and frowned at her.

"Don't look at me that way!" she said. "Please!"

He could not help grinning. This irritated the toothache, but he grinned on. She was such a damned nice-looking piece, this sly one.

And he would never be able to remove from his mind the memory of what she had done to him in greeting that afternoon.

"I should never have come," she said. Her voice was very emphatic, very serious. She was altogether serious now, and extremely nervous. She snapped two more quick glances at him, then walked swiftly to the window. She stood beside the window, out of range of the street, and pulled down the shade. Then she looked at him again, and this time she waited.

She wore a light tan coat, flaring open across a tight, dark green dress that revealed something of the body beneath it. From what Baron could see, the body was excellent, and promising. She carried a black beaded purse in her left hand. Her right hand was jammed into one deep pocket of the coat. Her hair was certainly the blackest Baron had ever seen, and in the scarlet glow from the lamp it was beautiful, as were her dark blue eyes. As he watched her, she touched her teeth to her lower lip, and for that single instant Baron thought she might cry. She did not cry, but obviously she came close to it.

"Lili what?" he said.

"Does it matter?"

"I think so."

"Laurent. Lili Laurent."

"Does he know you're here?"

"What? Who?"

"He sent you, is that it, Lili?"

"I might have known you would be like this."

"You the modern Mata Hari?"

She said nothing. She just looked at him. It was not a nice look, and Baron wished he did not feel as he did. How could he trust this one? What did she want with him?

"Or did you come to collect?"

"Collect?"

"On your promise, your little agreement, Lili." He stepped toward her. She did not move. She did not stop looking at him, her head tipped up, the sly light in her eyes showing through all the seriousness even though she might not have meant it to be that way. As he came up to her, he smelled the perfume again, as elusive as ever, and as sweetly good. "You know what I mean, Lili."

She nodded. "*Oui*, I know." She swallowed, searching his eyes. "If that is what you want ..." she said softly; then she said, "I am so sorry about your face. Did Joseph do damage?"

"How do you mean? He didn't cripple me. He hurt me, goddamn him, but that's all right."

"I am very sorry," she said.

"Oh, for Christ's sake!" He whirled, went over and sat on the bed, held his head in his hands. "Why are you here?"

He heard her heels on the floor. They reminded him of Elene. He glanced quickly at her, to make sure, unable to control the movement, then put his head in his hands again, staring at the floor. She came close to him and he could see the tips of her black shoes on the floor, the smooth curve of her ankles and calves. He could hear her breathing.

"I wanted you to know," she said. "That was the only way I could make you notice. By doing that. I am sorry, I–"

"Don't be sorry. My God, there's nothing to be sorry about. I can think of nothing more–I can think of nothing."

She laughed shortly, but when he looked up at her face was once again serious.

"Anyway," she said, "that's why I did that, to your palm, that way. I–I had to let you know."

"What? Let me know what?"

"That I am of them, but not with them, Monsieur Baron."

He stared at her and for the first time in all of this he began to sense warmth. He leaped at it, dragging at it with both hands, with all of him, giving himself to it. He was starved for any kind of reasonableness whatsoever. Was she a reasonable person? My God, how could he be sure? He rose, walked all the way around her, came back to the bed and sat down again. It could not be true. There was a catch to it. There had to be.

"Did it trouble you, what I did?"

"Yes. It might have troubled me still more, but I was in pretty bad shape."

She said nothing and he looked up at her again.

"Are you telling the truth?" he asked.

She nodded. "That's why I'm here. I had to let you know, you see? Back there, I could say nothing. I could think of no other way to startle you into thinking of me, so I took the quickest one that came to mind, the–"

"Never mind," he said. "Quit trying to explain. I understand."

"I'm glad."

She had not moved. She was so damned serious. He didn't know what to make of her, except that he liked her immensely. He couldn't help liking everything he had seen of her.

"I followed Gorssmann, the pig," she said. "And Arnold. And when they went out, I came in, you see? I had to find a back way, through the alley. I came upstairs the back way, and here to your room. But you were in the shower. I–"

"How did you know I was in the shower?"

She blushed slightly. "I peeked," she said. "Truly, that shower is not of much worth. Is it?"

"This is the damnedest," he said. "The very damnedest."

"Yes," she said. "You are right."

"You know all about what I'm supposed to do?"

"And more," she said softly. "And still more."

"Oh."

"Are we friends?"

He reached out, took her hand, and drew her toward him on the bed. She sat beside him, pulled one leg up under her, and leaned back against the foot of the bed. She laid her purse beside her and folded her hands in her lap.

He wanted to believe her. He felt that he should. He felt she must be truthful. But in the back of his mind, how could he believe? He thought of something.

"How is the girl Elene Cordon?" he said. He did not look her in the eye. He could not. It would give him away. She would know he knew something. "Do you get a chance to speak with her, Lili?"

When she did not answer immediately, he looked at her.

She was staring down at her folded hands. He watched her lips. They formed words several times, but she did not speak. Then finally she said, "The girl is dead, monsieur."

"Dead?" He knew the tone of his voice was not as it should be, and because of the quick look she cast him, he knew she suspected something. She would not know what.

"Yes."

"How?" He tried now to put anxiousness, worry into his voice. But it wouldn't work. He knew Elene was dead and he was not much of an actor. He was a very lousy liar. He had known this for some time. He wondered if Lili lied, and he found himself hoping strongly that she told the truth.

"They said it was an accident, monsieur. I don't know who did it. But"–she turned her gaze once again to her folded hands–"you can be sure it was no accident. Did she mean so much to you?"

"She was a good woman."

"I suspected as much. I'm sorry, monsieur."

He said nothing.

"You knew, didn't you? You knew she was dead."

"How could I know?"

She shrugged. "I can tell. You were not surprised. Did the pig tell you?"

He shook his head. He wanted to avoid telling her anything much as yet. He wanted to take her into his confidence, but he was afraid to. If Gorssmann had sent her to keep tabs on him–which might easily be the case–he had to be wary.

"Listen, monsieur," she said. She leaned forward on the bed, unfolded her hands, and laid them palms down on the bed as she looked at him. Her eyes seemed to become even a darker blue and very intense. "I know what is in your mind. But you must trust me. You must!"

He rose from the bed, walked over to the window. He turned and looked at her. She was still seated as he had left her, facing toward the head of the bed, where he'd been sitting.

He began to perspire again. Gorssmann was smooth. Every angle known to smart operation was in his command, and Lili could be a top mark on the page.

"I cannot escape them," she said. "There is nothing I can do. I have nobody, monsieur. You are the first one I have believed I might be able to trust in a long, long while. This is why I come to you. Between us, we must do something. Gorssmann must be stopped."

He still said nothing. Lord, how he did want to believe her! Not only that; he felt a strong desire to take her in his arms, and hold onto her, to crush her. It was a desire that had lurked in the back of his mind ever since she had entered the room. There was something quietly sincere about her and he hated the barb of doubt that clung there inside him, reminding him to take no chances.

"You work for Gorssmann?" he asked.

"I have been forced to do certain things, the same as you are being forced. I know all about you, monsieur. They have talked of nothing else for months. I have seen pictures of you. I have read the papers of your life. I know *all* about you. I know where "you have been, what you have been doing. And I know that I can trust you, monsieur. That is why I am here." She looked across at him now and she seemed very small and lonely, seated there on the bed. He wanted to go over to her and tell her he understood and that they would work something out together. But he could not do this. The gnawing worm of doubt was there and he could not evade it.

"You cannot bring yourself to believe in me, can you?"

He turned his back, stared at the lowered shade over the window. He moved to the dresser, peered into the mirror. He could see her back, the thick mass of coal-black black hair with the red highlights from the lamp, and the sag of her shoulders beneath the tan coat.

"Just after the war," she said, "Gorssmann contacted my father, who was a lens maker. He did something to him, I do not know what, and my father was forced to do something in turn. To work for him. My father nearly went mad, and my mother died of a stroke when she discovered that her husband was working with the enemy. The same enemy that had taken my brother and shot him, during the war. When I learned how serious it was, I told Gorssmann that I would do things for him, if he would only give my father freedom. Gorssmann lied. My father was very ill. He took me and trained me in various things. For instance, the painting of chinaware. It is a code, monsieur. An everyday code with which the agents in different cities and towns are kept posted on what is going on. What they are to do. It is extremely practicable. My father is in Austria now. I do not know where. Gorssmann insists that I stay with him, do what I have been doing, or my father will be put to death. It is very simple. I love my father. He is a fine man, but possibly as dead now as if he were buried. I think something must be done. I must make a sacrifice. But just leaving Gorssmann is no longer enough. Vengeance is not nice, but I must do something." She paused, turned her head, and looked at him very intently. "Between us, perhaps something can be done."

"I want to believe you, Lili."

She turned, rose from the bed, walked across to him. She stood very close to him, her head tipped back, her sly smile and her serious eyes somehow more than appealing.

"Also," she said, "I have no man, monsieur. This is continually on my mind. I am frank with the other, I shall be frank about this."

He could feel himself weakening. He could do nothing about it. He thought even of Elene just then and of what she would think, and Elene would have said, "It is to laugh," and he heard Lili speak again.

"Did you hear me, monsieur? I feel as if I have known you forever so long. I do not want just any man."

"You're a very peculiar person, Lili."

"No," she said. "I am simply honest, monsieur."

They were silent and she stood very close to him and he could sense her body and smell the perfume and her hair looked soft and rich and he wanted to sink his hands into it and grip it between his fingers; he wanted to crush her against him, and even with the thought, the desire, the want, he was doing just that. Her coat flared open and her body came against him, pressing close and tight and warm, and her lips opened almost wildly beneath his, damp and heating with the pressure. She trembled violently in his arms and he could not recall ever having kissed a woman's lips that were so sweet and angry, and he had never held a woman so anxiously tortured with desire. She was like something untamed, savage, in his arms. As though she were starved. Before his hands caressed her, her body caressed his hands as she came close against him, demanding, certain, frank not as Elene had been frank, but with a dangerously wild abandon that sent Baron plunging toward an understanding of her. She trembled and whispered frantically. Having seen her calm, he now realized her passion. He gripped her, wanting to hurt her, wanting with sudden bright anger to have her in hot forgetful endlessness.

She thrust herself away from him, backed to the bottom rail of the bed, and leaned there, breathing rapidly, watching him.

"I must go," she said. "I am sorry. I should not have come so close, monsieur. I cannot stay, not now. They will be wondering and we must be careful."

"Lili, please—"

"Yes. I know, but I cannot stay. Besides, you do not know if you believe in me as yet. Until you do, this would not be good. It would be good, but not perfect."

"Lili, that's just a woman's—You want to be honest, you say. You know that—"

She smiled, then laughed outright. It was nice laughter. It was laughter that did not often occur and he recognized the fact that she laughed seldom.

"They will want to know where I have been. I must go." She turned and walked over to the door, then looked back at him. "Monsieur," she said, "I will be the person that takes care of your daughter. I will let you know how she is. *À bientôt!*"

She was gone, quickly, and the door closed. He stepped hurriedly across the room.

"Lili! About Bette—"

She turned in the hall, smiled at him. "Don't worry, please. I will let you know." Again she smiled, and strode off toward the rear of the house, the back stairs. He started out after her, then stopped in the shadowed darkness of the hall. For a time he stood there, listening, waiting, and becoming conscious of all he waited for and of how small his chances were.

He returned to his room and stood for a long time staring down at the bed, thinking about Lili and what she had done and said. Then he lay down on the bed and consciously sought sleep. Somehow he missed sleep, though. It eluded him and he spent most of the night remembering Elene and how honest Lili had seemed. And in the back of his mind it gnawed and gnawed at him. Could he trust Lili? And he began to get Lili and Elene mixed up as he drew closer to sleep, until they merged and he slept.

## Chapter Eleven

THE TOOTH WOKE HIM UP. He lay there experiencing the pain, and everything rushed back into his mind, out of the deeply bleeding wound of sleep. He swung his feet to the floor, sick with the prospects of a new day. Today would be the real beginning and after a while he would know something about himself. He would know courage and he would know if he could lie to his friend Chevard and get away with it.

He bought clothes, had one decent suit made up while he waited. Returning to his room, he dressed. He was stiff in every bone. His muscles ached. He could not find the nerve to face a dentist. The swellings on his face had receded, and he looked fit above the collar and tie of his new shirt. He wore an Oxford-gray flannel suit, debated about the felt hat he'd purchased, decided against it, and flipped it onto the rumpled bed. The only comfort he discovered in his wrath of calamity was the clean, roomy sensation of new socks in well-fitting shoes.

Gorssmann had done something for him. Perhaps Gorssmann had bought him his funeral clothes.

It was early afternoon already and during the morning he became slowly more and more nervous. He could not wring Bette from his mind. He wanted to search Gorssmann out, see if Bette was all right. He wished Gorssmann would appear at his room. He wondered if he should hang around, waiting for Gorssmann. He knew that if he did, the fat man would not like it. For all Gorssmann had said about taking his time, Baron knew he was meant to get on with the job as quickly as possible.

He kept recalling Lili. If he could depend on her, if he could trust her, if she were truthful, honest ... If, if, *if!*

And all the time he kept forcing to the back of his mind the knowledge that he had to find Chevard and face him and lie.

He knew he should eat. He could not eat. Twice he went into cafés, twice he walked out with nothing but a double brandy under his belt. On an empty morning stomach, the brandy did not help.

The enormity of what he had to do was beginning to come through clearly to him. He was a spy, not merely an acting one, not a man posing as a spy–and he was from the wrong camp. One of the few men in the world who believed in him must be used, lied to, his faith undermined.

Baron knew he had to go through with it. He had no choice. Bette was in danger. There was the chance that neither he nor Bette would be alive when it was all over, even with Gorssmann's word. Gorssmann's word was an empty thing; a loud laugh in a wind tunnel. Yet he had to do as he was told.

Baron left his room, went out onto the street. His first move, since he did not know where Paul Chevard lived, was to find a telephone directory.

He went into a hotel nearby on Paradis, and found the phone and a battered directory. A moment later his finger prowled beneath the name. Paul Chevard. Baron's heart began to thud then, because he was this much closer and his nerve had to hold out, only it wasn't holding out. He stared at the telephone on the wall, with his finger still beneath the name in the directory. Baron reached for the phone. His hand actually touched the cold metal But his hand leaped away as though the phone were searing hot.

He stood there in the small telephone alcove, staring down at the battered directory. His hand with the finger pointing to the name was trembling, and beneath the crisp new white shirt, the blue tie, the immaculate gray flannel, he began once again to perspire and to shrink.

It's duty to yourself, he thought. To your daughter and perhaps even to that girl Lili. You've got to go ahead with it. Chevard himself would do the same, you know he would.

He leaned partially back against the wall of the alcove, and his tooth throbbed and throbbed in his head. How could it suddenly mean this much? Did it take this for a man to find out what he was made of? Was this the crisis in life?

Think, he told himself. Remember why you are in France. Remember back through those days, months, years–back to when it began. Who helped you? What did you decide?

And thinking this way, he felt a lessening of fear, a sharper patience, the possibility of victory. You want that man, he thought. That man who sits someplace, waiting. The man who ruined you and caused all of this in the first place. Think back, he told himself. Remember how it would be now if that man had not done as he did.

But he did and you swore an oath to yourself, he thought.

You're getting melodramatic, he thought. Get off it. Think straight and reason it out. Don't dicker with the consequences now. All that matters is the first move, then the next, and the next. Call Chevard, go see him, get it over with. You've got to!

Exuberance gripped him. He reached for the phone, took the receiver, heard the whistling whine of the wire as he placed the instrument to his ear. He glanced down at the directory, but his finger had slipped from Chevard's name. The operator was questioning loudly, emphatically. He searched almost frantically for Chevard's name. He couldn't find it. His nerve vanished like sugar poured into the ocean. He slammed the receiver back on its prongs and stood there in the telephone alcove, shattered, perspiring, the sweat trickling down his neck, under his collar. He stared at the directory, turned suddenly, and walked from the hotel.

He could not do it.

He turned up Paradis, walking dazedly. A loud voice argued with him in the back of his mind. You've got to do it! You can't back out now! What's the matter with you? And it was his own voice and his own voice answered back, I can't do it! Damn you!

All right. Go get a drink. Think it over. Only don't take too long, because Bette is here, remember?

He stopped dead in his tracks there on the street.

Look, he thought. Look what hangs on a telephone call. Maybe if you got drunk, he thought. Then maybe you would make some sense to yourself. Maybe you would find the nerve you should have, he thought. Maybe it's courage. Maybe you have no courage, maybe you have nothing. What's the matter with you? It's for somebody else. Weigh it, consider it. Is it from a selfish motive that you would put a whole country in jeopardy? Can you do this?

What is France to you, Baron? What is the world to you?

And as he thought like this, it became worse and worse. Because it was, in a sense, the world. It had happened before to other men, he knew. If cogs whirred right, if machinery were oiled properly, his making this phone call might very well be the first step toward instigation of war.

My God, he thought. Get a drink. Get a drink before you blow your fool top.

It had stopped being personal. He knew this. He was fighting with everything he had to keep it personal. From a purely selfish motive, he might be able to handle it. But when it expanded out of all proportion to his everyday thinking, it was beyond him. He could not deal with it. He had never been meant to deal with things of this sort. Gorssmann had said, "You are the man."

He walked swiftly now toward the Cannebière. He wanted to shy away from it. Because it wasn't for him, it had not been meant for him.

But it is you, he thought. You are the man walking down this street with this problem and you have to deal with it. Don't be spineless. At least face it. For God's sake, I am sick to death of you.

He turned the corner onto the Cannebière and walked into the first café at hand. It was a large place, with tables and chairs on the sidewalk, a large dining area, and a long zinc bar. He made for the bar. He almost ran.

"Cognac," he said.

The bartender eyed him wisely, raised his eyebrows, and reached behind him for the green bottle.

The first glass went down, the second, the third, the fourth, all in rapid succession, with the bartender standing there smiling pleasantly and pouring, then frowning and pouring, then hesitating.

*"Pardon, monsieur."*

They stared at each other. Baron flipped his roll of francs onto the bar, peeled off a thousand-franc note, and pushed it at the barman.

The barman smiled ingratiatingly. He reached behind him, under the shelf, and brought out a large brandy glass. He filled it brimming, until some of the brandy dribbled over the sides onto the zinc, carelessly. Baron liked the way the man poured the brandy. That was the way all brandy should be poured. Carelessly. He drank the entire glassful, gulping it, swallowing it like water, and motioned for the man to refill it.

Now, he thought. Now turn and run to the nearest phone. Quickly. You'll be able to do it now. You know you will. King Brandy has come to the rescue. Good King Brandy. It will be easy now, won't it?

"Perhaps something to eat, monsieur?" the barman said.

"No."

It was very early in the afternoon and the café was nearly empty. He stood alone at the bar. He felt the maggots begin their crawling in his blood now. He felt the pressure, the good pressure inside his head, the release and the relief. Bette was all right. Wasn't she?

And thinking of Bette, he leaned against the bar and drank from the glass, thinking and knowing that he had already passed the point where he could have made the telephone call. It had been but a minute ago and now it was miles behind him.

*"Encore, monsieur?"*

He nodded at the barman. The barman had not moved. He stood there with the bottle in his hand. Then he turned and opened a fresh bottle of cognac, grinned at Baron, and set it before him and walked away.

Baron leaned against the bar and quietly filled his own glass, letting it overflow and stream across the bar. He reached for the glass, started to raise it to his lips, and realized suddenly that he was drunk. He set the glass down and stared at it, watching it closely.

The brandy rose in his throat, turned over neatly, and settled, and he was quite drunk. He stood there and watched his glass and thoughts coursed through his mind like steel plates on a greased slide so that when he sought to grasp them and hold onto them, they slipped away and new ones took their place. It was simple and good and he was thoroughly drunk and nothing mattered.

Only in the back of his mind something did matter. He turned sharply away from the bar and walked out onto the street.

The sun was hot on the Cannebière. People streamed past in a blur of bright wandering imprints, flashing across his mind, and vanishing. The bright-skirted, flashing-eyed women. The flashing-eyed, bright-skirted women. The flashing-skirted, bright-eyed women.

He turned right off the Cannebière, walking swiftly. There was something he had to do. He knew there was something he had to do and as he walked rapidly along the slowly slanting sidewalk, rising smoothly beneath the elms, he remembered the telephone call and Chevard and then forgot and then remembered again in a haze of forgetting to remember, and remembering to forget.

Music soared, cascading against his ears like wet fountains of bright-slamming sound, bright and vivid and sparkling and dull, all at once, and he leaned on this sudden bar, staring, and somewhere off to his right in the dim fog of music and talking and laughter a woman sang and glasses clinked and he heard the loud pop of a cork. The wine.

He fumbled at the glass before him, trying to remember and fighting to forget.

*"Chéri?"*

He turned and she left, whoever she was. Whoever she was, he was too drunk for her, whoever she was. Her hips moved beneath the shimmering black skirt, like a tight taunt. He stood there recalling the redness of her mouth as she said the word, the dark conspiring light in her eyes. He turned back to the bar, watching the glass closely, and was surprised to see it was empty. He ordered again, ordering through the music that washed down over his shoulders, remembering Paul Chevard through the fog, thinking about Paul Chevard and of how long he had known him and knowing what he had to do.

On the street, walking, in the cool shade of night, he felt the wind that came down the street washing coolly against him, washing away the sound of the music, the pound and throb of it, and walking with him was the strong odor of cognac, like a laughing wrath. His wrath, his madness, his bitter grapes. Cultivate your vineyard, he thought. And the streets echoed to the pound of his hurrying heels, and he was out of breath standing against still another bar in the orange-colored night amid new music like the lilt of burlesque bounding, tightly insinuating a thousand pedigreed sounds and pictures, shoving the elbows that prodded him at the bar, thinking in direct hopelessness against the laughter and the talk and the laughter and the beat-beat-beat of the music.

"Monsieur?"

"Cognac."

Splash.

*"Encore?"*

*"Oui."*

"Upstairs, monsieur?"

"No, go away."

*"Autre cognac?"*

*"Oui."*

Splash.

He looked away from the bar at the suddenly naked woman over there through the fog between the heads and the tinkling tables, beyond the throbbing glare of red music, at the woman with the billy goat on the stage.

Good Lord!

He ordered another cognac, suddenly sober in the turgid scarlet interim of drunkenness.

They shouted out there amid the tables and the wild sound. They shouted for the billy goat. They shouted for the girl. They shouted and screamed for the both of them and everything went silent and he stood there listening to the slow, pulsing, whispering beat-beat-beat of the music, hearing them watching in the scarlet darkness and the whispering shriek of *le jazz hot,* the night, the patiently squealing night, and the slow, self-conscious laughter breaking like waves across the tables without applause, only laughter, the crazy press roll of the snare, the mad four-four steady rocking, and the sudden awakening of the waiters with fresh drinks.

He was reeling now in the shade of the moon beside a canal, the cement wall close beside him, dragging like sandpaper against his hand, still on his feet, still fighting the remembering.

He had met Paul Chevard during the war, long before any of the trouble, when he was in France. Paul had been in the air industry, even then, coming to it through his father. He had met Paul's mother and Paul's wife. He had lived at Paul's home in Paris. Later, Chevard had come to America to visit him, bringing along his wife and daughter. He wanted to see Baron's factories. And then during the Korean war, during the big mess, during the trials, Paul had written him that he must endure. If there was anything he could do he would do it, and at least he had friends who believed. In Europe, Chevard said, these things were of common occurrence, not so much importance was attached to them. They tried to free the seemingly guilty. They did not get excited, because they were used to sabotage. Sabotage.

He leaned against this new bar. The place was bright white with light. There was no sound. The barman read a newspaper at the far end of the empty bar. Baron staggered over there and read it, too. He read of himself, of Bette. Through a crazy blur of remembering and drunkenness, he read of Bette's drowning in Florida. Of himself in France. On page three it was, down in the right-hand corner.

"The paper, monsieur. I was reading it."

He hurled the paper at the barman and sprawled against the bar.

He looked at the woman who leaned over the bed. He was sick, viciously sick. He tried to hold his eyes open, won out, and kept watching the woman. A pretty woman, smiling, but anxious, too.

"Hello, Frank."

Beyond her head sunlight shone across a smooth ceiling and glittered on the glass of a chandelier. He was fully dressed, lying across a bed. He gagged, tried to say something.

She laughed.

"Give him a drink," somebody said. "He needs some hair of the dog."

His head ached angrily and he fought his way up on his elbows on the bed. The room whirled, and he sprawled back. He heard the clink of a bottle neck against glass.

"How did I get here?" he said, listening to his own voice.

"Through the front door," Paul Chevard said. He came close to the side of the bed and looked down at Baron. "You burst through the door at three-thirty this morning, Frank. Drunk as a lord. You smashed the lock on the front door."

"I'm sorry."

"Here," the woman said. "Don't you remember me, Frank?"

It was Paul Chevard's wife, Jeanne. She held the glass out toward him and he watched the glass, trying to fight his way up through despair.

## Chapter Twelve

PAUL CHEVARD LAUGHED.

"We sent the girl away," he told Baron.

Baron looked up at him. They were seated at the breakfast table in the dining room of Chevard's home. Jeanne was in the kitchen. Baron sipped at his coffee, not wanting to hear this.

"She was some girl," Chevard said.

"What girl?"

Chevard shrugged, chuckling. "You brought her with you. You said she had an inferiority complex. You insisted you had to cure her of billy goats. She was a good-looking one, all right," Chevard said, remembering. "An entertainer at some night spot. According to your story, she preferred billy goats to men. You were making strong attempts to teach her differently. She seemed to reciprocate, seemed to like you very much. You had her skirt off when you broke down the door, Frank. Yes, she was something. You insisted that we rent you a room so you could convince her that she was worthy of a man, that a man was better than a billy goat."

Jeanne laughed from behind Baron's chair. He felt the blood push into his shoulders, the sharp embarrassment.

"You *were* a picture!" Jeanne said.

"I must catch her act," Chevard said.

"You *will not!*" Jeanne said. "You saw enough last night." She rested one hand on Baron's shoulder. "You know, Frank, Paul really and truly wanted to give you a room. He told me maybe you were right. He said perhaps the poor child was repressed, or something."

"All she did was laugh," Chevard said. "She's a student at the Sorbonne, studying philosophy. Some philosophy." Chevard leaned forward across the table. "Listen, Frank, was she really–"

"Paul!" Jeanne said.

Baron sat back. He knew they were trying to make him feel better and he thanked them for it, but it did not help. He knew what he was here for. He was sick enough without that. In his drunkenness, he had made up his mind, apparently, and worked it out in his own way. He remembered nothing of the girl save the scarlet stage at the night spot itself and flashes of her laughter as she walked skirt-less through the night, her stockinged thighs flashing in the street lights. How long had that gone on? He must have returned to the place and picked her up. They had been in a park someplace because he recalled her lying on the grass with a fountain splashing over there through the trees and she was laughing even then.

He refused to try to remember.

"More coffee?" Jeanne said.

"Please."

He turned and smiled at her. He was feeling some better now. Chevard's wife was petite and plump, a small-boned redhead with one of the neatest figures Baron had ever seen. He knew she loved Chevard with a devotion seldom found. She looked lovely and fresh this morning, her eyes bright, her lips touched with laughter.

He drank his coffee.

"I've been looking all over Marseilles for you," Chevard said.

Baron glanced at the man over the rim of his cup. He knew he should say something, but he said nothing. Chevard wore a dark business suit. He looked tired and harried, worn out, his red-rimmed eyes sunken in a frowning face. The face frowned even when Chevard laughed and joked. His lips were tight and he was a man obviously under pressure. His shirt collar was too loose and Baron knew the man had lost a good deal of weight. Chevard moved nervously in his chair, ignoring his breakfast plate, drinking great quantities of coffee. His hand trembled slightly whenever he raised the cup.

Baron was surprised that his own hand was steady.

"Spent most of the day yesterday inquiring," Chevard said. "I read the story in the newspaper, about–" He paused. "You have seen the papers?"

"Yes."

"About Bette." Chevard frowned. "You know?"

"Yes."

"This is truly awful," Jeanne said. She came around and sat in a chair beside Baron and laid one hand on his arm, her fingers tightening. "What will you do?"

"There's nothing to do. I cabled," he lied. "It's all true. There's nothing I can do. Patricia is in Bermuda."

"Did you hear from her?" Jeanne said.

"No."

Chevard motioned to his wife. She turned and looked at him, gnawed her lip. "I'll get some more rolls," she said.

"Never mind," Baron said. He took her hand, grinned at her. "Sit down. I know how you feel, but there's nothing can be done."

"Is that why you came here?" Chevard said.

"Partly." He released Jeanne's hand, reached for his cup, then did not pick it up. He could not trust that hand now. He was lying now. He was in it now and he had to go through with it. The perspiration began, he felt it popping out on his forehead.

"What is it, Frank?" Chevard said.

"I've been trying to get up nerve to look you up for days," he said. "But I thought you were in Paris. I was checking a number in the telephone directory. I saw your name." He sat there, waiting that one out. It was a weak one and he wondered if it would get by. It did get by.

He saw the look Jeanne shot her husband then. Jeanne rose abruptly from the table, moved away into the kitchen. Sunlight streamed through the windows over Chevard's shoulders. It glanced off the brilliantly white tablecloth into Baron's eyes. He wished Chevard would suggest they move to another room. He felt ill. His tooth was beginning to throb again through the throbbing of his head and his stomach felt rather evil.

"What did you want?" Chevard said.

"I wanted to see you."

"Oh?"

"You'll be late, Paul," Jeanne called from the other room. "You're late now."

"It doesn't matter," Chevard said. He began nervously picking at crumbs on the tablecloth beside his plate. He saw what he was doing and stopped quickly. He let his hand lie quietly beside his plate. Baron recognized the effort in the movement and pitied Chevard.

He pitied the man for what he had to do.

"Are you going to return to the states?" Chevard asked.

Baron looked at the man. This would be the harsh beginning of the true lying and he did not want to begin. He wanted to walk out of this house and leave these good people. Unknown to them, they were embarking on a sure train to hell, and he was the conductor. He not only would punch their tickets, he would manacle them to their seats so they would be certain to arrive. Baron knew that when he began to speak now, it would mean the first mark toward destruction of all Paul Chevard lived for.

"Because of Bette? That what you mean?"

"Yes."

"No, I'm not returning to the states. Not now. There's nothing I could do."

"Don't you think you should contact Patricia?"

Baron glanced at his coffee cup. He shook his head. "We've managed this far without consulting each other."

"Is there no hope for finding Bette?"

Again Baron shook his head. "According to the authorities, no hope at all. She has drowned and they haven't found her body." And saying this, watching Chevard's face, he caught his breath and his mind stopped. Because he saw what it would mean. If he went through with Gorssmann's proposal, and if he eventually came through alive, with Bette, Bette would have lost her identity. It was a thought that even obliterated the throbbing pain from his tooth and the muddled, headaching fog of the hangover. What a fine life was in store for her! A young girl, starting out in life, having to take a new name, perhaps a new country, even. Any dream she had would be lost, turned to mud.

"I know something's on your mind, Frank."

"Something is. This business about Bette has thrown me, I guess."

Chevard said nothing.

"I thought she was perfectly all right with her mother. I find she hasn't been with her mother at all."

Still Chevard said nothings.

"But I'll have to forget that." He hoped he sounded convincing. He did not think he showed enough emotion regarding Bette. Lord knew, he felt the emotion, though not for the same cause Chevard suspected. Perhaps Chevard wouldn't notice. Baron knew his friend was tied up in a snarl of his own business.

Sitting there, Baron suspected that if it had not been for the deep drinking of the night before and the brandy this morning, he wouldn't be able to talk it through now.

"It's just this, Paul," he said. "I've come to ask a favor."

"Anything. You know that."

"Yes. I want to start over again. I've wasted time, pitied myself long enough. I've got somehow to begin, and make a way again. I'm going right back into the air industry. But I've got to have a way of beginning."

Chevard watched him closely, listening. Baron began really talking then. He went through it all, covering every angle, hating himself as he preyed on the man's sympathies. He found himself using every slight advantage he could think of. He talked it all out, in detail, and he watched Chevard's face closely. "When I'm back in the game, one way or another, and can see a way to some money, then I'll return to America and set up shop. In their faces. Somehow they'll know I was not at fault. They've got to know this. I'm—I'm flat broke, you know. I have nothing—nothing at all."

It was done. He had said all he had to say. If none of this worked, he would return to Gorssmann. He could do nothing else than this to begin.

He could not look Chevard in the eye right away then.

"You want me to help you?" Chevard said.

"There is nobody else. Nobody else I can turn to. They wouldn't understand."

"But your own country ..."

"I couldn't ask for help there," Baron said. He tried to keep the tone of his voice level, fighting against the desire to spill it all, the whole story. "It would be placing whoever I asked in the same fire with me. Here it's different. All I need is some kind of start."

"It seems to me," Chevard said, "that people in the United States would have cooled down about you by now. The war is over and they forget easily. You know that."

Baron waited now. He said nothing. He knew that if he spoke at all, he might give himself away. Too much hung in the balance.

Chevard shoved his chair away from the table. He was a tall man, and Baron noted the extreme nervousness. Chevard stepped away from the table over to the windows, with his back to Baron.

Baron sat there listening to the movements of Jeanne out in the kitchen.

"You know why I am in Marseilles?" Chevard said.

Baron waited a moment, then said, "No. I thought you liked Paris fine."

"I do."

"I see."

"No," Chevard said. "You don't see."

Jeanne's voice reached them from out in the kitchen.

"Paul, you'd better get going!"

Chevard did not turn from the windows, and he did not answer his wife. Baron sat there and suddenly saw how impossible it all was. How could Gorssmann expect him to work his way under Chevard's guard? Yet Baron knew that he could; that their friendship would cover that. He thought that it was only a matter of time before Chevard told him and told him everything.

Again he began to talk. He told Chevard of his reason for being during the past two and a half years, of how he had trailed the man who had sabotaged his factories.

"I thought as much," Chevard said. He turned from the windows, lit a cigarette, and stood there smoking quietly. The cigarette trembled between his fingers and his eyes looked haunted with worry and anxiousness. "And now?"

Baron shrugged. "I have not given up, if that's what you mean." And it was there in his voice, as it had been all this time, the defiance, the need to find this man. It was one thing he could never wipe out of his mind. Until he stood face to face with that man, his life would remain worthless. This he knew. "I'm going to go about it differently now. I've got to get back on my feet."

"I expected the newspapers were wrong," Chevard said. "I wish you had got in touch with me earlier." He came to the table and dropped the cigarette into his half-empty coffee cup. It hissed out and he glanced over at Baron. "This isn't easy," he said.

Baron waited. He watched Chevard straighten, walk back to the windows, and stand there looking outside into the bright, sunny morning. And as he watched Chevard and thought about what he was doing, Lili kept creeping into his mind, and a sensation of warmth and confidence came along with thoughts of her. He must remember to tell Follet about Lili and what she had said–if he ever again saw Follet. Perhaps Follet would view him on the same slab where two days ago he had looked down on Elene, with her throat cut.

Suddenly Chevard turned and looked at him. "Come," he said. "You come with me. Get your coat on." He walked swiftly out into the kitchen and Baron heard him talking with Jeanne. He took his coat off the back of the chair and slipped it on, his heart thudding stolidly against his ribs and into his throat. He knew very well this was it, and he hated to see Chevard doing it. He wanted to tell him it was all lies, but he could not. He knew Chevard would act the same. Wouldn't he? Wouldn't he? For the first time, now, doubt began to register in his mind. But he had to do it because of Bette. Yet, still in the back of his mind, he heard the question: Which was more to the point–a single person, or a whole nation?

Well, he thought, turning quickly away from the chair and the sunlight out there beyond the window, for me it's this way. For me it's got to be this way.

Chevard came from the kitchen. He carried a brief case now, and wore a stiff-brimmed felt hat. The hat made him look still more harried, the red-rimmed eyes peering at Baron quizzically, patiently, almost. Jeanne followed him and stood in the kitchen doorway, looking at Baron.

"Good luck to you, Frank," she said. "Please come and see us. Why don't you stay here while you're in Marseilles?"

Baron made as if to answer, but Chevard cut him short with a laugh. "We'll see," Chevard said. "Won't we, friend?"

Baron nodded to Jeanne and followed Chevard on through the house, out the side door. They got into a sleek, gray Italian Fiat 8V and Baron felt as if they were speeding even before Chevard started the engine.

"This is my baby," Chevard said. He sat behind the wheel, staring straight ahead. "Wait till I take you over the mountain roads." He hesitated, glanced at Baron.

"Where are we going?"

For answer, Chevard started the engine. The fine roar from twin exhausts sent leaves whirling in the driveway. "I have something to tell you," Chevard said. "I'm sure you will be interested."

He put the car in gear and they swooped abruptly from the drive, down into the street. Again Chevard shifted and Baron felt his shoulders come brutally back against the seat in a smooth, powerful drag. Trees flashed by, and the powerful engine whispered its challenge into the morning.

Baron's left hand lay half across the smooth, cool leather of Chevard's brief case there on the seat. He experienced a chill, knowing what might be inside that brief case. He was suddenly torn with a desire to look inside the case, and it was only with effort that he managed to keep from holding it in his lap and trying to look. This worried him. He began to wonder if he was losing control.

Soon they came out of Marseilles, to the south, and started up the mountain road on the way to Cassis.

"I don't much like Marseilles at all," Chevard said. They approached a curve, headed upward on the winding road, yet

Chevard only increased the speed of the Fiat. Down over the side of the mounting road, Baron made out Marseilles, spread like a relief map below them. The golden Virgin atop Nôtre Dame de la Garde shone brilliantly in the morning sunlight, and beyond the sun-bright and shadowed city the Mediterranean glistened and gleamed. Somewhere down there Bette waited, with Lili. Gorssmann paced and held his breath, betting on Baron, betting against the standards of humanity, betting against the world.

"I've had to leave Paris," Chevard said. "And I'm going to tell you why, Frank. I shouldn't, but for many years we have been friends. I think you should know. And when you do know, perhaps I then can be of some help to you."

Baron waited. He sat tightly in the seat, remembering now that Chevard had always driven much too fast, and on these roads it was frightening. Yet the car held tightly, even on the curves.

"I will tell you," Chevard said.

And he did.

## Chapter Thirteen

THE LATE MORNING turned hot as they drove through the thickly forested hills, after turning off the main road to Cassis. In the speeding Fiat, Baron wished there were something else to say. But Chevard was quite silent now, smiling behind the wheel, impatient to show Baron the things he had told him about. Baron knew he should not overquestion Chevard, yet he had to register just the right amount of enthusiasm and amazement. The only trouble was that Chevard had not once mentioned the cosmic breather. Perhaps it was too much to expect. Baron had waited, but Chevard talked only of the newly developed plane itself and of how they were reaching a peak of construction in the secret plant.

"And this is what you're doing in Marseilles?" Baron said. He kept trying to get Chevard to talk more. Nothing seemed to work.

"That's right. I'm in charge of the entire business," Chevard told him. "Otherwise I wouldn't be able to bring you here, Frank."

"Perhaps you shouldn't. Is it against the rules?"

Chevard glanced over at him, wheeled the car sharply around a banked curve on the dirt road.

"Not even governmental officials come here," Chevard said.

"No use getting the people you work with down on you."

Chevard laughed. "Suppose I put you on salary. What then?"

Baron grinned and said nothing. He didn't know what to say. Chevard was trusting him altogether too much. In one way, that is. On the other hand, Chevard hadn't told him enough. Baron did not like it. As it was now, if Chevard didn't tell him about the breather, Baron knew he would have to worm it out of his friend. It would be difficult. It would take time. During that time, he knew he would feel more and more sorry for Chevard.

Only a single thought held him solidly. Somewhere at the end of all this, he might meet the man who had originally begun the whole mess by sabotaging his plants in the States. So long as this desire burned in the back of his mind, he knew he was safe. Nothing would stop him.

But he was sick with it. Sick with all of it.

"I'm going to have to ask you to promise me one thing," Chevard said. He looked soberly across at Baron.

"Yes?"

"You must promise to say nothing of any of this to anyone. I don't like to ask it—I'm sure you wouldn't. But I have to ask it, Frank."

Baron forced a laugh. "You don't have to worry," he said, feeling the lie like a sharp-cornered rock in his mouth.

"That's good enough for me," Chevard said. "The future of France may well hang on this little enterprise."

Baron swallowed.

"I'd rather you would not mention to Jeanne that I have told you anything. All right that I've brought you out here. She knew you were coming. But about what we are doing, no. She worries. There have been certain troubles."

Baron waited for him to continue, but he stopped talking. What did Chevard mean?

The plant was not what Baron had expected. He had envisioned a vast, sprawling valley area, flat and sunbaked, with metal-roofed hangars and workshops and administration buildings of gleaming brick, their lawns and parking areas set out with grass and flower beds, sidewalks, and "For Official Cars Only."

It was not like that, nothing like back in the States.

They came upon the entrance to the plant suddenly, without warning. The road was abruptly blocked from a sharp hillside curve in the thick woods by a tall wire-mesh gate. Separated in the middle by the gate was a single-storied, one-room building, with doorways on both sides of the fence. Three guards stood by the gate, two on the outside, one on the inside, and they all carried rifles and wore holstered guns on their uniformed hips. They did not come to attention as Baron and Chevard approached and stopped in the Fiat, but Baron sensed a stiffening of tension, of control. None of the guards smiled and there was something immensely foreboding about the whole thing.

"Get out," Chevard said.

Baron opened the door and climbed out and stood beside the car. He glanced to the right and left, up the hillside and down, along the line of steel fence. The top of the fence jutted both inward and outward with a wild tangle of barbed wire and thrusting spikes. He noticed that the wire of the fence was nearly as thick as a pencil. It would be difficult material to cut through. No wonder Gorssmann had been stopped. The fence running up and down the hillside was camouflaged carefully, blending in with the woods and brush, and it had all obviously been erected with care. None of the smallest bushes or saplings near the fence had been broken or trampled in any way and the fenceline veered and curled and circled and zigzagged, following the natural inclination of the ground itself. It was not easy to follow the fence with the eye, or even to see it there in the woods. It was painted a dull green and he realized right away that he was being admitted to a place few even knew existed.

Beyond the gate, the road turned suddenly uphill and vanished from sight.

"Come," Chevard said. He walked on ahead into the building. Inside there was a desk, a typewriter, and a single chair. There was nothing else save a mounted .30-caliber machine gun sitting in the corner, with boxes of ammunition beside it. Under the desk was a wooden box with the top slats ripped off. Baron looked and saw that it contained grenades.

Chevard spoke to the one guard that had entered with them.

The guard sat quickly behind the typewriter and typed on a small card. He did not speak. He was a close-lipped young man, with eyes the color of shallow water beneath the black bill of his cap.

"This is an identification card," Chevard said. He handed it to Baron. Baron read it, reread it. It made no sense. The whole thing was in some kind of code. "It will admit you at any time," Chevard said. "Take good care of it. Only one such may be issued. Without that card, you cannot get inside the gate. Not even I could enter. Watch."

He walked on out of the building and Baron followed him. Chevard moved up to the gate and told the guard to open the gate.

The guard just looked at him. He did not move, nor did the other guard move. The one in the building came outside and stood there with his thumbs hooked into the brown leather belt that held his holster. Baron noticed that the man had cultivated a fine Western slouch.

"Come," Chevard said to the guards. "Open up. You know me, I'm in a hurry!" He spoke loudly, ordering them.

Still none of them moved or spoke.

"You see what I mean?" Chevard said. He drew his wallet from an inside coat pocket, flashed the card, then folded the wallet and put it away. Still nobody moved. He grinned then, withdrew the card from the wallet, and handed it over. One of the guards accepted it, seemed to feel of it between thumb and index finger, returned it to Chevard with a slight grin.

"Back to the car."

They climbed into the Fiat and Chevard put his wallet away as the gate swung open.

Baron was impressed, but for the first time this morning he began to perspire again. It had seemed almost too easy for Chevard to arrange with the guards about a card for him.

He questioned Chevard about this. There was no sense in letting it get by. He had to know everything there was to know.

Chevard grinned like a death's-head above the almost perpendicular steering wheel. "I was waiting for you to ask that, Frank. Good thing you did too,—you would have worried me if you hadn't asked." He shook his head. "I called in from home. A card was arranged for you and sent to the gate. That accounted for the third guard. He was guarding your identity card."

Baron looked straight ahead at the rushing dirt road. Yes, it was plain now why Gorssmann had found trouble. Nobody could get in there. He was coming in because of old friendship, and because Chevard trusted him; really trusted him.

"You notice nothing?" Chevard said suddenly.

At the instant he asked the question, Baron *had* noticed something. To the right, sunken into the hillside, shielded well by a large stand of pine, was the entrance to a eave, large enough to admit a full-grown battleship. Across the mouth of the cave, completely hidden from the air, and practically out of sight from the road, was another wire gate with two guards standing beside it. Through the gate, Baron saw a white stretch of concrete road, or street, stretching into the cave.

He craned his neck, peering back as they flashed by. Abruptly Chevard swung the Fiat off the road onto what resembled a bed of brown pine needles. The tires purred softly over solid-surfaced road, headed directly into a thrusting fall of greening forest that swung low, vine-clotted, to the surface of the road. He drove the car full tilt at the foliage.

"Look out," Baron said softly, realizing what it was even as he spoke.

Chevard chuckled quietly as the Fiat nosed into the mass of foliage at fifty miles an hour. Baron braced himself. It lifted away and the car zoomed into a yellow-lighted, low-ceilinged space that was immense. The floor was macadam, black and smooth. It was the parking area, and Baron sat tightly watching, his heart hammering, as he saw what he faced. It was a tremendous garage. Cars were ranked three deep along the far wall. Chevard circled the interior, swung into line with a grand old Lagonda-Bugatti black-top convertible, and the tires yipped impolitely as they stopped.

"What do you think of it?" Chevard said.

Baron saw another young uniformed guard clipping toward them across the floor. He seemed to have a long way to walk, his hard heels echoing. He walked with one hand on his holster, the other wrapped around the balance of a Garand Ml rifle.

"It's terrific." That was all Baron could manage to say.

Chevard climbed out of the car and met the guard. They spoke rapidly in French for a moment. The guard turned and waved and a jeep roared out of a far dark passage in the wall and veered toward them, tires squealing on the macadam. The first guard waited, watching Baron closely as he stepped over by Chevard. The other guard halted the jeep, waved at Chevard, and joined the first guard, and they started walking slowly back across the floor.

"Come," Chevard said.

He guided Baron over to the jeep and they got in. Baron saw that Chevard had not forgotten the brown leather brief case.

They headed for the dark passage and roared through, and Baron caught a glimpse of still another office, dimly lighted, with somebody seated at a desk behind a large glass window. Suddenly his head snapped around and his breath choked off.

"What's the matter?" Chevard said.

Baron turned back and stared over the hood of the speeding jeep. They took a turn in what was now a tunnel, lighted with orange bulbs set into the cement walls.

"Nothing," Baron said. "Nothing at all." But there was still a brassy taste in his mouth. A man had been standing beside the desk in that office as they passed. Baron could have sworn it was Louis Follet. And yet, as he thought back, trying to reconstruct in his mind the exact picture of what he had seen, he told himself he was mistaken. The man had been wearing overalls, he was sure. Yet he could not get it out of his mind. There had been something about the man's rigid stance, the way he held himself. What would Follet be doing here? But, he thought, it could not be Follet.

The tunnel went abruptly dark and Chevard switched on the jeep's headlights. Baron stared across the hood into the brilliant white splash of light with everything crowding at his chest, choking him into a kind of breathlessness inside.

Where was Bette right now? What was she thinking? What had Gorssmann told her of her father? How much did she believe? He wondered if she knew that he was a paid enemy agent, an international spy, already in the camp of the enemy because he had lied to the one friend in the world who believed in him.

Baron glanced over at Chevard. He knew that just as sure as he was going to keep hunting until he got his hands on the man who had sabotaged his Stateside plants, so was he going to do Hugo Gorssmann's bidding. He knew now that he would never renege, never fail.

Bette was worth that much. She was worth more. But right now, this was all he could afford to give her. He knew too that it well might be all he would ever be able to give her.

What was it Louis Follet had said behind the shredding tobacco and pale smoke of his cigarette? That there was only death to look forward to, when Gorssmann was finished.

"Everything is underground," Chevard said.

Baron snapped himself back to the present.

"The large entrance we passed," Chevard said, "is for the planes to take off from, in case of emergency–in case we have to clear the plant quickly."

"You mean to say the whole business is down here?"

"All, Frank. It was originally a natural cave. I purchased the land and built a home on it. I even have a few small vineyards. Just to make everything seem right. Meanwhile, we installed the plant. Good, eh?"

Chevard drove the car off the main tunnel onto a narrower artery, dimly lighted again, and parked in a small space beside a blank wall.

"Outside."

They got out and Baron stood there waiting. Chevard stepped up to the wall beside the jeep and pulled a chain that hung beneath a gleaming orange bulb. The wall swung open. The door was not concealed, but until it had opened, Baron could not see it. They walked into a well-lighted, efficient-looking office. Two desks behind a wooden barricade faced each other, and at each desk sat a girl. One was typing, the other reading a sheaf of papers and checking things with a pencil. Both girls were extremely good-looking, Baron noted. One was an ash blonde, the other brunette. They smiled and waved at Chevard.

"This is where you keep them?" Baron said.

"This is it. Aren't they beauties?" He grinned at Baron. "Which do you prefer?"

"The blonde," Baron said.

"That's Lucinda. Lucinda," he called, "Mr. Baron wishes to say he admires you greatly."

The girl smiled. The other one looked up, smiled at Lucinda, then returned to her machine-gun-like typing.

Lucinda was extremely chesty, and wore a form-fitting, light tan dress with a big gold buckle under her chin. Every time she breathed the buckle seemed to bend. She turned in her chair, crossed her legs, and looked straight at Baron. Her legs were very long and the skirt hissed up over the knees as she crossed them.

"Lucinda," Chevard said, "show Mr. Baron that you like him." Chevard gave Baron a light push toward the wooden gate that led through the barrier. "Go ahead, Frank—meet Lucinda."

Baron strode through the gate. Lucinda's hand came up. Her hand held a big black automatic. Baron stopped, stared at the large, dark hole in the muzzle, then at Lucinda's pale smile. She waggled the gun barrel slightly.

"Don't go any farther," Chevard said abruptly. "They have orders to shoot. If you had come in here without me, they would already have shot."

"*Magnifique,*" Baron said. He came back to the other side of the gate. He looked back at Lucinda. She tossed him a heavy, round-lipped kiss off the barrel of the automatic and dropped the gun into the desk drawer just over her lap. It clanked against something.

The other girl laughed shortly, and Lucinda returned to her sheaf of papers.

"The dark one is Georgette. She also packs a rod, Frank, as they say in America." Chevard cleared his throat, opened a door leading from the outer office into a smaller room. "They are my girls," Chevard said. "I think Georgette likes you, Frank."

"How?"

"Lucinda seldom tosses kisses that freely and Georgette dislikes Lucinda. You understand?"

Baron grinned, then his face sagged as he stepped into the smaller room, and Chevard chuckled again beside him as the door closed.

"Something, eh?"

Baron looked across the room. The far wall was made of glass, opening into a vast cavern. He had never seen anything like it. Rank upon rank of sleek-bodied planes were strung out, leading from near the window to a dimly lighted distance. Baron could not see the end of them. They were jet jobs, he saw, with the most extreme deltatype wings he had yet seen. They were almost like row upon row of torpedoes, squatting on three spindly legs. They looked nasty. They looked mean. The tricolor of France was stamped on the dull crimson side of each plane, beneath the cockpit. Those wings were like the folded wings of an insect, narrow and frightening. They were thicker than any he had ever seen, the trailing edges stepped once, deeply. Beyond the cork-lined walls of the office, he heard the high tight whine of machinery, the staccato sock of a riveting machine, and far down at the end of the cavern, white sparks showered brilliantly in streaming arcs. Men walked around, hurrying like ants among the planes, crawling over them like ants.

He hadn't expected anything like this. A single plane, yes–other types, perhaps–but countless jet jobs, never.

"Now, you see why all the secrecy?"

Baron glanced at his friend. "No," he said. "I don't."

"I have told you this is a fast plane," Chevard said.

"So?"

Chevard looked out across the ranks of planes, his eyes brooding. His voice was mellow when he spoke, and Baron sensed the strain of excitement in the man.

"It is the most fabulous plane in all the world, Frank," Chevard said. "The fastest man has yet seen. I do not mean by a few miles per hour. I don't mean the sort of advancement of speed we are conditioned to reading about in the newspapers, seeing in the newsreels. This plane is amazing." He went on talking, telling Baron many of the things he knew and suspected, other things that he hadn't known. But as yet he did not mention the breather. "It has more hours of flying time than you could imagine. Refueling has been reduced to a negligible worry."

"Atomic power?" Baron asked quietly.

"Ah," Chevard said.

Baron was half listening, and half thinking of the cruel mess he was in. There had never been anything like this mess, either. The Secret Police would nail him if he made a slip. The guards–yes, even the women secretaries here at the plant–would kill him at the drop of an eyelash. He supposed those girls in the outer office went to target practice twice a week, packing their big black automatics. Gorssmann would remove him and Bette as lightly as he would squash a bug on his desk blotter if he slipped up. Paul Chevard would quite possibly turn on him and shoot him between the eyes with the gun Baron was certain he must carry. Suddenly he wanted very much to get out into the fresh air again. He wished he were drunk. He wished he could be with the billy-goat girl.

Suddenly a door at the other end of the office opened. A uniformed guard stepped halfway out into the room, peered at Chevard, seemed to shrink in embarrassment. "I am sorry," the guard said. "I expected my relief."

Baron saw Chevard frown and the man's mouth twisted. But he said, "It's all right. Close the door."

But Baron had seen what he wanted to see. Beyond the open door was still another room. He saw a desk, chairs, and against the far wall a gray metal safe. Somehow he did not have to be told that that was where he would have to go. That was where his journey would end—and begin....

The guard closed the door. There was no lock on it that Baron could see. Chevard turned his back, then slowly whirled again and frowned at Baron. He began to speak, then waved his hand and grinned. He said nothing at all.


"Would you care to stay on with us?" Chevard asked.

He and Baron stood in the parking area beside the Fiat. Chevard had shown him around the plant some, but Baron had begged off any further tour, because of his still pressing hangover. He did not give the true reason, that he had seen all he needed to see. He wanted to see nothing else. He wanted to get away from Chevard. He could no longer stand before his friend and lie. He tried to find something about Chevard that he could hate, but failed. The man was too trusting. Yet Baron did have to smile inside. Chevard had never mentioned the breather.

"What would I do?" Baron asked.

Chevard shrugged. "There's plenty to do. For a few days, suppose you nose around here at the plant, get the lay of the land, as they say.

Then I will put you to work." He paused, watching Baron carefully. "If that is what you want."

"You know I do."

Chevard clapped him on the shoulder. "You take my car, then. I have another here at the plant. Go home and get some rest. Come around whenever you care to. You are welcome, and trusted, Frank."

"Thanks." He looked across the parking area. "I don't like taking your car, though."

"How else will you get around?"

"All right. I will. Will I always find you here?"

Chevard smiled. "I practically live here, Frank. And as for Georgette and Lucinda, so long as you don't cross the line, you'll be all right."

Baron wanted to ask him about the little room off his office, but he refrained.

"I don't have to remind you about what you have seen, and how much it means, do I?"

Baron shook his head. "No, Paul," he said. "You don't have to remind me." He looked sharply away, stepped over to the Fiat, climbed in behind the wheel.

"Tomorrow?" Chevard asked.

Baron nodded. "I'll call you." His nerves shrieked for him to leave, yet Chevard stood there watching him almost casually.

"Call my house, then–at night. This phone's not listed, here at the plant."

"All right." Baron stared at the spokes of the steering wheel. They seemed to spin before his eyes.

Chevard banged the side of the door with his fist, turned sharply, and walked off across the parking area. The sound of his ringing heels burned into Baron's mind. He started the engine quickly, swung the car out into the immense area, wanting to obliterate everything.

He whipped the car down the road, drew up at the outside gate. The guards carefully inspected his identity card, did not smile, waved him on.

Driving down the tortuous mountain road, with the cliff dropping off beside him, Baron felt utterly lost. He knew now that he was already beyond any explanation. He knew there was no turning back now.

## Chapter Fourteen

HE SPENT THE BETTER PART of an hour, after arriving back in Marseilles, prowling the streets north of St. Charles Station. He took the Fiat up one street, down another. He tried one alley after another, seeking the entrance to Hugo Gorssmann's headquarters. He knew he would recognize it, but the more alleys he attempted, the less confident he became. He found nothing. He discovered many doorways, and tried them all. None was the one he sought. He watched every car carefully, searching for the small gray Opel.

Hugo Gorssmann was well hidden.

Baron drove back toward the Rue Paradis. His head ached dully and his tooth throbbed in time with the headache. He felt dirty inside and out. He knew he was doing what was right, yet he had to keep reassuring himself.

And already he was beginning to dislike Paul Chevard. He could not prevent it, and did not want to. It was better that he hate the man. When all was done, complete, there would be no turning back of time. They could never again be friends. He knew he would never again be able to enter the air industry. He wondered who he would be, where he would be.

He wondered truly if he would be anybody or anywhere.

Above all now he wanted to contact Gorssmann, get word of Bette. He drew the car in to the curb and parked, looked up at the windows of his room at 77 Rue Paradis. That was a hot one, all right. Paradise. He had used to joke with Elene about that, and now Elene was gone and he hoped she had found some sort of paradise wherever it was you went, but he doubted it, believing only in the endlessness, the darkness, the complete emptiness and unconsciousness of sleep.

He felt tired, groggy from last night, fogged with the memory of what he had seen this morning. That place out there near Cassis would have been very interesting if it hadn't been for his problem. He felt that he could have remained out there for days, just looking, watching. But now, sitting in the car, he had consciously to summon energy to climb out and slam the door.

He stood a moment on the sidewalk, staring up at the gray-brick face of the building he lived in. Two feet of lawn, almost the only lawn on the street along here.

He stepped over the gray grass, his foot crunching on a rusty sardine can, and went through the door.

Inside his room, he closed the door, and saw the door to the closet on the other side of the bed move. He said nothing, waiting. The room smelled musty, as it always did at midday. The bed was still unmade. He stood there staring across the room, seeing himself in the mirror. He looked haggard, worn out. His eyes were slightly wild.

"Oh–thank God, it's you."

Lili stepped from the closet, cast him a quick, sly smile that vanished instantly.

Looking at her, he was suddenly tremendously glad to see her. Again that good feeling seeped into him, up through him, and he knew he wanted her. He wanted her badly and with a calm, stolid abruptness that was pure need. He did not know at first whether it was Lili, or merely surcease. He did not care. Just seeing her standing over there across the bed from him washed the fatigue from his system. She was sharp and clear and waiting.

"You've come back," she said. She swallowed, still not moving. He wondered if she sensed the way he felt. He wondered if he recalled rightly what she had said the night before about not having a man, with the intimation that she wanted one. He knew she was not a street girl, not a casual lover, perhaps not even an uncasual lover. Thinking he might not be able to have her when he wanted her like this excited him, and he stepped toward the bed, then stood still, watching her as before.

"Yes," he said. "I've come back. How long have you been here?"

"Not long." She stepped to the foot of the bed, gripped the bedrail with one hand. She looked very good to him. There was something reedy about her, yet full and lushly desirable. She was wearing the pale tan coat again today and now she peeled it from one arm, flipped it across her back, let it slip from her other arm onto the bed. She shook her thick head of black hair, tipping her head back, watching him from beneath slightly lowered lids, with the eyes sly and conspiratorial, and maybe patient. She wet her lips lightly with the tip of her tongue, not smiling, quite somber, contained, patient.

"I'm on an errand," she said. "Paint." She nodded toward the dresser, and he saw a small parcel. "Oh."

"Yes." Her fingers tightened around the bedrail and she did not move. She wore a pink dress of flannel, with a high curling collar, the throat slit open to the waist. A silver chain with a padlock on it swung from her smoothly rounded waist. The padlock swung like a pendulum, tapping lightly against the full round thrust of her right thigh. Each time it struck soundlessly against her thigh, Baron saw the tiny indentation, almost a shadow, and it drove down into him angry and hot.

She moved from the foot of the bed, walked slowly around, and stood looking at herself in the mirror.

He could not, did not want to, take his eyes from her tightly sheathed hips. The immaculately smooth surface of the pink flannel cloth was drawn just tightly enough around the swell and curve of her hips; it clung to her thighs, stopped at the first outward curve of rounded calf tightly snug in sheer black silk. She wore high-heeled pumps, the heels like two thinly tapered pink promises.

The flannel across her hips was shadowed slightly where the twin curves were separated and he could see the fine movement to her body as she waited.

"I see you," she said.

He glanced into the mirror, met her gaze.

"I've been watching you watch me," she said.

"I want to watch you."

"Yes."

Wind blew the curtain on the window, came across the room, dallied a moment with the smooth hem of her skirt, laying it in a molten caress against her leg, and for that moment her leg was completely outlined to him He saw where her stocking ended, where the stocking was gartered high on the thigh, and the garter was the only obstruction to the flawless fit of pink flannel.

"You want me," she said.

He could not answer. It was in his throat, the wild need. He felt as if he were rooted to the floor. Then he went over to her in one step, whirled her around tight in his arms.

"I've had no man," she said. "I have grown up with Hugo Gorssmann. I was fourteen when I last saw my father." She held tightly to him and he wanted to crush her completely. It was all he could do to restrain himself from tearing her dress off her body as she bent to him, arching her back, the warm depth of her thighs cleaving to him, the faintly harsh movement of her body a taunt. Her words rushed at him between parted lips, her breath hot and fierce against his face, her eyes wide and unafraid.

"You knew you were coming here, didn't you?" he said.

"Yes."

"You planned it. You planned this, didn't you?"

She nodded, keeping her eyes on his. "Yes. Yes, all of it. Yes."

They spoke against each other's breath and her breath was sweet to him, and he held her against him, rocking her against him, and she rocked with him, whispering to him, moaning low. And in the back of his mind still was the thought that he could not trust her, that she was doing this for a reason, setting him up like tenpins, to be socked into a crock. He tried to rid himself of the doubt, to stop caring. You fool, he thought. You goddamned fool, forget it!

"You still don't believe me," she said.

It no longer mattered whether he believed her or not. He lifted her, carried her to the bed, moving with mountainous care, feeling like cement, grooved, set, established. He sat on the bed and stripped her, while she stood there in front of him, doing it slowly, and she watched his eyes all the while, not moving to help him, only waiting, and they came onto the bed together, savagely, intent and fused....

She had not lied. She was ready. She had waited....

And with the moment of spending, with her body a still dying crescendo of laughter and tears, spent yet still spending, Baron heard the knock on the door.

They froze.

For one instant their eyes locked.

His guts seemed to turn to water. In one movement then they were off the bed. Again the knock came.

"Baron!"

It was Gorssmann.

She stood like a rock. She could not move, not speak, not anything. He knew it. He shoved her into the closet, retrieved her clothes. He threw them in after her, seeing only her half-closed eyes sharp with memory as he closed the door. He had forgotten her coat. He took that over, stuffed it in.

"I'm coming," he said, saying it slowly.

All Gorssmann had to do was try the door. It would flip open like an eyelid.

### Chapter Fifteen

BARON GRABBED HIS WADDED ROBE from the foot of the bed. He whirled toward the door, slipping the robe on, and now the door opened. He was covered with sweat, his heart slamming in his chest, and he knew he would look anything but composed. He glanced quickly toward the closet. The door was closed, not tightly, but partially, and the closet was in shadow. He could not think straight, and as the huge hulk of Gorssmann came through the door, he slumped to the bed.

"Well, Baron," Gorssmann said. "Sorry to disturb you."

Baron looked up at the man. Gorssmann stood beside the door, a smirk on his lips, his eyes faintly sneering. He wore a dark blue suit today, with a white checked vest. He carried a derby and a white stick. "Sleeping?" he asked.

Baron said nothing. Sitting there, he tried to keep his breathing level, seeking to calm it down slowly. With the tail of his robe he mopped the sweat from his face. He wanted to say, The hell with Gorssmann. But he knew he couldn't. He still could not be sure of Lili, God bless her. He did not know what to do about Lili.

Gorssmann turned beside the door and, watching Baron from the corner of his eye, spoke toward the hallway.

"You wait there, Arnold."

Baron heard Arnold mumble something. There was disagreement in the tone, but he couldn't make out the words.

"Kindly refrain from speaking to me that way," Gorssmann said.

Arnold said something again, snapping it at the man.

Baron watched. He saw Gorssmann's hand come up suddenly. The stick lashed out. He heard the smack, the cry, the rapid steps as Arnold scurried from the doorway. Gorssmann thrust his head forward and spat past the door into the hall. Then he closed the door and looked at Baron. He was smiling politely.

"Well?" he said. "What is the good news, Baron?"

"How?"

Gorssmann rapped his stick on the floor.

"You know precisely what I mean, thanks."

"What's the idea, barging in this way?"

Gorssmann stepped over to the window and looked out. Then he turned and blinked at Baron. He hung the derby on the back of the chair by the window, but held onto the cane. He glanced toward the hall door and pursed his lips, and Baron heard the dry whistling hiss of his breathing.

"I knew very well where you were this morning. Also of your–shall we say–picnic last night. Poor Joseph is so drunk I've had to confine him to his bed. He was appointed your shadow last night. You didn't know that, did you? Joseph is silent in more ways than one." Gorssmann paused, paced over by the dresser, and stood there.

Baron noticed something and his energy began to pick up again. Gorssmann's hand was not a half inch from Lili's package of paints, there on the dresser. Gorssmann had laid his hand on the dresser top. He twiddled his pinky, close to the packaged paints.

"How is your friend Monsieur Chevard? He is well, eh? He took great pleasure in seeing you?" Gorssmann chuckled, panted, blinked slowly at Baron with his head thrust slightly forward. "Come, come, Baron–loose the tongue. A close-mouthed habit does not become you. Please relieve my anxiety."

Baron knew he would have to talk. There was no point in holding back. He wanted to get everything over with as quickly as possible. He knew he had to, and the hate inside him seemed to grow with this thought. Hate for everything–hate for himself. And looking at Gorssmann, he recalled something else. If Joseph, the deaf-mute, was in bed recovering from too much drink, and Arnold was in the hall, and possibly the chauffeur outside in Gorssmann's car, then that left but two persons who might be relegated to keep tabs on him today: the man who had originally been in the rear seat of the Opel that first night, and Lili.

It was an evil thought after what had happened between them, and what he had discovered about her But suppose she were here under Gorssmann's orders? Suppose Gorssmann even knew about that package on the dresser, knew what had happened, perhaps? It ate down into him like a frothing acid. Lili, standing inside the closet, there behind him, perhaps smiling and giggling to herself about this. And Gorssmann brooding quietly as he stared at the bed, knowing possibly what had happened there. He could even imagine Gorssmann giving her the order: Keep him happy. Sleep with him— it's high time you slept with somebody, thanks.

He wanted to rise, go over there, and fling the closet door open.

But he didn't.

"Yes," he said instead. "Everything is well with Paul Chevard."

Gorssmann waited and Baron saw the impatience, the dim light in the huge man's squinting eyes. Gorssmann licked his narrow lips, and his hand moved out and he clutched the package of paints unconsciously. He did not look at what he had in his hand.

"I went out to the plant. I think I spotted where what we want is," Baron said. "I can't be sure, because Chevard said nothing. But I'm pretty certain."

"Good. Good." Gorssmann's tone was throaty, yet high-pitched with excitement. He was holding himself down tightly.

"That's all there is," Baron said. "I'm free to come and go as I wish. Frankly, he trusts me too well."

"No, no. He is your friend. He trusts you, that is all. Don't you comprehend human nature? You say he has not told you of the breather?"

"Never mentioned it." Baron felt truly bad now that he had spoken. It hit him all at once, hard, knowing what he had done. He had betrayed the last confidence he would ever be likely to get in this world. He stared down at the floor between his feet, thinking about it, and wondering almost frantically if Lili were in it with Gorssmann. If so, all right—then it wouldn't matter.

But it would. That was the trouble. Having her had settled nothing. He realized he wanted more from her than just that. He wanted her. He sensed something in her he had never before found in a woman. Elene had been fine, and true, and she had given her life, yes. It hurt to know this. But nevertheless, he had never felt with Elene what he did with this little sly one. And this had been only the third time he'd seen her. When he came through the door, he had wanted her, and now that he'd had her, he still wanted her, more than ever.

"You are very silent," Gorssmann said. "I should think you would be happy."

"Yes."

Gorssmann chuckled again. He picked up the package of paints, glanced at it, dropped it back atop the dresser, went over and sat heavily in the chair by the window. He sort of backed into the chair, and he had to jam himself between the arms. He was obviously uncomfortable and Baron liked knowing this.

Gorssmann said, "You have discovered something else, I see."

He's wise, Baron thought. He's wise about Lili!

But it wasn't that. "You have discovered hate regarding your friend Chevard already. So soon, Baron? It takes the best of us a little while. Even I. Here nor there." He waved his hand, tried to settle himself more comfortably in the chair. He hissed short laughter. "Perhaps we should keep you in my employ. Would you like that? I have a little enterprise in South America. We will take that up as soon as this is off the hooks, eh? Baron, what do you say?"

"Go to hell."

Gorssmann leaned forward in the chair, the arms creaking with his weighted pressure, and he blinked solemnly.

"Very well," he said. His voice was sad with concern. "*Alors,* tell me everything—everything, Baron!"

Baron did not want to. He felt that if he retained some small part of what he had seen out there at the plant today, it would boost his morale. But as he looked at Gorssmann, he knew the man would know if he lied. So he told it, and hated himself some more. He rose from the bed and went over to the dresser, unconsciously hiding the package of paints now, because it had been on his mind.

Gorssmann sat there, gloating.

"I want to know about Bette now," Baron said. "All about her. And I'll tell you this," he said, looking into Gorssmann's glistening eyes. "You harm one hair of her head, or let her get hurt in any way, and I'll blow this whole thing sky-high."

Gorssmann laid his head back in the chair and hissed quiet laughter at the dingy ceiling.

"You forget," Gorssmann said. "We have her. As to your question, Baron, Bette is fine. Yes. I took her shopping yesterday, we bought all sorts of pretty things." Gorssmann's eyes turned inward with remembering and Baron began to feel ill. "She is a beautiful girl, very beautiful," Gorssmann said. "Young and coltish, and gorgeous. A body that would destroy–" He glanced up, caught Baron's look, waved his arm. "Here nor there." He smiled, trying to smile away remembering. Baron saw that Gorssmann wished he had not spoken as he had.

"Just remember what I said," Baron told him.

Gorssmann raised his hand. "I shall treat her like my own daughter, never fear. Just as I have treated Lili. Lili has been like my daughter, Baron. Don't you think she's a sweet one, though?"

"Very nice."

"Yes. Bette is getting the best care." Gorssmann looked up quietly at Baron. "I heard, through Joseph, about something," he said. "Ah, my taste, as it were, in women. Baron, is it true about this girl–this one with the goat?"

Baron continued to feel more and more ill. Bette was in this man's hands and he could see a dry evil flame in Gorssmann's eyes now.

"I should much like to meet this woman," Gorssmann said. "You might say I collect such creatures. They interest me." Gorssmann writhed slightly in the chair, the arms creaking against his weight.

Baron was close to exploding now. It was all he could do to stand there and know the man Gorssmann was.

Gorssmann shrugged, rose to his feet. The chair rose with him. He wriggled his hips and the chair clattered to the floor. Gorssmann's derby bounced to the floor and rolled over by the bed.

"Would you kindly pick it up for me?" Gorssmann said.

"No."

The big man loomed beside Baron. He stepped over, fished for the hat with his cane. He had no success.

"I will ask you again. Please. I cannot. Would you hand me my hat?"

"You will leave then?"

Gorssmann waited. Baron went over and picked up the hat, flipped it to Gorssmann, waited. Gorssmann passed him a slow tight look, turned, and walked out through the door. Baron waited. The door opened and Gorssmann stepped back inside.

"Please act immediately. As soon as you can, Baron. I will keep in touch." He turned and the door closed. Baron heard him speak to Arnold, then the slow descent of the stairs began, and he thought how good it would be to push Gorssmann down those stairs, to see his huge body tumbling end over end with the high song of fear bubbling on his lips.

He knew what he had to do.

She stood stiffly in the shadows of the closet and stared at him.

"Come on out," he said. "I'm in a hurry, Lili.'"

She reached for him, her fine body beginning to tremble again, and Baron did not know what to do.

"Darling," she said.. "Darling."

He left her there, hurried across the room to the front window. He heard her padding along after him, her bare feet whispering on the worn carpet.

If he could follow Gorssmann ... He looked down and the big man and Arnold were standing by the gray Opel, parked behind the Fiat. Gorssmann brandished the cane, pointed across the street. Arnold said something.

"Please," Lili said. She held to him, gripping him and pressing her warm soft body against his back. "Please, Frank!" He felt her breath against his neck and her thighs tightened on him, her body moving against him. He wanted her, but he had to try to follow Gorssmann. He did not exactly know what was in the back of his mind.

"I did not know," Lili said, holding to him. "Frank, I love you. I love you, *chéri!* It is magnificent and I never knew. I love you. Come to the bed again, Frank. Please, darling!"

He pulled her around and held her against him. The smell of her hair was like heady musk in his nostrils and he held her there against him, looking down to the street.

Gorssmann whipped the cane against Arnold again. Arnold shrugged his shoulders and the two men crossed the street in front of the Opel and entered a café. Baron saw them sit at a table near the door.

"I am a grown woman and I never knew!" Lili said. She whispered it against his throat, pressing herself against him, whispering again and again that she loved him.

He held her way from him, keeping one eye on the café, trying to arrest the rise of passion that again confronted him. He wanted to take her over to the bed. He wanted her perhaps even more now than before. She seemed to be trying to let him know that she was completely his, and the sly look in her eyes was there all the time. He wanted to believe her, trust her. Abruptly, then, he tore off his robe, whipped it across her shoulders, held it tightly closed.

He moved across the room, gathered up his clothes, returned with them to the window, and began to dress.

"Listen, Lili," he said. "I don't want to stop now, either. There's nothing I can do."

"Yes." She watched him. The robe began to sag open and he kept his eyes on the window. She was the most tantalizing woman he had ever seen.

He fumbled nervously, dressing, trying to forget that Lili stood there, pleading with her eyes.

"Is what Gorssman said about Bette true?" he said.

She nodded. "He did not go shopping with her. He says those things to tease you. Bette is well. Tonight I will talk with her. She said to tell you she is all right and that she understands."

"But do you understand?"

"Only that I have found love, Frank."

He said nothing. He got his tie around his collar, knotted it, realizing he had his collar under the tie, unknotted it. He saw Gorssmann and Arnold come out of the café. Gorssmann carried a paper bag. They looked up and down the street, then moved on across and climbed into the Opel.

"I've got to go," he told her. For a single moment he held her against him, kissed her warm lips.

"You are going to follow them? Why?"

He said nothing. He could not bring himself to tell her about Follet. He still could not trust her.

"Gorssmann is bad," she said. "I must tell you this, so you'll know. Quickly!"

He glanced down the street. The Opel still hadn't moved.

"What, Lili? What?"

She stepped away from him, turned her back, and went over to the bed. "He does bad things, I know they are bad. He has never touched me, but he makes me dress up all in black. With black pants that you can see through, Frank. Then he makes me do things. Like– stand on my head. Sometimes he pins the skirt of my dress over my head and makes me dance for him on his bed. Always on his bed. He has a huge bed. Once he painted me with black paint all over and–He has a peephole cut into the wall of the–I never know when–It's truly terrible, Frank. I thought you must know."

He stood there staring, and his stomach turned slowly. He wanted to go down there and kill him. He knew now that he had to act, and quickly. Already he had seen the man's eyes when he spoke of Bette. Bette did have a wonderful body, as lovely as Lili's, and if ... He left the thought unfinished, rushed through the door and down the stairs.

As he reached the front door and opened it, he saw the Opel draw away from the curb. He climbed behind the wheel of the Fiat and drove quickly out into traffic. He kept the small sloping rear end of the Opel in view, two cars ahead.

As he headed out Paradis toward the Cannebière, he remembered with a touch of panic that he hadn't told Lili that Gorssmann had handled her package of paints. If Lili was honest and the alert Gorssmann happened to see the package when she reached his place with it, there would be trouble. Because Gorssmann would remember.

## Chapter Sixteen

BARON WAS FRIGHTENED. He knew he was doing the best he could, but the sense of fright and panic would not leave him. He was dealing with things over his head. He had already realized that his life had not been meant for this. This was the kind of thing you looked at in a movie, or read about in the morning paper over coffee with your first cigarette. Yes, he thought, drying one palm after the other on his trousers, then grasping the sweat-slippery steering wheel of the Fiat, Only you are in it. And now you've gone and begun to cross the fat one.

And thinking of Gorssmann, he recalled again what Lili had told him as he left the room. The man was a monster. Imagine, painting a girl with black paint! He had never heard of one just like that before.

Somehow he had to keep Bette out of his mind. Thinking of her only brought more pain.

He knew he should insist that he see Bette. Suppose Gorssmann was lying? Suppose Lili was, too? Maybe Bette's knife-sliced body already lay on the banks of the canal, her blood tinting the waters crimson. Like Elene.

The Opel drew to the curb before a bakery, just ahead. Baron came to the curb and waited. For the moment, his mind cleared, and he tried to remember what it was Follet had said he should do if he wanted to find him.

Yes. Café Demoiselle on the Prado, somewhere around the Place Castellane. He would find it. It was a gamble, but lately everything was a gamble.

He would try to see Louis Follet and talk him into staging a raid on Gorssmann's headquarters. That way Bette could be saved, and Gorssmann would be put behind bars, where he belonged, with the rest of his crew. And surely among Gorssmann's effects there would be some lead to the head man. Baron wanted that as much as Follet. He prayed now that Follet would take the chance. He knew the agent wanted the big boy, not the middle man. Nevertheless, he must go along with it. He had to.

He saw Gorssman at the bakery door. He went inside, and Baron waited. Arnold got out of the car and stood on the sidewalk in front of the bakery, looking up and down and carefully brushing his hat.

Gorssmann returned, striding across the sidewalk with two long loaves of bread beneath his arm. He nodded brusquely to Arnold, and after they were inside, the Opel pulled away into traffic again.

As he followed, Baron realized he was hungry. Seeing the bread had done it. He passed the bakery and the loaves were racked fresh and flaky and brown in the windows.

The moment the Opel turned off the main street into the alley, Baron knew for sure it was the spot. He remembered it from the first night, and he also recalled that he'd been past here today. How he missed it he didn't know. But to make doubly certain, he parked the

Fiat and ran across the sidewalk to the corner of the alley. The Opel was nowhere to be seen.

He stood there.

For an instant he went sort of blind inside. He was about to move down into the alley when a grape arbor on the right side, shielding the rear of a home, rustled, and Gorssmann stepped out. He looked up the alley.

Baron ducked back. When next he looked, Gorssmann, Arnold, and the young driver were moving through the door into the corridor that led to the garden.

Baron turned and made for the Fiat. Exuberance picked him up, and he headed back toward the Prado.

*"Oui,"* he told the thin, red-haired woman in charge of the Café Demoiselle. "Room Two."

She stepped back from the side of the small bar, took hold of the beer spout, and looked him over. She was very tall and very thin. She wore a gray dress with a white apron, and her eyes were like the blued heads of freshly tempered horseshoe nails. Her long nose hooked out over her upper lip and her chin hooked up. Her mouth was a buttonhole and Baron saw suddenly that the red hair was a wig. It was disconcerting. From beneath the edges of the red hair, just around the woman's large pendulous ears, fine gray-white hair peeked in fuzzy knots and knobs, like the gray gobs of dust that collect beneath beds.

"Room Two?"

*"S'il vous plaît,"* Baron said. He watched as the woman arched her head back and swallowed.

"Whom do you seek to find, monsieur?"

"Simply Room Two, please."

She frowned question marks at him.

"This is the Café Demoiselle?"

*"Mais oui, monsieur."*

"You are–the madam?"

He could have sworn that she blushed. She nodded.

"I was told that I should ask you for Room Two."

"Who told you that, monsieur?"

"A man—a friend."

"Ah." She released her grip on the beer spout, moved around behind the bar, pushed the cork tight in a bottle of *vin ordinaire*. She held the bottle up to the light, toward the street, looked at it, then looked at Baron over her shoulder. He could have sworn now that she was trying to look coquettish. It was his turn to blush. He whirled around, stared out the front door of the café. A man who had been at the back of the café, playing the pinball machine, walked past him.

The man nodded and waved a cigarette at the woman.

The woman waved the bottle.

"Well?" Baron said to the woman.

"Would you desire a glass of beer, maybe?"

"No."

She shrugged, put the wine bottle down, and stared at it. She scratched her head. The wig moved back and forth with the itching movement of her fingers. When it moved, Baron saw the pink scalp just about the tufts of gray hair. It was somehow grotesque, horrible, frightening.

"What kind of man was this man who sent you to Room Two?"

He stared at her. "Maybe I should go," he said. He knew very well that he could not go. Had Louis Follet been making jokes?

A young girl with an extremely flagrant behind entered the café. She went to the bar, ordered a double cassis, drank it, did not pay for it, and left. She did not once look at either Baron or the red-haired woman.

"You are sure you do not desire one beer, maybe?"

"All right."

She smiled, picked up a glass, held it under the spout. She pressed the handle. When the glass was full she held it up to the light, inspecting it. She found something. She wiped her index finger across her apron, dug into the beer for the something, had some success, wiped the finger on her apron and wiped the bar with the apron and set the glass carefully on the bar just beyond the spot she had wiped. She grinned steadily above the glass of beer.

He paid her. He did not drink the beer. She rang the money up on the cash register. The grin vanished.

"Come."

She motioned to him and walked rapidly ahead of him across the café floor, through some bedraggled violet drapes into a hall smelling strongly of fish and cabbage. She went to the end of the hall, opened a door, and stood aside as Baron entered. He saw the numeral 2 on the door. Inside he turned just in time to have the door close in his face. Not loudly.

An hour and a half later, Louis Follet entered the room and stood there looking at Baron. He took his hat off, stuck it beneath one arm, prodded his pockets for tobacco, and rolled a cigarette.

"Sorry to keep you waiting. I had a long distance to come to arrive."

"Forget it."

Baron had been sitting in one of the two chairs by the small circular table in the center of the room. There was an ash tray in the center of the table. Otherwise the room was empty. Baron was so tired and sick now he did not care what Follet did. He could not even see through the one window in the room. It had been painted a peculiar color sometime along about 1912, maybe.

He was so worked up, thinking about Bette and how he had sold Chevard out, that he could just barely stand looking at Louis Follet. He hated Follet. He hated everybody he knew. He could think of no one he did not hate vehemently and with glass-smooth, easy-flowing, unadulterated hate.

"Madame said she did not know whether or not to trust you," Follet said. He chuckled. It was a dry sound, like sand poured down a cellar door.

"Good Lord," Baron said. "Who is that harridan?"

"We keep her on," Follet said. He came across the room. He dropped his spent match into the ash tray, rocked on his heels, dropped his broken hat on the table, and sat down opposite Baron. "She was, believe it or not, one of the very most famous spies in the Allied forces during the First World War, and she caused the firing squad and the rope, too, and even suicide for many an unhappy one." He mused quietly above his cigarette, coughed lightly, like a beetle cleaning its wings, while he picked shreds of tobacco from the cigarette. He shook his head. "You perhaps saw the wig?"

"How could I help seeing?"

Follet nodded. He did not smile. "They did that to her, too. She was captured. They burned her hair off, Baron. Then they cut her scalp into small checks, like a chessboard, and plucked the pieces out one by one. Her hair never grew back, of course. She escaped, and came across to our lines with her head bandaged, as a prisoner of war, disguised, you know? When they took the bandages off, there was only the skull–the shiny white bone. They performed surgery–plastic surgery, you know?–and saved her. It had already started to–" He made loopy motions with his finger. "But the hair, it never became again, except some tufts near the ears." He shook his head. "She was content that she lived, even grateful. She continued with her work. She even managed to return and somehow kill the very officer who cut her scalp. She cut his throat. What was it you were going to say about Madame?"

Baron said nothing. The picture in his mind was bright and horrible.

"Not many know of these things that happen during war," Follet said. "Or during peace, either. The ordinary person has no conception of what is gone through, perhaps." He smiled behind the thin cigarette smoke. "It is, as they say in America, a tough proposition–rugged."

"Were you at the Cassis plant this morning?" Baron said. He did not want to think about what he had thought of the woman.

"What did you summon me for?"

"All right." Baron sighed, rose from the chair, and searched for a fragment of calm. Some calm had to be someplace. He paced the room and told Follet why he'd wanted to see him. "You've got to do this," he insisted. "You've got to."

Follet ground his cigarette out in the ash tray. He rolled himself another, coughed around it, and lighted it.

"It stands to reason, it's a good chance all round."

Follet nodded.

"I can't take the chance, with this Gorssmann. Not now," Baron said. "They've got my daughter." He looked over at Follet. The man sat quietly smoking, staring at the flyspecked wall beyond the table. Baron came quickly across the room, smashed his fist onto the table. The ash tray leaped up, flipped out its ashes, slammed back in place.

Follet brushed the ashes off the table into his hand, emptied them back into the ash tray, and looked at Baron.

"I'm sorry, damn it! Can't you see how I feel?" "I did not disagree with you, monsieur," Follet said. "I was merely thinking about the prospect and how we should best approach it. All right, we will try."

Baron felt relief like a cold shower on a hot day. He settled into the other chair and suddenly felt extremely tired and hungry. He leaned his head on his arms on the table, then peered over his arms at Follet, saying nothing.

"Tonight, then. You will come?"

"Try and keep me away."

"Good. The sooner, the better. Just after dinner, then. Let me think." He took out a large round gold watch from his vest pocket, inspected it, put it away. "Two hours, eh? Good. I shall play the fool."

"The fool?"

Follet shrugged and said nothing.

"Then what now?"

"You meet me here. At a quarter after seven, good? Yes?"

Follet rose, uncrumpled his hat, put it on, and ground out his cigarette. "I will go. You wait five minutes. Then you go."

Baron nodded.

Follet went on out and closed the door.

When the five minutes were up, Baron walked out into the café. The woman was behind the bar. She did not smile at Baron. He walked over to the bar.

"A beer, please."

She drew the beer, inspected it in the failing late-afternoon light, and set it on the bar. He paid her. She rang it up, brought him his change. He drank the beer, and discovered to his immense surprise that it was absolutely excellent beer. The woman smiled at him now and he left. He felt somewhat better for the moment at least.

He had never seen so many policemen. They converged on the blocks surrounding the alley leading to Gorssmann's headquarters, and Baron sat tensely waiting beside Follet in the Fiat, until Follet would give the word to move in.

"In case anything goes wrong, you will have your own car," Follet had said. "It would look peculiar if Gorssmann found you wandering around loose–if he got away."

So, sitting in the car, Baron went over everything and tried to make himself believe that this was the right thing to do. Some of the excitement came through to him, and by the time Follet said, "We'll go now," he was ready.

There was something about it from the very beginning. The opaque silence as he followed Follet down the alley toward the corridor door seemed too quiet, the night a soft shroud that held a kind of impatience that worked its way into Baron. He wanted it over with. And when it was over with, he would go to Chevard and talk. He did not care whether Chevard could be understanding about it. He wanted to get it off his chest, free himself of the nearly deliberate anxiousness, because of deliberate falsehood.

"That the door?" Follet asked.

Baron nodded. "That's it."

Three other officers came from the other direction in the alley. Two were with Follet and Baron. One remained outside.

The door was open. Baron had told them about the Opel, but they were unable to locate the car. They moved down the corridor, through the still garden with the smell of jasmine thick in the night. When they finally reached the door that led to the rooms in which Gorssmann lived, Baron knew. He knew from the way things had happened. And he was right.

Nobody was there. The rooms were empty. Gorssmann had left.

"I was afraid of this," Follet said.

Baron said nothing as Follet ordered his men back to headquarters. They would not be needed now. Baron walked through the rooms. All of the furniture had been left behind, but it seemed to have been swept with a vacuum cleaner. The place was immaculate.

"There won't even be a fingerprint," Follet said. He was obviously disgusted. Baron saw that he did not want to look him in the eye. The secret agent walked through the rooms, rubbing, looking, checking every crack, every drawer, every closet.

Baron sank into the chair beside the huge desk, the same chair he had sat in that night that seemed so very long ago. He pointed out the room in which Joseph had beaten him, and Follet frowned.

"You know what you have done?" Follet said.

Baron looked at him.

"You have ruined chances of any help from us. It took a great deal of argument to pull this off. Now it is finished."

"I'm sorry."

"Being sorry arranges the least of nothing, monsieur. I said I would play a fool. I have. I should have known better."

"You think somebody tipped Gorssmann off?"

Follet shrugged. "It matters little. They have flown. We can do nothing now."

"You're a great goddamned help," Baron said.

Follet looked at him.

"What the hell are you birds for, anyhow? What the hell good do you do, anyhow?"

"This is the last time I can help you, monsieur."

"Fine."

"But you had better achieve something soon, Baron–very soon."

He felt the fear coming strong into him again.

"Don't worry." His voice rose then, and excitement took him as he told Follet what he was going to do, how he was going to rifle the safe at the plant, get the plans for the breather, because he felt certain that's where they were. "I'm through fooling around."

Follet pursed his lips. "As you wish."

"You don't like it?"

"It gives with the bad odor."

Baron stood sharply. He stared at Follet. "Anyway, that's it. And as soon as possible, with or without your help." He turned and started across the room. He walked out past the Chinese screen that still stood by the doorway. Another door across the first room was open. He went over there and looked into a bedroom. He saw something beneath the bed, clothes, sticking out by one of the legs. He kicked the clothes with his foot, picked them up.

There was a skirt, a black coat, and a pair of dirty gray gloves. They were marked with the name of a shop in Atlanta, Georgia.

Holding the clothes, he knew they were Bette's.

Whirling, he stalked into the other room. Follet was standing with his hand on the knob of the door leading into the corridor.

"Yes?" Follet said.

Baron shoved the handful of clothes under Follet's nose.

"My daughter's, see?" he said. "Look at them! Do you know what that means? Do you?" He wanted to hurl them in Follet's face.

Follet looked at him for a few seconds. Then he turned and walked out of the door. Baron stood there in the room with the clothes in his hand and it was very quiet.

## Chapter Seventeen

JEANNE CHEVARD stood in the doorway and smiled at him.

"No, Paul hasn't come home yet," she said.

"Think he's going to stay out there a while?"

She shrugged. "Maybe. Why don't you come in?"

Jeanne was wearing a thin, dark blue dressing gown. She looked very appealing, and when she invited him to come in, she smiled in a way that troubled him. She stood that way at the door, too.

"Paul isn't home much any more," she said. She kept on looking at him that way. "Nights especially, he's often gone until very late. Sometimes he doesn't get home until morning."

"Well."

She stood there in the doorway with the light from inside the house shining through her hair and over her shoulders and through the dressing gown, too. He could see the full outline of her body through the gown. When she smiled he saw that her lips were wet, but she kept the gown closed. She wasn't going to press anything. He knew she was lonesome. He didn't blame her. He knew she loved Chevard, but she was just so damned lonesome.

"You don't know when he'll be back, then?"

She shook her head, never once taking her eyes from his. "Certainly, not for hours yet. I can tell you that for certain."

They watched each other. The light shone in her hair.

"My daughter's staying at a friend's house tonight."

"It wouldn't be right," he said. "I wouldn't feel right."

"All right."

Maybe the excitement and the way the night had been and the way he felt had done it. He knew he should have turned and left the instant she said Paul was not there. She moved now, in the doorway, from one foot to the other, shifting her weight, and he saw that she wore absolutely nothing beneath the gown.

"It's been a terribly long time since Paul has stayed around the house for more than a few hours," she said. She kept on looking straight at him. "He isn't like me, you see. I mean, there's a difference. He's wrapped up in his work."

"I'm sorry."

"You're so damned noble," she said. "Why do you men have to be so damned noble?"

"I–"

"Forget it."

"All right. I'd better be getting along."

"You had damned well better. No, listen–it's all right." She smiled at him. "Say hello to Paul."

"Sure."

"I could fix you some coffee, Frank."

They both laughed then, and it was all right. He waved his hand and turned away, and she closed the door.

Driving over the road to Cassis, he began to think about Patricia and how the way Jeanne had been reminded him of Pat. He had been too busy, too. Only there was a difference. Jeanne would stick with Paul and everything would turn out all right. He knew that. She wasn't the same as Patricia.

He remembered Graff. John Graff. A tall, broad-shouldered, blond roamer with a scar across his forehead that humped up like a pencil. Graff had been around before and during all the mess at the factories. He hadn't realized until later that Graff was with Patricia every night he was away, and all of the days. He should have known. It must have been perfectly obvious to everybody. Graff was a smooth one, though. And when the trials came up, he disappeared. It was during that time, just before Patricia left, that she told him.

Somehow, he had not hit her. And anyway, what good would that have done? Graff was gone, and she didn't care about that, either. And she got Bette, anyway. There was nothing he could do about any of it. And all the time he had been on friendly terms with John Graff.

He lived in a hotel then. But he had returned to the big house one afternoon and the shades were all pulled, the air smelled close, and the sun shone yellow through the shades with the dust motes crawling in the beams of sunlight, and he walked from room to room, picturing them in his mind because he couldn't help it, and that same night he had tried to find Graff. He failed. Graff was gone.

"Mr. Graff gave me a present, see, Dad?" Bette had said the day before. It was a brooch, a gold brooch studded with fine stones, and Bette was crazy about it.

"Yes?"

"Isn't it lovely?"

And he had asked to see it. Something uncontrollable took hold of him and he dropped the brooch to the floor, there in the hallway on the terrazzo floor, and smashed it with his heel. Bette stared at him, maybe a little wild.

He told her he was sorry. He would get her another brooch just like it.

"It's all right, Dad," she said. "I think I know."

And she turned and left and came back and looked at him and said, "It's because of that night Mr. Graff stayed in the guest room, isn't it?"

He hadn't known about that, either. He hated the way Bette wised up to things. She had a mind that snapped out and caught at everything very quickly. "Yes," she said, "Patricia"–Bette always called her Patricia when she was mad about something–"took him a tray. She told me they were going to talk and play cards. She never came to bed that night. I know because I checked twice and I thought I heard her crying in the guest room, only now I know what it was."

"Run along, Bette."

And a week later he was putting on one of his shoes and he saw something sparkle. It was a ruby jammed into the leather heel of his shoe. He remembered sitting there on the edge of the bed, staring at the ruby in the leather. Patricia and Bette had already left town and he was due on the witness stand that day.

Lucinda and Georgette were not in the outer office. Baron walked past the wooden barrier and the door leading to Chevard's office was open. He stood there a moment, looking in, and Chevard was seated at his desk, looking at some papers in a large folder.

Chevard looked up and saw him and grinned. Then he frowned down at the papers, and Baron stepped quickly into the office and stood there.

"What brings you?"

"Stopped by your place and Jeanne said you were out here. I'm feeling some better. Thought I'd take a run out, for something to do." He was lying like all hell. He was beat. He was starved. He hadn't eaten a thing all day and had not had a moment's rest.

"I see."

"Sure."

Only, he thought, you don't see at all, you poor fool. And you'd better damn well get home right now. Or maybe you had better wait. Your wife might be out someplace for a time.

Chevard looked dead tired. His eyes were red-rimmed hollow sockets, with the pupils glaring.

The door leading into the room where the safe was was open. Baron noticed, without actually looking, that the guard was in there, seated on a chair. The door to the safe was open and his mind began working, planning it all even without consciously thinking it.

He had the feeling the papers on Chevard's desk were the papers he wanted. He began to tremble down inside, standing there, and Chevard was plenty nervous about something. It was too quiet and he did not know quite what to do. He wanted to sit down, but he could not move from in front of Chevard's desk.

Then Chevard rose. Baron could see that the papers were blueprints and his heart rocked.

"Jeanne all right?" Chevard said. He edged around to the side of the desk and tried to shove some books over the folder. Then he must have thought better of it and Baron knew Chevard was fighting it out with himself as to whether or not he should tell him about the breather. It was very plain and Baron began to feel sorry for the man again. Chevard's eyes kept snapping up at him with the excitement in them, and Chevard wanted to tell him about that breather. He had to tell him. Because he trusted him, only he wasn't supposed to say anything, only he had to, and Baron began not to feel sorry for him. He tried to summon hate.

"You didn't answer me," Chevard said.

"She's fine. She looked lonely, though."

"Suppose so. Well, I can't help it." He kept looking from the folder to Baron, then to the folder again. Then he made some kind of decision and he picked up the folder.

Baron knew what he was going to do. It had been in the back of his mind all along, about the safe. If the papers were kept in the safe, then how in hell was he ever to get it open? Because the combination would be memorized–by Chevard and possibly a couple of others. He didn't have the time to find out who the others were, and he knew what he was going to do–what he had to do.

It had to be timed exactly right and it could fail miserably and easily, but right now it was his only chance. He already knew that tomorrow was going to be the day, too.

"Just a moment," Chevard said. He dropped the folder in a large envelope, tightened a string clasp, glanced at Baron, and walked into the other room.

Baron knew he was meant to wait here, where he was. He didn't. That was part of the plan. Disconcertion. He followed Chevard into the other room.

The guard stood up and looked at them.

Baron saw Chevard's shoulders tighten as he realized Baron was in the room, too. It was nothing, really, because they were friends. But just the same, it bothered him, and Baron was beginning now to understand just exactly how important those papers were.

The guard did nothing. He was young, with a blunt face; a stolid man who would be difficult to push.

Chevard put the papers in the safe, straightened, and closed the door with one hand touching the dial on the front of the safe. All he had to do was twirl that knob once, and Baron knew the thing would be in the soup worse than ever.

He spoke quickly in the silence, praying and with the perspiration streaming down inside his shirt and beading across his hairline.

He struck straight at what Chevard was thinking about, knowing it was the best psychological jar. The safe door was closed, Chevard's hand was a finger's breadth from the knob.

"That where you keep your skeletons?"

Chevard snapped erect, looking sideways at him. The hand came away from the door.

"Good Lord," Baron said. "I didn't mean to scare you, Paul!"

The guard's leather creaked and Baron began talking in a steady stream. He felt that if Chevard moved toward that knob now, he would jump him.

He told him he was sorry he had startled him, talking steadily, standing close to Chevard. "The way you began creeping around here when I came in, it's sure something, Paul," he said. "Listen," he said. He reached out and took hold of Chevard's arm, then dropped his hand. "I need a drink and you look like you could use one. Keep anything around?"

He grinned at Chevard, and, turning, winked at the guard. The guard grinned back.

"Come on," he said, reaching out and rapping Chevard lightly on the shoulder. "You must have a bottle stashed away somewhere. Remember Paris, during the war? You had bottles in every room in the house. Say, remember that night we took the case of cognac to the Follies?"

Chevard grinned. "I sure do."

"Well, come on. You got anything?"

Chevard snapped his fingers, moved toward the other office. "By God, I *could* use a drink," he said. "I haven't had a drink in days."

Baron followed him into the office. He did not look at the guard now. He could hardly see. His head thrummed and thumped like a kettledrum.

For the moment, the safe was open. He knew it. All you'd have to do would be to turn the handle and pull....

They sat there in the office and drank two thirds of a liter of cognac. After five drinks, Chevard began talking about the breather, and Baron sat there by the desk and cursed himself for the worst kind of heel. The brandy had grabbed hold of Chevard like a steel clamp. The man was dead tired, exhausted, and with the first drink his eyes had glazed and his mouth twisted and he was licked. He talked all right for a time, sitting there behind the desk, pouring the cognac into a couple of inkwells. He had emptied the ink into the wastebasket and cleaned the glass receptacles with paper. They didn't hold too much, but they served.

The guard in the other room kept watching them, but Baron knew better than to offer him a drink. Pretty soon the guard could no longer stand it. He came over and silently closed the door and Baron began to feel safe.

He did not think about what he had to do tomorrow. He wished he had the nerve to do it tonight. It would take more than a bottle of cognac, though. A hell of a lot more.

"I should not tell you this," Chevard said. He tried to hold his stiffening lids open, forcing them upward, his eyebrows up all the time now. It didn't help any. His lids closed even with the eyebrows up like that. He looks like hell, Baron thought, like pure hell. But don't feel sorry for him.

"All you've told me is something about a gadget you put on this plane. I keep thinking it's maybe atomic. But how could it be? It would be out, somehow–wouldn't it?"

Chevard leered at him. He drank from his inkwell and refueled without spilling a drop.

"A breather," Baron said, prompting him a little.

"A *cosmic* breather," Chevard said.

"The hell with it," Baron said. He did not want to hear any more about it. It would be better that way. He felt completely evil and rotten. Even the brandy didn't seem to help. He hoped Chevard would shut up now.

"I'm drunk," Chevard said. "It's a good thing I know you, Frank."

"Sure."

"I could be shot for this."

"Oh, hell."

"It's true. We all took an oath, Frank. But I know you. I said to myself, Chevard, you old son-of-a-bitch, this man is your friend and he lost his faith in himself because he thinks everybody's lost faith in him. So, I said, you've got to show him that you trust him."

Baron stood up by the desk with the inkwell in his hand and stared at Chevard. Right then he came very close to telling the man just how wrong he was to place any faith in a lying bastard like himself. He put the inkwell on the desk, turned, and walked over to the door. "I'm going home."

"All right." Chevard coughed, drank, looked at Baron. "We begin production on the breather next week," he said. "Maybe I can ring you in on that. Everything's ready. It's going to be something, all right. Never been done before."

"Next week."

"Correct. Think I'll last through to the tests? I've been under some terrible pressure."

"You'll be all right."

"It's a question of air," Chevard said. "You see? The higher up you go, the less air there is, you see? Got to have it. Got to breathe. A question of breathing. It's so damned simple it's obvious, we all know that. Only how? That's the simple part. Well, we've got it. Fly to the goddamned moon. A question of breathing, that's all on God's green earth. Nobody hooked onto it, though. By God, no." He drifted off into a long tirade in French, rattling on and waving his arms, with Baron catching perhaps two thirds of it. Baron knew he had to get Chevard to leave with him. He could take no chances on Chevard's staying here all night, and maybe checking the safe to see if it were locked properly.

"Why hasn't anybody else caught on to this thing?"

Chevard stood and came around the desk and stood rocking and weaving in front of Baron. "It's staring them in the face, understand? They want to make it intricate. They've missed it, had their hands on it hundreds of times, and missed it. People look but they don't see, that sort of thing."

"I'll drive you home."

"Yes. All right."

Baron saw that Chevard was close to collapse. They left the office and piled into the jeep. Baron drove Chevard home in the Fiat. Chevard slept all the way. Jeanne and Baron helped get him into the house.

She grinned at Baron, with Chevard slumped in a kitchen chair, snoring.

"See what I mean?" she said.

"Yes."

"It's all right, though. It's all right, Frank."

He looked at her but she was already poking Chevard awake, so she could get him upstairs. Baron left in the Fiat, and he knew what he had to do. There weren't many hours between now and the doing, either.

He drew up at the curb in front of 77 Rue Paradis. He sensed the shadow by the door of the Fiat before Arnold opened the door.

"Good evening, Monsieur Baron," Arnold said. "Come with me."

He was about to tell him to go to hell. He thought better of it. He didn't know what he wanted to do and maybe it was just as well that he see Gorssmann. Perhaps he could see Bette.

All right, he thought. Where's your gun?

"We will go in my car," Arnold said. "Please, quickly."

"I'll follow you," Baron said.

Arnold said nothing. He waited by the open door of the car. The Opel came up the street then and parked beside Baron's car. The rear door swung open.

Baron went over and got inside the Opel.

"Proceed," Arnold said to the driver.

This time Baron was alone in the rear seat of the car. They're beginning to trust me, he thought. Somehow it was a kind of consolation in the midst of all the distrust and lying and confusion. Then he sat there and laughed. At first he laughed quietly to himself, but finally the laughter burst past his lips.

Arnold hung his chin over the rim of the front seat and watched him, his face gleaming pale as they passed street lights.

## Chapter Eighteen

THIS TIME THEY DROVE through quiet moonlight on the Corniche road. Out there to the right, the Mediterranean lay peacefully black and moon-shot, and Baron tried to think of nothing. He concentrated on the word itself, but it was no use. Bette would be wherever he was going–and Lili. As they drove along, he thought about Bette and his thoughts turned to Lili and he knew that he loved her. He wished that he did not, but there was nothing he could do about it. Because perhaps she was with Gorssmann on this thing and that would be bad–for him, not for Lili.

"You've moved?" he asked Arnold.

Again Arnold turned and looked at him over the rim of the front seat, his eyes glistening wetly. He did not answer.

The hell with him, Baron thought. He realized that he had picked up something along the way that helped him not to care. He wondered what it was and where he had got it. He wondered whether it was a good thing. He decided it was. At least in this case it was.

He had so many things to consider and to worry about that not caring about a couple of things seemed to help release the pressure. Then he got to remembering about how Follet had acted and the places where the pressure was released filled up and he felt worse than before. Why couldn't Follet have been just a good egg? But they can't be, he decided. They've got to be a little mysterious and opaque and all that. They can't just be straight and to hell with it. They've got to let you know that they're onto something that you don't grasp, that you can't understand. Maybe that's what's so maddening about them.

Damn them all.

Damning them did not help.

They rounded a curve, and Baron saw a swimming pool cut into the rock, back from the sea, down there to the right. There were some dim yellow bulbs burning above the doorways to bathhouses and he saw two women sitting on the boardwalk wrapped in towels. It was far from warm and the breeze from the sea had ice in it. What the hell was the matter with these people? Nuts, he thought. It's not the people, it's you.

Rounding the curve beyond the pool, the Opel turned suddenly to the left, straight into the Corniche cliffs, and up a road cut through the solid yellow-gray rock. They lurched in ruts, swung up and up and around and under huge trees and roared across an immense lawn, disregarding a semicircular driveway. It was one of those big châteaux up there on the cliff overlooking the sea. Baron saw that it was an old one, the moonlight touching it in places, and he thought of the old castles and witches' temples in a Disney cartoon of midnight on Halloween.

They jerked to a stop in front of the house. A light burned in one of the windows upstairs and all of the downstairs lights seemed to be glowing. Wooden blinds were drawn, but the light shone through the slats.

"He laughs," Arnold said to Gorssmann. "He laughs like the clown."

Gorssmann blinked at Baron. They were sitting in a large flagstone-floored room, in immense hand-carved black mahogany chairs. There was a large fireplace opposite Gorssmann. At the end of the room a weathered-looking grand piano was quietly going to hell beneath a wrought-iron stairway that circled upward to a balcony. Off the balcony, Baron could see doors leading to rooms.

"The laughter is merely tension," Gorssmann said. "Not so, Baron?" Gorssmann was wearing an orange-and-blue-checked robe. The sash was too small for his girth and it kept coming loose and beneath the robe he wore black pajamas. He kept tying the sash, but every time he moved, it slipped loose. Finally he tied the sash into a tight knot and from then on was obviously extremely uncomfortable.

"What do you want?" Baron said.

Gorssmann sighed. "I expect this may trouble you some," he said. There was a kind of sadness in his voice. "I have had orders. Things are, shall we say, getting hot? It was, as you see, necessary to move." He waved his arm.

"Why?"

"Here nor there. The man I am dealing with is impatient. He says we must act immediately."

"I have good news, then," Baron said. He heard the bitterness in his voice. He wished he could rid himself of that, but it seemed to come from down inside him. "I've decided not to wait at all. Tomorrow is the day."

"Good." Gorssmann leaned forward in his chair and smiled. The sash pained him and he leaned back again. "Very good, Baron. You see, something has been decided. If you fail, we are supposed to blow up the plant at Cassis."

Baron stared at him disbelievingly. "But that's only destroying your own ends!"

"Try to grasp this," Gorssmann said. "I don't care at all what is done, so long as I am paid. The sum I am to receive is the same, either way. If you fail in accomplishing this mission, you are to be put on the other one. That is, if you are not, shall we say, out of the running?"

"I won't fail."

"Optimistic? Well, that's a good sign, sometimes. All right."

They discussed it for a time and Baron told him what he had planned. He kept his eyes and ears open, hoping for some sign of Bette. So far there was nothing.

Gorssmann was working himself into a slow fit, thinking about what would happen in the morning. He had begun to perspire and breathe heavily. Arnold stood over by the door, watching them. Baron listened to Gorssmann's hissing breath.

Gorssmann said, "As soon as you succeed in getting those papers, Baron, return here. You know how to get here now?"

Baron nodded.

"We'll be waiting."

"Is that all?"

Gorssmann nodded. "Arnold, you may take Baron home now." He was staring at the floor, his eyes slightly protruded, staring intently. "You must not fail! Do you understand?"

Baron nodded. "I want to know something," he said. "I want to know about Elene. Where is she?"

"You have seen the papers," Gorssmann said.

Baron knew then that the newspapers must have printed the story.

"Don't feel badly," Gorssmann said. "It was unavoidable. She was the cause of her own demise." He did not look at Baron. Baron came out of his chair, strode across the room, and looked at Gorssmann. The fat man turned his eyes up to Baron and tried to smile. But he could not smile. "I promise you," Gorssmann said. "If you fail–"

"You know what I want to know."

"Your daughter is perfectly all right."

"I want to see her. Where is she? You lied to me about Elene. You would lie about anything. I know that, you know it. I want to see Bette."

"I am profoundly sorry. You cannot. Arnold," Gorssmann said. "Show Monsieur Baron out, please."

Arnold started across the room. He was already wearing his hat. His face was quite grave and he walked stiffly, with one hand near the pocket of his suit jacket. The jacket pocket hung down slightly and Baron knew there was a gun there.

He also knew they would not hurt him now.

"Why did you lie about Elene?"

"Because you did not have the proper attitude to assume the responsibility of knowledge. You still haven't, but that cannot be helped."

He heard a voice calling to him. It was a young woman's voice and he knew it was Bette's. It came from one of the rooms up on the balcony. Gorssmann lurched to his feet, reached to grab him, fumbled.

"Arnold!" Gorssmann said.

Baron turned, twisting from Gorssmann's grasp, and leaped toward the stairway.

"Baron!" Gorssmann said loudly. "You fool! You ass!"

Arnold ran in front of him, waving the gun. He still had his hat on, and somehow, even in the violent rushing, it was comical. Baron straight-armed Arnold in the face and Arnold sat down on the floor, still holding the gun.

"Bette!" he called. "Bette!"

He heard her yell then. She yelled bloody murder and he started up the stairs. He was scared. He was as frightened as it was possible to be.

He ran full tilt into Joseph, who had started down the stairs.

"Bette," he called, trying to get past Joseph.

There was no sound from upstairs now. He went slightly berserk. Joseph frowned, lifted his foot, and centered it on Baron's chest.

"No, Joseph!" Gorssmann screamed from the foot of the stairs. He had forgotten Joseph could not hear. Baron felt himself leave the stairs and he hurtled backward through the air, over the banister.

Gorssmann yelled something. He yelled it close to Baron, and Baron landed on something that gave, scrambling and yelling. He had landed on Gorssmann. They rolled across the floor. He leaped up. Joseph was already there. Joseph stepped toward him.

Gorssmann was groaning on the floor. He saw Joseph coming toward Baron and shouted, trying to get to his knees. He could not rise. Baron saw he could not get by Joseph.

"Bette!" he shouted. "Are you all right?"

There was no answer. He nearly wept. Joseph did not move. Gorssmann kept trying and trying to get to his knees, but he could not manage.

"Arnold, help me!"

Arnold came over and finally got Gorssmann to his feet. The huge man stood reeling, staring at Baron.

"Have Joseph take him outside. Take him home. Now!" He turned on Baron, and he was in pain. He panted heavily, his breath hissing and whistling, tears in his eyes from the pain, his lips twisted like a baby's.

"So help me, if you've harmed her—"

"Get out, you fool!"

Joseph got the wind of things then, through Arnold's gesticulations, and he came and took Baron's arm and they moved toward the door at the far side of the room.

"Hurry," Gorssmann said. "Go along, Arnold—take that maniac home. And Baron," he called. He limped painfully to the chair and sank into it, wiping his face with both hands. "One mistake—one, you hear!—and your daughter will—you know! You know what will happen. Now, go and we will see tomorrow."

In the car, Arnold turned and looked at Baron over the rim of the front seat.

"It is true," he said. "You are a fool. Hugo becomes mixed up when things like this happen. He is apt to do anything. One never knows."

Baron surged forward. Joseph reached over and grabbed his arm. Baron quieted down. There was nothing he could do. He had heard Bette's voice. She was there, in that monster's house.

A few hours, he kept thinking. Just a few more hours.

But what would those hours bring? He did not know and he was too worked up to guess. His leg began to pain him and he knew he had hurt it when he sprawled down the stairs. He looked over at Joseph. The man stared straight ahead, his face utterly without expression as they drove down onto the Corniche road and turned toward Marseilles proper.

Baron tried to look at things coldly now. He knew what he had to do and he was going to do it. Morning would come soon, and he would cross Chevard once and for all. It would be done.

He hoped it would be done. Anything could happen. If he failed, he did not know what he would do.

"Arnold," he said, "I've got to have a gun. You can understand that, can't you?"

"Yes, but I do not know if Hugo will think—"

"Let me worry about that."

Arnold debated for a time. They came around past the harbor, and turned up the Cannebère.

"Well?"

"Yes, all right." Arnold reached down onto the front seat, handed Baron a gun. "You will return it, *non?*"

Baron did not answer him. He examined the gun. It was a .32 Savage automatic. He put it in his pocket. They turned up the Rue Paradis.

"Let me off at the restaurant, right there. The café on the corner."

"Sorry," Arnold said. "My orders are to take you to your home. That is the way it must be." They sped on past the café.

The Opel drew to a stop exactly where they had picked him up earlier, beside the Fiat. Baron climbed out and looked back at Arnold's glistening eyes.

"I must tell Hugo about the pistol," Arnold said.

Baron turned and walked away.

"I don't know what Hugo will do," Arnold said.

Baron climbed into the Fiat, pulled swiftly away from the curb, turned, and headed back toward the café. He was ravenously hungry. The gun was uncomfortable in his hip pocket. He changed it to his side jacket pocket.

He was going to go through with it. Why did he keep telling himself that? He knew he would have to, he must.

Eating in the café, he was extremely nervous. It seemed to him that everybody watched his movements. Even the waiters seemed to hover unnecessarily close. Nevertheless, he forced himself to eat, because he did not know what tomorrow would bring. He knew he would need strength.

He sat back then at the table in the café and laughed at his half-empty plate.

## Chapter Nineteen

THE QUESTION OF WHETHER OR NOT the supposedly constructed model of the breather was in the safe along with the papers did not occur to Baron until he was already inside the plant the following morning. Now, thinking of it, he knew what he was going to do. Whether he found it or not, he would tell Gorssmann he *had* found it, and destroyed it. He would tell him he smashed it, maybe burned it. This pleased him, because just now he was very anxious and worried and nervous.

He parked the Fiat and climbed out and stood there in the parking area. It was quite early. He felt certain Chevard would not be here now. There were few cars in the parking area. He was glad of that, because seeing anyone would raise hell with what little composure he had.

He started walking across the parking area toward the dispatcher's office. They apparently had expected no one in this early and weren't watching, because no jeep came tearing across the area toward him.

He was scared deep down inside now. But he kept walking steadily, not allowing himself to think beyond the first move. His heels echoed across the nearly empty parking area.

The place was so large. So very large. He had known this, but now it seemed out of all proportion. He knew he would have to go deep underground, to Chevard's office, to reach the safe. Worse than that, he must return calmly and drive away, past the parking area, past the gate with the close-lipped guards.

He opened his mind freely because he couldn't stand it any more and admitted the fear. It came into him like a kind of wisp of smoke, like a new kind of soul, this bright fresh vital fear. A nation's right to live and grow crossed the floor with him, walking along with him. Bette's life and liberty and perhaps Lili's happiness; surely his own, if Lili ...

The dispatcher was sleeping at the desk in the front office. He lay across the desk with his head on the telephone. Baron closed the office door, took the first jeep at hand, and pushed it straight out into the tunnel, without starting it.

When he figured he had gone far enough, he jumped in and turned the ignition on and drove on down the tunnel, then finally turned into the artery leading to Chevard's office.

He parked the jeep. He had turned off the motor quite a way back and coasted to a stop before the door in the artery wall.

Now he sat there in the hard-seated jeep and stared at the windshield folded down across the hood. He gripped the steering wheel hard, and perspiration oozed from between his palms and the rim of the wheel. He wiped his hands on his trousers, then took hold of the wheel again, just sitting there.

Every muscle in his body was tense and aching. He tried to relax, but he couldn't. He did not know what was on the other side of that door and he had to go in there and find out and he was afraid, damned well afraid.

He breathed deeply. The breath shuddered his whole body.

He climbed out of the jeep and stood there. He looked up and down the artery, toward the main tunnel far up there, and down into the blackness, the other way. Right now somebody might be standing down there watching him. But he had done nothing, so far.

All right, goddamn it! He walked over to the wall and found the chain under the dim bulb and pulled and the door swung open.

Lucinda looked up from her desk. Georgette was typing. She kept right on typing.

It was a horrible shock and he almost faltered, but somehow he went right on in with the swing of the door. If it hadn't been for the door, he knew he would have stopped. He had not expected them to be here. It was perhaps seven o'clock now, and he had not planned for them to be here, to see him.

He kept right on walking. He walked over to the barrier and stood there, looking at the blonde Lucinda. She turned in her chair, crossed her legs with a professional hiss, and smiled broadly at him.

"What is it you desire?" she said in very brisk French.

"Monsieur Chevard in yet?"

"Not yet, my cabbage."

He gripped the edge of the wooden barrier, then pulled his hands away. She kept watching him and then Georgette looked over at Lucinda and then at him. Georgette winked at him.

They both watched him now.

"Well, guess I'll wait for him." He grinned at them both, turned, and walked at a medium rate into Chevard's office. He felt their eyes and he felt them strongly. He somehow managed not to look back and to keep moving all the time, and got inside the office and closed the door.

The door leading into the room where the safe was was open. The guard was sitting in there, wide awake, reading a magazine, and looked up at Baron. He said nothing, he did not smile, he simply looked. He was not the same guard that had been there the night before. Baron tried to remember whether he had ever seen this man before, and then he remembered that he had been on duty the first morning he was here. It was a stroke of luck, and it was something he had not counted on at all.

He waved to the guard. "Morning!"

The guard did not even nod. He stared for a moment longer, then began reading his magazine again.

"Just waiting for Chevard," Baron said. He went over and stood in the doorway. He watched the guard. The guard immediately began to fidget. He could not read the magazine, yet he must somehow keep his eyes on it because for some reason it was embarrassing with Baron standing there. It was embarrassing because the guard knew the door should be closed and he should speak to no one and he was conscientious, or maybe frightened, and too young for his job. He also knew Baron was Chevard's friend and perhaps if he closed the door in Baron's face, or ordered him away, Baron would say something to Chevard and the guard would lose his job, or be reprimanded, or both, and he could not take that. He was too young. Baron saw all of this with a kind of cynical satisfaction.

"Must get boring, sitting there all the time."

The guard's head jerked up, then his eyes went back to the magazine. He said nothing.

Baron tried hard to hate the guard. He called him names in his mind. Nothing worked. You jerk, he thought. You crazy dumb young jerk of a guard, don't you know what I'm here for? Haven't you got the guts they're depending on? Get the hell over here and order me away, close the door, pull a gun.

He walked into the room, over to the small table, and sat on the table, watching the guard.

It was too late for the guard to do anything. He was young and he sat there, still pretending valiantly, violently, sickeningly, to read. It was painful to watch him. He was beginning to perspire beneath his cap.

Baron waited a little longer, watching the suffering.

How could Chevard have been so dumb as to hire a guard of this sort? A young, helpless, honest, trustworthy, faithful jerk?

The guard deserved death, at the very least.

The guard was positively in agony now, seated there with his fool magazine. There was perspiration running down his nose and he did not even trouble–could not trouble–to wipe it away. He could not move. He was trapped and Baron knew it.

Baron left the table, went over to the door and closed it, and drew the gun from his pocket and walked back to the guard and shoved it in his face.

"Get up. No, sit still!"

The guard's mouth came open and remained that way. Baron could see that the guard had many fillings in his teeth and that he needed a filling badly in one tooth at the front of his mouth. The magazine fell to the floor. Baron reached down quickly, took the guard's gun, and slipped it into his pocket. He kicked the magazine under the table.

Time, time, time! It shrieked at him abruptly in the back of his head and his ears began to buzz with the tension he did not really realize he was under.

"Do not move, not a hair. Don't even breathe," Baron said slowly, in his best and most precise French. "If you do, I promise you, I will kill you. I mean that. You understand?"

The guard's head bobbled like a puppet's and Baron kept slowly moving around the chair behind the guard. Now came something he had to do and suddenly he stood there not able to do it. He stared at the guard's head and he could not do it.

He began to think the guard's cap bothered him. He knocked the cap off onto the floor. The guard's shoulders jerked, but he said nothing and he did not again move.

Baron stared at the man's head. He had brown hair, straight, and combed in a very neat part. All around his head Baron could see in the shining grease the man used the imprint of where the cap had been.

He had to strike this man on the head with the gun. He had to knock him unconscious.

How in all hell could he do it? He remembered everything he had read. He tried to think of the war, thinking back, but he had never in his life struck anybody on the head. They claimed that if you struck too hard it would kill. Hell, he did not want to kill this jerk.

Where should he hit him?

Behind the ear? That's what he had read someplace. He looked behind the ears and goddamnit, he could never hit a man there with heavy steel! There was a hump of bone behind the ear and he knew it would go crunch and that would be that.

The guard said something. Whatever it was stuck in his throat and it scared Baron.

Baron's arm came up, holding the .32, and he brought it down with everything he had, just under the bump on the back of the skull, where it turned in to the neck. It made a hell of a noise and the guard sat there stiff and straight and Baron did it again, still harder, with that almost maniac-like violence with which you kill a mosquito in the middle of the night.

The guard sprawled out of the chair, face down on the floor, out cold.

He went over and opened the safe door and began searching. He found the envelope he was looking for. He had not felt anything at all when the door opened. He did not even think, This is great! Suppose the door had been locked?

He tore the envelope open and tried to make out what was in the folder. Blueprints, all sorts of plans, and a sheaf of solid manuscript, and it was the breather, all right. My God, yes! Now it came to him hard, reaching him with the solid, substantial force of something accomplished and a hell of a way to go yet. He shoved the stuff back into the envelope and checked on through the safe. There was some correspondence pertaining to the industry, signed documents, a lot of loose papers, but nothing else pertaining to the breather. He closed the safe door, as it had been, and wiped it free of his fingerprints.

Then he opened his jacket, undid his shirt, and pushed the envelope and papers into his shirt and around the back, so his belt held them securely. He rebuttoned his shirt, put his gun away, and stood there breathing like a small steam engine.

He quickly went over and inspected the guard. His head was bleeding. Baron turned him over. The man was out absolutely cold. Baron felt of the pulse. It was weak and slightly erratic, but it was there. He took the chair over and leaned it against the wall. He was laughing to himself now, down in his throat. He knew he was a bit mad. He dragged the guard over to the chair and pulled him up and sat him there, with his head hanging, his arms hanging. He got the magazine and propped it on his lap and looked at the guard.

How long would he stay unconscious? Would striking him again help? He knew he could not do it, anyway.

You are no longer a jerk, I am sure of that, he thought. When you wake up, you will be a man, and you will trust nobody. You will probably become so goddamned belligerent you'll never make another friend in this world.

He turned, walked rapidly across the room, out of the door into Chevard's office. He closed the door and went on out into the outer office and looked at Lucinda and Georgette.

He closed Chevard's door. The papers in his shirt seemed to crackle with every move he made and he was certain they bulged his coat out, so anybody could see them plainly. It made him walk oddly, sort of sideways, and he realized this and knew he had to act natural.

"I believe I'll go on outside," he told Lucinda. "If Paul comes in, tell him I'll be back."

She nodded and smiled broadly at him. He did not look at either of them again. He strode toward the outside door. As he stepped up to it, it opened, and Chevard walked in.

## Chapter Twenty

"WHAT IN GOD'S NAME are you doing here?" Chevard said.

Baron made the effort to speak. The words caught in his throat and he swallowed with doom ticking in his ears. He waved his hand back at the two secretaries and grinned, then his voice broke through strong and clear.

"Came by a little early." He looked at Chevard. "But I'm going home, Paul. I feel lousy. After I left you last night I stopped for something to eat. Must have been bad. Awful stomach cramps this morning. They just seem to be hitting me." He grimaced slightly, and avoided Paul Chevard's eyes.

"I'm pretty much of a mess myself," Chevard said. "Hope I didn't cause you too much trouble last night. I must be in terrible shape, the way that cognac hit me. Ordinarily, I can drink brandy all night long."

"You're tired." Somehow or other, he had to get Chevard away from the office, manage time enough so he could get away from the plant.

"I guess I am tired." He stepped closer to Baron, and Baron saw the anxiousness in the man's eyes. "I talked a great deal last night, didn't I? I told you something, didn't I?"

"Yes. Forget it. It was nothing. What I mean, you have a wonderful thing in this breather, Paul. It's an amazingly wonderful discovery. I can see why all the secrecy now, and I admire you."

"Thanks."

"I'm going on home," Baron said. He felt the papers in his shirt and he distinctly heard them crackle. He watched Chevard's face closely. "Why don't you ride out to the parking area with me? You could bring this jeep back."

Chevard glanced over at his office, then back at Baron.

"Come on," Baron said. There was anxiousness in the tone of his voice, he tried to make his voice light. "We can talk. You can spare the time."

"All right," Chevard said.

They went on outside and climbed into the jeep and Baron hardly talked at all. He had difficulty in keeping his foot easy on the accelerator.

"You seem troubled," Chevard said. "I thought we were going to talk, Frank."

"I'm sicker than I thought."

"You get on home, then. Listen, why don't you go to my place? Jeanne will fix you up."

Oh, good great God, Baron thought. He doesn't know what he's saying, the poor fellow.

"I'll see," Baron told him. They came into the parking lot and he drove the jeep over to where the Fiat stood. He climbed out immediately, and the papers crackled. He wondered if they would be worth a damn by now. They would be sweat-soaked, but the envelope would protect them.

"Listen, Frank," Chevard said. "For God's sake, please never say a word about what I told you last night."

"You don't have to ask me that."

"I know, but I am asking you. One slip and all is lost. And that's not being dramatic." His face looked intensely worried.

"Just don't bother yourself about it," Baron said. "I'll see you later. Maybe tonight?"

Chevard nodded quickly. "Yes. Come to the house."

Baron was already in the Fiat. Chevard kept looking at him, wanting to say it again and again, that he should not say anything about the breather, the story he had told him last night. Baron could read the fear in Chevard's eyes.

"Tonight," Baron said. He started the Fiat, drove swiftly out of the parking area. Once outside, he stomped on the accelerator, careened down the curved road toward the gate. In his mind's eye he saw Chevard climb into the jeep and start back for the office. He slowed the Fiat on the last curve and rolled slowly to the gate.

Already, he knew, the phone might have rung in the gatehouse. The guards might be waiting.

They weren't. They came out and one of them took his identification card, then handed it back, and the gate opened. He drove through with the card still in his hand. As soon as he was out of sight, he turned the Fiat loose. He saw the card in his hand blow abruptly out the window, and made a wild grab for it. He was already doing eighty-five miles an hour and the car swerved on the road and he straightened it out, perspiring, his hands wet on the steering wheel.

He hit the main road, finally, and opened the car up all the way. The Fiat roared and became a light, foolish, wild thing in his hands, but it stuck to the road. He saw by the speedometer that he was doing 168 kilometers, and went through the familiar mental steps to translate the kilometers into miles: 105. This speed on those particular roads was out of the question. There were no guardrails and the road began to peel down now, around the mountainside. He came off the macadam onto a stretch of gravel where they were doing repair work, and the car hit it lightly, cuttingly.

He began to let up then, going down, and as he approached the first really wild curve on a cliffside, he looked straight out there and saw the sea and Marseilles bright and shining in the morning light. If he held the wheel perfectly straight, it seemed that he could ride right on down there, coast to the Cannebière.

He wanted to take those papers out of his shirt.

He made the curve and it was close. For one long horrible moment he could see from the corner of his eye out the car window straight down and down and down to treetops and the bare side of the mountain with the road curling and a vineyard.

He took it a little more easily then. But not much.

There was nobody in the Café Demoiselle except the woman with the red wig and the horribly interesting background.

She looked at him and shook her head.

"I do not know if I can do this thing, monsieur."

"That's not the question," Baron said. He was very nervous. He knew every minute counted, that Gorssman was very smart, and that he might have had him followed. If so, he had managed to elude the shadow. He had driven up and down several alleys and had seen no one. He knew, however, that he had to reach Gorssmann's place, and fast. Bette was in the back of his mind, like a poised dagger, and Lili was there with her, and he was going through hell and now this woman had to act this way. "You've got to get word to Follet, see? Tell him to come here and wait here until he hears from me, until I get here, something! Understand? There's not a single moment to lose, madame."

"I should not divulge this, perhaps, but this I know: Louis Follet will no longer help you, monsieur."

Baron just stared at her.

"All right," he said. He whirled around, all the way around, then faced her again. It would be easy to walk out. He could not do it. He had thought for an instant that he would be able to leave it this way, let them soak in their own stinking broth, let them lose everything. He could not do it.

"Just get word to him. Will you try to do that much?"

"Yes, but as I tell you ..."

"Never mind that. Tell him to wait. Tell him things are under way. Tell him that I am going to do everything I can, that–Oh, hell!"

"I understand," she said. Her face became abruptly kind, serious. "I do understand, believe me." She stopped speaking French and spoke perfect English. "I have been through these things, Mr. Baron. I know about them. I promise to do all I can to persuade Louis Follet."

"Thanks." He reached out and took her hand. She smiled at him.

Then she shrugged. "But Louis is stubborn. He thinks you did a wrong thing."

Baron nodded. He could think of nothing else to say. He left, running across the sidewalk to the Fiat.

Damn Louis Follet, he thought. Damn them one and all, singly and together. Damn them.


Hugo Gorssmann stood on the porch of the sprawling stone house on the Corniche. As Baron turned the Fiat's engine off, he glanced up toward Gorssmann. The big man was nearly dancing up there, rocking back and forth, from one leg to the other. He reminded Baron exactly of an elephant dancing at a circus.

"Success?" Gorssmann called carefully from the porch.

Baron said nothing. He climbed from the car, walked toward the porch. Gorssmann wore a light tan suit and it looked spanking new. He also wore a large-brimmed felt hat of pale gray and it looked fine and rich in the midmorning sunshine. He could hardly wait for Baron to reach him. He had his hands stretched out, waiting, his tongue batting his lips.

"Baron–Baron, did you–"

Baron clipped up the steps, stared at Gorssmann.

"Baron!"

He walked on past the huge man, into the house, on into the sprawling living room. He stood over by the fireplace and waited.

Gorssmann came slowly into the room. He paused by the door, looked bright, then sad. He was afraid to ask anything now. He moved across the room, moving effortlessly, it seemed, like a battleship coming into dock.

Abruptly he turned his gaze to the floor.

"You have failed," he said quietly. "Something went wrong." He looked at Baron, then suddenly tears sprang into his eyes. His shoulders shook, his chins shook. He folded his hands in front of him, as if he were praying, took a single step forward, and stood like that, his face thrust slightly forward, tears streaming from his eyes. He wrung his hands, weeping, his lips curling like a baby's, curling down with his chin puckering. It was a sight.

"Take it easy," Baron said.

"Oh, Baron!" he cried. "Baron, Baron, Baron!"

"You poor son-of-a-bitch," Baron said. He was awed. He could say nothing else, do nothing.

Gorssmann trembled and tried to prevent his chin from puckering. With all his might he tried. Nothing seemed to help.

Baron reached inside his shirt, wrenched it around, came up with the papers. The envelope was soggy. He stripped it off like damp, rotten cloth, let it drop to the floor. Then he banged the sheaf of papers and blueprints against his other hand.

"Here they are," he said.

Gorssmann said, "Oh, Lord!"

"Arnold!" Gorssmann called. "Arnold!"

"You want to know something?" Baron said. He backed away until he was pressed against the fireplace. Gorssmann kept coming, lumbering, wiping his eyes dry, smiling now. "You make me sick."

"Give them to me," Gorssmann said. He had changed again.

"Stay away from me," Baron said. "I'm warning you."

"What is it?" Arnold said, coming across the room. Joseph followed behind Arnold. They both saw the way Gorssmann was acting and saw the papers in Baron's hands. Arnold made a happy sound. Joseph just kept coming.

Baron drew the gun and pointed it at Gorssmann. "Stay right there. All of you," he said.

Gorssmann stopped. He observed the gun closely, then nodded. "Yes, yes," he said. "Tell us about it, Baron."

"All of you sit down," Baron said.

Gorssmann looked at Arnold and Joseph. Joseph stopped walking and looked at Arnold. Arnold made a sign. They all went and sat down, Gorssmann in a chair and the two men on a wooden settee.

Baron relaxed.

"Please," Gorssmann said. "Put the gun away, Baron. I was excited, nervous. Have you not been this way? A great deal depends on this. Excuse it, please. Now, the gun—I do not like seeing the gun, thanks."

Baron thought about it, put the gun back in his pocket.

Everybody was very still. There wasn't a sound. Then coming through it, spearing it, was Gorssmann's breathing. It was angry breathing, mad breathing, and Baron looked into the man's eyes and he saw the evil there.

"Where is Bette?" he said.

"Bette?" Gorssmann looked at him. He folded his hands in what lap he had and looked quietly, almost sadly, at Baron.

"When I see Bette, you get these papers," Baron said.

Gorssmann waved his hand. "Come, come, now," he said. "Such a bargain, Baron. Is that any way to talk to me? How do I know what papers you have there? They could be any sort of papers. I have to see them."

"You'll see them. When I see Bette."

"I'm afraid we can't come to terms this way. Bette is, I assure you, Baron, in perfectly excellent hands. Lili's, to be exact. You certainly can trust Lili, can't you?"

"I don't know, frankly."

Gorssmann did not even smile.

"But I do know this: Until I see Bette in this room, you don't see these papers." He stood there by the fireplace. To the right of him, on the settee, Arnold watched him, his face quite sober. Joseph stared straight ahead.

"I mean it," Baron said. He stepped forward and looked down at Gorssmann. He was trembling and he could not help it. He felt like kicking Gorssmann in his fat face. He did not like the man's composure.

Gorssmann seemed to be debating about something. He looked up at Baron, then down at his feet. He unfolded his hands, then folded them again.

"All right," he said, shrugging. "Arnold." He nodded his head, waved his hand toward the rear of the room and the stairway, leading up to the balcony.

"Are you sure?" Arnold said. He rose from the settee, looked at Baron with slow amazement, then at Gorssmann.

"Go–hurry!" Gorssmann snapped.

Arnold frowned, walked on across the room. Baron watched him go, watched him start up the stairs. His heart beat and beat inside his chest, he could feel it beating, feel the push of blood and the heat of it in his neck and shoulders.

He heard Gorssmann's chuckle. At the same instant he felt the arms come down around him. He fought with crazed frenzy, knowing the arms were Joseph's, that he had been tricked. At the same time, he told himself he had to hang onto those papers. He kicked and cursed Gorssmann, trying with all his strength to get loose from Joseph.

Gorssmann nodded at Joseph. Baron was released. He sensed it, then felt it. A harsh, smashing blow caught him across the back of the neck. He flew sprawling past Hugo Gorssmann's chair into abrupt darkness.

"He moved. Arnold, simply hold a gun on him. He knows there's nothing he can do. Ah, yes—these *are* the papers we wanted!"

Baron looked up from where he lay on the floor. His head throbbed dully, and when he moved his head, his neck hurt. Otherwise, he was the same as before. Joseph stood a little way from him, watching him. Arnold sat on the settee with a gun resting on his knee. Gorssmann was thumbing through the sheaf of papers and the blueprints.

"You know, Baron," Gorssmann said, "I just thought of something. It would take some daring, of course. And I won't do it now, because I'll have enough money from this to tide me over for some time. But the thought did occur. To me, that is." He peered down at Baron, and strummed the papers across his enormous belly. "I could have perfect facsimiles made of these papers. Then I could sell them to different persons I know of all at the same time."

Baron said nothing. He knelt, then stood, rubbing the back of his neck. He stared at Arnold, looked around the room. There was no sign of Bette. He went dead inside.

"Where is she?" he said. He sprang toward Gorssmann.

Joseph stepped in, grabbed his arm.

Gorssmann shook his head at Baron. He took his hat off, laid it on the chair, began waddling slowly up and down the room with the sheaf of papers in his hand. As Baron watched, Gorssmann seemed to expand in girth, if that was possible.

"Where is she?" Baron shouted. He cursed Gorssmann. He shouted curses at the man, feeling the futility of it deep inside him. Gorssmann did not even bother to look at him. "Tell me, damn you! Tell me! Where is my daughter?"

"Please," Gorssmann said. "Relax, Baron. I always hold to my bargains. Believe me, yes. Always, thanks."

He tried to get hold of himself and his voice leveled out. "All right," he said. "Tell me where Bette is!"

Gorssmann did not answer.

The big man moved across the room to an empty bookcase beside the fireplace. There was a phone on one of the shelves. He looked across at Baron, grinned, and began a phone call that endured in a steady muttering from that corner of the room for over an hour.

Baron went through all the hell possible during this time, or thought he did. Arnold did not once move from the settee, and Baron lifted Gorssmann's hat, dropped it to the floor, and sat down. Joseph came across the room and sat in the chair opposite Baron. They looked at each other and waited while Gorssmann muttered and mumbled and argued over the phone.

He was trying to settle some dispute.

Baron began to know then what those papers meant to these men. To Gorssmann in particular, but also to Arnold, and very likely to Joseph. He could not tell what kind of man Joseph was. There was really no telling. The deaf-mute's immobile features gave no inkling of what went on in his head. He hardly ever looked at anybody, only seemed to wait and stare solemnly into space.

Baron tried to force his mind away from the one fact that drove him close to insanity during this time. If they would not produce Bette now, then it must be that they could not produce her.

He refused absolutely to admit that she was dead. They could not do such a thing. And Lili? He slumped in the chair, listening to the interminable, indistinguishable mutter of Gorssmann's voice at the phone, trying in his mind to find some solution to the way these men acted.

He refused the obvious.

Finally Gorssmann hung up, returned to the center of the room, then came over and stood in front of Arnold. Baron knew better now than to try anything. It was hopeless. He did not want to admit this hopelessness, but it was there.

"It's all settled," Gorssmann said. "I had a time, but it is settled. Their radios were not in perfect order–something. Anyway, we have little to worry about now."

Arnold gave a big sigh, relaxed on the settee. "I was worried, to tell the truth," he said. "The man is unpredictable."

"I know," Gorssmann said. "A truly bad man to deal with."

"You're certain?"

Gorssmann shrugged, paced back and forth between the settee and the fireplace. "As certain as it's possible to be. Of course, we must allow for the chance."

Arnold stared at Gorssmann's feet.

"Come, come!" Gorssmann said. "Think optimistically. Be like our good friend Baron." He glanced at Baron, frowned. "What? You are no longer so optimistic, Baron?"

Baron said nothing.

"Hugo," Arnold said. "How much longer? This waiting kills me, it tears the heart out of me."

Gorssmann drew out his watch, glanced at it, put it away. It was a fat silver watch without a chain, carried in his vest pocket. It had a silver chain fob, very short.

"We can't do a thing until dark. Until at least seven." He cleared his throat. "Of course, I will go before then. Just before dark, that is."

"You."

Gorssmann nodded.

"Alone?"

Again Gorssmann nodded, paying no attention, it seemed.

"I might have known," Arnold said. He was wearing a neat blue suit, light colored, and a yellow tie. His hair was very smooth and slick and dark. He seemed to turn into himself, sadly, forlornly.

"What?"

"What about me and Joseph?"

"You will wait here–with him." He pointed at Baron and Baron saw the man's eyes and knew the only way Gorssmann would ever be any good was dead.

"I see."

"Listen, you fool!" Gorssmann snapped. "I have never let you down, have I? Do you think I am such a fool as to run out on you now, to try to? You ass–you unspeakable fool! Don't you know I could never rest if I did? Don't you know how–Listen. I will go and I will come back and we will have the money. I guarantee it."

"All right, Hugo."

"Yes. I planned this, and I planned it well. Things must progress in an orderly manner from start to finish."

Things progressed very slowly. The afternoon passed in this manner and Baron realized that he walked a narrow ledge. He did not once move from the chair.

Joseph remained perfectly calm, only taking an occasional stroll around the room. Arnold had fits of bad depression, and held long arguments with Gorssmann that Gorssmann always won, one way or another.

"Listen, Arnold," he said at last. "Understand me. It is getting later and I must depend on you. I must return here. You must trust me."

"Where is Lili?" Baron said finally. It was the first time he had spoken in hours. Gorssmann had begun to show nerves now and his head snapped around at Baron.

"Kindly shut up," he said.

Baron did shut up. There was nothing to say, nothing he could do.

By the time dusk fingered the windows, Gorssmann was in a bad state. He had placed the papers in a brief case, and he marched up and down the room with it, taking long swinging strides.

"I am going," he announced at last.

Arnold came off the settee, running. He ran across the room and stood before Gorssmann.

"You won't come back!" he screamed. "I know you. You will leave us here and we will sit with that person all night and all tomorrow and you will never come."

Gorssmann swung the brief case hard. It caught Arnold across the side of the head with a loud splat, sent him spinning over against the wall with the gun dangling from his arm.

"You are a fool," Gorssmann said slowly. "An utter fool!"

Joseph had not moved in his chair. He turned then and glanced toward Arnold. Their eyes met and Joseph nodded. Baron began to feel more ill than before. He had been thinking of Louis Follet. He knew now that Follet would not have waited at the café, even if he had ever come.

For fifteen minutes they sat there after Gorssmann left. Then Arnold rose and began to pace the floor with the gun in his hand. Occasionally he stood before Joseph and talked to him with the quick gestures of sign language. Whatever it was Joseph said, it seemed to frighten Arnold.

Baron knew that if he expected ever to do anything, it had to be with these two men and it had to be right away.

"He's not coming back, you know," he said to Arnold.

"Quiet," Arnold said. "Don't talk that way."

Baron shrugged.

And sitting there like that, he summoned the last of his strength and courage in an effort to think it out clearly, and face the issue the way it stood. He was certain now that Bette was not here. He could never admit to himself that she was dead. Why didn't they kill him?

Somehow he had to get away. Right now Gorssmann was starting out to meet the head man, the same man Baron had been after all these years. But where? It was like a solemn voice inside his head threatening dark laughter.

"It's true," he said to Arnold. Arnold turned and came over and stood in front of him with the gun in his hand.

"What is true?" Arnold said.

"I'm not trying to frighten you," Baron said. "But Hugo Gorssmann is not coming back. Can't you see that? Why should he return here? It is foolish and you are a fool, just as Gorssmann said. Where is Lili?"

"She is gone. She has gone to Belgium. Hugo sent her on an errand."

A piece of Baron chipped away. He swallowed, forcing a grin. "How do you know this is true?"

"Because!" Arnold cried. "It has to be true."

"Sure. Where is my daughter, Bette? She was here, wasn't she?"

Arnold looked at him and said nothing. The wheels were beginning to turn around inside his head, faster and faster. Baron could see this easily. He wished he could get his hands on that gun. Arnold carried it very loosely, carelessly. Joseph was preoccupied with some inner conflict. The man's face twisted this way and that way and his gaze was glued to the ceiling.

"One thing," Arnold said. "You can forget your daughter."

He turned swiftly away, went over to Joseph, and began waving his hands again. He set the gun on a table by Joseph's chair as he talked with the man.

Baron came out of the chair running. He struck Arnold across the back, reached for the gun, got it in his hand. Joseph was already lunging at him. Baron moved backward, tripped, sat down on the floor.

He took careful aim and pulled the trigger of the gun three times. He saw the slug tear into Joseph's right knee. He saw the shock on the man's face, the abrupt demolishment of satisfaction and orderliness, and Joseph sprawled on the floor. He clutched at his knee, felt of it, lay back and rolled and twisted on the floor with his mouth wide open, his tongue working in wild, silent screaming.

"Don't move!" Baron said to Arnold.

Arnold did not move. He stood quite still, watching. His eyes were very bright, intense, his face deadly pale.

"I'll kill you," Baron said.

"Yes."

Baron rose carefully from the floor, looking at Joseph. The man still lay there, twisting and groveling like some kind of animal, his mouth wide open screeching and screaming horrible silence. Blood trickled down his pants cuff and onto the floor, and as he moved about, it trailed in a bright stain on the flagstones, as a snail leaves a trail.

Baron pointed to Joseph. "Tell him not to try anything. That if he does, I will kill him."

Arnold talked quickly to Joseph, above his face, with his hands. Joseph watched the hands and answered. Arnold turned to Baron.

"He says to go ahead, to kill him. He asks it, please. He cannot stand pain. He is of the type that cannot bear pain, any pain."

Baron stepped up to Arnold and slashed the gun across the man's face as hard as he dared. He was worked up inside, coming closer and closer to a crazed pitch of wild hate, and this helped.

"You see," Baron said, following Arnold as the man stepped back, holding his face. "I know you. I have watched you carefully and I know you don't want your face smashed. Well, I am going to smash your face," he said slowly. He followed the cringing Arnold. "I am going to break your nose and your teeth. With this!" He held up the gun, never ceasing the prowl after Arnold.

"Please, no! God–mercy, mercy!"

"I will do this, then–unless you quickly tell me exactly where Gorssmann went, and where the meeting is to take place."

Arnold's voice was steady. He looked straight at Baron. "He would kill me."

"All right. As you choose."

"I will tell you. He takes a motor launch from the Vieux Port to the Château d'If. You know of this place?"

"Yes, yes. Tell me."

"God save me." Arnold looked across the floor toward Joseph. Baron followed his gaze. Joseph was lying peacefully on the floor, staring at the ceiling. There was a large puddle of blood pooling around Joseph's foot.

"Well?"

"On the other side of the island, he meets a ship–a yacht, that is. The *Esmeralda*. This is the name of the yacht."

"And the name of Gorssmann's boat?"

"I cannot." Arnold moved past Baron and went over to the settee. He sat down quietly and stared at the floor. He did not move. Then he looked up at Baron and his mouth opened. It closed. He looked at Joseph and he said, "The *Sea Grape.*" He put his head down in his hands and rocked himself back and forth.

"When?"

"At ten."

"Precisely?"

"*Oui.*"

"You do not lie?"

He rocked and rocked and rocked and said nothing. Baron went over and stood in front of him. He touched the muzzle of the gun to Arnold's head. Arnold flung his head back as though he'd been shot, his eyes horrified.

"If you lie, you know, things can happen. I am very mad," Baron said. "I am mad enough to kill without worrying at all, you know?"

"I do not lie," Arnold said. He let his head down into his hands again. "But it does not matter. It no longer matters."

"Is Gorssmann's boat a big boat?"

"He is hiring it, renting it. No, not so large. Large enough–large enough to go to Italy." He rocked and rocked and rocked. There was no sound at all in the room.

Baron went over to the phone and finally managed to get through to the cafè. He expected the woman to answer. Instead, he recognized Louis Follet's voice over the crackling wire.

"This is Baron," he said. He talked rapidly, told him everything to date, and where the meeting was to take place, and when.

"You expect me to believe this?" Follet said.

Baron said nothing.

"You recall how the last turned out?"

"You know the papers are stolen? I have made the delivery to Gorssmann!"

"Chevard has put in the alarm, yes. All right, I will try."

Baron hung up and looked at Arnold.

"Take care of Joseph," he said. "Try to stop the bleeding."

Arnold looked up at him from where he sat on the settee.

"He would not have come back, anyway. He would have gone on with everything," Arnold said. "Tell me that is so, monsieur."

"He would not have come back," Baron said. He looked at the two of them, the one on the floor and the other one on the settee. Then he went on outside. The Fiat was still there. He saw no other car. It was very dark and the wind from the sea was a dead wind. It barely moved and it was sick and slow and moist. He looked up at the sky and saw the stars burning in the black ceiling, but they gave no light.

He returned to the house. He did not want to do what he had to do. He entered and walked across the large living room. Arnold and Joseph were as he had left them. He went up the stairs and went through the rooms and he found where Bette had been. For a moment he sat on the bed in the room where she had been, seeing her clothes, and he wondered that he was able to feel anything at all. He searched the entire house, then, but Bette was not there.

He went on outside and looked back toward the house. One light was lit in the big living room. He supposed he should have done something for Joseph. He did not have time. He supposed he should have tied them up. He knew somehow that they would remain there, that they would do nothing.

Somehow he knew that they would stay right there and wait. And wait....

## Chapter Twenty-one

HE FOUND THE *Sea Grape* down the quay. But he saw Gorssmann first. He parked the car and moved over onto the side of the quay. Gorssmann was pacing up and down beside a large launch, perhaps a fifty-footer, with a long deck cabin. As Baron looked, a man stepped from the launch to the quay and brandished his arms at Gorssmann. Gorssmann said something loudly, and his voice carried on up the quay.

All he knew was that he had to get aboard the boat. He saw only one way, and decided to use it. Several rowboats were moored close to the side of the quay where he stood. There were no oars in them, but he did not need oars.

He let himself down into one of the boats, released the mooring rope from the huge iron ring fastened to the quay, pulled himself out beside another boat, then slowly turned his boat and began working it down the quay in the slow, dark, still waters of the harbor.

He came in against the side of the quay and dragged his hands along the old pilings, working the boat slowly and softly. There was no wake at all in the water that he could see and he was in deep shadow. As he reached other boats, he worked his way around them.

If the launch Gorssmann had hired left before he reached it, he did not know what he would do. He worked in a kind of frantic vacuum now, not allowing himself to think very far beyond the present, yet holding the future there in the back of his mind as a kind of promise.

The big boy. The head man.

This was the promise. And after that–Gorssmann. He wondered, as he pulled himself along, whether or not Follet would manage to come. He told himself that certainly the man could not afford not to come. But he could not be sure. Follet was peculiar.

Bette was dead. He was certain of this now. Bette and Lili too, probably. The whole thing was shot to hell. Chevard knew by now, knew of the whole sordid mess, and he wondered vaguely what Chevard thought of him. It no longer mattered. Nothing mattered save that he somehow be on hand when Gorssmann made the delivery of the papers out there on the sea.

He was nearly there now and he could hear Gorssmann talking with another man.

"One engine, two—who cares how many engines?" Gorssmann said. "I have hired this boat. Listen, we must go now. You hear, now!"

"Very well, monsieur. But the other engine, it works not well. It works not at all."

"You have one engine?"

"Ah, *oui.*"

"Then let us go."

They were standing on the quayside, talking. Baron gave the rowboat a hell of a push, thrusting it away from the quay and under the bow of the launch. It was a big boat, all right. A beauty, though the paint was flaking. Gorssmann's back was turned to him and the tide was low. Neither of the two saw him. He remained in shadow and the rowboat slowly slipped beyond the launch's bow. It kept right on going, toward the middle of the harbor.

Instantly he was frantic. Panic had him and he swung wildly in the boat, trying desperately to grasp something on the launch. He did not succeed. The rowboat bumped solidly against something, commenced to turn very slowly around, and bumped again and yet again.

It was a buoy. Baron felt for it in the darkness, caught it, his hand grasping slime and sharp barnacles. He held on tightly, cursing under his breath, trying to see what they were doing back at the launch. The two of them still stood out there on the quay, talking.

He felt the buoy anchor. He pulled on it with all his strength, and the rowboat swung and drifted toward the hull of the launch again.

He came in amidships and caught the launch with both hands, holding the rowboat from slamming against it. His heart rocked and his mouth tasted brassy. The launch rose, lifting high with his slight weight. He felt the rowboat back away from him. He reached, clawing up the side of the launch. The rowboat continued to slip faster back into the water as he desperately tried to find a hold, any hold at all. He was a bridge now, with the water below him. If he slipped now, all would be gone, and the toes of his shoes clung to the side of the rowboat and he felt the ship's rail.

He grabbed it, swung his feet to the side of the launch. The rowboat splashed, gurgled, and slued around. They stopped arguing there on the quay.

He waited, hanging dismally to the rail, his feet dragging in the black water. There was the strong, biting odor of dead fish and garbage and creosote and somewhere cognac. It hung in the air like a cloud.

They began to talk again.

"We will go," the one man said.

"Good," Gorssmann said.

"Double the money, for certain," the man said.

"For certain," Gorssmann said. "Double the money." Then he said in English. "You conniving bastard, you! You have stalled the other engine, to hold me up for more money."

"What is this?" the man said.

"It is nothing. I was saying a prayer," Gorssmann said.

They came aboard. Baron swung himself up over the rail, lay on the deck. Beside the deck cabin, on the deck, was a dinghy. It was tied down. He rocked it up on its side and looked beneath. It seemed all right. He crawled in there and lay panting, wishing his feet weren't wet.

He lay there and thought about Bette and of how he had failed her. He had failed everybody so far, including himself. There wasn't much left to fail at now. There was something, though, and it was all he had left. He wondered in a kind of daze whether or not he would fail at this. He lay on his back and stared into the blackness.

Underneath the dinghy, he could see out onto the harbor and far up the harbor toward the town. The lights of the Cannebière and the specks of people walking up there by the cafés. The women and the men and the both of them together. There were still some fish stalls left out there on the sidewalks in front of the shops and the cafés along the harbor.

He saw a sailor wrestling with a girl against the side of a brick wall, a café wall. He was wrestling the hell out of her. But she was a wise girl and wanted her price first, apparently. She brought her knee up quickly and the sailor stepped back, doubled over, his cry reaching down the harbor in a string of obscene cursing, and the girl ran, and Baron heard and felt the engine turn over, catch, and burst loudly across the harbor.

The sailor turned, still bent over, still in pain, still cursing, and looked to see what the hell kind of boat was making all the racket at night.

And watching so, not thinking about anything, because the nerve exhaustion was too great, Baron felt the rocking and looked and his nose was not three inches from Gorssmann's feet. The feet were planted well apart, just on the deck beside the dinghy.

Something crawled over Baron's hand. He did not move. It stopped on the back of his hand and preened itself. He wondered what it was. It took great care with the preening, and he watched Gorssmann's feet, hoping it was only a beetle.

Finally whatever it was started off his hand, then decided to have a look around. It paused, came up to the wrist, and must have taken a good look up the long dark tunnel of his sleeve.

The man down in the boat someplace shouted something.

"What?" Gorssmann said.

The man cursed.

Gorssmann muttered something and rocked from one foot to the other. Then he stood quietly again and the engine of the launch wound up and the launch took headway, away from the quay. Baron felt the throbbing and the movement of the launch on the water and he stared out under the dinghy at Gorssmann's feet, thinking, I could pitch him over. He would sink. No, he would float. He would float out and meet the *Esmeralda*. He wouldn't even get the papers wet. He wondered if Gorssmann carried the papers.

Whatever it was on his hand wandered on up his sleeve clear to the elbow. He tried to squash it against the deck by pressing his elbow. It wouldn't work. The thing got out of the way fast, and went on up to the shoulder and down by the collarbone, exploring slowly and preening.

Baron itched horribly. But he could not scratch. The thing wandered down onto his chest, making slow headway now because of the low ceiling, then it suddenly was gone and he knew it had somehow gone out the front of his shirt. The relief was so enormous he nearly shook.

He waited patiently, perspiring, expecting whatever it was to crawl into his ear. But nothing happened and Gorssmann did not move, either.

Baron lay there, thinking about it, about everything. He could not move and he dared not try to sleep, although sleep would have been good. Bette is dead, he told himself. I hope she is dead, because ... But I do not hope she is dead. But she is, he told himself. And Lili? She is dead too. If she is in Belgium. That story was weak in the knees. It was a rotten one, all right. She is not in Belgium, unless that canal where they found Elene is called Belgium.

He lay there imagining Lili lying half in and half out of the water of the canal, on the bank, on the abrupt fall of the bank where her face gleamed in the moonlight with her throat ... You've got to stop, he thought. Because you can't take any more of this, because you're done, you're finished.

Not yet, he thought. Not by a long damned bloody shot.

Why did he have to go and love her? Why was it that such a thing had to happen? Why couldn't she just have been another one in the bed? She wasn't, though. And he guessed somehow now that he could trust her. Place the trust after the thing you trust has vanished, he thought.

He looked and as he looked Gorssmann's feet moved. The launch was moving swiftly out of the harbor now. The lights were dimming and he saw the bridge over the water and they were fast leaving everything behind.

He lay there quietly blinking into the darkness of the overturned dinghy.

They don't have to tell me, he thought. She's dead and that's all there is to it. It's a good thing that I understand about that, anyway. That when it's done, it's done. He rolled over under the dinghy, then rolled back because there wasn't room enough, and he lay there and, looking out now, he could see nothing. God, she did have wonderful hair, soft and black, like this night. And did she love him, wherever she was?

"We are here," the man said. "This is it."

"All right," Gorssmann said. "Good."

"What shall I do now?"

"Don't do anything."

The man was exasperated, plainly. He thought it was a fool's errand, coming out here at night, and aside from that, he was extremely suspicious of Gorssmann. He did not like Gorssmann.

"Anchor the launch," Gorssmann said.

"The depth is great."

"I don't care about the depth."

"Monsieur, must we just sit here?"

"What time is it?"

"Nine o'clock."

"We sit," Gorssmann said. "Please, with the anchor."

The man cursed.

"What?"

"I was praying," the man said.

He heard the sound of the other engine coming close. He heard it through the converging blackness underneath the dinghy and he knew that this would be the *Esmeralda*.

It seemed hours and hours ago that the anchor had splashed into the sea. The launch rocked and Baron twice had been able to make out the dark thrusting outline of the Château d'If, and he had lain there going over the story of the wily Count of Monte Cristo.

"*Merde,*" the man said.

"Look, a ship," Gorssmann said, and the excitement was in his voice and Baron wished he could see. He heard the yacht coming closer to them.

"Flash a light," Gorssmann said. "The flashlight."

"Here."

"*Merci.* It doesn't work!" Gorssmann's voice was edged with fear.

"The button, push the but—There! See how it lights?"

"Out of the way, thanks."

The man cursed. Baron saw the light flash out on the water. A spotlight splashed brightly from some distance, and dashed him coldly in the face under the dinghy. He instinctively shrank back, though he knew no one could see him under here.

The yacht came in close and Baron saw her sides and the ports yellow out there.

"Hello," Gorssmann called.

Somebody shouted something.

"A boat?"

"No, fasten to the side," Gorssmann said. "I can't–" He stopped, then said softly, "How could I get into a boat?"

"We can't hook on," somebody said from the other boat. "It would make things very bad."

"All right," Gorssmann said. "What shall I do?" he asked the captain of the launch.

"My boat leaks," he said, apparently referring to the dinghy.

"You'll have to come over here," Gorssmann said.

"Is it ready?" somebody said.

"Certainly."

Baron could hear Gorssmann breathing. The hissing of the man's breath reached even above the sound of the yacht's engines.

"All right," somebody called. "We're coming over."

Gorssmann was standing near the dinghy softly muttering curses in English.

"Let us not pray now," the captain of the launch said.

The yacht's engines ceased. Baron heard the oars.

"You are alone?" somebody in the rowboat said.

"Certainly," Gorssmann said. "As I promised."

"Good."

The boat bumped alongside. "Stay there," somebody said. "Hand me up."

Gorssmann muttered futilely to the captain and the captain came down beside the dinghy where Baron lay and knelt and reached overboard, and pulled up a hand and an arm. Baron watched quietly underneath the dinghy and saw the face come up into his line of vision, the eyes turned sharply up, watching.

And it drove down into him coldly. The blond hair came up and the blue eyes and the smile and the thick scar on the forehead. John Graff. The man kept right on coming and finally stood and Baron looked out at the feet of John Graff.

"Well, Hugo," Graff said in English. "We meet again."

"True," Gorssmann said. "True, true. Exciting and of extreme pleasure, I assure you."

"Still the same old Hugo, eh?"

Baron lay there with his memories.

"We will make this fast, Hugo. I haven't much time. I'm going straight to Italy."

"Which means you are heading for Spain," Gorssmann said.

"Well," Graff said.

And each time he spoke it was as if somebody drove another spike deeply into Baron and he twisted upon the spike, feeling the pain of it. This was the man. The man he had sought for two and a half years. The man who had taken his wife, and destroyed him, ruined him–the man who had been the cause of Bette's ...

"The money?" Gorssmann said.

"Right here," Graff said. "I must see the papers."

"Start the engine," Gorssmann said to the captain.

"*Comment?*"

"Leave us! Fool!"

The captain stumped back along the deck. Baron watched their feet. They moved forward on the launch's deck and they were facing away from him. He felt for the gun. He got it in his hand. He was dizzy with wanting to see Graff, wanting to show him the gun, wanting to get his hands on the man. He went out of his head then. He knew what was happening, but the control was gone. He held the gun and thrust the dinghy up and came out, springing to his feet.

They had not even heard him. A man beside the launch in the rowboat called, shouting.

Graff turned and saw Baron.

"Well," Graff said. He had one hand on the rail of the launch. The man in the rowboat kept shouting. Baron glanced quickly toward the yacht over there and saw them running up and down the deck.

Gorssmann was staring at him, his eyes protruding in his head. The pale darkness was sliced from the yellow glow of the lights in the launch's cabin.

Gorssmann clutched the papers and Graff held a small black leather brief case, about half the size of an ordinary brief case.

"You didn't tell me this would happen," Graff said to Gorssmann.

Still Gorssmann could not speak. Baron stepped lightly along the deck, until he could see Graff quite plainly. Graff had not moved. He was a tall, broad-shouldered man and he wore a dinner jacket and white shirt, but no tie. He stood stiffly at the rail. Then abruptly the hand with the case swung out, striking Baron's gun arm.

Gorssmann began to run toward the far side of the deck cabin. Baron snapped a shot at him, saw Gorssmann go to his knees, and bright blinding lights suddenly shot all over the launch.

Baron swung the gun across at Graff. Graff swung the leather case again.

"Afraid to shoot?" Graff said.

The lights flashed into Baron's eyes and he dived at Graff. He felt the man's face against his hand and he battered, and Graff cursed and Baron heard a splash.

"For that–" Graff said.

They came together, wrestling on the deck. Graff was a tremendous man and Baron found that he was strong, too. He battered at him. He still held the gun.

"Stop!" somebody called. A shot banged and the slug whined, ricocheting off the cabin.

Gorssmann yelled something. Somebody was shouting over on the yacht. Baron slammed and slammed at the bright-dark figure before him. Graff's face was twisted with fury, and he lashed out at Baron with his fists. Baron swung the gun and felt it contact with Graff's face. Then the gun spun from his hand.

"Get the boat ready!" Graff called overboard.

Nobody said anything. Baron went after him. Graff turned and ran along the deck. Again the gun shot and again and again. The lights were bright and Baron saw they were coming from still another boat that was quite near, a low launch. Two lights splayed from the bow.

Baron leaped past Gorssmann, who still knelt on the deck. Graff turned and watched him come, leaning against the rail. He cursed Baron, then ran straight at him.

"Everybody stand still, don't move!" a voice called loudly over a loud-speaker.

Graff kept coming. Baron dived at him and Graff leaped over him and the voices shouted over the loud-speaker. Baron turned, getting to his feet, and he saw John Graff poised on the rail of the launch getting ready to jump, and from the other launch with the searchlights out there, Baron saw the sudden flashing arch of the tracers and heard the machine gun and John Graff stood on the rail receiving the slugs in his white shirt and in his throat.

Graff crumpled, still standing, his knees bending with the slugs pounding into him. The machine gun stopped yammering. Graff folded and sprawled out and down into the water.

"Get a boathook," somebody called. A rowboat was coming from the other launch. Baron stood by the rail and watched and he heard Gorssmann bubbling nearby. He turned and looked. Gorssmann was still there on his hands and knees, spitting blood across the sheaf of papers and blueprints still clutched in his hand.

Baron stood on the quiet deck of the police launch and talked with Follet. They watched them fish Graff's body from the water and a medic was on the deck of the other launch trying to help Gorssmann now.

"Well?" Follet said.

Baron looked at him. He could not think. He could do nothing but listen and watch. He had talked for a few moments, but now he could not speak. All he could do was think of the image of his daughter.

"I cannot tell you all," Follet said. "I want to thank you, though, monsieur."

Baron watched him. He saw Gorssmann over there, seated on a canvas chair. The big man sat quietly, staring out across the sea, into the night.

"Look," Follet said. "I–"

"Never mind," Paul Chevard said.

Baron turned. Chevard had come up out of the companionway. He stood there with the light passing over his shoulders. Then he closed the door and came across the deck and said to Follet, "I'll explain."

"*Merci,*" Follet said. He grinned at Baron, then began touching his pockets, probing for his tobacco.

Baron stared at Chevard.

"It was a dirty trick, in a way," Chevard said. "Follet and I have worked together on this, Frank."

Baron turned away. The rowboat with Graff's body was alongside now. He could see the wet crumpled figure lying across the bow of the rowboat. He listened to Chevard speak, the words filtering aimlessly into his mind.

"Those papers weren't real, Frank. It was the only way Follet could get to Graff, you see? It simply happened this way. I'm sorry, but we are very proud of you. You thought you were lying to me, and I thought I was lying to you–so now ..." Baron turned and saw Chevard shrug. "Everything is the same as before, see? These things come to pass, Frank."

"I see," Baron said.

"Frank," Chevard said, "I know what you've been through. But don't you see, this will clear you of everything. I am coming to the States with you. We will get you set up again."

Baron kept on watching him, not letting the thoughts come into his head at all, and he was dead inside, all dead, and his head was like the night out there.

"Frank," Chevard said. "I have something for you–something that will make you feel better." He walked over to the companionway and opened the door and Lili came out, bringing Bette with her. Bette broke free of Lili's hand and rushed to Baron.

She came into his arms. He did not know whether to hold her or what and he could not think at all. He could not speak.

"I didn't know what to do!" Bette said. "Lili took me and we ran away last night. We've been with Monsieur Follet ever since. Lili is wonderful, Dad." She stepped back and looked at him. He stared woodenly. He looked up past Bette and Lili smiled at him.

"All right?" Chevard said.

Lili smiled slyly at him and moved across the deck toward him. Bette turned and watched her. He stared at Bette, at the way the freshening wind blew her coat, at her hair, at his daughter and his hope.

Then Lili was in his arms. And suddenly he began to wake up as she pressed close against him, speaking softly against his throat. He closed his eyes and let her continue to speak softly against his throat like that, and her fine dark hair brushed against his face.

"You trust me now?" Lili said.

He opened his eyes and held her off and looked at her. Somebody coughed, and he heard Follet giving orders about Gorssmann, and Chevard slapped him hard on the back.

He just kept right on looking.

## THE END

Ingram Content Group UK Ltd.
Milton Keynes UK
UKHW010806190623
423681UK00015B/621